THE DEVIL
INCARNATE

Praise for the Cain Casey Saga

The Devil's Due

"A Night Owl Reviews Top Pick: Cain Casey is the kind of person you aspire to be even though some consider her a criminal. She's loyal, very protective of those she loves, honorable, big on preserving her family legacy and loves her family greatly. *The Devil's Due* is a book I highly recommend and well worth the wait we all suffered through. I cannot wait for the next book in the series to come out."
—*Night Owl Reviews*

The Devil Be Damned

"Ali Vali excels at creating strong, romantic characters along with her fast-paced, sophisticated plots. Her setting, New Orleans, provides just the right blend of immigrants from Mexico, South America, and Cuba, along with a city steeped in traditions."—*Just About Write*

Deal with the Devil

"Ali Vali has given her fans another thick, rich thriller...*Deal With the Devil* has wonderful love stories, great sex, and an ample supply of humor. It is an exciting, page-turning read that leaves her readers eagerly awaiting the next book in the series."—*Just About Write*

The Devil Unleashed

"Fast-paced action scenes, intriguing character revelations, and a refreshing approach to the romance thriller genre all make for an enjoyable reading experience in the Big Easy...*The Devil Unleashed* is an engrossing reading experience."—*Midwest Book Review*

The Devil Inside

"*The Devil Inside* is the first of what promises to be a very exciting series...While telling an exciting story that grips the reader, Vali has also fully fleshed out her heroes and villains. *The Devil Inside* is that rarity: a fascinating crime novel which includes a tender love story and leaves the reader with a cliffhanger ending."—*MegaScene*

Praise for Ali Vali

One More Chance

"This was an amazing book by Vali…complex and multi-layered (both characters and plot)."—*Danielle Kimerer, Librarian (Nevins Memorial Library, Massachusetts)*

Face the Music

"This is a typical Ali Vali romance with strong characters, a beautiful setting (Nashville, Tennessee), and an enemies-to-lovers style tale. The two main characters are beautiful, strong-willed, and easy to fall in love with. The romance between them is steamy, and so are the sex scenes."—*Rainbow Reflections*

The Inheritance

"I love a good story that makes me laugh and cry, and this one did that a lot for me. I would step back into this world any time."—*Kat Adams, Bookseller (QBD Books, Australia)*

Double-Crossed

"[T]here aren't too many lesfic books like *Double-Crossed* and it is refreshing to see an author like Vali continue to churn out books like these. Excellent crime thriller."—*Colleen Corgel, Librarian, Queens Borough Public Library*

"For all of us die-hard Ali Vali/Cain Casey fans, this is the beginning of a great new series…There is violence in this book, and lots of killing, but there is also romance, love, and the beginning of a great new reading adventure. I can't wait to read more of this intriguing story."
—*Rainbow Reflections*

Answering the Call

Answering the Call "is a brilliant cop-and-killer story…The crime story is tight and the love story is fantastic."—*Best Lesbian Erotica*

Lammy Finalist *Calling the Dead*

"So many writers set stories in New Orleans, but Ali Vali's mystery novels have the authenticity that only a real Big Easy resident could bring. Set six months after Hurricane Katrina has devastated the city, a lesbian detective is still battling demons when a body turns up behind one of the city's famous eateries. What follows makes for a classic lesbian murder yarn."—*Curve Magazine*

Beauty and the Boss

"The story gripped me from the first page…Vali's writing style is lovely—it's clean, sharp, no wasted words, and it flows beautifully as a result. Highly recommended!"—*Rainbow Book Reviews*

Balance of Forces: Toujours Ici

"A stunning addition to the vampire legend, *Balance of Forces: Toujour Ici* is one that stands apart from the rest."—*Bibliophilic Book Blog*

Blue Skies

"Vali is skilled at building sexual tension, and the sex in this novel flies as high as Berkley's jets. Look for this fast-paced read."—*Just About Write*

Beneath the Waves

"The premise…was brilliantly constructed…skillfully written and the imagination that went into it was fantastic…A wonderful passionate love story with a great mystery."—*Inked Rainbow Reads*

Second Season

"The issues are realistic and center around the universal factors of love, jealousy, betrayal, and doing the right thing and are constantly woven into the fabric of the story. We rated this well written social commentary through the use of fiction our max five hearts."—*Heartland Reviews*

Carly's Sound

"*Carly's Sound* is a great romance, with some wonderfully hot sex, but it is more than that. It is also the tale of a woman rising from the ashes of grief and finding new love and a new life. Vali has surrounded Julia and Poppy with a cast of great supporting characters, making this an extremely satisfying read."—*Just About Write*

By the Author

Carly's Sound

Second Season

Love Match

The Dragon Tree Legacy

The Romance Vote

Girls with Guns

Beneath the Waves

Beauty and the Boss

Blue Skies

Stormy Seas

The Inheritance

Face the Music

One More Chance

Call Series

Calling the Dead

Answering the Call

Forces Series

Balance of Forces: Toujours Ici

Battle of Forces: Sera Toujours

Force of Fire: Toujours a Vous

Vegas Nights

Double-Crossed

The Cain Casey Saga

The Devil Inside	The Devil's Orchard
The Devil Unleashed	The Devil's Due
Deal with the Devil	Heart of the Devil
The Devil Be Damned	The Devil Incarnate

Visit us at www.boldstrokesbooks.com

THE DEVIL INCARNATE

by

Ali Vali

2021

THE DEVIL INCARNATE

ISBN 13: 978-1-63555-534-9

This Trade Paperback Original Is Published By
Bold Strokes Books, Inc.
P.O. Box 249
Valley Falls, NY 12185

First Edition: February 2021

CREDITS
EDITORS: VICTORIA VILLASEÑOR AND RUTH STERNGLANTZ
PRODUCTION DESIGN: STACIA SEAMAN
COVER DESIGN BY SHERI (HINDSIGHTGRAPHICS@GMAIL.COM)

Acknowledgments

Thank you, Radclyffe, for the opportunity to tell one more Cain and Emma story, and thanks to Sandy for all you do for everyone in the BSB family.

A big thanks to my editors, Victoria Villaseñor and Ruth Sternglantz. Victoria, thank you for your ongoing lessons that make me think of new ways of doing things. Ruth, as always, you're a treasure. I appreciate you both. Thank you, Sheri, for another great cover.

Thank you to my beta readers, Cris Perez-Soria, Lenore Benoit, and Kim Rieff. You can't know how much I appreciate you all.

To the readers, you know every word is written with you in mind. Thank you for all the encouragement to keep going. These characters are like old friends, and it was nice going back for a nice long visit.

Thanks to my quarantine partner, C. You do make every adventure fun. *Verdad!*

For C
and
For the Readers

CHAPTER ONE

"Ah, ah...Jesus...*ohhh*...don't stop," Emma Casey said, exhaling into Derby Cain Casey's ear. "I'm coming...Harder, baby...I'm coming." Her body arched, and then she went still. "Good Lord, mobster," Emma said, opening her eyes lazily when Cain pulled her fingers out. "You do give new meaning to *good morning*. That was fantastic."

Cain moved to lie on her back and opened her arms to her wife. She loved these early mornings after Emma fed Billy and he went back down for a few more hours. It'd been four months since the birth of their third child, and they were enjoying the routines that revolved around the baby. Watching Emma with him made her thankful for all they had.

"Those are the chances you take by exposing your breasts in here," Cain said, running her hand down Emma's back to her butt.

"I'll have to remember that." Emma moved to lie on top of her, smiling when Cain put both hands on Emma's ass. "You make me feel so good."

"That's my job, and only my job." She gave Emma a mock glare. "Remember, I'm the jealous type."

"The truth is, you've ruined me for anyone else, so no worries." Emma lowered her head and kissed the side of her mouth. "And I'm beginning to think my hormones will never get back to normal." Emma rolled them over again, seeming to like the position this morning.

"Are you okay?" She pressed her thigh harder between Emma's legs when she started rocking against her again.

"I'm fine, but I'm afraid of wearing you out if the craving for sex doesn't start to slow." Emma lifted her hips when Cain put her hand between them. "It wasn't like this the last time."

"Lass, IRS audits are something to complain about," she said, pressing her fingers against Emma's clit. "You craving sex isn't something I'll *ever* think of as a bad thing." She kissed her way down Emma's body until she reached the top of her sex. "That you're wet and ready for me is a gift, never a hardship."

"I love the way you talk to me, but right now I need you to shut up and put your mouth on me." Emma lifted her hips and spread herself open. "Fuck," she said when Cain flattened her tongue and swiped up hard and fast. Emma grabbed Cain's hair and held her in place. "Put your fingers in…I need you to put them in."

The way Emma moved and demanded she go harder proved that the first orgasm of the day hadn't done much to calm the need in her. Cain smiled when Emma slammed her legs together, effectively trapping her head between her thighs. She didn't let up and stilled her fingers when Emma let out a long moan and then pulled on her hair to get her to stop.

"I love you so much," Emma said when she came up and held her. The declaration sounded weepy, but Cain was getting used to that as well. It was true that Emma's hormones weren't back to normal, but the doctor had said she was a long way from postpartum depression and to give it time.

"You okay?" she asked a few minutes later when Emma wiped her face with the sheet.

"This time it's more from you overwhelming me than from anything bad. You're that good, so live with it."

"That's true, but if you need to talk to me, I'm here every night." She was used to the kidding as well, but she still worried that there might be something lurking under the surface that brought on the tears. Emma was here, and she'd never been happier, but she'd never take her job as Emma's partner lightly. Her life would be empty without this woman.

"That I know and give thanks for all the time." Emma lifted her head and kissed her. "You and the kids are the best things in my life."

"We love you, so don't ask me not to worry a little bit," she said, wiping away the rest of Emma's tears.

"I know that about you too, and do you know what the best thing is to knock the worry right out of your head?" Emma moved to put her knees between Cain's legs.

"What's that?" She almost forgot how to form words when Emma dragged her hard nipples over her chest and down her abdomen.

"My mouth on your clit."

"Shit," she said as Emma sucked her in. The feel of Emma's tongue on her clit made her close her eyes and lift her hips. Emma was relentless, and she kept her hand behind Emma's head until Emma was done driving her insane. When she could finally speak again, she said with a smile, "You would make a fortune as a psychologist. Your bedside manner is impeccable."

"You're right, but I'm dedicated to the one patient I love," Emma said and laughed. "Now that you've performed your marital duties, what's on tap for today?"

"I've got Muriel coming over. She called last night and has some news. Then I have to talk to Fin." She spoke softly as the room started to fill with light. In an hour, everyone in the house would be up and getting ready for the day. Their lives were fast paced, and these quiet times with Emma were what fortified the armor she needed to navigate her days.

"Still nothing when it comes to Fin's situation?" Emma sat up and held out her hand. "Want to share a shower with me? You reek of sex," she said, winking.

"With any luck, I'll be in the same situation tonight." She got up and scooped Emma into her arms, getting a squeal out of her.

"That's a given." Emma kissed her all the way to the bathroom and stood behind her when she put her down to adjust the water temperature. "Are you free for lunch?"

"I am, and I already made a reservation, if you don't mind Remi and Dallas joining us. Remi said Dallas had some questions about their reception, and your valuable input is needed."

"I keep telling her the woman standing next to her is the most important part," Emma said, putting her arms around Cain's waist. "But I'd be lying if I said I didn't obsess over every little thing too, until I got that ring on your finger."

"You know damn well that I was yours, ring or no, from the day you spilled beer on me." She jumped a little when Emma pinched her nipple.

"Don't go rewriting history, mobster. I had to chase you down plenty before I convinced you that you couldn't live without me. Remi is cut from that same cloth, and I give you both credit for being spectacular at the partner job once you commit." Emma ran her soapy hand over her chest and kissed the spot over Cain's heart.

"Thank you, my love, and there's no doubt I'm all yours. As for

Remi, she's in the same boat I am. When you talk to Dallas today, go ahead and tell her our idea for the reception. It's a way of controlling the guest list as well as keeping the watchers out."

"We can cover it at lunch, and then I'm getting the rest of what we'll need for the end of this week."

Mardi Gras was in full swing, and the city was full of tourists as well as locals enjoying the free show. They were a block from the St. Charles Avenue parade route, which had necessitated doubling the guards on the wall around the property. Big crowds heading to the parades meant a large number of strangers walking around the house, and the guys on the wall discouraged loitering. She wasn't letting her guard down again when it came to her family.

"Anything you need me to do?"

They were flying up to the house they'd built on Emma's father's property, and they were taking a crowd with them. The remote area known for dairy farming was a godsend, allowing them to get away from the ever-present FBI agents who followed her around daily. They'd added five guest cottages on Ross Verde's property, leaving the house by the lake for just them and the kids.

Hayden and Hannah were finally enjoying cousins to play with, thanks to Fin's return, and Abigail's three children. As the family grew, so would the accommodations to house them all. That's what all the hard work was about. Having her family around her was why Cain dedicated herself to making their lives bulletproof. The money was secondary to the sanctity of family.

"Just tell me we're ready to go." She soaped Emma's back and spent more time than necessary on her backside.

"We are, but have you broken it to Hannah yet? She's not going to like leaving Lucy behind." Their daughter Hannah had grown attached to her school pal Lucy, who had divorcing parents and constant drama in her young life. The little girl seemed to spend more time with them than at home, and that meant more interaction with Lucy's mother, Taylor Kennison.

"I wanted to talk to you about that," Emma said, stepping out as she shut the water off. "Don't give me that face, honey."

"I'm not giving you a face, but please tell me you didn't invite the fictitious Drew and Taylor." She accepted a towel and thought about those two again. No matter how much Muriel, her law associates, Finley, or Merrick dug, they didn't exist in any database. She had enough to worry about without adding any more unknown elements to her plate.

"As if, but I did want to talk to Taylor about Lucy coming with us, if you agree," Emma said, kissing the top of her shoulder from behind. The woman had come by their house a couple of times to complain to Emma about her cheating husband and his shitty ways. Cain wasn't buying that either.

She turned and laughed as she kissed the top of Emma's head before moving to hang up her towel. "Why are you even asking me? If I say no, I'm the bad guy."

"That's not true and you know it." Emma pressed up against her naked back. "I did want to clear it with you, though. I'll agree that there's something not right about these people, but Lucy is stuck in the middle. It's not fair to her, and she's really hurting."

That was true, and it was never fair when kids got caught in their parents' drama, whatever it was. "Talk to Taylor and see what she says. They might want to keep Lucy in town for the holiday, but she might enjoy spending time with Finley's three as well as Hannah."

"You're the best, mobster."

"I know," she said, slapping Emma on the ass. "You said it a few times this morning."

Cain finished dressing and headed downstairs as Emma got Hannah and Hayden up for school. Both kids looked like her, but they took after Emma and her love of sleeping in. It took everything short of dynamiting them out of bed to get them going in the morning.

Muriel was waiting for her in the office, reading over a file. When she glanced up, Cain wanted to groan at Muriel's expression. "Go ahead and tell me." Cain stared at the ceiling and shook her head, waiting for Muriel's report. It sounded like a stampede of out-of-control cattle above them, and she smiled at the sound. Hannah knew only one way to move in the world, and that was at full throttle. "No matter what you've heard, I seldom kill the messenger."

"There's always a first time," Muriel said and laughed.

She smiled, liking that Muriel was almost back to the cousin she'd grown up with. After the death of her Uncle Jarvis, she'd been afraid she'd lose Muriel to the pain and guilt. Muriel had been hard to reach, but what had cut through all that was the same thing that had saved Cain when she'd lost so much. The love of a woman had finally given Muriel hope for her future. That the union had the potential to bind their family to the Jatibons was an added bonus.

"I understand that life is a bag of shit sometimes, cousin, but we have no choice but to shovel through it. That or throw it back in the yard it came out of." Cain sighed and lowered her head. "Helping Fin and Abigail wasn't up for debate, but…" She sighed again. "But it's going to haunt us until the ghosts of the past are put to rest in a more permanent way."

Special Agent Finley Abbott of the FBI was now on her payroll, and she'd given her the keys to the kingdom. Fin was her first cousin and someone she didn't feel any differently about than Muriel or Katlin—her trust in her was absolute. After dedicating herself to hunting down scum who dealt in human trafficking, Finley had retired because of her last case. That's where she'd met Abigail Eaton and her three children. Fin had fallen in love with Abigail as well as the children, but she'd also taken on Abigail's problems. Those problems weren't simple to fix, even with Cain's inventive problem-solving skills. Getting it wrong would come with stiff penalties.

"Do you honestly think Nicola Eaton is still alive?" Muriel appeared skeptical, but Cain believed Abigail, the one woman alive who knew Nicola best.

Nicola Eaton, or Nicola Antakov, had been Abigail's partner and also owned the Hell Fire Club in town. Cain had kept an eye on it from the opening, but brothels weren't her style. There were plenty of supposed bad guys in New Orleans, but the Russian mob was a whole other animal, the kind you never turned your back on. Then again, there were brothels, and then there was the Hell Fire Club.

Hell Fire was a place where every sexual appetite, no matter how depraved, was catered to. That was fine—whatever two consenting people thought was fun was okay. To each his own. The problem was that only the customers were having fun. The women under Nicola's control were trapped in servitude and not many escaped alive.

"Nicola's parents David and Valerie are the only two I'm sure about." The Eatons were a dead subject. They'd met with her and asked for Abigail's head on a pike, selling a story about being poor grandparents losing a battle to see their grandchildren because of their bitch birth mother. That lie—not to mention the reason they really wanted Abigail found—was why they'd paid at the end of Finley's spray of bullets. "All I know is to trust the person who knew her best, and Abigail says she's not dead."

"But why the ruse?"

"Fin might be the answer to that, or should I say Special Agent Abbott holds the answer. Fin's investigation was getting close, so Nicola did the best thing she could to get her head out of the noose. If you're trapped with no escape, what better than death to throw the feds off your ass?" She thought about the tall woman who'd introduced herself as Nicola Eaton the night they'd met at Ramon Jatibon's club, and the way she'd carried herself. There was no denying Nicola was a bitch, no matter what last name she went by. "So go ahead and tell me what you have to say."

"I got a call from an associate in New York, and she told me there's plenty of money on the street here for any information about you. Whoever can get the full story on you is in for a big payday."

"I had no idea I was that interesting," She glanced at her watch when she heard the running above her heading for the stairs, with Emma talking loudly. "Any idea who's behind it?"

"Not yet, but I offered up more cash to make it a two-way street of information."

"Good, that's one more thing we'll have to discuss when we head somewhere I don't feel so hemmed in. Do you have time for breakfast?" She stood and took off her jacket, then draped it over the back of her chair.

"Lead the way."

"Hannah Marie Casey, if you don't stop running I swear..." Emma said as Cain reached the bottom of the stairs in time to catch Hannah when she jumped from the seventh step up. "Why must you encourage her?" Emma asked as she gripped the railing and seemed to start breathing again.

"Because fearless people come to rule the world," Cain said, kissing Hannah's cheek. "Isn't that right, Hannah girl? What do you say?"

"Sorry, Mama," Hannah said, appearing anything but as she gazed up at her mother with a smile.

She put Hannah down when Emma handed her the baby. "You're as incorrigible as she is." Emma's hand stayed on Cain's arm as Emma stuck her tongue out at her.

"Lassie, you say that like it's a bad thing," she said as she put her free hand around Emma's waist.

"I should spank you for teaching your daughter bad things, but you're not lying. You always follow through." Emma shook her head as they headed for the kitchen.

The baby jumped in her arms when he saw their longtime housekeeper Carmen and lunged at her when they were close enough. There'd been plenty of changes around the house with the addition of family, but none more surprising than Ross and Carmen's budding romance. She had a feeling Dallas and Remi weren't going to be the only ones planning a ceremony in the future now that Ross was almost free of Carol.

"Mom, don't forget I'm going to the movies with my friends after school," Hayden said when she sat down.

"I haven't forgotten, and here." She handed over three twenties.

This was the fourth time he'd mentioned it, so she was starting to suspect the friends weren't his buddies from the all boys school he attended. "Remember that Mook stays with you," she said of Hayden's longtime guard.

"You know it, and I'll be home by seven or so."

"Make it seven on the dot," Emma said, and her tone meant it would be unwise to argue. "It's a school night, so lose the pout, son. Besides, I'm sure the girl's parents will agree with me."

"Yes, ma'am," Hayden said, and Cain had to laugh.

"Now you see why I never step out of line," she said to him and winked at Emma. "Finish eating, and Mama and I will give you a ride to school."

She smiled as the kids talked nonstop about their friends and school. The only surprising thing was that Hannah had stopped talking about Lucy as much. That she hadn't mentioned her once today meant there was something wrong, but Hannah had a way of clamming up whenever she asked too many questions about her best friend.

"Do you feel okay, Hannah?" Emma asked, seeming to have figured out the same thing.

Hannah nodded but stayed quiet as she shoved eggs in her mouth. "Are Liam and Tori coming with us to Grandpa's?" Hannah said after a long pause, clearly changing the subject.

Abigail's youngest two were common sights around their house after they'd fallen in love with Hannah. Sadie, the oldest at ten, liked to read and help her mom with her siblings, and Hannah loved her as well. Cain was hoping Fin would move the relationship along, which meant taking legal responsibility for Abigail's children. It was the honorable thing to do, and it would also drive Nicola out of whatever hole she was hiding in. Not that she wanted to use the family as bait, but that was one of the only ways to find someone who'd died as effectively as Nicola.

"Everyone's coming, so you'll have plenty of people to play with. Are you finished?" she asked, pointing at Hannah's plate.

"All ready, Mom." Hannah picked up her dirty dishes and handed them to Carmen.

They left with an entourage of guards, and Cain stared at the van a house down from them. This time it was a plain panel van, and she got a kick that the neighbors took turns calling the police about it. It had been months since she'd seen any of the people inside, but they were always there. She couldn't imagine such a boring existence. All they did was watch her bring her kids to school, take her wife out on dates, and go to the office. The slipup they were waiting on was never going to happen unless she lost her senses. Wishful thinking on their part if they thought that was in their future.

Hayden was dropped off first, and they headed back uptown for Hannah's school. She walked Hannah to the front door and shook hands with the young woman who was now Hannah's teacher. The old bitch who'd given their daughter such a hard time was history, and the young woman who'd taken her place was someone Hannah adored.

"Are you going to be good?" she asked Hannah as she crouched to Hannah's level.

"I'll give it my best shot," Hannah said, smiling because her answer had made Cain laugh.

"That's the best we can ask for, kid."

"Is there trouble in paradise?" she asked Emma when she got back in the car. "Lucy is usually waiting for her at the door, and Hannah never mentioned her this morning."

"I'm not sure, but I'll talk to her this afternoon," Emma said, taking her hand. "Want me to call Dallas so you and Remi don't have to listen to wedding plans?"

"You have me all wrong, darlin'. I love weddings. It's the romantic in me."

"You are that, and you gave me a wedding I loved." Emma rested her head on her shoulder and sighed. "Then do you mind if I go shopping before we meet them for lunch? We have that thing tonight, and I'm not quite down to my usual size."

Cain hadn't been around when Emma had given birth to Hannah, but she was like this after Hayden. Emma wasn't vain about her appearance per se, but at times it took a little persuasion on her part to convince her she looked good. "You're not upset, are you? I happen to love the size you are, so buy whatever you want, but forget about any crazy diets. You're beautiful and sexy." She lifted her arm and put it around Emma's shoulders.

"You're good for my ego, honey. If you want, drop me at home, and I'll have the guys drive me."

"I'm headed in that direction, and I have some time to kill, so I'll come with you."

Emma looked at her as if she wanted to say something but ended up smiling and putting her head down on her shoulder again. She pulled Emma close, thinking. There was some inkling at the edges of her subconscious that understood what was coming. She'd taken something precious from Nicola Eaton, and there'd come a time when she either had to pay for that or mete out more punishment. Killing enslaved women to save your own ass proved what kind of people the Eatons were. That meant Cain's family was fair game.

That terrified her more than anything she'd ever faced. She'd lost her parents and her siblings to dishonorable men, but losing Emma or any of their children would put her in the grave. Planning and vigilance were the only ways to face this, but Nicola was coming, and when the day arrived, she wanted to be the one left standing, with her family unharmed. Until then, all she could do was stay close and worry in silence and hope that she'd put enough layers between the threat and those she loved.

"You can talk to me too, you know," Emma said softly as she stuck her hand in her shirt and rubbed the skin of her abdomen. "I'm easy to find most nights."

"That I know, lass, but sometimes I have to find a way to put things." She kissed Emma's forehead and exhaled deeply. "Do you understand?"

"I understand it's more like you trying to figure out how to say it so it won't worry me," Emma said, lifting her head and kissing her. "I love you more than life, but you're so infuriating sometimes."

"No sugarcoating, huh?"

"See, that's why they made you the head of our clan. You get the answer right without a lot of prompting," Emma teased and kissed her again.

"We've come a long way from that beer bath, lassie." She wanted to chuck the day and spend it naked with Emma.

"We have, love, but there's plenty more road to travel. All I'm asking is you keep showing me the map."

The car stopped, and it was too early for the shopping center to be open, but a man in a great suit stood outside waiting. "I promise, and I'm sorry for stewing in silence."

"Don't worry. I'll whip you into shape once I get you alone again."

CHAPTER TWO

"Do you know what my father used to say about failure?" Nicola Antakov asked Nina Garin. Nina had been the only one her father had trusted with the fact she was still alive, and she was the one who'd come and told Nicola the news of their deaths.

"No, ma'am." Nina put her teacup down and maintained eye contact.

"It's a sign of weakness. You show weakness and the world will finish you off." The apartment in Trump Tower was beautiful and a gift from her father, but it had become a prison. No matter how beautiful the bars.

"There was no way to know that Casey would double-cross Mr. Antakov and your mother. That's more a lack of honor than a failure," Nina said, as if knowing exactly what she wanted to hear. "But to be fair, I can't prove Casey had anything to do with this. From what your father reported, she'd agreed to help them."

"I don't believe that, so don't insult me by repeating it. It's time to join the land of the living and get what's left of my family back." She'd been living as Crista Belchex for the last year and a half, and she'd used the time to heal. It was no lie that the plane carrying her and her twin, Fredrick, had gone down, but death wasn't in the cards. "I refuse to let my children grow up not knowing me."

"We need to shore up our support before we can do that," Nina said, clicking her mouth closed when she seemed to realize she'd overstepped.

"What did I just say about failure?" she screamed. The pain that shot from her jaw to her right temple made her stop and breathe deeply. There were certain injuries the doctors had told her wouldn't go away, and the nerve damage she'd sustained was something she could do nothing about. The other most noticeable souvenir the accident had left her with was her limp. "Damn."

"The family lost plenty of ground when your cousin gave over all the ledgers. Please don't take that as an insult—it's fact." Nina didn't stand but did appear wary. "She's never been found, and your aunt Yula is worried about her sons."

Her father had placed too much stock in family. Just because you carried the Antakov name didn't buy you loyalty. Linda Bender was her cousin, her father's niece, and she'd screwed them and run. Linda had been trusted with the ledgers that contained their entire operation, going back to her grandfather arriving from Russia. The day her parents had left for New Orleans to cut a deal with Casey about Abigail, Linda had allowed the FBI to raid the warehouse where all the paper was stored.

"Don't say her name in my presence." The other person who'd pulled a disappearing act was Boris, her father's fixer, and that couldn't be a coincidence. Who knew such a big man could run so scared? "And don't say we can't prove what she did."

"I wouldn't," Nina said, "because that one I know for sure. Linda took enough money to fund her disappearance with her brothers, and it'll take time to find her. I also know we need to regroup and formulate a plan going forward, Nicola. What you need to understand is all this has left us in chaos. The men aren't ready to accept you as the boss, even after you come back from the grave after Yury's death. They see you as taking the easy way out while some of them went down without backup from the family. We need to give them something that'll solidify their reason to follow you."

"How about a few of their heads on a plate? I'm my father's heir, and they're going to have to accept that or die," she said, rubbing her temple. The pain in her head was just slightly less than the pain in her hand, but that was an old injury. "Be ready to move. I'm going to deal with Abigail and her betrayal, and I'll deal with the rest when I get back."

"Who do you want to bring with you?"

"Let's keep it small. There's no reason to invite trouble if someone notices us. Choose the people you know aren't going to be a problem. The ones who know who's boss." She motioned Nina away, wanting to lie down for a little while. "And make the flights to Biloxi, not New Orleans."

"What's in Biloxi?"
"Money, casinos, and answers."

The sound of the pounding surf was relaxing Jerome Rhodes as he got a massage on the balcony of his room. He'd escaped the tourists overrunning Cabo San Lucas in search of warm weather and had come to Malibu to find some quiet. He'd brought only a few men and his new bedmate, Daniela Navarro. Once Gustavo—formerly Juan Luis—and his mother, Gracelia, were dead, he'd returned to the house Gracelia had owned and taken over. No one had questioned him, and the number of men he now had meant no one ever would.

Unlike the Luis family and the rest of the thugs like them, he was taking it slow and building his business so it'd be impossible to penetrate. The first part of his methodical plan to not only start his own operation but to be the biggest distributor in the United States was to get rid of the competition without firing a shot. That was the most important lesson he'd learned watching people from small shitty vans. Cain Casey ruled an empire, and the bitch used her brain more than her muscle.

Casey would be no competition, though. Drugs weren't her game. No, the current king, Hector Delarosa, had gotten soft with his move to New Orleans. All he'd done from his arrival in the city was chase Casey like a lovestruck teen, but nothing he did got Casey to bend. It was like he kept trying new ways to change her mind and couldn't accept Casey wasn't into drugs. It was rather pathetic.

No, Casey had grown fat and rich off liquor and cigarettes, but she didn't have the stomach for where the real money was. Casey was a wannabe in a man's world, and when the time came, he'd pay her back for the loss of his life and name. He'd gone to Rodolpho Luis, then his nephew Juan, as a last resort to bring the smug Casey down, but the only thing he'd accomplished was to lose everything that had defined him. He'd screwed up so badly, there was no going back. Anthony Curtis was dead, and he'd be Jerome Rhodes to the grave.

"Señor," his right-hand man, Pablo Castillo, said softly. "I'm sorry to disturb you, but I have news."

"Take a break," he told the masseuse. The woman they'd sent up had good hands and was beautiful. After he dealt with Castillo, he was going to offer her enough to spend the rest of the afternoon massaging something else for him. It didn't matter that he had Daniela with him. When you were the boss, you could indulge in whatever you wanted.

"The men call me—" Castillo started, but Jerome lifted his hand to shut him up.

"Not out here," he said, already annoyed. "I keep telling you— there's always someone listening." That he knew for sure from his old life. Listening and watching people get rich doing whatever the hell they wanted had fueled his rage once upon a time. Now he knew power belonged to those courageous enough to take it. "What?" He turned the television on and brought his tone down considerably.

"The men call me, and Hector's fields are burnt. There will be no more plants for long time," Castillo said in broken English that was getting better.

"They did what I said?" He took a cigar from the small case he carried with him. He'd seen Casey and the Jatibon woman share a smoke sometimes and had given it a try. The Cuban Cohibas were an indulgence worth every penny he paid for them.

"Yes," Castillo said, laughing. "They spray and the ground die like you say. This will make the price go up, and we can start to sell."

"Give it another month." He blew the smoke out in rings and smiled. "The junkies who can't live without a fix will be willing to kill to get a hit. Once the money starts coming in, we'll take care of Hector and his crazy bitch of a daughter. That'll clear the way for us to take over."

"The men only worry about Carlos." Castillo appeared almost afraid to bring up the name of Rodolfo Luis's son and heir. The man who'd stood behind Rodolfo for years had been an effective leader who'd cobbled his father's empire back together and had become a force to be dealt with.

"That's not our problem right now, so tell them to relax. Concentrate on putting Hector out of business, and the rest will come when we're in charge." He sat and adjusted the towel around his waist, ready to get back to his massage. "I have something I need you to do for me, and you're the only one I trust to get it done."

"Whatever you want."

"It has to do with my father."

CHAPTER THREE

Emma twitched the new dress, getting it to lie correctly right above her knee. She'd picked it when Cain sat in the dressing room and smiled in a way that telegraphed what she thought. That welcome intense stare had made her want to come home again. It was the same look she was getting now, and it made her nipples hard.

There was no time, though. They were attending a dinner at Vincent Carlotti's restaurant, which had now become a quarterly thing for the families doing business together. Business only took up a small portion of the evening, and the rest of the time was spent laughing and catching up on each other's lives.

"You look more beautiful by the day," Cain said, putting her arms around her from behind.

"Stretch marks and all?" She loved all her children, but the little suckers did a number on her body every time.

"You can keep trying to change my opinion about something I believe with all my heart, but you're never going to succeed. To me, you are my picture of perfection, and you always will be." Cain kissed her neck and turned her around. "At the risk of being overly sappy, I happen to love every one of your curves, as well as every inch of you. It's why I try to get you naked every chance I can."

"You are a little sappy, but that's how I love you." She turned away again to put her earrings on and to have Cain help her with the necklace she'd chosen. "Anything interesting tonight?"

"Remi, Ramon, and I wanted an update on what Jasper Lucas and Vinny are up to," Cain said, sitting on the bed to watch her finish getting ready.

She smiled before putting on lipstick. "Are they up to something you're not happy about?"

"Not exactly, and it's more me being a worrier than anything else," Cain said, leaning back on her hands. "We'll get into it in more detail when we get home later, but Muriel told me there's someone paying for information about us."

"What kind of information?" She turned and gazed at Cain, knowing she wouldn't try to keep the truth from her. The way she was sitting also made her want to do things they didn't have time for. Cain laughed when she put her hands over her breasts. "Stop laughing at the big horny woman and tell me."

"Anything anyone has to offer up. Remember what I told you about Napoleon Bonaparte?"

She laughed at Cain's conversation tangents. "Something about supply chains losing him the war," she said, tapping her chin with her index finger.

"That's me right now, and it's driving me a little batty." Cain chuckled. "When there's too many variables out there ready to pounce, it makes me nervous. I don't have enough muscle to cover everything I think needs covering."

"This is when you should concentrate on the things that are rock solid in your life, mobster. The most important thing is you're loved. Granted, I'm at the top of that list, but there's plenty of people who feel the same." She leaned over Cain, pressing their lips together. "I know you're never going to let your guard down, but remember that I'm right here."

"I know," Cain said, kissing her again. "Need anything before I can't kiss you again?"

"You can kiss me whenever you like, lipstick isn't going to stop you, but go check on your daughter before we go. She's still not talking, and I'm about to take a wet noodle to her to see what's bothering her."

"My guess is Lucy, but she'll spill it when she's ready." Cain stood and squeezed her fingers before walking off.

Hannah's silence was starting to bother her, but Cain was right. They couldn't force the kid to talk. She finished with the lipstick and went to stand outside Hannah's door. If Hannah would talk to anyone, it'd be her idol. Hannah loved everyone, but she adored Cain. That had been true from the first time Hannah saw Cain, and Cain's love had transformed the skittish little girl into a child who knew her mom would always be there to catch her if she stumbled.

"Hey, kiddo," Cain said and whatever Hannah had been tinkering with stopped. "You look a little down. Is something wrong?"

"No," Hannah said, not convincing anyone that was true.

"Come see," Cain said, and Emma stepped into view. Hannah was sitting in Cain's lap with her head down.

She sat next to Cain and took Hannah's hand, not minding the silence that stretched on for a few minutes. Hannah didn't seem uncomfortable with the silence and dropped her head to Cain's chest, and Emma waited to see if Cain would say anything.

"You know what the best thing about meeting your mama was?" Cain asked, and that got Hannah to lift her head and shake it. "I had someone to talk to when I was sad."

"And I had someone to talk to when *I* was sad," Emma said, kissing Cain's cheek, then wiping off the lipstick she'd left behind. "The best part was, no matter what I said, your mom never got mad."

"Then you and your brothers came along, and your mama and I want to hear if something is making any of you sad. You can tell me whatever it is, and I promise I'll try to fix it." Cain jiggled Hannah, finally getting her to smile. "What's wrong? Did Lucy and you have a fight?"

"No." Hannah's head went down, but at least she'd answered.

"Then did something else happen?" Emma asked, glancing at Cain for a moment. "Did she say something you didn't like?" That got her a nod. "Please tell us," she said, kissing Hannah's hand.

"Lucy said her mom and dad are mad all the time, but there was something that would make them happy." Hannah glanced at Cain then quickly at her. "She said I had to do it, so they wouldn't give her away again. If that happened, then she'd have to go back to bad people."

Emma had to take a minute to try to understand what Hannah was talking about. From Cain's expression she'd already made up her mind as to what this was about. Before her partner drove to Lucy's house and beat both her parents until the truth came out whether they wanted it to or not, she had to get Hannah to say it.

"What did you have to do?" Cain asked, sounding calm. The set of her jaw was what gave her away. Her wife was a compassionate soul when it came to her and the children, but there was a rage that built in her when someone threatened to upset any of them. That rage had a way of building until she found the best release valve, and at times it meant someone ended up dead, but that didn't bother Emma. The way Cain protected and stood up for them was what made her want to have as many children as Cain wanted. That overprotectiveness was an important part of why she'd fallen in love.

"You promise you won't get mad?" Hannah asked, looking at her before turning her eyes to Cain. Whatever this was, Hannah was more worried about upsetting Cain, so she squeezed Cain's arm to keep her calm.

"Hannah girl," Cain said, kissing the little girl's forehead. "No matter what, your mama and I will never be mad."

"She said I had to put something in your office and see if you found it," Hannah said as fast as the words could come out.

"That doesn't sound so bad," she said, staring at Cain over Hannah's head. She shared the anger she saw simmering in Cain's eyes.

"Mom doesn't like anybody in her office, and I told Lucy that. She said we can't be friends because I wouldn't do it." Hannah sounded miserable and started crying.

Cain's expression softened, and she closed her eyes momentarily. "You did the right thing, baby," Cain said, holding Hannah tighter.

"I'm sorry, Mom. I should've told you." Hannah turned and threw her arms around Cain.

Their daughter was a lot like their first-born son in that both of them loved their parents, but they didn't ever want to disappoint Cain. Not that Cain pushed them too hard or gave them a bad time, but it seemed to be an innate thing that had something to do with the Casey genes. Their mother's disappointment was way worse than her anger.

"You don't have to be sorry," Cain said, holding Hannah as she cried in earnest. "What Lucy did wasn't your fault, and it's not something a real friend would ask." Hannah gazed up at Cain as if she wanted to believe what she was saying. "The thing is, you have to forgive Lucy because it really wasn't her fault either."

"It wasn't?" Hannah put her hand on Cain's face, and Emma smiled.

"You have to understand that it was her mom and dad who asked her to do that. That wasn't a nice trick they asked her to play with you, but we're not mad. Do you promise to tell me if she asks you something like that again?" Cain winked at Hannah and tickled her.

"Yes," Hannah said, her tears and upset forgotten.

"Good. Now forget about that for tonight and have fun with Grandpa and Abuela."

Hannah jumped off Cain's lap and ran out like the normally carefree child she was. The smile on Cain's face disappeared as soon as Hannah left the room. Emma moved her hand over Cain's fist and nodded. "I know you're mad, but remember something else you always tell me."

"What's that?" Cain sounded winded.

"There's a time for everything, and right now it's not time for whatever's going through your head. Not that I don't agree, but you need to find out exactly what this is." She moved closer and leaned against Cain. "This isn't what it seems, and you can't go in blind."

"Everyone with honor knows that children are off-limits." Cain looked at her when she framed her face with her hands. "Hannah is an innocent, but so is Lucy."

"I know that, but who can we ask about what Lucy told her? And what did Hannah mean when she said if she didn't do this, Lucy'd have to go back to bad people? That isn't something a mother tells her child no matter what she's after." She caressed Cain's cheeks with her thumbs and understood perfectly the rage that she could see in Cain's features. "We already knew they weren't who they pretended to be when Taylor left a bug in the house. I thought Lucy was real, though. Now maybe that's not true. Maybe she's adopted."

"It has to be the feds. No one we're having problems with deals with state-of-the-art listening devices. The crew outside must be lowering their standards, because Taylor came to visit, and we found it after she left."

"They never had standards to begin with. Barney Kyle tried to kill you while he was their boss. That told me all I needed to know about that." She kissed Cain like they didn't have to go out, but it was the only way to make them both feel better. "Now take me out and show me a good time, honey."

"Are you sure you don't want to stay in?" Cain's hand had crept up her leg, and she laughed.

"I'm positive. If we make this a big deal, your kid will think it's a big deal. She's happy, so let's go."

"You're the boss," Cain said, standing and holding her hand out.

"There's only one clan leader, baby, and that's you. I love you, and because of you, we'll be fine."

"May I always live up to your expectations, lass."

❖

"What'd you do last night?" Joe Simmons asked Shelby Phillips as they sat in the back of the van across from the Casey house.

The only thing coming through the high-powered microphones pointed at the house was a repetitive techno beat. They weren't sure how Cain did it, but the music seemed to be aimed right at them no matter where they tried listening in, and it was always aggravating. They didn't think there could be anything more annoying than the song the big purple dinosaur sang, but this was torture.

"Stayed home and tried catching up on this series I'm watching," she said as she saw the car pull to the front door. "It was hard to leave last night."

"The series or this?" Joe said, putting binoculars up to his eyes.

"This," she said. The front door opened, and Cain came out first to open the car door for Emma. "There's something off, and I can't figure out what it is."

"There's always something off about these people. It's catching them at it that's been the problem." He laughed and she had to smile. Joe had pulled back the hostility aimed at Cain a thousandfold and concentrated on their jobs. "What are you talking about?"

"I'm not sure. It's like having a bum knee before a big storm. You know something's coming, but you have no idea how bad it's going to be." She belted herself into her seat as they pulled away.

"If the chatter is right, something is going on, but nothing concrete. We need to meet with the other teams in town to see if there's any overlap with what Casey has going on." Joe read from his notebook as they turned toward downtown. "Tonight is probably nothing more than the meeting of the evil minds."

She laughed, thinking that sounded like something her father would say. Her grieving over their murders hadn't completely ended, but she'd started healing once she knew the people who'd killed them had paid. Cain had given her that gift and had kept her word about leaving her to decide what would happen to the men. On the books, she didn't owe Cain anything for the privilege, but she knew that wasn't strictly true. There was always a price. It was a debt she'd gladly pay, but first there was one more person on her list before she paid anyone anything, and that was the man who'd ordered her parents' deaths to begin with.

How could a man who had worked so closely as part of their team double-cross her by ordering the deaths of her family? The question had no reasonable answer, but that's what Anthony Curtis had done before running off with the Luis family.

"What are you hearing?" she asked. Cain's car crossed Canal

Street into the French Quarter, and it appeared Joe was right. They were headed to Vincent's place.

"There's some new players in town, and they're looking to map the landscape. Once they do, they'll stick a pin in it and declare it theirs."

"Try to remember this isn't a James Bond movie, and speak so we can all understand." She laughed and was joined by their newest team member, Dylan Gardner. The blonde looked more like a surfer beach bum than an agent, but she was the replacement for Brent Cehan, who was serving a fifteen-year stretch at Angola State Penitentiary. He was still screaming about his innocence and how Cain set him up, but they'd all testified and corroborated Cain's alibi.

"One of the snitches familiar with the situation—" Joe stopped talking as Cain and Emma got out of the car and stared at their vehicle as if they could see them sitting inside. "Someone is paying for information about the people we follow around all day, and plenty of it. If that's true, your premonition might be right on the money. I mean, who pays for information unless they plan to use it for something?"

"Want to take Dylan inside?" she asked.

"You two go. You're not going to get anything, but at least you'll get a decent meal out of it. Vincent's a killer, but the guy knows how to make a mean sauce."

"Dylan, do you like Italian?" she asked, shaking her head at Joe again. "Call the guys assigned to Remi and Vinny, and see if they have something we don't, Joe. They shouldn't be hard to find since they're probably parked right next to us."

"All right, smartass. Get going and bring me a cannoli."

"Let's go, Gardner. It's time to run with the big dogs." She put her jacket on and headed to the restaurant where she found the Caseys still in the lobby greeting Vincent Carlotti. "Table for two please?" she said to the host.

"Are you having a nice evening, Ms. Phillips?" Cain asked as Emma took her hand. "It's been a while, and I haven't met your friend."

"Wait, you don't know who she is?" She was pushing it, but she did like to yank Cain's thin leash every so often. "I'll have to tell the boss you really don't know everything."

"Ms. Gardner, welcome to the city. It shouldn't take you long to figure out Ms. Phillips doesn't have a sense of humor. I don't care what she tells you to the contrary." Cain held her hand out and Dylan took it with a slight widening of her eyes. "You were kicking ass in Los

Angeles for the last four years, so I'll be sure to be on my best behavior. You seem like the kick ass and take names type."

"You know who I am?" Dylan asked.

"Like I tell Phillips and all her playmates all the time, it's only fair. You know all about me." Cain smiled and Emma laughed. Shelby had to laugh as well. Cain Casey was aggravating as hell, but she was entertaining. "At least you think you do. Life's more interesting if there are some mysteries left. Don't you think so?"

"Stop scaring the new agent and get going. We're only here for dinner," she said but did give Cain a small smile.

The host agreed to where she wanted to sit, so they were close to the room where the heads of the top three organized families in the city were meeting. She'd love to finally hear what they talked about just to satisfy her curiosity, job be damned. They took their menus and ordered two teas.

"I'd be nice to order a big glass of wine every so often," she said, and Dylan smiled at her.

"With your luck, you'd shoot someone in the kitchen if you got tipsy," Joe said in their ears. "It would be hard to explain if you let the killers escape because you can't walk a straight line."

"True, and we ordered tea, so get out of my head," she said, rolling her eyes. They ordered a meal after the drinks were delivered, knowing Cain and company would be a while. They always were. "Are you liking the new assignment so far?" she asked Dylan.

Their new team member was beautiful and seemed casual about everything except her job. They hadn't spent a lot of time together, which made it hard to get an idea of what made her tick. All she knew was that Dylan had transferred for safety reasons. She'd been made by one of the drug cartels, and the bureau had found it necessary to move her not only out of the state, but out of the public eye until things calmed down. Surveillance in the back of a van was certainly out of the public eye.

"I'm used to being in the field, but this isn't too bad." Dylan buttered a piece of bread and glanced at the closed room Cain had disappeared into. "Casey is a different animal than what I'm used to."

"What do you mean?" There was silence coming from her earwig, so Joe had taken her joke seriously. If they needed anything, she'd have to turn it back on.

"Drug lords get to the top not because of brains but muscle. The

king of the hill is the guy who climbs to the top of the most bodies."
Dylan sounded detached from what she was saying, but to stay sane
after that much blood, you'd have to have that mindset. "They kill
indiscriminately, but Casey doesn't strike me as that."

"Believe me, she's killed her share of enemies, but you're right.
Taking out innocent people to make a point isn't her style." She
swallowed around a lump that formed at the thought of her parents.
She'd blamed Cain at first and had come close to killing her even if
she would have landed in the cell she'd wanted to cage Cain in for
years. "I've learned that lesson the hard way, as have the people you're
working with."

"She's wicked smart, isn't she?" Dylan asked, a slight Boston
accent slipping out. All her time in California didn't seem to have killed
it off completely.

"It wouldn't be wise to underestimate her. Cain is more of a
tactician than a murderer, but she's as deadly as they come."

Dylan nodded, and she stared at Shelby, her features softening. "I
read the files Agent Hicks sent me, but official reports don't always tell
the whole story, do they?"

"Reports are written for court. Blunt can lose you a trial when the
accused is this charming and well known, and every agent knows that."
Shelby didn't mean to sound patronizing and hoped it didn't come
across that way.

"True, so tell me your take on all this." Dylan's smile widened.
"And don't take this the wrong way, but I'm used to getting results."

"Results?" she asked, already knowing the answer.

"We had a good close rate on all our cases, and none of them took
this long. So what's the deal?"

"Ah, you think we've been incompetent up to now and let her
skate. Is that your take?"

"I didn't say that. In California, we investigated and brought
people down. All those guys are sitting in maximum security and will
be old men before they get out. Your team has followed this family
around for years and made no significant progress. I don't get it."

A put-down like that didn't sound any better when the asshole
delivering it had a great smile and a beautiful face. "Our first supervisor
shot Casey on the order of another mob boss the first few months I
was here. That was followed by another one of our team members
going to work for the Luis family. That special guy was responsible for
killing my parents. He figured the most expeditious way of getting rid

of Casey was to become what we spend our days trying to bring down. Never mind that he was part of our team from the moment I started working on it."

"Hey, I didn't mean anything by it," Dylan said, putting her hands up.

"Please, of course you did. If you had the guts to say it, then have the guts to own up to it, Special Agent Gardner. Things here are way more complicated than anything you've dealt with before. What I haven't read about is your team bringing down anyone up the cartel chain. Investigating and bringing down low-level guys isn't rocket science."

"Hey, I *said* I didn't mean anything by it."

"Your delivery needs work, then, and I'm sure an attitude like yours will get you promoted, but it'll get you nowhere fast down here, especially with Casey. She'll take that superior attitude of yours as a challenge, and you'll pray for the days of the stupid drug folks you're used to dealing with." She got up and headed for the bathroom, giving Dylan a look that dared her to follow.

She headed to the restroom at the back of the restaurant and leaned against the closed door when she got inside. The sudden bouts of anger were something she had to work on in general, but sanctimonious bitches wreaked havoc on her rationality. This had the makings of another Anthony Curtis, and she wasn't going through that again.

"That was a short honeymoon period," a soft voice said from the other side of the bathroom. "Though, I've learned through the years that the best people don't often go into law enforcement. In the movies it's always the noble at heart that pursue the bad guys, but that's far from the truth."

"Mrs. Casey, you might be a tad skewed in your thinking," she said to Emma as she lifted her head and faced her. "Were you waiting for me?"

"What a conceited thing to say. Sorry to disappoint, but my bladder has a mind of its own," Emma said as she washed her hands. "You don't look like you're taking a true restroom break. Anything the matter? Feel free to tell me." Emma winked.

"I didn't realize you were moonlighting as a shrink."

"I'm not, but it's my way of trying to figure out how an organization as respected as yours lowers their standards to use a child to do your dirty work," Emma said, lifting her hand. "Please don't insult us both by denying the truth. A word to the wise, Agent Phillips, Hannah and

Hayden are off-limits. You've chased Cain for years, her father before that, and God only knows who before that. Don't compound your failure by trying to lure children into doing things they're ill prepared for."

"I know you're not going to believe me, but I have no clue what you're talking about." There were days she wished she had the forethought to stay in bed. Today was at the top of that wish list. "Hannah is in kindergarten. The bureau doesn't hire that young."

"Really, Agent Phillips, I know how old my child is. If you truly have no idea, then you have another problem on your hands. Let's hope you deal with it before we have another fiasco that leaves someone in my family needing medical attention. Don't pretend to not know what I'm talking about when I say that." Emma dried her hands and faced her. "If you'll excuse me."

"Could you talk to me a second? I'd really like to know what you mean." Her anger at Dylan evaporated, and any information from Emma might get them somewhere.

"Tonight isn't the time to unburden our souls, so move." Emma stepped through the door she opened for her.

Shelby rested her head against the closed door once she was alone. "Joe," she said, calling his cellphone.

"Yes, are you done talking about me?" he joked.

"We might have a big problem, and it's not our new asshole team member." She moved to a stall and lowered her voice.

"Can you explain? I'm not sure what you're talking about," he said, sounding as confused as she felt. "Wait, Dylan's an asshole?"

"She's underimpressed by our lack of results, since that's all she got when she was the legendary sheriff of Bumfuck, California."

"We'll talk about that later. What's the other part of this?"

She told him what Emma had said, and he hummed for a minute. "Do you want to call Annabel or do I?" Shelby asked. Fuck, she wanted to go home and lie down. She'd been right. There was something off, but hell if it wasn't in her own house. "Actually, it's your turn, but keep Dylan out of the loop for now. We're going to have enough problems."

And that was the story of her life lately.

CHAPTER FOUR

Cain glanced at the door when Lou and Emma walked back in. Her wife appeared angry, which was a change from when she'd excused herself to the restroom. "Did they run out of hand soap or something?" she asked, putting her arm around Emma's waist.

Her question made Dallas laugh. "You do look like you've lost your good humor," Dallas said.

"I ran into our favorite FBI agent in the bathroom and lost my cool over what happened with Hannah," Emma said, accepting a glass of wine from one of the waiters.

"Whoa." Remi put her hand up. "What happened with Hannah?" Remi was as overprotective of their children as she and Emma were. That had doubled when they'd named Remi and Dallas godparents to Hannah and Billy.

Cain told them about the talk they'd had with Hannah and what the little girl had admitted.

"That's terrible," Dallas said. "Using a child to do something is one thing, but trying to teach her to lie to you and Cain is unforgivable."

"Cain told Hannah that and made her feel better about not admitting what happened right away. It makes me angry when I think about how much time that little girl spent in our home and what else she might've left behind." Emma toyed with her fork.

"The boys are good about checking for things that need to be fumigated, lass, so don't worry about that." She rubbed Emma's side and kissed her temple when Vincent asked everyone to sit down. "Try to let it go for now, and we'll talk about it later."

Emma nodded. "Sorry, I told you to cool it before we left the house, and it's me who loses her shit when I see that bitch in the bathroom. And before you say anything, Shelby is no better than the rest of them.

I don't care what her excuses are. There should be a limit to how far you go even when it's something you want so badly you're willing to sell your soul to get it."

"I'm not disagreeing with you, but right now let's enjoy our night." Cain stood from her chair, taking a moment to observe Marianna Jatibon. Ramon's wife had come a long way in accepting what Dallas meant to her only daughter and seemed to genuinely enjoy her company. "I'll be back in a bit."

She went through a back door and headed down to the private room under the restaurant that was swept daily for bugs to keep prying ears out. This was the council her grandfather had set up years before—a way to iron out any details or head off any problems they were having with joint ventures, and a means to offer help to whoever needed it with minimal blowback.

"Thank God the city is getting back to normal after that fucking storm," Vincent said as an opener. It had been almost a year since Katrina, and with the exception of a few sections of town, most of the citizens had come back and business was good again. "It's easier to get lost in a crowd now that there's actually a crowd."

"True, but we need to discuss Jasper and Vinny's business. How's that going?" Cain asked.

"I'm glad you brought it up." Vinny poured them each a drink of the Irish whiskey Cain had gifted Vincent. "Someone just put the final nail in Hector's business, and that's going to bring nothing but problems. If any more fields are destroyed, there's going to be a shortage of supply, and that's going to mean war."

"Hector's not my favorite person, but does he have any idea who did this? Whoever it is, they had balls, considering the size and strength of his operation," she said, taking a glass. "No one needs a war right now, but we'll back you up if it comes to that. Who knows, it might give you the opportunity to expand if that's what you want."

Remi and Ramon nodded as the door upstairs opened and Remi's twin brother Mano came down. "I'm sorry I'm late, but there was a small issue I had to deal with that couldn't wait," he said, glancing at Remi, then Cain.

"No problem," Cain said, holding up her glass. "Here's to another good month, and to friendship."

"Saluto," Vincent and Vinny said, draining their glasses.

"We were talking about Hector Delarosa's problems," she said to

Mano. He'd recently moved back from Las Vegas and was running their casino interests in Biloxi as well as other things for his family.

"I asked around after the first fields went up in a ball of fire," Mano said, "but whoever's responsible isn't talking. That's smart considering what Hector would do to them if he found out."

Cain accepted another drink from Vinny and took a breath, already aware of Hector's problems. It was never good to project weakness, but Hannah was worth mentioning. "Something happened with Hannah I'd like to discuss."

She gave them the gist of the conversation, and Vincent appeared the most upset. The man was as tough and lethal as they came, but his one weakness in life was children. "That can't stand, Cain. What are you going to do about it?" Vincent asked.

"I'm not sure yet, but this kid's mother left a device in my house the day she came to introduce herself. The house had been swept that morning, and then it was there. It had to be her. Muriel checked her and her allegedly problematic husband out, and they don't exist. All those signs point to our friends outside."

"Those fuckers would stoop this low?" Vincent asked. He punched the top of the table and raised his voice.

"Emma just ran into Agent Phillips in the bathroom and told her something about it."

"Who the hell is that?" Vincent asked.

"You remember her as the friendly flight attendant planting bugs in your plane," she said, and Vincent flattened his hand.

"See?" He pointed at her. "You should've let me throw her out over the Atlantic on the way home. I wouldn't have minded the long way around."

"I agree, but there are two other feds I'd like to eliminate for trying to intimidate a child into doing their jobs for them. Don't worry, though, I'm going to be good. There's no sense inviting someone to crawl up our collective ass if two agents show up missing or dead."

"Thanks for that visual," Ramon said and laughed. "What these people did is not acceptable, and something must be done. Does everyone agree?"

They were in unanimous agreement, which was good, but they still had to proceed cautiously. "Thank you, but let me dig deeper into this. When I tweeze the ticks out, I don't want any part left behind to fester."

"Damn right," Vinny said. "These fuckers have been building up to something like this for a while. We either take it or not."

"I'm not taking it, but like I said, I need more information. There's plenty I'm willing to take, but when it comes to my children, I have a low threshold when it comes to bullshit. And this is nothing but bullshit." She lifted her glass again and everyone did the same. "To friendship."

"To friendship," Ramon said. "We'll keep an eye on the situation with Hector, but on this too. If the feds are going this route with you, we won't be far behind."

"Going to war with the feds isn't something I'm going to do lightly," she said, and that was all she needed to say out loud. Action didn't require permission from the other families, and they didn't expect her to ask.

"Let's have dinner, everyone," Vincent said, putting his hand on her shoulder.

They went back upstairs, and Cain winked at Emma when she faced her. "You know what I'm in the mood for?" she asked, whispering in Emma's ear.

"If it's anything but crab salad, wait to share that information until later," Dallas said, making Emma snort.

"I'm thinking more about drinks and dancing at a place named after my wife, lady with a dirty mind," Cain said, making Dallas and Emma laugh. "How about a double date after this?"

"I'm always up for dancing," Dallas said, "and Emma's is the only place I don't get hounded by people who think I'm dying to dance with them. It's crazy to ignore the overprotective big bear with me, but people aren't always the smartest." As a movie star, Dallas was never incognito, and she enjoyed the time with the family that meant she got some space.

They enjoyed dinner and talked about anything but work. Vincent embraced Cain and kissed her cheek before they left. He wanted her to know he had her back and always would. That made her think of Vincent's friendship with her father. They'd grown up together, and Vincent had stayed loyal long after her da had died.

"Vincent, you're a good friend, and I'll never forget that." She kissed both his cheeks and took his hand. "I live every day to make my da proud, but your continued friendship also makes me fortunate."

"You never have to worry about either of those things. You do his name proud," Vincent said and gave her a bag of cannoli for the kids. "Don't forget I'm always a call away."

"Thanks, Vincent."

There was plenty unsaid, but it could be deciphered between the lines. Life was like a puzzle where there were always missing pieces, but you needed to see the entire picture. It was the only way to survive in this particular profession. In truth, the picture could never have all the pieces in place in full view—that way you kept prying eyes from seeing what you knew was there. The fewer visible pieces you could get by with, the more successful you were.

"Let's have some fun," she said, opening the door for Emma. The restaurant was full but she didn't recognize anyone from Shelby's team still inside. "Maybe they didn't like the food," she said to Emma.

"Maybe the truth of what scum they are made her lose her appetite." The venom in Emma's voice meant she wasn't over her visit with Shelby.

Cain had gift-wrapped the two guys who'd killed Shelby's parents and left her in the position to take revenge without fear of it coming back on her. That favor should've bought her more goodwill than Shelby was showing, but Cain wasn't surprised that she wasn't willing to show gratitude. Revenge was one thing, but the love her cousin Muriel had once had for Shelby was deep, and Shelby had chosen her job over that. That proved the best thing about Shelby was her consistency. She couldn't be trusted because her job defined her.

"Father Andy tells me that God sees all, whenever I question something," she said, putting her arms around Emma and holding her.

"It's in the Bible, love." Emma put her hand back in her shirt and scratched the skin she could reach. "What does that have to do with anything?"

"It takes me a little longer than God, but eventually I find what I need to see. The moment I do, there'll be hell to pay for whoever did this." She tilted Emma's head up and kissed her. "In my gut, I don't see Shelby being behind this."

"I trust you, but you can't trust her. She's not going to care that you helped her. All those people hiding in that van are loyal only to themselves."

"That's the first lesson Da taught me, and I've never forgotten it. Right now, though, I want to dance with my wife."

They held hands as they bypassed the line into the nightclub, and there was a waiter waiting by their table in the back corner. She was happy to see Muriel and Kristen already there. "Hey, sorry we missed dinner, but I was swamped at work," Muriel said.

"Forget about it. We'll catch up tomorrow." The waiter took their order just as Remi and Dallas walked in. "Mrs. Casey, would you dance with me?"

"I'd love to." Emma took her hand and followed her to the dance floor. They didn't get to do this often, not wanting to leave the kids too many nights, but she loved holding Emma as they moved to the music.

"The best thing that ever happened to me was meeting a girl in an Irish pub a lot of years ago," she said as she lowered her head so Emma could hear her. "That balances out whatever bad things we have going on, lass. So stop worrying—we're going to be okay."

"I know, because you'll take care of us. This may sound hypocritical, but I want you to make them pay. Had it been anyone but Hannah, maybe it would've been forgivable, but I can't forget that it was."

"We'll leave the forgiveness to the Lord, my love. That's not in my job description."

Emma smiled when she turned her head up and kissed her chin. "That's okay, I'm more interested in the devil I know."

Chapter Five

S top talking shit and answer my question," New Orleans Police Detective Elton Newsome said. The two feds sitting across from him in the café across the lake in Slidell briefly glanced at each other but didn't say a word. "You two dipshits don't seem to understand that you've blown my world to hell, and there ain't no going back."

"You knew the risks going in," Special Agent Barry Knight said in a condescending way that made him want to put a bullet in his head.

"If you say that one more time, I'm driving to the New Orleans bureau office and making an appointment to talk to Annabel Hicks. Call me crazy, but I'm willing to bet the ten bucks I have left to my name that's she's going to be interested in what I have to say." He finished his coffee and decided to stop giving a fuck. Playing nice hadn't gotten him anywhere, and it was time to make other plans.

He'd fallen for the bullshit these two had fed him when they'd approached him months before. Their plan, which involved Emma's mother Carol, had seemed foolproof. They'd take Casey down, Carol would get what she wanted, and he'd get the credit for the bust. That feather would've come with major promotions at the NOPD. The one thing he should've considered wasn't the future glory, but that it was Casey he'd be pitted against. Well, that and that their plan involved Carol Verde, that crazy bitch.

"Detective Newsome," Special Agent Christina Brewer said, following him out. "Stop before things are said that we'll all regret. Forget about what Barry told you, and tell me what it is you want."

"How about a million dollars and I'll make like the wind," he said, making a sweeping motion with his hand. "You'll never have to worry about me again."

"What exactly do you think you've done to make you worth a

million dollars?" Barry asked, coming out with his wallet in his hand. "You were given an assignment, you ad-libbed, and you fucked it up. You did a shitty job of keeping Carol Verde in line, and your mistake has put us back months."

"You two didn't do much better. You promised that crazy-ass bitch a lot of things you couldn't deliver on, so don't blame me. Your mistake was thinking Carol would be enough of a distraction to throw Casey off her game." Elton took his keys out and moved toward his car. "All she wanted was that kid, so she could save her soul from the perverts, and she wasn't sitting around waiting on your timeline."

"You're going to have to be patient, Elton. I understand what you want, but that's not going to happen." Barry reached over and took his hand, squeezing to the point of it being uncomfortable. "Believe me, if there's something we can do for you, we'll do it. Until then…" Barry let him go and moved so Christina could hand over an envelope.

He counted six hundred-dollar bills. "Is this a joke?" He laughed and slapped the envelope against Barry's chest. "That won't buy a tank of gas and groceries. If you're going to lowball me, then you give me no choice but to move to greener pastures."

Barry grabbed him again but bent double when Elton punched him in the gut. "Fuck," Barry said, letting out a whoosh of air.

Elton had his gun in his hand in case either of these fuckers tried something stupid. "That's right, you're fucked. Now stay away from me. We're done."

❖

Cain smiled as Merrick Runyon walked into the house. Cain was waiting for her in the foyer, thinking of the days they'd spent together when Merrick was the one person in the world she trusted to keep her safe. She now trusted Merrick to do that job for Emma. She'd almost given her life to do just that, and for her act of bravery, Cain owed her the world.

"Breakfast?" Cain asked as her cousin Katlin followed Merrick in. Merrick and Katlin had been lovers for a while now, and she was happy for both of them. "Then I have something I need you to do."

"Whatever you need," Merrick said as they headed to the kitchen. The kids were already eating and talking about the trip they were getting ready to take. "Hey, guys, ready for tomorrow?"

"We're going sledding, Aunt Merrick," Hannah said in a way

that made Cain think that she'd forgotten all her sadness from the day before. "Do you want to come?"

"I can't wait," Merrick said, kissing the top of Hannah's head.

"I have a surprise for you," Katlin said to Hannah. "Can you guess?"

"What?" Hannah said, standing on her chair. The little girl slapped her hands together before holding her arms out to Cain.

"Aunt Fin told me Victoria is starting at your school today, and she's coming with us tomorrow," Katlin said, having heard what happened the night before. "Do you think you can be a good friend today? Aunt Abigail is counting on you."

"Yes!" Hannah said, screaming her answer. She wiggled enough that Cain put her down. "Let's go, Mom. I want to see Victoria."

"Calm down a little and finish your breakfast," Emma said, coming in with Billy in her arms.

Cain took the baby and placed him against her shoulder. "Have fun today and listen to your mama."

"I'll be taking you guys today, so let's not be late." Emma patted her chest and blew her a kiss. "Want me to take him?"

"He's okay," she said as Merrick and Katlin followed her to the office. "Did Katlin talk to you last night?" she asked once the door was closed.

"I did, and Merrick isn't any happier than I am about it."

"That's true," Merrick said, "but there's ways of handling this. Is the bug in the living room still active?" Merrick sat and took a note pad off her desk.

"It has its purposes," she said, cradling Billy.

The little boy looked up at her as if he had something on his mind. She had a feeling this one was going to be her wild one, followed by Hannah. Once they hit puberty, her life and Emma's were never going to be remotely the same. If Billy was anything like her brother, she'd be gray way before her time.

"I didn't want Taylor Kennison, or whatever her name is, to think I was on to what she'd done. What I do want to know is who Taylor and Drew Kennison are. We both know those people, along with Lucy Kennison, don't exist. Muriel has checked and rechecked but hasn't found anything." She glanced up at Merrick. "This needs your special attention."

"True, but they aren't figments of our imagination. They're real, here and have found a way in. The bug in the living room proves that."

"It's time to put a little more effort into this, Merrick. I want to show these people the same hospitality they've shown me. I'm thinking the best way in is to start with Lucy. If she's not their kid, she had to have come from somewhere." She made a face to make Billy smile. The sight of it made her anger come down a few notches. "Do we have everything to get that done?"

"We do, but I'll have to finesse who goes. You don't want to tip your hand, and with your permission, I'm going to put some guys on these people." She made a few notes and tore the page off, folded it, and put it in her pocket. "The best way to follow breadcrumbs is when they put them down themselves."

"What about our friend Newsome?" The other secret to success was never forgetting anyone who'd done them harm. Detective Newsome had brought Carol back into their lives, and the bitch had kidnapped Hannah. That would never be forgotten or forgiven. She didn't care if he was the chief of police—Newsome had a bill to pay, and it was overdue.

"He's in Slidell and getting desperate. I have someone on him, and so far, all he's done is order pizza and catch up on all his television shows. Whenever you're ready, we can take care of that too." Merrick crossed her legs and stretched her fingers. "According to the guys in the department, they're still looking for him, but haven't had any luck."

"They must not be trying too hard."

Merrick laughed. "It could be that I'm that good."

She smiled as she heard the loud voices in the hall. "That's a given, but now you have to get to work. How's Dino working out?" she asked. Lou's nephew had just joined them.

"He's good with the kids, and he pays attention. Lou taught him well." Katlin took Merrick's hand as she stood and opened the door. "Go ahead and stop worrying about this."

"Keep me in the loop," she said on the way out.

"I'll take care of it, and whatever happens, we won't be in town," Merrick said.

Cain went out and kissed everyone good bye. "See you this afternoon," she said to Emma as Carmen took the baby. "I have a meeting with Finley about a few things, and then a few stops."

"Be careful and don't be late." Emma turned so she could help her with her coat. "And don't forget to stop at Dickie's Sporting Goods. You'll have a disappointed daughter if you don't."

"I'm not that forgetful. I'll see you at four."

Finley's brother, Neil, was still driving Finley so Cain could keep her out of the sight of the feds. Introducing her to the operation was going to take time and finesse. The people watching had long memories, and she didn't want to put Fin in a tight spot. All the information she had on the agents who watched her had nothing to do with Fin's time in the bureau. The feds, though, were never going to believe that.

"Lou, what's the status on the shipments coming in from New York?" she asked as she glanced in the side mirror on their way to the office.

"On time and they got everything you asked for." There was a lot of horn blowing behind them and Lou sped up a little.

A car had gotten between them and the van following them and almost caused an accident doing it. "Someone's in a rush," she said of the nondescript black SUV that resembled the one they were in. "Call ahead in case they have a bad case of road rage."

Lou did as she asked and went through a light that had just turned red to try to lose them. Surprisingly the vehicle stopped, trapping them and the van at the corner before her office. If this was something to do with her, they'd given up easily.

"We got company, boss," Lou said when he slowed to turn. Another SUV was parked outside the warehouse she owned along the river.

There were enough men patrolling the grounds to take care of whoever followed them in, so she was more curious than worried. They drove in and the guys by the big doors waved in the driver behind them. She and Lou waited until they'd checked out the car and her visitors emerged. Hector Delarosa must've come from the airport here because her information had him in Colombia trying to save his business.

"There's a man with problems, Lou, and a really slow learning curve."

"He's a man with a crush for sure."

"If that's true, he's a man with no concept of what Emma Casey will do to him."

She took a breath and opened her own door. Tomas Blanco didn't appear pleased when her man took his guns and patted him down in case there were some other additions to his wardrobe. Tomas always resembled a disgruntled basset hound, but Hector had told her he'd been by his side for years, so he must've been as effective as Lou.

"Good morning, Hector, and welcome back." Cain held her hand out and he took it in both of his. "Am I your first stop after your trip home?"

"I arrived last night, and there's so much to catch up on." Hector held her hand a second longer than what was appropriate. "My home has changed so much here that I don't recognize the town when I get back. Marisol had so much to say."

"Not everything is different." She waved him to the seats close to her office. One of her guys put down coffee and poured Hector some. "Your absence didn't give me an overwhelming desire to join your business, so I'm at a loss as to why you're here."

"I spoke to Michel Blanc while I was gone, and his daughter Nicolette has disappeared. She was here to do business with you, and then she turned to us."

"Nicolette and I were never going to be what Nicolette had in her mind. Her friend Luce is the one who decided not to do business with us, and I was fine with her decision on behalf of Michel. My interest in the deal was to help Michel get out of a situation that could've cost him his family's business, that's all." She took a sip of coffee and glanced at Fin and Neil, who were seated across the room from them. "The only misunderstanding we had was hers and Luce's decision to visit my club and make wild accusations that attracted people neither of us would ever invite into our lives."

"Like I could give a fuck what happened to Nicolette Blanc, Cain," he said, tilting his head to the side. "My daughter and her became friends, but she is of no importance to my business. I said this to tell you that her family is looking for her, and they might come here to ask."

"I'll give Michel or anyone he sends the same story. I've got nothing to hide."

"Think of your children. If something happened to one of them, it would make you crazy, so watch your back, my friend." Hector put his cup down and rubbed his hands together. "That is all I have to say about that."

"Which brings us to what you really want to say." She smiled and waved him on.

"You already know what has happened to my business, Cain, and maybe you are happy."

She shook her head and interrupted him. "Hector, we're neighbors who are friendly, but we aren't friends. The most important thing, and what I keep telling you, is that I'm not your enemy. I don't wish you, your family, or your business ill." She leaned forward and tapped the tips of her fingers together between her legs. "I've heard what happened, and no one I do business with had anything to do with that."

He nodded and sighed dramatically. "I know that, but someone is responsible."

"And you don't know who?" That wasn't the answer she was thinking he'd admit. With the amount of money he must've offered here and at home, something should've shaken loose by now.

"This is a move to take me out," Hector admitted, shrugging. "That too might make you happy, but ask yourself something." His Spanish accent slipped more than she thought he meant it to.

"What's that?" She smiled again and he did as well. They'd never be anything more than this, but she had to admit Hector possessed an infinite amount of charm. "Better the devil I know?"

"Yes, because all my money has found only one name. My problem is I don't know who he is, but maybe you do."

"Who is it?" If their businesses or multitude of problems overlapped, it was better to have as much information as possible.

"Jerome Rhodes."

It was a name she knew. The man who'd been Gracelia Luis's lover was a mystery, but he seemed so inconsequential. She remembered him pacing and smoking on the levee like a caged rat, and she'd figured he was concerned because he was in over his head. He hadn't been there when Gracelia was taken, and he'd disappeared after the dust had settled on whatever Gracelia's plan had been, one they'd never fully know since it had failed in spectacular fashion. It didn't have anything to do with them, so she hadn't worried about it at the time. Her only concern with the whole thing was finding Juan Luis and turning his mother over to Carlos Luis.

"Gracelia Luis brought him with her when she came back to exact her revenge with her son. That's who's done this to you?" Just what she needed, another piece on her chess board to worry about—because Jerome Rhodes was a name she'd heard before. Had he really been in on plotting her downfall all along? It had occurred to her that Rhodes might be Anthony Curtis until she laid eyes on him. She doubted the FBI agent would have done what Juan had to hide his identity. No matter what Shelby and the others said, there was no way Anthony wasn't working undercover.

"His is the only name I hear whenever I ask anything."

"I don't know who he is."

Hector nodded then leaned forward as well. "I know that you can find out. If Rhodes was here with Gracelia, then he knows you. She wasn't here to only take from me, Cain, and you need to remember who helped you when you asked."

"I've returned that favor more than once, and there are nicer ways to ask." She softened the reprimand with a slight smile, but this guy was good at pushing buttons. "Let me see what I can find, and I give you my word that I'll share whatever I discover with you. Now, if there's nothing else, I have a few things I have to attend to."

"I am grateful, and you will not be sorry to work with me."

She waited until the doors closed again and sighed as she headed for her office. "Are you ready?" she asked Finley.

"I got everything you asked for, and all you need to do is your part," Finley said as her brother Neil sat next to her. He seemed to be enjoying working with her.

"How much time do you need?" she asked as she glanced over the paperwork Muriel had left her. When she was done, it went into the shredder. Later one of the guys would put it all in the incinerator they'd installed outside. There'd never be a room full of feds taping all this shit back together.

"We can do everything in twenty minutes." Finley glanced at her phone when it buzzed. "Have Lou call when you're ready. Neil, Shaun, and I will get in and out."

"No trace, Fin, that's important."

"I know what you want, and we'll get it done." Fin glanced at her phone and smiled.

"Do you need to go?" She'd kept up with Fin's career from a distance, but she seemed happier and more settled now that she'd come home with Abigail and her children.

"The kids started at their new school today, so Abigail was giving me an update. Victoria is thrilled her buddy was waiting for her, and they're all looking forward to tomorrow."

"Get going and be ready around eight. You got a burner?"

"I've got everything and won't let you down. Is Delarosa going to be a problem?" Fin had a complete bird's-eye view of her business and had filled in some holes even her old tech guy had missed before Gracelia had him killed.

"Hector is more of a pain than a problem. His main issue is not knowing the meaning of no, but someone has done a number on him.

Our issue is going to be getting caught in the middle of the war this is going to start. The one good thing is we might get some answers out of all this." She drummed her fingers in an uneven pattern and thought about all the moves they had to make. "Anything on Nicola?"

"The easiest path to her is to talk to my old boss, but I'd rather not do that. I'm working on the best ways to find her, but our best option, her cousin Linda Bender, has done a good job of disappearing." Fin handed over a sheet that had Nicola's family tree on it. "Linda was a reluctant participant in the business, and she was smart enough to know when to get out."

"Is she the one who handed over all that information your old team found?" Sometimes it was better to be an outlaw than a lawman when it came to finding your own kind.

"That's the rumor, and I want to believe it." Fin stood and pointed to the references about Linda's family on the page. "Her mother is still looking for her, because Linda didn't disappear alone."

"She took her brothers with her?" She glanced up at Fin and saw a glimmer of possibly finding an easy way out of all this. The cousin was the key. "Maybe I can help you with that by looking somewhere you might not have thought to."

"I'm not turning down any help, and she did go with her brothers. There's no way to be sure, but I think it was her way of severing the connection to what she hated in her family. Without the Antakov influence, there was no chance of her siblings becoming what Nicola and Fredrick turned out to be. Both boys were doing well in school and were involved in sports." Fin showed her pictures of the two young men who'd just started high school. "I have to admire her for that."

"There are things you'd rather starve than do, and this family crossed every line of decent behavior. Exploiting women and children makes you a good candidate for a bullet to the head." The evil twins had the same smile, but Nicola's had a coldness in hers that made Cain want to hurt her until she begged for death. "We can't let Nicola or anyone in her organization anywhere near Abigail and the kids."

"I know that better than anyone. Like those guys across the street, I spent a lot of time looking and studying these people. They're the bullies who exploit because they can, but they're good at evading justice."

"That's the only thing we have in common. I'm sure our friends across the street think I'm a bully, but Nicola's brand of strong-arming responds only to one thing," she said, standing and embracing Fin.

"You started finding your answer with the parents, and we end it with Nicola. That's the head of the snake that'll kill the body." She hugged Neil next and gave them both a warning. "Don't take any chances tonight. In and out."

"Stop worrying and take off. We'll see you tomorrow at the airport," Neil said, kissing Cain's cheek. "I'll take care of my little sister."

"You remember to keep your cool tonight." Fin hugged her again.

"Believe me, I'm doing that even if I rupture something trying to keep it together."

CHAPTER SIX

Finley had Neil drive her to the parking lot of the shopping center at the end of Canal Street where she'd left her car. Her life was different with Cain but gave her more time with Abigail and the kids. "I'll meet you at the bar close to Carrollton at six. Remember to bring everything, and make sure Shaun does the same."

"We got it covered, and this is some serious shit if they went through Hannah. Cain should deal with it in a more permanent way." Neil tapped his fingers on the steering wheel and stared straight forward. "I remember when Emma brought her home and how Cain fell in love with that little girl. Using her to bring her mother down isn't right."

"We have to find out who is behind this before she decides on a course of action. These aren't the type of people you're used to, but I agree with you. Hannah or any child shouldn't be used like that." She'd examined the bug the woman calling herself Taylor had left. It wasn't anything you could buy on Amazon. It was sophisticated and complex, and there was only one organization that used this kind of stuff. That led her to believe her old employer was using questionable tactics, but maybe Cain had finally driven them to break the rules.

"No, that's true. Juan Luis was an asshole like I've never seen, but he stayed away from the kids. His big weakness was Emma. Who goes after a child?"

"We're somewhere between someone like that and the people I used to work for. That scares me more than a thousand Juans." Someone working on the outskirts of the law usually felt everything was okay as long as they brought down whoever they were after. She'd met agents like that, but they didn't last long.

"You think the feds would do some shit like this?"

"That's what we're trying to figure out. The more answers we have, the better the response we can plan. Don't be late tonight." She watched him drive away and waited ten minutes before driving home.

This was Abigail's late day for clinic, and she wanted to catch her before she left. On her late days she dropped the kids off, then went home for a nap before heading to work. They usually were able to spend a few minutes alone even though Abigail's parents were still living with them. She was glad, since Abigail's dad was overseeing the construction of an addition to the house, so everyone would be comfortable. She didn't want a repeat of what had happened to Cain when they had to remodel their house. No one who wasn't personally vetted by her was allowed on the construction site.

"Hey, baby," Abigail said, looking up when she walked in. She was sitting in the kitchen with her mother having coffee, still wearing her sweats and a T-shirt. Liam was sitting in her lap having juice, but he seemed to perk up when he noticed her. The youngest of the Eaton children had a sort of radar for Fin whenever she was in the house. No matter where, he found her and liked engaging in long conversations.

"Fin!" Liam got down, ran to her, and wrapped his arms around her leg. "Look." Liam held up a picture. She picked him up and sat down next to Abigail and kissed her, then admired Liam's masterpiece.

The crude drawing had seven stick figures and what appeared to be the lake behind the house. The people had to be her, Abigail, his grandparents, and his siblings, but it was his name that captured her full attention. The preschool they were sending him to was showing him how to write his name and he hadn't quite gotten the scale down, but he'd spelled *Abbott* correctly.

"Wow, buddy, this is a beautiful picture. Is this your homework?" she asked, trying not to cry.

"Me and Vicky want to be Abbott, like you. I wanted to show my teacher." He kissed her cheek and went with his grandmother when she said it was time to go to daycare. "That's okay, right?" He turned and ran back. This kid was so earnest she had a hard time saying no to whatever he wanted.

"We'll have to check with your mom, but that's okay with me." She walked them to the door and waved as they pulled out. Abigail put her arms around her waist as she stood in the doorway.

"Before you accuse me of anything, he and the girls came up with that on their own. It's the name the girls wanted to put on their school records when I signed them up last week, and how they introduced themselves today when I dropped them off."

"You dropped them off in this?" She plucked Abigail's T-shirt before picking her up and letting her wrap her legs around her waist. It was clear she wasn't wearing a bra, and she doubted she wore underwear.

"I'm sorry, but have you met me? No, I changed when I got home, hoping I could take a nap before I have to head to work." Abigail bit down her neck, and she stumbled a little before hitting the stairs. "Do you have time to join me?"

"I do." She didn't stop until they were in the master bedroom with a locked door. "And you don't have to worry about the kids. You know how I feel about them."

"I do know that." Abigail held on to her as she sat on the bed.

"You're scared I'm going to freak out and run screaming into the night. You don't say it, but I know that worried expression of yours."

"No." Abigail couldn't seem to look at her as she protested.

"Yes, you do, but I'm going to keep telling you I'm not going anywhere until we're in our eighties. By then you might believe me. You have to trust that not only do I love you, but I'm not going to run because of Nicola. Once we find her, she's not going to be a problem. I know that sounds harsh, but I don't want anyone hurting our family." She leaned back a little to see Abigail's face, and Abigail nodded at what she'd said. "As far as the three kids, if you let me, I'd adopt all three of them today."

"You mean that, don't you?" The way Abigail asked was full of wonder.

"How we met isn't exactly dating app material, love, but we found us. We work, and I understand better than you give me credit for that the kids come as part of the package. I love them, and the only thing I'm sorry about is that I haven't been here from the beginning."

Abigail combed her hair back like she did some nights to relax her. "I do give you credit, baby, but I can't help but worry. Doesn't all this scare you? Nicola is out there, and she's probably planning her next move, how to take you away from me. Hell, she probably wants us both dead. After what happened, I'm convinced all she wants is the kids. Not because she actually wants them, mind you. She just wants a legacy."

"Nicola is going to wish she stayed dead. You keep thinking I gave up my career for you, but I did it for us. That's the most important reason, but I also left so I could close this case."

"What do you mean?" Abigail kissed her lightly.

"I didn't really know who I was chasing when I started this case. All those hours of investigating left me with the knowledge of all their atrocities and a far better understanding of what kind of people they are." She ran her hands up and down Abigail's back. "I know all that now, and I might eventually be able to gather enough evidence to bring them to court."

"I know that's what you were working toward."

"I was, but I have all the evidence I need to know I want to handle it a different way. Your ex and her family are bad people, but they'll pale in comparison to Cain when her family is threatened. Her sense of justice is harsh and swift, but that's the way it should be when it's family. You're my family now, and you have to understand that makes you her family."

"I know that she'll protect us like you will. Like I said, all Nicola and her parents wanted were the kids. This was never about me." Abigail let out a sharp laugh. "That's what's so screwed up about all this. She didn't want the kids when she was married to me and living in the same house. Now they're willing to kill me to get them back. It's a joke."

"I realize you're not wild about me working for Cain, but it puts us in the best position for what has to happen. It's also going to give us a better future in the long run when I'm at home every night. I'm tired of living in all that darkness and skulking around in vans all the time. It's not a way to raise a family." She sat Abigail on the bed and stood up to take her shirt off. "I should say every night except tonight, for a little while. Neil and I have a thing."

"What kind of *thing*?"

"It's a fishing expedition," she said, then recapped what happened with Hannah. "Nicola is someone Cain knows how to bring down, and I have to help her load the weapon it'll take to do that. I got her into this by asking for her help with the Eaton family, but rogue agents are a different animal. We need to know if this is what someone put in place."

"Promise you'll be careful," Abigail said, lifting her shirt over her head.

"I'll do that if you promise me something." She lay down and covered Abigail's body with hers.

"What?" The question seemed hard to ask as Abigail ran her fingernails up her back.

"That you think about talking to Muriel," she said, squeezing her hand between them. "Jesus, I love when you get this wet."

"Concentrate, honey. Talk to Muriel about what?" Abigail sucked in a breath when Fin stroked her fingers over her clit.

"She took care of Cain and Emma's adoptions. I'm sure she'd do the same for us."

"Let's talk to them and ask, but right now I need you to finish what you started." Abigail spread her legs and lifted her hips. She groaned when Fin only ran her fingers over her clit. "Not the time to tease, Abbott."

"I love teasing you," she said, moving down Abigail's body and stopping at her nipples. "You can complain, but you love it."

"I love you, and you can't adopt my kids."

She stopped what she was doing and took her hands off Abigail. "What?"

"You have to ask me something too, or it's no deal. I'm not going to be the only one here with a different last name. I'm not keeping Eaton, even if you don't change my name properly." Abigail rose on her elbows and smiled, giving Fin's body permission to breathe again.

"You scared the hell out of me," she said, kissing Abigail to keep her from saying anything else. "And I'm not asking empty-handed. Trust me, I want to do it right."

"Good, now do something else right," Abigail said as she put her hands back on her. "Oh...good God."

Fin put her fingers in and sucked Abigail's clit against the roof of her mouth. From their first night of intimacy Abigail had taken her breath away with how beautiful she was when she let go. "Tell me," she said, lifting her mouth off momentarily.

"Don't stop, baby. I want to come," Abigail said, grabbing the top of her head. "Harder, baby."

She could feel the walls of Abigail's sex tighten around her fingers. Abigail was trying to hang on and make it last, but the way she was moaning into the pillow meant she couldn't stop the orgasm that was building. No matter what was going on in their lives, she never wanted to stop showing Abigail how much she loved her, and touching her in a way that made her know she'd be the woman in her life until it ended.

"Faster, baby, please." Abigail bent her legs and put her hands behind her head to make her suck harder. She obviously needed more pressure to relieve the ache, and she was going to give it to her.

She kept pace with Abigail's hips, and she felt ten feet tall when Abigail screamed and went limp under her. "Let's hope they're not working in the hall today." She turned her head and kissed the insides of Abigail's thighs.

"They'll be lined up to ask you some hard questions. I doubt any of them have ever made a woman make this kind of noise in their life." Abigail laughed and straddled her hips. "Now," she said, putting her finger under her chin and bringing it slowly down between her breasts and over her abdomen. "Do I need to torture details out of you?"

"About what? I'm a retired agent. I don't talk that easily." She smiled when Abigail moved down some more.

"Is that so?" Abigail was beautiful all the time, but there was no sexier sight than her kneeling between her legs. "That sounds like a challenge."

"Mm-hmm." The pressure of Abigail's mouth on her and the way she used her tongue made her hang on to the sheets in an effort not to give in right away. That was impossible when Abigail was this relentless, and she closed her eyes as the pressure built. Abigail didn't stop no matter how she moved, and she sucked harder when she fisted a handful of her hair, needing to be connected to Abigail somehow.

"Fuck." She said it softly as she bucked her hips, unable to control the need to come. It was like holding back the tide with a spoon, so she gave in and gave Abigail what they both wanted.

She was limp by the time she was done, and she lay there as Abigail crawled back up and put her head under Fin's chin as she held her. It wasn't often she thought of Nicola and who she'd been in Abigail's life, but she sneaked in when she let her guard down. How Nicola could've neglected this gorgeous, sexy woman was something that didn't compute.

"What deep thoughts are you contemplating?" Abigail asked as she rubbed small circles on her abdomen.

"I'm trying to figure out where all my control went," she said, kissing Abigail's forehead. "If you had been interrogating me, I'd be telling you whatever you wanted to know right now."

"I just want to know if you love me."

That was a strange thing to say. She rolled over and looked down at Abigail. "With all that I am." The tears did her in. "What is it?" Abigail turned her head as if to hide the tears that were coming faster. "Baby, tell me what's wrong. Is all this too fast for you?"

"No," Abigail said, wiping her face. "I just want you to be sure. I love you so much, and I don't think losing you is something I could do. That would cut deeper than Nicola ever did."

"Hey, you're not going to lose me. What's wrong? I know it's not that."

"I was with someone who eventually only saw me as a vehicle to cement her legacy through children. I became invisible in that relationship once I had kids, and you seemed to fall in love with my kids before—"

"I love your kids, baby, and I'll be honored to raise them with you, but what sold me on a future with you, is *you*. You're the woman I want, and invisibility is never going to be something you have to fear." She kissed Abigail in a way that she hoped conveyed how she felt. "My problem is focusing on anything *but* you sometimes. I'm sure your parents must think I'm a horndog who can't get enough of their little girl."

"I had to go through hell to find you, lover, but I'm so glad I did," Abigail said, kissing her again. "Thank you for loving my kids, but for loving me too."

"You know," Fin said, leaving the bed and heading to the closet and the drawer at the bottom of the built-in chest, "I was planning a romantic dinner in the perfect setting, but I don't want another second to pass with you doubting how much I love you."

She got down on her knees on Abigail's side of the bed and took her hand. "Everything I do in my life, I want to do with you. No matter what comes, it'll be okay because I have you. Abigail, you have all of me—I hope you know that. What I want now is for you to spend the rest of your life with me and be my wife." She opened the box with the ring Emma had helped her pick out. "Will you marry me?"

"Yes," Abigail said, the word sounding muffled because her hands were pressed to her cheeks. "Oh my God, yes."

"I owe you that romantic dinner and perfect setting, but I couldn't wait anymore."

"This is perfect, and it saves you from my father's lecture about your horndog ways," Abigail said as she put the ring on her finger.

Fin felt like her heart could burst and every cheesy romantic movie ever made suddenly made perfect sense. "I talked to him last week, and we did in fact talk about that. Bob isn't a big guy, but he does get his point across with plenty of menace."

"He didn't." Abigail laughed as she pulled her back on the bed.

"I'm not telling on him, but convincing him to give me his blessing wasn't a cakewalk," she said, lying on Abigail but holding her weight off her. "He and your mom love you, and they're both happy for us.

What I can tell you is that I promised him I'd take care of you and the brood."

"That's a given." Abigail put her thigh between her legs.

"I also said I'd try to convince you to give him another grandbaby. He thinks four is a much rounder number." The admission made Abigail stop. "I couldn't promise that, so don't worry."

"You should've told him that was a given too. I've seen the kids in your family, and planning a couple more Abbott kids will change what we'll do to the house, so you might as well go ahead and give in now before the renovations are done." Abigail lifted her hips and placed her hand on her sex. "You don't want to disappoint my father, do you?"

"Not him, not you, not ever." Everything she'd done in her life had led her here, to this woman, to this family, and to this life. It was hers. She was claiming it, and she'd fight to keep it all safe.

❖

"Did you finish everything at the office?" Emma asked as she came out of the bathroom in her panties and a sweater.

"I did, and thank you for packing for me. This is the last thing on our to-do list, and then we're set for tomorrow." She pulled a cable-knit sweater on and put her phone in the front pocket of her jeans. "This reminds me of our first days together."

"If you want, I'll even wait some tables tonight and spill something on you," Emma said, winking at her as she pulled on a pair of jeans. "It's been ages since I've been to the pub."

"I thought these people would be more comfortable in a public setting where I'm less likely to bite." She put her money clip in the opposite pocket and waited for Emma to get her boots on. "Hannah looked a lot happier and back to her old self."

"We can thank Victoria Eaton for that." Emma put on earrings next. "The strange thing is Lucy wasn't in school today. I told Sabana to see if Lucy tried talking to Hannah," she said of Hannah's guard. Since the kidnapping incident, Sabana now sat outside Hannah's classroom, and the kids loved playing with her when they were at recess. "I don't want to punish Lucy, but I do want to know what's going on."

Cain had wanted Hannah to form a relationship with her personal bodyguard early, like Mook had done with Hayden, and Sabana wasn't disappointing her. "It's pathetic we're having to jump through all these hoops. I find threatening to shoot someone's fingers off is a much better way of getting answers."

"I know, honey, but there's no way I want to take chances by doing nothing or you landing in jail. I'm willing to overlook and forgive a multitude of sins from these people, but messing with our children isn't on that long list." Emma pulled her hair back in a loose ponytail and held her hand out. "Once we get this done, you can buy me a drink for real and sing some Irish drinking songs, so I can pretend I'm still that young woman who managed to get your attention."

"I hate to break it to you, grandma, but you're still that young woman who drives me to distraction. The only difference is, you don't kiss me at the door and send me home hard and in pain." She whispered that part as they headed down the hall. Victoria had asked to spend the night, and the girls were playing in Hannah's room.

"You're so mean, mobster. Now I'm wet and expected to go out and be entertaining."

"I'm here to please," she said as they stopped in the doorway to Hannah's room and saw Hayden sitting on the floor playing a board game with the two little girls. "There's no money riding on this game, is there?" she asked, and Emma backhanded her on the stomach.

"You guys have fun," Emma said, "and we'll be back in a little while. Dinner is in an hour, so don't give your grandparents any trouble."

"Can Mook take us for ice cream later?" Hayden asked.

"Let Sabana and Merrick know, and go easy on the chocolate. You all need to sleep a little before tomorrow," Emma said as she bent to kiss everyone good-bye. Victoria hadn't taken long to feel like part of the family and put her arms around Emma when it was her turn.

"Thanks, Aunt Emma," Victoria said, giving Cain a hug next. "Hannah said we're going to have fun on the farm, and I can't wait."

"Hannah's right, and I have a little surprise for everyone when we get there," Cain said, kissing Hannah next. "Be good, and get some sleep."

They walked through the kitchen to the garage to avoid the pouring rain and let Lou drive them into the Quarter. The backstreets let them avoid the parades rolling that night, but the Quarter was packed with tourists and locals out enjoying all that carnival season was about. That meant drunks, women showing their breasts for beads, and the religious zealots out with their signs and megaphones telling them all they were going to hell.

"Will you get me one of those nice long strands of beads if I show you my boobs later?" Emma asked thoughtfully.

"If I have to bring cheap throws to see these beauties, I must be doing something wrong," she said, squeezing Emma's chest. "But if party favors are your thing, I'll pick some up."

"You're being frisky tonight, baby, and I'm loving it. All you need is that wonderful mouth of yours, and I'll show you whatever you want." Emma turned her so she could reach her lips. "What exactly is our plan tonight? I'd rather have fun with you than this, so the quicker we get to it, the better."

"Let's play it by ear, but all we are tonight is concerned parents. Our kids aren't getting along, and we don't know why," she said as Lou stopped at the door of the club, and two of her guys came out with umbrellas.

"Have our guests arrived?" Emma asked as they made their way to the reserved table the longtime manager Josh had set up for them.

"Not yet, but it's good to see you," Josh said, hugging her. "What's your pleasure?"

"Tall Irish women," Emma said, making him laugh. "But for now, I'll take a Guinness and so will Cain, but bring hers with a Jameson chaser."

Josh went off to pour their drinks himself, and Emma sat on her lap as the band started playing. The place was crowded, but her guys were spread through the place, trying to not stick out. She gave Emma what she wanted and sang to her as they waited, stopping when Josh joined them after setting down their order.

"How's business?" she asked, putting her hand on Emma's hip.

"The crowds have been steady, and we've had a line all week. I wanted to let you know that the place next door is up for sale and would be a good pickup if you're really interested in expanding. It would give us a Bourbon Street entrance." Josh tapped his shot glass against hers and slammed back the Jameson he'd poured for both of them.

"Call Muriel and have her set up a meeting with the seller. Business is good, but it can only get better with more space."

Emma slid off her lap and pointed discreetly to the door. "They're here."

"Josh, have the band take a break, and send one of the girls over in a few minutes," she said as Emma waved the couple over.

"You got it, boss."

Drew and Taylor Kennison appeared wary as they made their

way through the crowd. It reminded her of the day she'd met Shelby Phillips on Vincent's plane. Undercover work was a tightrope of trying to get information and wondering if the people you were trying to bring down knew what you were doing. In this case she wasn't sure yet, and that bothered her. Information meant survival, and these people were standing in a blind spot.

"Hey, thanks for inviting us," Taylor said as Drew pulled her chair out for her. "I don't know if I'd have the patience for the line out there."

"The public knows a good thing when they see it." Emma smiled but it didn't reach her eyes. "Thanks for coming."

"Cain," Taylor said, "Emma, this is my husband, Drew."

Drew shook both their hands, then put his arm around Taylor. "I've never been here before."

"If you like beer and ale, we've got a good selection. That goes for whiskey as well." One of the waitresses came and took their order, leaving them with only the noise of the crowd. "We wanted to meet you to talk about Lucy and Hannah," Cain said as Emma nodded.

"What about Lucy and Hannah?" Drew asked, glancing at Taylor as if waiting for her to clue him in.

"I'm not sure, but they've gone from best buddies to Hannah not saying much at home. Did Lucy mention what the problem might be?" She didn't need to look at Emma to know exactly what she was thinking from the way she was gripping her thigh. The two assholes sitting with them were like guppies swimming in a shark tank desperately trying not to be noticed.

"Lucy asked to spend some time with Drew's mom, so we sent her ahead of the upcoming break. She wasn't in school today, so I'm not sure about any problem." Taylor leaned in to her husband, and they didn't appear to be a couple on the verge of splitting up. "Hannah didn't say anything to you?"

"No, but I'm sure it'll blow over," Emma said. "Maybe Hannah's just feeling a little off."

"They're just kids," Drew said as if that answered everything. "If there's something, it'll be forgotten by the time everyone gets back."

"Where does your mom live?" Cain asked and received a lost look from both of them. "Is it a secret?"

"No, I just don't know why that's important," Drew said, finally seeming to remember he had a mother and where she lived. "But it's outside Atlanta."

"It's good Lucy has somewhere to go that she likes. There's

nothing like spending time with the one person who lives to spoil you," she said, and Emma squeezed her leg again.

"Sorry to cut this short, but we've got another stop tonight," Taylor said, grabbing Drew by the bicep and practically lifting him out of his seat. "Happy Mardi Gras."

"Same to you," Emma said and neither of them stood. "It's a shame Hannah won't get to see Lucy before we go."

Cain gazed at Emma and smiled. Her wife had become a very wise woman in their time together, and she leaned in and kissed her for using her head. If she was a gambling woman, she'd bet the pub there was a listening device under the table. Emma's time with her had taught her plenty, and the first thing when it came to dealing with the feds was never to underestimate them. She didn't have to look to see if there was a bug—it was there, operational, and Emma had given them nothing. She was the perfect partner.

"I'm sure they'll be thrilled to see each other in a week," Cain said. "It'll be nice to just have the family around, though, so it'll be a quiet week."

The non-couple nodded and gave quick, uncomfortable smiles before they left, Taylor practically dragging Drew from the club.

Cain signaled to Josh, and the band started up again, and Emma moved back to her lap. Another round of drinks came, and if whoever these people were wanted to listen in, they'd get everything they wanted when she started singing along.

"We need to do this more often, honey," Emma said into her ear.

"Whenever you like, lass. We're due a little fun."

They stayed another hour only because Muriel and Kristen joined them. Their conversation revolved around Kristen's school schedule, and Cain teasing Muriel about helping her with her homework.

"Baby, if anyone should be blushing, it should be me, not you," Kristen said, kissing Muriel's cheek. "And thanks for inviting me to tag along."

"You're family now, so of course you're coming," Emma said. "Once you get a load of all the cousins together, you might run screaming for the hills."

"I'm not going anywhere, don't worry. It took me long enough to get this one not to see me as just some kid with a crush, so nothing scares me."

"Careful with this one, cousin," Cain said. "She might be the one who breaks you of your solitary ways. Come on," she added, patting

Emma's bottom. "Let's get some sleep before we have to peel the kids off the ceiling."

"I'm sure they're in bed," Emma said.

"Um, what's their last name again?" Muriel tapped her chin with her index finger.

"Good point," Emma said, shaking her head. "Let's go, Casey, so I'll have someone to blame when I have to ground everyone in the house."

"You know I'll plead the Fifth."

Emma pinched her cheeks and laughed. "I wouldn't expect anything else, lover."

CHAPTER SEVEN

Nicola sat in the bar across the street from where Casey was sitting with a blonde in her lap. That was the last face her parents had seen before they were killed like dogs in the street. There was no doubt in her mind—that piece of shit was responsible for their deaths, and she was going to pay, along with her bitch of a wife, Abigail. She'd seen Abigail in the hospital, but somehow she'd gotten in and out without her figuring out how she was arriving, and where she was going.

"If you hit her, you might want it to be quick and unexpected," Nina said as she sat next to her. "She might not look like much, but Casey has an impressive organization that had nothing to do with your business. Are you sure this is who you're looking for?"

"Do you think Abigail armed herself and shot my parents?" She tapped on Nina's forehead hard enough to make her flinch. "Think."

"I am thinking," Nina said, backing away from her. "What would Casey gain from their deaths? She has nothing to do with anything that would encroach on our business."

"The most logical answer is Abigail somehow got to her." She stopped talking when that theory sounded crazy even to her, but she knew she was right. "Papa was here to talk to her about helping him find Abigail," she said. "Less than two hours later, he and Mama are dead. Explain that to me."

"I can't, but I also know we don't have the muscle to get into a war we can't win. Hate me if you want, but you have to concentrate on solidifying your hold on the family. The person we should be looking for is Linda. She holds the answers to what happened to Yury and your mother. Their deaths are on Linda's head as much as whoever pulled the trigger."

"She'll be easy enough to find once I'm done with this bitch. I'm sure her parents died at home in their own beds."

Nina shook her head and appeared to be losing patience. "Her father was killed by her cousin, and her mother was killed by an enemy. They died much like your parents, so I think she understands the lack of honor it takes to kill someone like that." Nina tilted her head toward Cain. "Her sister was gang-raped, then killed by her cousin and two other men. This is a woman who understands pain and loss."

"Perhaps, but I don't give a shit about any sad stories." She clenched her fist and hit the table to emphasize her point for the last time. "Stick to the subject before I beat it into you. Do you know where Abigail is?"

"No." Nina took the hint and backed down. "I think she's tried to hide as best as she can and still make a living after what happened in New York."

Nicola's father had massacred a bus full of women to protect their operation from the people getting too close. A few lives of unimportant people were worth it to not take any chances. He'd tried to deal with Abigail at the same time, but her ex had lucked out. Her survival after that and how she'd effectively disappeared made her think Abigail'd picked up a guardian angel along the way. An Irish angel with good taste in women.

"There is only one person who could've sanctioned this hit, and it wasn't Abigail. Now, I need to know whatever you can find on this woman so I can plan how to take her down with as much pain as possible."

"What about the family?"

She took a deep breath and held it. This conversation was getting tiresome. "They will either fall in line, or I'm going to personally make some examples of the loudest voices. Once that's done, we'll get back what's rightfully mine."

"But you want to deal with Casey before that?"

Nina was persistent. She couldn't deny that. "Compared to what we faced in New York, Casey will be as simple as brushing my teeth. What I don't want is her death, and her family's deaths, to drive Abigail underground with my children. It's time they start learning their place in the world."

"Their place is with you."

"I don't need you to tell me that." She stretched her hand out to ease the pain that lanced through it. "They're the future of the Antakov family, and I'm ready to start their education."

❖

Emma ran her hand through Cain's hair as she sang the song the band was playing, and it made her smile. Cain loved seeing that smile. When Emma was having fun and this carefree, it reminded her of their first days together. It had taken some time for the shy country girl to get used to Cain's faster-paced life, but Emma had enjoyed all their nights out.

She took a sip of the new Guinness Josh put down and kissed the side of Emma's neck. They'd been planning to head home, but she'd asked Emma for a few more minutes after they'd gone into the office together and talked. Their short vacation was cutting into some things she had to get done, and there was no reason she couldn't tick one thing off her list before they left.

"Having fun, lass?" She spoke loud enough for Emma to hear her, but she wasn't her only audience.

"I always have fun with you." Emma kissed her, and Cain pressed her hand to Emma's backside. "I love you."

"I love you too, and I'm going to spend a lot of time in the next few days showing you how much. Are you ready for what comes next?" She whispered in Emma's ear, then cocked her head back to gaze at her wife. The thought of how complicated life was crossed her mind, but the truth that her feelings for Emma never were complicated knocked the worry down some. Loving Emma was simple and easy, and the depth of her emotion was endless.

"Are you sure?" Emma put her lips next to her ear, and the warmth made her hard.

"I am, and I trust you to do it." She rubbed her hand up Emma's back, and that got her another smile. "Do you trust me?"

"With all that I am." Emma knew to speak right into her ear because of the bug that was most likely under the table. She didn't need to tell Emma not to tip her hand. "Need anything from the bar?" Emma's voice went back up.

"How about one more round, and then we head home." Emma stood and pressed her hand to her cheek before she walked off. She headed to the office first, and Cain smiled at the waitress coming toward her. The girl took Emma's place on her lap and kissed the curve of her ear. The move surprised her, but not enough to move her away.

"Did you enjoy the beer?" the girl asked, kissing the same spot again.

"I did, and I couldn't help but notice how you've been looking at me all night. Is there something you want?"

"Don't deny your reputation. You haven't been married that long, have you?" The woman combed her hair back and kissed her cheek this time. "All those kids at home must take a lot out of you. How about something a little different to overcome any boredom you might be feeling?" Her waitress spoke loud enough to be heard in the noise of the crowd.

She smiled at that and was about to lean in for a kiss when she felt the sting of Emma's hand to the side of her face. The blow was hard enough to knock her head back and killed the sound in the room. Everyone looked their way, as if to see what she was going to do in retaliation. Emma cocked her hand back when the woman stood, but Cain caught it before she was able to hit her again.

"Only the first one's free, lass. Think before you do anything stupid." She didn't speak too loudly, but it carried enough menace to get her point across.

"Think? Is that what you were doing? Thinking of me and all those empty promises you keep spouting off?" Emma turned and walked away without another word, but from the set of her shoulders she was pissed.

Cain motioned for Lou to follow her out, and the band started up again as the squeal of tires faded outside. The ache in her face matched the one in her chest, but she stayed at the table alone until her drink was done. When she stood, she stopped when the guys at the next table made a few jokes and laughed at her expense. It didn't last long when she glared at all three of them. In the mood she was in, a good bar fight would take the edge off.

"So much for a fun night." She headed toward the office and shook her head at Josh when he went to follow her. The men she'd stationed around the room followed her to another ride waiting in the alley behind the pub, and the waitress was still sitting in the stockroom where she'd run off to.

"Home, boss?"

"Let's make one stop and then home." She glanced in the side mirror to see if they had a tail, but so far, the street behind them was empty of traffic. "Pull into the parking garage on the right."

The old hollowed-out building was a private parking structure not good for anything else without major renovation. She spotted the car close to the back and told her guy to stop. The older model Impala was tricked out with everything you'd expect from a young punk who spent more on his ride than anything else in his life. The airbrushed bullet holes, along with his initials, were a nice touch that went with the pistol door handles.

"Ms. Casey," the young man said through the open window. "I cleaned the back seat out for you, so if you want, lie down and relax."

"Thanks," she said, getting in and doing as he said. The owner of the lot had a back way out, and that's how they were leaving. "Did Jasper give you the address I need?"

"Yes, ma'am, and I can't wait to see it. I thought he was fucking with me when he told me where we're going," he said, then shook his head. "Sorry about the language, Ms. Casey. Jasper told me to not act like an asshole, and I didn't mean no disrespect."

"Don't worry about it, and I think Brandi is enough of a legend that everyone thinks she's too good to be true. She runs a good business, though, and her girls are world class." She laughed at the memory of the first time she'd visited the famous red door. "They don't come cheap, so if you're interested, save your money."

"Jasper don't pay me enough to try peaches like that." He laughed. "You mind if I turn the music up? We're about to hit the street and we want to fit in."

"Crank it."

She closed her eyes and listened to the lyrics that seemed to be a string of curse words set to a thudding, repetitious beat. It was probably official. She was getting old since this did nothing for her except make her want to run from the car or put a bullet through the stereo system. By the second song, though, she was starting to see the appeal and blamed it on the number of drinks she'd had at the pub.

He turned it down when they left the crowds of the French Quarter for the quieter section of town with large homes that, like hers, were behind large gates. Brandi Parrish's place was a mansion where she lived with the women in her employ. None of Brandi's business happened within the walls of the house, and the vetting system to get a date was extensive, protecting them from law enforcement, though Brandi had been around long enough that she had enough law enforcement on her payroll to take care of any problems that arose.

Cain had never paid for sex in her life, but she'd met Brandi when she'd been invited to a party at the house when she was in college. Brandi had made her feel welcome, but that had more to do with her da than with her. The only way to survive as long as Brandi had without major complications was to have powerful friends.

Dalton Casey was as powerful as they came, and befriending his daughter and heir was a calculated move, but Cain had never seen it as a lack of respect for her father. Brandi was someone she'd liked from their first meeting, and she'd never minded doing the occasional favor when Brandi was in need. They'd never be business partners, but she'd always been a firm believer that nothing sexual was off-limits if everyone involved knew the rules of the game. That's something Nicola and her family had never learned.

"You want me to wait?" the guy said when he stopped and whistled at the size of the house.

"What's your name?" She sat up and combed her hair back into place.

"Sam Johnson, ma'am, but my friends call me Skeeter."

"Okay, Skeeter, park it and come inside with me. You can practice talking to girls respectfully while I finish with my meeting." She studied the street, and there were a few people walking around, but they appeared harmless.

"You think the people inside mind if I'm packing?"

"You're with me, so it won't be a problem." She shook his hand when she got out, before leading him to the gate. "Did you want to wait in the car? I don't mind going in alone."

"No, ma'am. Jasper told me to make sure nothing happened to you, and I'm trying to keep my ass in one piece. If something happens to you, Jasper promised to chop me into little pieces."

She laughed as an older African American gentleman opened the gate and gave her an embrace when they stepped into the yard. Wilson had been with Brandi from the time she was sixteen, and they were the only family each claimed. He took care of Brandi and the girls, and he was the one she'd called for this appointment. He was an excellent gatekeeper, buffering Brandi from anything and anyone she didn't want to deal with.

"Thanks for carving out some time for me, Wilson. I'd ask how you are, but you don't ever age, my friend." She smiled when he didn't drop her hand as they started for the bright candy-apple red door. That color was like a neon sign announcing who owned the house, but Brandi wasn't one to hide.

"You're a good liar. It feels like I get older by the day, but I can't complain when I'm living such a good life. You come to talk to my girl about that place on Poydras?" He led them inside and the velvet couches in the foyer appeared new. "That's been bad for business." Wilson's slow drawl was relaxing to listen to.

"That's exactly what I want to talk about, so could you keep an eye on my escort for the evening? Actually, if anyone is around to keep him company, I wouldn't mind if you joined us."

"You one of Jasper's boys?" Wilson asked Skeeter and the young man nodded. "Wait here and mind your manners." A few girls came down after Wilson made a short call upstairs, and then he led her to the office.

Brandi stood and smiled when Wilson opened the door. The jeans and sweater, much like what Emma had been wearing, didn't fit the role of infamous madame, but Brandi seemed to be relaxing for the evening. Brandi was a beautiful woman no matter what she was wearing, and her smile made Cain believe she was hiding a secret. Considering Brandi's client list, it was more than likely quite a few secrets.

"Why is it that all the tall handsome butches in my life are taken? You've been a stranger for too long, Cain." Brandi stood on her toes and kissed her cheek. "But from what I hear from our mutual friend Sept Savoie, you've got a houseful of cute kids and a beautiful wife. I guess even the wildest of beasts can be tamed."

"They keep me busy, and all it took to civilize me was a farm girl from Wisconsin." She sat next to Wilson as Brandi moved behind her desk. "Wilson tells me you've heard of the Hell Fire Club."

"It's appropriately named. That place was nothing but a pit, and the owners didn't mind dealing in human trafficking from what I hear." Brandi stood and poured them all a drink. It was the last thing Cain wanted, but she also didn't want to be rude. "That's not your gig, though, so what do you need?"

"It's not my business, but—" She stopped talking, realizing Brandi, like her, wasn't walking on the right side of the law. "Is this room clean?"

"I check every day, Cain, so feel free to say whatever's on your mind," Wilson said.

"It's not part of my business, but it is yours," she continued, and Brandi nodded. "When the club was open, did you meet Nicola Eaton?"

"That bitch tried her best to put me out of business. We lost one girl to her offers of better money. That lasted a month, and I had to hide the poor thing for a couple of months when Nicola sent her dogs to bring her back. She made it clear that once the girls worked for her, she owned them." Brandi pressed her hand flat onto the desk as she spoke through gritted teeth. "That bitch was an animal with no soul. When I heard she died, I wasn't exactly torn up about it."

"What if I told you she was alive?"

"No way." Brandi downed her drink and closed her eyes. "We took in a few of the girls they left behind." There were faint worry lines around her eyes when she opened them. "Are they safe here? Are the rest of my girls?"

"Brandi, you know I'm not letting anything happen to you or your girls. I came to offer my protection and leave a few guys around who'll keep an eye on anything suspicious. But I wouldn't do that without your permission." She poured Brandi's next drink and glanced at Wilson and thought he looked relieved.

"What am I going to end up owing you?" Brandi's tone wasn't overly suspicious, and it seemed more like a programmed response.

"I'm your friend, and in this case *I* might end up owing you. Right now I can't tell you why, but if Nicola is coming for anyone, it's going to be me." She sat back down and crossed her legs. "I have a feeling, though, when she comes back, you're going to hear about it before I do. Places like the Hell Fire Club are all she knows, and they're what built the empire her family had."

"I hear her family is dead. Someone shot them until there was very little left in front of the building where the business was located."

"That's true, and the police are looking into that."

"I'm sure," Brandi said and smiled. "What exactly do you want me to do?" Brandi moved to the front of her desk and leaned against it. "I'm not good at acting like bait, and I wouldn't ask my girls to do that."

"That's the last thing I want from you. I'm here to offer my protection, that's all. If you hear from this bitch, then I want to know about it." She reached for Brandi's hand and smiled. "You know me better than to think I'd put you in danger, but Nicola Eaton is a dangerous woman. Someone like that might try to rebuild by taking a shortcut through an already successful business to get back on top."

"I do know you, but that goes both ways. You know Wilson and I can be trusted with what all this is about." Brandi sandwiched her hand between hers. "Did you talk to Sept about Nicola?"

"It's not something I can share with Sept without her wearing her detective hat, so you're going to have to trust me." She stood, ready to go. No matter how good her intentions, she couldn't force Brandi to take her help. "If you don't want my help, that's okay to say, but please be careful. Eaton, whose real name is Nicola Antakov, by the way, is an animal, and I don't want you, your girls, or Wilson getting hurt."

"I'm not turning you down, darling. And if you can't talk about it, you can't talk about it. I'm also not an idiot, so have as many of your guys over as you can spare. Just tell them no freebies."

"That's not going to be a problem, and don't engage with this woman if she does come by. I don't want anything to happen to you." She stood and put her arm around Brandi.

"Do you honestly think she'd try to take me out?" Brandi asked, leaning against her.

"Think about who this woman is, and you'll have your answer. If she has enough muscle, she'll take you down to take what's yours, and sleep the sleep of the innocent after she does." She kissed the top of Brandi's head and let her go.

"I'll do whatever you want, but promise me you won't let any harm come to my girls."

"No harm is coming to you or anyone in your life, Brandi. I give you my word, but give me yours that you won't do anything stupid. Wilson, don't let her take any chances."

"I try my best, but Brandi don't take too much coddling."

"This time, coddle away. It's important that the only one in the unmarked grave that needs to be dug is Antakov and no one else."

Chapter Eight

Emma pressed against Cain's back in the shower, kissing her shoulder. "I didn't leave a bruise, did I?" Cain turned and showed her the slight blue mark under her eye. "Jesus, honey, I'm so sorry. I didn't mean to hit you that hard, but—"

The smile on Cain's face telegraphed that she didn't have to ask for forgiveness. "But you saw some woman about to kiss me, and you lost it even though we asked her to." Cain kissed her until she put her hands around her neck. "Do you think I would've acted any differently if it had been you?"

"No matter what happens, you'd never hit me. That's something I know for sure." She tightened her hold on Cain's neck and gazed at her, wanting the morning alone, but they'd have a houseful of people in an hour. "It's not something I've ever worried about."

"I'm sure there are plenty of people who warned you to run as fast as you could out of here, but you're right. Whoever was trying to kiss you, though, might've had a problem," Cain said, bringing her hand up to touch Emma's cheek. "You didn't do anything I didn't ask you to do, so stop beating yourself up."

"Do you know what my life would've been if I hadn't gone with you? Had I not had the courage to choose you?" She lowered her head and rested it on Cain's chest. "I'd be empty without you, so don't ever tell me about what other people would have warned me about. None of that matters. You are my life, and you've made me a very happy woman."

"That's who you are to me, my love. You're mine, and I'm going to love you for as long as I have breath. I'm going to love you even if you give me a black eye." She smiled and kissed the tip of Emma's nose.

"That's not funny," she said, kissing Cain's neck. "It's not," she said when Cain laughed.

"It is, and I think you're going to have to call Josh and tell him you haven't taken a hit out on my life. That, and I'm sure he's fired that girl by now." Cain soaped a sponge and ran it down Emma's back. "Forget all that and get ready to have some fun."

"Are you ready for this many people and kids?" She turned so Cain could reach the front.

"The question is, are you? There's going to be a lot of Casey family running around."

"I happen to be a card-carrying member of the Casey family, so that doesn't scare me."

"If we're lucky, the kids won't walk away with too many bad habits," Cain said and laughed again. "Come on, Mrs. Casey. Let's go round up our troops."

"Do you think the guys out there are going to follow us up there?" She pointed to the street. "I want us to relax and spend some time with Maddie and Jerry without feeling like a bug under a microscope."

"I have a solution to that, but we don't have time to worry about it now. Did your father mention anything about Carol? That was the only thing I forgot about." Cain was still pissed at what Emma's mother had done, and Emma didn't feel any differently. The lengths her mother had gone to get her hands on Hannah surprised even her, and that was something when she considered that she'd believed her mother had hit rock bottom.

"She's living with her brother Morris, and the divorce is almost final. According to Muriel and the guy she has working on this, no matter if she shows up or not, it's done." She rinsed and accepted a towel. "I called the sheriff and told him about the restraining order. He'd be happy to take her in if she comes within a mile of us."

"I'm still sorry all that happened with her. Carol isn't my favorite person, but she is responsible for my favorite person." Cain kissed her again and led her out to the bedroom.

"My mother isn't someone who should've had children," Emma said. "It was more about survival than anything else when I was growing up. The only bright spot was my father." She followed Cain into the closet. "I'm sure you have your opinions about him, but he did try his best."

"I love your father," Cain said as if trying to put her at ease.

"He also loves our children, which buys a lot of forgiveness for any shortcomings he might have."

They dressed, then ran into Hannah and Victoria in the hallway as the girls headed for the stairs at top speed. After a lecture on how to act in the house, both girls took off at a slower pace that could in no way be described as a walk. There were a slew of guards in the front yard when she glanced out the window, and the number made her think about ordering more food.

"Do you think we're going to have room for all these people?" she asked Cain.

"I had some temporary space brought in, so we'll be fine. With the number of guys out there, it'll put a wall between you and the unfriendly people across the street." They walked into the dining room where most of their guests were eating the spread Carmen and her staff had put together.

Remi and Katlin greeted them both but asked to speak to Cain alone. There was something going on, but it wasn't the time for Emma to question Cain about it. Emma turned her attention to Abigail and Dallas. Both appeared happy to be getting away, but Emma saw how Dallas looked at the kids running around as well as the baby Carmen was holding.

"Marriage first, my friend. Then you can start planning that family I know you want," she mock-whispered to Dallas, and Abigail laughed.

"Are you sure you want some of these wild things in your house?" Abigail asked.

"As many as I can talk Remi into."

It hit Emma then what Cain must think at times. All this they had, how easy would it be to lose? What would happen when the enemies at their gates decided they had to pay for the slights they'd thought Cain had committed against them?

"You okay?" Abigail asked.

"I think I need a vacation," she said, and Dallas put her arm around her.

"While our partners are talking about whatever it is they run off and talk about, how about a girls' night of wine and gossip?" Dallas suggested.

Emma tapped her finger against her lips and nodded. "That sounds like a great idea. We might as well get used to each other's company. We're the only ones we can trust to keep our secrets." And that was true. Her mother might not have understood family and loyalty, but Emma did.

"Count me in," Abigail said, lifting her hand. The move made Dallas whistle.

"Man, have you been holding out on us," Dallas said, grabbing Abigail's hand and studying the diamond ring. "You have some explaining to do, Miss Abigail."

"Fin proposed yesterday, and I accepted. We also want to talk to Muriel about Fin adopting my three." Abigail sounded like she'd won the happiness lottery.

"You can say plenty about our partners, ladies, but damn if they all don't have great taste in jewelry," Emma said and hugged Abigail. "Congratulations, honey, and welcome to the family. Cain and I will be happy to throw you as big a party as we're planning for my pal here."

"Thank you," Abigail said, gladly accepting Emma's hug, then Dallas's. "Sometimes it's hard to believe Fin is real, but she's everything I've ever wanted."

"And I can tell by how she looks at you that she feels the same way. It's going to be a long night of wine and gossip if this is where we start," she said and laughed. Her thoughts, though, were on the other room and Cain.

❖

"Jasper got hit last night," Remi said as they sat in the office to have coffee. "He lost a couple of guys and has no idea who did it. Simon told me this morning, along with a message that Jasper would be calling you today," she said of her personal guard. "Vinny is ready to go to war, but you know Vinny as well as I do. We need to aim him correctly before he goes off and slaughters everyone who looks at him funny."

"Anyone talking?" Cain asked as she stared out the window. "We all know some of these guys can't wait to brag. And you're right, Jasper needs to put a muzzle on Vinny. It's not the time to blow up the world."

"That's the thing that worries me," Katlin said as she sat next to Remi. "The corners are quiet as church on Sunday. That means either a professional hit or whoever this is brought in outside muscle. As for Vinny, you've known him longer than any of us. How reasonable do you think he's willing to be?"

"Reasonable isn't in Vinny's vocabulary. He's hyperactive and has poor decision-making skills, which is why I put him with Jasper. I thought the two would balance each other out. Where did this happen?" If it was anywhere near Jasper's Aunt Maude, Vinny wasn't the only one who was going to lose his shit.

"You know that club he opened in the east?" Katlin asked, and Cain and Remi nodded. "They were hopping last night, and someone did a drive-by and took out two of his men standing outside doing business." Katlin put her hand up before Cain could say anything. "I know this sounds like a few other incidents around town, but they didn't just spray the outside with bullets. They aimed and took out the two guys tied to Jasper. It was a calculated surgical hit."

"It shouldn't be hard to narrow down," Remi said.

"That depends," Cain said, trying to figure out the angle. "What we need is to talk to my favorite neighbor, but I'm not missing that plane."

"How do you want me to handle that?" Katlin asked.

"He's always so happy to hear from me, so let's give him a call. Get Fin in here," she said, prompting Katlin to go.

"What are you thinking?" Remi asked.

"I just want a phone conversation, but I don't want to rile up the guys outside. With Fin's help, we can leave them in the dark."

Cain briefed her, and then Fin set up some equipment and made the call. Once Hector got on the phone, Finley gave him some directions and they waited.

"Cain, good morning," Hector said, calling on the line Fin had specified.

"It's not a good morning for everyone." She drummed her fingers, not wanting to waste another moment of time than she had to on this guy. "I need to know who hit Jasper Luke last night."

"You are not going to believe me, so why do you call to ask? Jasper is someone who works against me and would be happy if it had been me who was killed." Hector said a lot for a man who didn't really say anything at all.

"That makes no sense, and I'm not accusing, I'm asking." This was a waste of her time, but it was the only way to get through these conversations with the sensitive guy. "I know you've had your problems, so I'm sure you don't want to get into a war. I'm not sure, but I'm guessing you don't want too much more loss."

"That sounds like a threat."

"It's an observation. Jasper's a friend and I care about what happens to him. A move against him is something I'm not going to forget."

"That, too, sounds like a threat. The operation Luke and Carlotti have is not big enough for me to worry about moving against them. You have my word it wasn't me, and if you're interested, I got hit last night too." Hector paused as if for dramatic effect. "I am surprised you don't know this."

"I keep telling you, I'm not interested in your business. What happens around your world isn't something I keep tabs on unless it spills onto whatever I have going on." She smiled at the group listening in with her. Of course, she knew his place had been shot up too, but there was no need for them to know that. "Do you have any idea who would've had the guts to do this to you? Granted you're in a tough spot, but you're not exactly an easy target."

"I have no idea, but think of this," Hector said as what sounded like a closing door came from his end. "If they do not respect my business, it will be no time before they do not respect yours."

Hector's English was improving but he still hadn't gotten the hang of contractions, making him sound more formal in his speech. "Do you have any idea or not?"

"There is someone trying to either kill me or take away what I have. If they want to rule the streets from here to Florida, that means your friends Vinny and Jasper will be in danger." Hector made a lot of sense, since they were all in the same game. "If you have given them your protection, you will be pulled into this too."

"Hector, that might sound like a threat," she said, repeating his words.

"As you keep telling me, amiga. I am not your friend, but I am not your enemy. Mi mama did not raise a stupid man who will go to war with a woman who is now in a position to take what I have built. Even if she would give it away because she says she is not interested." The admission sounded so truthful it stunned her into silence. "You did not think I had the cojones to admit that. Now you know I tell the truth. I have given you the bullet that will kill me if you choose that."

"I'm not your enemy, Hector, and you've helped me enough in the past with information that if you do go to war, it'll never be with me unless you make a move on my family." She looked at Remi as she said it and her old friend nodded. "The wolves at your door have nothing to do with me or mine."

"I believe you, but I need you to tell me you will share with me what you find."

"I'll do that, if you make the same promise."

"Perhaps we will never do business, but friendship might not be bad," Hector said and laughed.

"Perhaps, and I'll talk to you soon." She hung up and sighed. "Just what I don't need on top of everything else."

"True, but I'm shocked to hell he admitted he's in that bad a position," Finley said. "I'd think a guy like Hector would rather cut his tongue out than verbalize a weakness."

"He's not lying. The destruction of everything he has will make it tough for him to keep his standing. We're going on vacation, but you need to work on finding whoever this Jerome Rhodes is," she said, standing. "Ask Merrick for some help and maybe you two can make headway on him and the Kennison family. All these damn unknowns are driving me batty."

"I've found all there is to find on these people. They're not real and the trail ends when the people you know as Drew and Taylor Kennison came into being," Finley said. "The only thing I have to wonder is if this has anything to do with Nicola."

"The Kennison duo arrived before you and Nicola's parents did," Katlin said. "This has your guys in the feds written all over it."

"I'm not with the feds any longer, cousin, so cut me some slack. We should get some answers after last night sooner or later, but we might not have that kind of time. The only way to know for sure right now is if I ask my old boss, but I'm not sure if that's a good idea or not."

"For the next day concentrate on your beautiful partner and children. Work will come soon enough, and with time the traps we've set will either work out or not." She motioned toward the door, ready to have breakfast before they left.

"We set traps?" Finley asked.

"We did, and when we're airborne they'll send a clear message." She put her arm around Finley's shoulders and walked her out.

"What's that, exactly?"

"That we're a weak pack of women waiting to be taken down." She smiled when Fin looked surprised.

"How is that helpful?" Fin asked, stopping.

"Did your mom ever tell you the story of a small rooster everyone bet against?"

"No." Finley looked even more confused.

"Then let me educate you," she said, telling the story she'd shared with Emma when they'd first gotten back together. "Whoever takes the bait will find my talons are still sharp when I bury them in their neck. Nothing teaches a better lesson than death."

Jerome buttoned his shirt and glanced at the bed. The short trip with Daniela had left him with the need to see his family—rather, his dad. According to his father, his mother was now living with her sister in upstate New York. When the FBI sent agents to pump his parents for information to help them find him, they'd listed his misdeeds and reminded his mom of all the old accusations against his father as well. His mother had never been one to understand the meaning of loyalty, and she'd blamed his father for the troubles he was having now. Their divorce had been swift and not fair at all to his dad.

"Where are you going?" Daniela asked as she sat up and let the sheet fall.

Her body was perfect, but in a strange way it didn't excite him as much as Gracelia's had when they'd been together. That bitch had been totally crazy and still hung up on the loser who'd fathered Juan, but she'd been the most passionate lover he'd ever had. Her death at the hands of her nephew Carlos must've been horrific, considering how Gracelia had killed her brother, Carlos's father, but he understood revenge. Still, in a small way, he missed her.

"I've got to make a short trip, so I'll have one of the guys take you home. Go shopping or whatever you want. I'll be back in a few days." He picked a tie and had started tying it when he felt her arms go around his waist.

He'd found Daniela on the beach in Cabo with a group of girls who'd taken the day to sunbathe on the mostly deserted beach. She was the only one who hadn't turned away from him when he'd walked up on them skinny-dipping. It was like she'd seen in him a way out of the life she had in the slums out of sight of the tourist hotspots. The money had made her agreeable to whatever he wanted or did, and that was the way of the world as far as he was concerned.

"I want to go with you." Daniela pressed herself to him and put her hand on his crotch.

The feeling of being in a porn film always came over him when she acted like this. There was no way she was this into him, but he didn't care about that. Love was an illusion created by the weak as a promise to keep you stupid. He hadn't gotten to where he was by being stupid.

"Not this time. Go back to the house and wait. I won't be long."

"Please, Papi. I want to go with you. You know I'll be good."

"Dani, don't make me tell you again. I'm going on business, not fun, so go home." He kissed her forehead and went back to his tie. There was a knock on the door—he was expecting Pablo—and Jerome pointed to the bathroom so Daniela would cover herself.

"Who did you send?" he asked Pablo when he opened the door. Pablo had been a peon in Gracelia's orbit, but she'd overlooked the best thing about him. He followed orders to the letter and never complained. That was the kind of loyalty he'd demand going forward from everyone.

"Abril Rojas, señor. She say she go where she know no one looking." Pablo handed over an envelope. "For you. This what you ask for."

He took out the driver's license and credit cards solidifying his identity as Jerome Curtis, since he didn't want to go back to the Gulf Coast with an identity someone might remember. One final gift from Graciela. "She knows what to say? I didn't get to call, so she's sure about what I wanted, right?"

"She know, and she no let you down. The men are still there, señor?"

There was one thing he knew about Annabel Hicks, and that was she didn't like giving up. His father had tried and failed to stay on Giovanni Bracato's payroll, and he'd completely covered his tracks. The bureau, though, had suspected and driven him out without proof. All he'd been trying to do was better his family's situation, and they'd made him pay for that. He'd succeeded where his father had not, and Annabel was going to do what it took to bring him in. What Annabel didn't know was that he and his father were going to fuck her and the rest of her team into embarrassment. She had to pay for what had happened to his family.

"They're still watching, so it's important Abril gets it right. The grocery is the best place."

"She know and she already there." Pablo helped him on with his jacket, and Jerome tilted his head toward the door. Pablo took the hint and left and almost immediately, the bathroom door swung open.

"Remember not to leave the house alone," he said to Daniela and took her hands before she could touch him. "And be careful who you invite back here."

"I remember, but you should take me with you. I can help you."

"I'll call you," he said, letting her go. There was no time for circular conversations.

They drove to the airport, and he rolled his own bag, wanting to blend in as a businessman taking a short trip. He smiled at the niggling fear that surfaced when he was in the security line. If he was stopped and fingerprinted, he was done.

"Here you go," the TSA agent said, handing him back his boarding pass and ID.

Pablo didn't talk to him as they sat in the concourse having coffee, nor on the flight when he reclined his seat and closed his eyes. He thought of Cain Casey right before he fell asleep and her poise no matter the situation. He'd heard what had happened to her when Cehan had taken her in and laughed at the big goon sitting in prison. When was his old team going to learn that Cain played to win no matter the penalty shots? He'd learned a lot from the bitch, but it was time to surpass her in the dangerous game they played.

They landed in Houston and waited forty-five minutes before catching the connecting flight to Biloxi. The house Pablo had rented across the street from the beach wasn't as private as he would've liked, but he wasn't planning to lie outside tanning himself. He was in the den having a drink when the door opened, and he heard his father's deep voice.

"Jerome," Matty Curtis said loudly from the kitchen.

"In here," he said, not enjoying his father's use of his fake name. The loss of his identity was one of the things he was angriest about. His name was something he'd been proud of since it carried his father's legacy into the future. That was lost to him now.

His father put his arms around him and held him for a long while. It had been months since they'd seen each other, and he'd missed the only man he'd ever trusted completely. "Anthony, I've missed you, boy."

"Dad." He couldn't stop the tears that came at the feel of his father against him. Nothing in life replaced the feeling of having someone in your corner who'd never betray you. Family was the one thing that proved you weren't alone. "I'm so glad to see you."

"Me too. You've done good so far, but we need to talk about the rest," his father said while their heads were still close together. "There's still a lot left undone, but I'm here to help."

"I've done plenty, but there's some stuff that can put us at the top of the game if we get it done right. It's a gamble, though."

His father sat down and put his hand on Jerome's knee. "That's what I'm here for, son. Nothing is too much of a gamble if you stack the deck."

CHAPTER NINE

The number of vehicles that pulled away from the house off St. Charles made Nicola think Casey was running like a scared bitch, and it left her with nothing to do but wait. The windows on every vehicle were tinted so she couldn't see who was in the entourage, but that didn't bother her as much as trying to figure out where they were going. With the feds following, she couldn't get too close as they headed to the airport at the lake. All Nicola saw was the cars driving into a large hangar and two planes leaving. It was a lost opportunity to riddle the vehicles with bullets and deal with them all at once.

"Do you want to go back to the city?" Nina asked as they drove back toward their hotel. "I'll leave a few guys behind to watch for when they come back, if you want to head home."

"What you need to do is find out where they're going. If Casey figured out we're here, she's running scared, so I don't mind following her." She made a fist and relaxed it in a methodical motion, trying to ease the pain in her hand. Today it hurt much worse than the ache in her head, and she blamed the damn humidity in this swamp. "Try to remember that I'm in charge, so keep those helpful hints to yourself."

"What would you like?" Nina asked as if resigning herself to the boredom of the coming days.

"A nap, and then we're going to find the information you haven't been able to get. I'll show you how easy it is, and why you should think about shutting up and leaving the decisions and ideas to me." She headed straight to her hotel room, then closed the door and lay down after taking a pain pill. There'd have to be a trip back to New York, but she didn't want to give Nina the satisfaction of giving in so easily.

She opened her eyes when her phone chirped at midnight but

decided on a shower to be fully conscious for what had to be done before she talked to anyone. Nina and another one of her people were waiting outside when she came out and motioned to the door.

"Where to?" Nina asked.

"The school the girls are in," she said and almost laughed at how Nina was looking at her. "Abigail moved them this week. I called the school we had them registered in, and they told me where the records were sent."

The school was prestigious from what she'd read, but their security system was not. They went in through the back as soon as Nina picked the lock, and she remembered the few times Abigail had dragged her to some function or other the old school had concocted to drain more money out of them. Sadie had been the only one in school back then, and she'd been so excited when Nicola had shown up. She'd been waiting until they were a little older before she started spending time with them. She had no patience for giggly little girls and what they found exciting.

It was Abigail's job to get them to a point where she could start teaching them who they were and what was expected of them. They might have had to give up the Antakov name, but their legacy was a rich one filled with power and money. The only time she interfered with what her lovely partner was doing was when she thought she was leading them in a direction that would've made them too soft. Abigail had no concept of how only the truly strong could come to rule their empire.

She stopped at the door to the office and cracked her neck. "Open it," she said to Nina.

The filing cabinets behind the counter would hold all the information she'd need to lead her to Abigail and, more importantly, her children. She had Nina and the other guard wait outside as she placed a penlight in her mouth and opened the drawer with the *E*s. She got to the slot where Eaton should've been.

"What the fuck?" she whispered as she looked through every file, thinking someone had made a mistake. She had no choice now but to start at the beginning because they had to be there.

That didn't take long since she found them in the *A*s. She would have driven a dagger through Abigail's forehead had she been standing next to her when she saw the pictures of a smiling Sadie and Victoria. They'd grown up quite a bit since the last time she'd seen them. Had Abigail figured out their true name and registered them under *Antakov*?

No—their information listed their name as *Abbott*. That was something she didn't expect.

"Who is Finley Abbott?" she muttered around her flashlight. From what was listed, this Finley had as much right to remove the children and make decisions for their care as Abigail did. She made note of Abbott's address, and what classrooms the kids were in.

She walked the halls and stopped at Sadie's class first. Sadie's name was on her desk along with some *welcome to class* sticky notes clearly done by the other students. When Nicola went through her work, she squeezed her hand into a tight fist when she saw how Sadie had signed her name. Eaton had been replaced by Abbott, and the sight of it intensified the pain in her head.

"What's wrong?" Nina asked, having obviously noticed the change in her demeanor.

The anger coursing through her prevented her from saying a word as she went to Victoria's kindergarten classroom. There, along with all the pictures the children had done of their families, was Victoria's effort. The tall stick figure with dark hair and blue eyes had to be the Abbott who'd convinced her children to forget her and their family.

"Why did she write Abbott?" Nina asked as she stared at the same thing she was looking at.

"Are you familiar with the name Finley Abbott?"

"There was a cop in New York who was under Brock Howard. Abbott and some other woman were assigned to Howard when a transmission was found coming out of the precinct regarding the operation at the quarry." Nina stared at the picture as if it held all the answers. It bothered Nicola enough that she tore it down and crumpled it into a small ball before dropping it on the ground. "What's a NYPD investigator doing with your kids?"

"Get us back to the city tonight. I don't care what you need to do, but we need to get there now."

She kicked the wad of paper away as they walked out. It was time to put Casey on the back burner until she had found some answers to the slew of questions she had. Before all that, though, she'd have to deal with Sacha Oblonsky. Her cousin wasn't hyped about a woman running the family next and had told Nina that when she'd informed him she was still alive.

"Do you want to set a meeting with the family?" Nina asked.

"No, I want to talk to Sacha. He might have something important to say before I pull his balls off and shove them in his mouth. That message will get through to the rest of my loving family when I display his head at the next family meeting."

❖

Emma finally closed the door of their bedroom after a night of catching up with her old friends the Raths and their beautiful boy JC. The older the little boy got, the less he resembled the family he was born into. That Giovani Bracato's grandson would grow up to be a dairy farmer was probably bothering him more than the flames of hell if he could see beyond the grave.

"God, I can't wait to take this bra off," she said as she locked the door. Cain was already undressing by the bed, and she stopped to watch.

"Need help with that?" Cain asked, facing her with her shirt open.

"You know something, mobster?" she asked as she stepped closer.

"What's that?" Cain lifted her sweater over her head and threw it on the floor.

She wasn't about to fuss about misplaced laundry now. "From the day we met, I've craved you touching me. You'd think it would've calmed down after all these years, but the urge only gets stronger." She smiled when Cain reached behind her and unfastened her bra. "Is it like that for you?" Cain glanced down when Emma put her hands on her belt.

"Always, lass, you know that. There's never been a moment I haven't wanted you."

"I don't know if that's exactly true, but I'm glad it is now." She left the belt hanging open and started on the buttons of Cain's jeans. They were both tired, but she'd been staring at Cain all night and hadn't been alone with her since that morning. She put her hand between Cain's legs and smiled at her hard clit. "Can I do something for you, baby?"

"You can now," Cain said, her voice tight.

She dropped to her knees, taking Cain's pants with her, and didn't waste time putting her mouth on her. Cain's knees bent a little, but she stayed on her feet as Emma sucked her in and didn't let up on the pressure. They both moaned when Cain put her hand at the back of her head, and Emma knew from the way Cain flexed her thigh muscles that she was coming.

"Damn, that was way too fast." Cain stepped out of her pants and kicked them aside. "I'll pay you back for that before we get interrupted."

"What does that mean?" She wrapped her legs around Cain's waist and pressed their lips together. She lay back on the bed when Cain put her down and pulled her jeans off as if in a hurry to do so.

"There's about to be a spectacular display of my weakened position in town, and I'm sure either Merrick, Katlin, or someone else is going to be banging on the door in about thirty minutes." Cain climbed in after her and rested her weight on her elbow.

"I'd ask what the hell you're talking about, but I don't care at this moment." There was nothing on her mind when Cain's hand came to rest between her legs. She arched up into her when Cain put her fingers in easily. She'd been wet for a while as she'd been watching Cain downstairs no matter who she was talking to. "Yes," she said as the end came as fast as Cain's had.

"Is the plan you have in mind going to keep us from sleeping in tomorrow?" she asked as she put her head under Cain's chin. "I need you alone for as long as I can get you."

Their time was up when she heard the knock. Emma wanted to curse, but going through the steps of necessary evils got them to the ultimate goal of peace. When those steps interrupted intimate moments like this, it was hard to remember the greater good.

"Give me a minute, lass."

Katlin was the one who'd come to the door, and Emma heard her talking for only a minute before Cain closed the door. "What happened?" she asked when Cain sat on the bed.

"Emma's, the pub, and the office were all shot up. It'll be seen as a move to make me come back to town and hit back." Cain spoke calmly, but the news didn't really call for calm.

"You're going back?" She gripped the sheet at the thought of Cain going back without her. When things were going great, it ramped up her fear that there'd be a price to pay. She'd give anything but Cain. That was unacceptable.

"No," Cain said dropping her robe and getting back into bed. "The way I figure, the club needed remodeling, and the pub was going to be expanded and closed for renovation anyway."

She sat up, straddled Cain's waist, grabbed her wrists, and held them above her head when that was all she said. "Don't make me beat it out of you."

"Whoever wants a piece of me, my darling girl, is going to think it's okay to take a bite. When they try, though, I'm going to rip their heart out and let them watch it stop beating in my hand." Cain put her hands on her hips and smiled. "Sometimes bloodying the water is the best way to get the sharks to come out and play."

"Are you sure about that?" She knew who Cain was. She'd always known, but love was love no matter if she was the devil incarnate. She could no more deny her feelings for Cain than she could stop her own heart from beating. "Inviting sharks to a party doesn't sound like a good idea."

"I can't live with the not knowing, love. You and the kids are the most important people in my life, and I can't stand that I don't know when all this will crash down on me." Cain moved her hands higher, and she came down to lie on her. "Bringing things into the light lets me take my shots without missing."

"Just as long as you understand this family can't survive without you. Hayden needs your time to learn what it is to be a clan leader, and Hannah and Billy need you to show them who they are." She lifted up a little and framed Cain's face with her hands. "Don't leave me out of any of this."

"You know better than that. Tonight wasn't about leaving you out, but letting you enjoy your night without having to worry about all of it." Cain shook her head when she opened her mouth. "And don't insult me by accusing me of treating you like a feeble female. That's not what it was."

"I wasn't going to do that," Emma said but smiled because it had crossed her mind. "But how do Ramon and Vincent fit into this?"

"Mano stayed behind to help Ramon put out the narrative I want. Vincent is going to do what I asked him."

She pinched Cain's side and widened her smile. "I think I *will* have to beat it out of you."

"If I'm seen as weak, the next targets will be Vinny and Jasper because it's well known they're under my protection, even if our businesses don't overlap. Someone already took their first shot at them, and if whoever that was thinks I can't back them up, they'll deliver the killing blow."

"I'm not sure how you're not tired all the time," Emma said. "You've got to do a lot of thinking in the span of a day." She kissed Cain and pressed her sex down against her abdomen. "I'm going to have to do my best to make you relax as often as I can."

"Is there something I can do for *you*?" Cain ran her hands down her thighs and back up to her hips. "The next few days is all about you and the kids. All the traps I've set will either work out or they won't."

"The kids get you in the morning, but right now I want you all to myself," she said, kissing Cain with as much passion as she could manage. "You're not blowing anything else up tonight, are you?"

"Yes, but I promise no one is going to knock on the door for what I have in mind," Cain said, putting her hands on her ass. "My aim now is you."

"Good answer, baby. Show me how good your aim is."

CHAPTER TEN

Shelby sat in the diner the next morning and studied the pictures that had been emailed to her the night before. Someone had taken a major shot at Cain's life last night, and that meant there was some major shit coming their way. They'd watched Cain long enough to know that she'd never take something like this lying down.

They'd staked out a spot for surveillance the night before, but all they saw was Cain and her cousins hanging around the fire pit. For an instant. Before the bright security lights came on. They were so bright it was hard to make out anything. That was something else Cain loved doing—finding clever ways of messing up what the feds were trying to do was a hobby of Cain's.

"Do they have any idea yet?" Joe asked as he slid into the booth. The temperatures outside were frigid, so they were both in heavy winter gear.

"No, but with any luck she'll go back to deal with this and we can warm up again. It's chilly in New Orleans, but nothing like this." She laid out the pictures showing no spot had been spared. "What do you think this is about?" They were waiting for a call from Annabel, so they'd left Dylan and the guy filling in for Lionel at the farm.

"I'm not sure, and that bugs the hell out of me. We're always in the dark, but in this case, we haven't seen anything out of the ordinary in the last few months that would've made anyone retaliate against her like this." He put his hands around the mug the waitress put down. It didn't feel hot, and the woman was never friendly. "Do they not know how to heat up coffee in this town?"

"You're not the big tipper in town, so don't expect anything to be hot. They all seem to know who we are and what we're about, so expect cold coffee to go along with your cold eggs." She opened her laptop as Joe studied the pictures, and she found an email from the contact they'd made with the DEA. "Do you remember David McCulla?"

"DEA guy, right?" He stacked the pictures and put them back in the file. "This is going to put Casey out of business for at least a couple of months. When she finds out who's behind it, there'll be hell to pay."

"McCulla is with DEA, and his team is following a problem with Jasper Luke. There was a drive-by at his club, and two of his men got killed." She clicked through the file and glanced at the one Joe had just closed. "Do you think the two are related? They're friends, after all."

"What does McCulla think?" Joe accepted the laptop and read through what was sent. "The only difference is there was no one hit with Casey's problem. If this was a way to get her to engage, it was a bad idea. That's a given, but Jasper lost a couple of guys. He's not known for sitting shit like this out. It's the only thing he and Casey have in common."

"Like I said, they're friends." She smiled at the waitress when she delivered breakfast and laughed softly when it wasn't returned. "All this is going to do is start a war." Her phone buzzed but they couldn't take a call from Annabel in the open. "Want to go to the bathroom with me?"

Joe laughed and waved her out of the booth. "I can't wait."

"Hello, ma'am," she said as they walked toward the back. "Please hold on a minute."

"Take your time. Believe me, this call is going to be the best part of my day," Annabel said.

They locked themselves in the ladies' room and set up the laptop for a video conference. "We got the reports from what happened last night. The DEA also sent us pictures of Luke's issues," she said as Joe nodded. "Any new information?"

"The word on the street is Casey's power is waning, and she's vulnerable. That someone hit her when she left town and was able to get away with it because she didn't have enough muscle to prevent it has us wondering if that's true." Annabel shuffled the papers in her hand and glanced up when she seemed to find the one she was looking for. "I have another team on the ground here looking into this, and they've only gotten to a couple of informants."

"Do you know of anything else in the works when it comes to the Casey family? From our side, I mean."

"Aside from you and Joe and your team, nothing, except the guys I have looking into what happened last night. Why do you ask?"

"It's something Emma Casey told me in the bathroom at Vincent's. I didn't approach her, but we did have a conversation." She remembered how adamant Emma had been, and she also knew how protective both Emma and Cain were of their children. "Usually she does a good job of pretending I don't exist, but not this time. I think if she could've gotten away with it, she would've slapped me."

"You didn't mention it before you left," Annabel said but she didn't sound upset.

"To tell you the truth, Joe and I started checking before we shipped out to see if there was something to what she said. We asked around to try to tie this to anyone else, but Emma was convinced someone from our side approached Hannah or Hayden Casey."

"The Casey children aren't people we're interested in. Maybe years from now if they go into the family business," Annabel said with a small laugh. "But she has to know we have higher standards than that."

"I thought it was strange and laughable, but believe me, Emma Casey wasn't kidding. She also holds what she believes is the higher moral ground because of Cain getting shot."

"That's going to haunt us for years, but none of us are at fault for that."

"I doubt she sees it that way. Are you sure no one who would take the chance of using their kids has anything going?"

"No matter what the Casey family thinks about us, that's not our style. Children—I think we can all agree, no matter what side of the law you're on—are off-limits. I'll check, but I doubt there's any merit to this. How is everything else working out? How's Gardner fitting in?"

"Not to belabor the point, ma'am, but something triggered Emma to say that." She hated to complain about Dylan, but hopefully Annabel would transfer her when the rest of their team got back. "When are Claire and Lionel coming back?" Their team members had been in training for weeks, but that would be ending soon.

"You should have Lionel back by the end of the week, and that didn't answer my question. Is Gardner working out?" Annabel gave them her full attention by looking directly into the camera.

"She's okay, but if you give her a few minutes, she'll tell you how fabulous she is. She's used to more arrests and convictions than we get with the people we follow around." So much for not complaining. "Sorry, but it sounds like she's used to much simpler cases and subjects." Joe poked her in the side where Annabel couldn't see. "We'll give her time and bring her up to speed about the games Casey likes to play."

"She'll have to be happy in the back of the van for a long time to come. The people who made her aren't going to forget her anytime soon, and they're out for blood." Annabel glanced at her watch and grimaced. "Let me run, and I'll call up the chain and see what I can find out about the situation with the kids, but I doubt we'll come up with anything."

"I appreciate it, ma'am, and we'll keep you up to date."

Joe's phone rang, and he stepped away to answer it as she shut the video call down. "What's wrong?" he asked to whoever he was talking to. "We're on our way."

"What?" she asked, and he put his finger up.

"Hang tight and we'll be right there." He hung up and shook his head. "We've got to go, then try to figure out how to work around this."

"What, exactly?" She didn't really want to know, but it was unavoidable.

"Wait and see."

❖

"I don't want to hear it's humiliating," Hector said to his daughter Marisol. She was sitting across from him, and he could almost feel the murderous thoughts flitting through her brain in rapid succession. Ever since their move to the city of New Orleans, Marisol had tried to break out on her own and had made decisions not approved by him. None of it had turned out well, and she hated him for pointing it out, but her real anger was aimed at Tracy Segal. It was one thing for him to tell her she was an idiot, but when Tracy did it in her subtle way, Marisol went insane.

Marisol's problem was his growing relationship with Tracy, and how much he relied on her. Tracy was young, but she was good at finding problems in the system and, more important, finding solutions to fix those problems. And Tracy was fearless even when it would be better for her to lie because of his temper. She'd started to take responsibility away from Marisol, and Marisol didn't like it.

"Meeting with some small-time hustler isn't humiliating?" Marisol asked, spitting the words at him. "Is this her idea?" She pointed at Tracy, then glared back at him. "Do you think this is going to make you look strong?" They spoke in Spanish, but he knew Tracy had enough grasp of the language to understand every insult Marisol tossed her way. Her uninterested expression never changed, though.

"Your problem is you never could see the big picture. It's not about looking weak or strong, but about survival. You were born after I fought my way to the top, so you've never had to really fight." He shook his head at the only one of his children interested in taking over for him. "All you've done is run around beating your chest and acting like an idiot off what I gave you."

"What you gave me?" Marisol laughed as she ran her finger along the scar next to her eye. He'd put that there for beating on Tracy.

"Tell me one thing you've done that got us something new? One thing and I'll give you the whole thing and fucking walk away." He understood the anger. That's what had gotten him to the top, but you could never rest once you got there. Once you were at the top, anger wasn't enough to keep you there. All this shit proved him right. The shiny pedestal he'd been standing on was starting to teeter.

"I got us the deal with the Blanc family." Her quick answer made him laugh, which of course only made her angrier.

"The great Blanc family," he said seriously. "Of course, how could I forget? Nicolette is dead, and her father is as interested in doing business with us as he is in getting shot in the balls." He sat back and shook his head again. "I'm tired of arguing with you. If this is beneath you, then don't go to the meeting."

She finally smiled as she turned her glare on Tracy. "Fucking send her. She might find the *pendejo* a better fit than you." That made her laugh more than he'd heard in the last five months.

Her lack of respect finalized his decision, even though it hurt his heart. "The thing you have to learn is to find people you trust to do what's necessary. The other thing you have to learn is how to make it on your own." He stood and buttoned his jacket before holding his hand out to Tracy. "The world is a scary place, but it won't be a problem for you."

"What's that supposed to mean?"

"It means go and make your own way. Show the world how strong and smart you are. You've outgrown us." He held Tracy's hand and glanced back at Marisol. It was a mistake to turn his back on her even if she was his daughter, but he trusted Tracy with his life. His friends would say that was a mistake as well, but he knew something about Tracy everyone else had overlooked. She had no one but him. That sad fact would make her loyal to her last day.

"What's that supposed to mean?" Marisol asked again. Her tone had changed from condescending to fearful.

"It means you're a free agent and no longer part of my organization. You think me weak, and I'm not going to try to change your mind about that. I'm not so weak, though, that I'm going to sit and take this kind of shit from you. Get the fuck out of my house."

"You can't do that. I'm your family, your heir." Marisol lost her bravado as fast as he'd made up his mind to cut her loose. "Papa, don't do this."

"What are you talking about? You've sat here telling me how whatever I need is beneath you. Leave before I have you thrown on the street with nothing." He tugged Tracy ahead of him and opened the door for Marisol, who seemed glued to the spot where she stood. "Don't make me say it again."

"I don't want to go. If you need me to go and meet with Carlos, I will." She was as close to pleading as she'd ever been.

"Get out, and be grateful you're not dead, Marisol. I've given you too many chances, and I'm done, daughter or not." He motioned for the guard, but Marisol moved before the guy could touch her. "Be careful what you do next."

"You should do the same," Marisol said with a conviction that made him smile.

"I'm not the one who's a slow learner, mi hija. Your usual way is to smash everything in sight, but not everything in life needs to be broken. Remember that, and don't get in my way."

❖

Cain leaned against a tree about a hundred feet from where Shelby and Joe drove up and stopped on her property. Both agents were staring at the spot where two camp chairs, various cameras, and what appeared to be surveillance equipment were set up but abandoned. She smiled at the three large German shepherds standing on their hind legs barking and snarling around one tree.

The three dogs were part of a pack of fourteen that now patrolled the outer grounds as backup to the guards she'd posted closer to the house. They'd been trained to stay away from Jerry's cows, but federal agents seemed to be their specialty. Granted, if the feds had a warrant, there'd be no way she could keep them off the property, but her new pets weren't illegal.

She'd been walking with Lou when he'd released them to the spot she knew Shelby and company had picked, but she didn't immediately recognize the two agents who'd scaled the large elm. It had been pretty funny watching them climb as fast as they could in heavy winter gear trying to get away from the sharp teeth. One dog had managed to rip a piece off the woman's jeans, but thankfully it'd missed skin since there'd been no cries of pain. She had enough headaches to deal with.

Joe lowered his window and pointed his gun at the elm, prompting her to start walking. "Good morning," she said from behind them. She had to put her hands up when he swung the gun toward her. "Shoot me or the dogs, and you're going to want to turn it on yourself when I'm done with you."

Lou shouted a command from where he was standing, and the dogs sat but kept their heads turned upward toward the two people they'd treed. "Come," Lou said, and the dogs went right to him.

"Get them the hell away from us," the woman in the high branches called. "And keep them over there until we get down."

She finally recognized the new agent when she hugged the trunk on the way down. "Do you have a warrant?" she asked Shelby. "I'm sure you noticed the posted signs on the way in."

"You left the gate unlocked, so we didn't think you'd mind," Joe said.

"A lock is what it takes to make you literate?" Her question made Lou laugh. "Good to know. The other thing to know is there are plenty more of these guys, and next time they won't be so nice. If you decide to chance it, pray Lou is out here to call them off. Considering how quick you are with your gun"—she pointed at Joe—"my first call will be to PETA if you harm one of these guys."

"You can't impede our work," Dylan said as she pulled her pants up. It was comical since now one leg was shorter than the other.

"Again..." She sighed, losing patience. "Do you have a warrant?"

"No, but you know why we're here, so cut the crap," the guy with Dylan said.

"You all are a nuisance back home, that is true." One of the dogs moved to stand next to her. "But you aren't allowed in the yard there, either. Not unless you have a warrant. And you're not allowed in this yard."

"This is ridiculous," Dylan said. "We should bring you in for threatening a federal agent."

Cain smiled when Shelby's head dropped. Training young hotheads was always a pain in the ass. "It's more like harassment, Agent Gardner. I'm landlocked back home, so you park those ridiculous vehicles pretty close. That I can't do anything about. You're on city property and there's nothing stopping you. Here, though, my yard is acres and acres. You haven't been invited in, so I should warn you about the ordinance the town council passed when it comes to trespassing."

"Is it a dollar fine?" the male agent asked, laughing. "Here you go." He fished a buck out of his wallet.

She heard the sirens getting closer. "It's actually a little steeper than that, so you might want to save your money. You might need it." Haywood had a small sheriff's office, and all of them were now between them and the road. "Hey, Sheriff." Cain smiled at her old friend as he sauntered up the path.

"Cain," Ignatius said, resting his thumbs on his utility belt. "These people invited?"

"Trespassing, actually." She pointed to the camp chairs, and Lou joined her. "Don't forget to bag all their stuff. We wouldn't want to be accused of stealing."

"You've got to be kidding," Joe said when the deputies got their cuffs out as if they'd practiced the move. "Casey, come on."

"Thanks for everything, Sheriff." She waved as they headed back to the house. The screaming she left behind was humorous, but it was time to get back to work. The night in jail and the thousand-dollar fine would give her a window to get a few things done. Thank God for the tension between local cops and the feds that meant there was no love lost between them. It was something she could always count on.

All that was important, but she also wanted to spend some time alone with Emma. Since Billy's birth, Emma had been clingier than usual, and she wanted to make sure Emma was okay before business started demanding more of her time. She needed to get answers to all the problems she had, but not at the expense of her wife and her happiness.

"Everything ready?" she asked Lou.

"Your ride is due in an hour in the middle pasture. Are you sure all you want with you is me and Sabana? Chicago can be a dangerous place."

"It's one night, Lou, and one meeting. We'll be fine."

When they got closer, she saw Hannah following Hayden to the side of the house, and she smiled at his promise to help her build a snowman. From the sounds right inside the back door, Abigail's three were ready to join them but didn't have coats on. Mothers were mothers no matter what was going on, and they walked in on Abigail and Fin trying to get everyone buttoned up.

"Victoria, step outside without a hat, and you're staying inside all day," Abigail said in a voice that left no doubt she was serious. "All day inside doing homework."

Cain picked up the pink unicorn hat on the table and put it on the little girl. "Hurry or your buddy Hannah will get all the good snow."

"Thanks, pal," Fin said when the comment sent Victoria into a motivated panic.

"No problem." She headed upstairs to change. Emma was dressed and putting on makeup when she closed the door. "Ready, lass?"

"Yes, so hurry."

They'd said their good-byes to the kids, so Lou drove them to the pickup point and the waiting helicopter she'd hired. Lou and Sabana were spending the night in Chicago with them for a date night with a little business mixed in. The helicopter was the fastest way to the commercial airport since she didn't care if Shelby and company knew where they were going.

"I can't remember the last time we went out overnight," Emma said. The road was bumpy, so Lou took it slow.

"That means I'm doing a lousy job in the spouse department." She looked at Emma and smiled at how beautiful she was.

"No, you're not, and I've enjoyed sticking close to home and enjoying the kids. It's nice to have you all to myself, though, and that I don't feel totally frumpy is a bonus."

"Anyone who calls you frumpy is in for a beating." She kissed Emma as Lou came to a stop. "Are you sure you don't mind a little business first?"

"Not at all. I'm looking forward to meeting this guy. He sounds a little different but interesting, given your description."

She carried Emma to the helicopter to keep her heels from sinking into the mud, and it took them thirty minutes to get to the airport.

It was strange to not have anyone standing around trying to appear inconspicuous while watching them, so they'd shaken the feds for now. That was a rare treat, and she planned to take advantage of the small window.

After the short flight they walked out to a couple of waiting cars and the extra guys she'd flown in from home to make Lou more at ease. The trip into the city was faster than she expected, considering Chicago traffic, and a glance at her watch told her their guest would already be waiting in their suite at the Ritz-Carlton.

"We've never been here together," Emma said as they drove down Michigan Avenue toward the river.

"We should plan more short trips like this. It could be like an extended date night."

Lou opened her door as Sabana opened Emma's, but Emma waited for her to come around to get out.

"There's no denying what a romantic you are, my love." Emma took her hand and laughed as they entered the lobby with a number of heavily armed men. It seemed like everyone around them turned and stared. "You also know how to make an entrance."

Cain laughed as one of their guys from New Orleans held up a key card. Their rooms were on the top floor, and there were already two guards outside their door. Once she and Emma were in for the night, the guys would head next door, but for now she wanted to limit access.

"He's waiting in the sitting room, ma'am," the older of the two said.

She opened the door and went in first with Emma's safety in mind. Not that she thought Nathan Mosley was in any way a threat, but old habits had kept them alive, and she was never going to change. "Nathan," she said. He stood up when he saw her.

The small man had on a purple pinstripe suit with matching purple shoes, and she smiled at his outlandish sense of style. Considering what he did for a living, she would've thought he would've been a lot lower key.

"Ms. Casey." Nathan held his hands out and stepped forward. "I never expected to hear from you, but it is a pleasure to see you again."

"Cain, please, and before we begin, I'd like to introduce my wife, Emma."

"However do you leave the house and leave this woman behind?" Nathan said, letting her go and taking both of Emma's hands in his so he could kiss them. "You are a beauty."

"Thank you," Emma said, sounding delighted.

"What can I do for you, Cain?" Nathan asked after kissing Emma's hands again.

"Before we start, I'd like to tell you that I'm not asking what I did before. Your integrity is important to your reputation as a businessman, and I'm not going to compromise that."

"What you asked for when we first met was in the spirit of keeping my work intact. I didn't mind giving up a few of my secrets to keep such a wonderful young woman safe." Nathan sat once they had and crossed his legs, bringing his red socks into view.

"Thank you for all you did for Dallas. She's my closest friend, and she deserves all the peace your work has given her." Emma was sincere, and Cain would do what was necessary to keep her as well as those they cared for whole.

"It was my pleasure, but Ms. Montgomery is a done deal, so what is it you need?"

"I'm having problems with the Russian mob, and I'm looking for a way to solve them."

Nathan laughed and shook his finger at her. "You know all roads don't lead to me, right?"

"In this case I don't think you know this woman at all, but she did effectively disappear. There's either someone out there who is as good as you, or she did it herself, and her technique is spot on." She took her phone out and handed it over. Finley had given her a picture of Nicola's cousin, Linda Bender.

"I've never seen her," Nathan said, studying the picture before handing it back.

"Like I said, I didn't think you had worked with her, but I figured you could point me in the right direction to find her. Like with Dallas, there has to be a crack in the armor that lets someone inside. I need to know what this woman's crack is before she plugs the hole like I did for Dallas and her sister." She put her hand up when he started to speak. "I don't mean her any harm, but she has some answers I need, and I'm not going to get the insight I would from anyone else. If anything, I'd like to do for her what we did for Dallas."

"If you give me the file, I'll do what I can and get back to you tomorrow. Will you still be in town?" Nathan asked, and Lou stepped forward and handed over the file.

"We'll be here, and I appreciate your help."

"Please, I think you're a good friend to have, and now that I know

I might see your beautiful lady again, I'll try to make myself useful."
He stood, buttoned his jacket, and bowed his head slightly before
walking out.

"That was interesting," Emma said, glancing at her before looking
back at the closed door.

"He's a little different, but he gets results. If we ever decide to start
over with new identities, he's the go-to guy."

"You'd give up our name?" Emma leaned in and kissed her.
"There's no chance I'll ever let you do that."

"Not to worry, Mrs. Casey. If you want to go hunting, the smartest
way to find what you're aiming for is to get the best hunting dog."

CHAPTER ELEVEN

Elton Newsome jabbed his fingers into the blinds and cracked them less than an inch. He'd left his sister's house and rented the cheapest room he could find, but the constant sound of sirens was making him paranoid. His conversation and threats to agents Knight and Brewer hadn't gotten him any more money, so it was time to kick things up a few notches. If they wouldn't reward him for what he'd tried to do to help them, then it was time to get his old life back.

He'd been just eight short years from retirement, and he'd fucked himself out of his pension to get a little payback when it came to Cain Casey. Really it was her cousin Muriel who'd pissed him off and humiliated him in front of the feds that day Casey's house had been shot up.

"Fucking bitch," he said as he drank from the bottle of Southern Comfort he'd purchased, not trusting the glasses in this place. "You were so fucking smug, and that agent was creaming her panties for you. It wasn't fucking right." He screamed that through the crack he'd made in the blinds, not caring if anyone heard him.

"No one goddamn well rewards you for playing by the rules. Those Casey fuckers prove that, so why not me?" The whiskey sloshed out of the bottle as he waved it to make his point. "I've seen every perverted thing there is to see in that cesspool of a city, and no one paid me big money to keep looking at it."

The police rolled up and started hassling some guys in the parking lot, so Elton went back to sitting on the bed. "I tried to do what no other cop had the guts to do, and I fucking end up here." A cockroach the size of a mouse crawled over his foot, and he kicked out, almost falling off the bed. "That ends tonight."

He took another swig from the bottle and reached for his phone. If those assholes that were working with him weren't going to help him, then he had no choice but to contact Annabel Hicks and get her to force the police hierarchy to take him back. There was no way they could deny he was a good cop, no way.

"Put Annabel Hicks on the phone," he demanded when an operator answered. That surprised him since he figured he'd have to navigate his way through one of those automated things.

"Can I ask who's calling?" The woman sounded like a brick wall who wasn't about to give him what he wanted.

"Look, she's going to want to talk to me, considering she's probably been looking for me for weeks. I'm not going to hold forever."

"May I place you on a brief hold?"

"Tell her this is her only chance," he said, loud enough to make sure she knew he was serious.

The on-hold information feed had to do with the various programs the FBI had available in the community and how responsible citizens could get involved. The mechanical sounding voice had gotten to the rewards people could claim when it shut off, and all he heard was silence on the other end.

"Agent Hicks?" he said trying to sober up and sound respectful.

"Who am I speaking to?" The voice sounded female, but she really didn't say who she was.

"Is this Agent Hicks?" He wasn't dicking around with any more flunkies. "If it's not, I'm gone."

"This is Special Agent Annabel Hicks, and I'd like to know who this is before we go on. You demanded my time, so give me a name."

"This is Detective Elton Newsome, and I want to come in and talk to you, but only if you can guarantee my safety." He lifted the bottle to his lips again and decided not to take another sip. He'd probably regret it later, but if she agreed to his demands, he had a long drive ahead of him.

"That's interesting, considering you've been MIA for weeks. Your involvement in the Hannah Casey case has left quite a few questions that need answers. Carol Verde has refused to give her side of things, so that leaves you." Annabel sounded like a woman who didn't take a lot of shit from anyone.

"I'll tell you everything you want to know, but the feds got me in this, and you're going to give me my life back. I'm not going down because your people fucked up." He had to stop and take a breath before he started screaming. "What happened isn't right."

"Where are you?" Annabel suddenly sounded like she was more interested than she was letting on. "I can have you picked up if you're worried about your security."

"I'll drive myself to your office. There's no way I'm trusting anyone but you. All I tried to do was help you, and I lost everything. Now I want my life back."

"I'll be waiting, but I need to know where you are. Trust is a mutual thing, Mr. Newsome. If you don't show up because something happened to you, I need a place to start looking."

"I'm at a dive off the interstate in Slidell. That's all I'm giving you right now, so you'll have to wait an hour if you want the rest." He hung up before she made any other demands and took a moment to get his balance when he stood up to grab his keys.

The thought of packing crossed his mind before he opted to leave everything behind. With any luck he'd leave this crappy place for his crappy apartment in the city. The liquor in his system was making him a little woozy, but he still had the presence of mind to crack the door and study the parking lot before he stepped out.

There wasn't any one thing that increased his paranoia, but his gut told him he was on borrowed time. He walked as fast as he could to his sister's car and took it slow out of the parking lot. To throw off anyone following him, he headed north out of Slidell to the Causeway toll bridge, which would have less traffic than usual at this time of night. The woman at the toll booth to the Lake Pontchartrain Causeway barely looked at him as he handed over his money, and he gripped the wheel as he started driving the nearly two dozen miles of elevated roadway.

He relaxed as he hit mile ten and leaned in to turn the radio on. Wondering why he hadn't thought of this course of action before now made him want to slap himself, but all he needed was to tell Hicks everything, and he'd be back to where he was before he met Christina Brewer and fell for her grand plan. Whatever happened to Carol Verde likely wasn't bad enough, but that crazy bitch was out of his life for good.

The song that came on made him smile, but that happy feeling disappeared as the car passing him sideswiped him hard enough to make him fishtail badly. Heart pounding, he overcorrected and went over the guardrail on the left-hand side of the road. The splash came quickly, and he panicked when the waters of the lake plunged him into total darkness.

"Fuck," he said as the coldness hit his legs. It didn't take long for the water to go past his chest, and he couldn't find a way out of the car. He hit bottom and took one last breath as he pulled on the door handle. The burning in his lungs made him open his mouth, and he gagged, choked, his chest bursting. His hands fell away from the seat belt, his body jerked as it tried for a last gasp of air, and his last thought as he saw the shapes of two people looking down at him from the bridge was simply… *Fuck*.

❖

Matt Curtis stared straight ahead as the guy behind the camera took his picture. Jerome looked on as he took a sip of the drink he'd made himself and couldn't wait for this guy to finish. Once his father had a new identity, they could leave for New Orleans and not get picked up right away by their old employer. If his father was going to help him grow the business, he couldn't do it under his own name.

"How long?" he asked once the guy took down the sheet behind his dad's head.

"Give me two days, and I'll deliver it to wherever you are."

"I'll call you, but it'll be New Orleans. Make sure it doesn't take longer than those two days." He took a wad of cash out of his suit coat pocket and handed it over.

"Don't worry, I'll be there. You want the whole workup?"

"Everything including credit cards, and it has to hold up for a trip south of the border. Trust me, if we get caught, I'll find a way to hunt you down and shove the camera up your ass." He signaled to Abril Rojas, and she led the guy out. When Abril came back, his father smiled at her, the pretty woman who'd first approached him about meeting in Biloxi. "Make sure you put someone on him until he gives us what we need."

"I sent Roberto to follow, and he know not to lose him."

"Good, if everyone is ready, we'll head out."

They got into the back of the SUV with heavily tinted windows while the men put their bags in the vehicle in front of them. Before he left for Mexico there were a few decisions that had to be made, and he was running out of time to make them. Choosing wrong, though, would negate all the advances he'd made. It was the last thing he wanted to do, but it was time to make a decision one way or the other.

"What are you thinking about?" his father asked as they got on the road.

He looked out the window for a long time before he answered. This area had been part of his days for so long, and then he'd had to run. It was funny that it was only now that he realized he missed it. Biloxi was the new playground for people like Casey, and New Orleans was where she ruled. He didn't miss running around behind her all day, trying to gather evidence that she was blatantly flaunting breaking the law.

"I need to see how Delarosa is doing after his setbacks, and how Nunzio Luca did after all the fuckups he's had lately. We're sitting in a good position—we have the product, but it won't mean shit if we can't move it into the US." He put his head back but kept his eyes trained on the passing landscape. "The safest thing is to sell it before it leaves Mexico, but the real money is in street sales. It's how Delarosa made enough money to climb to the top."

"You have any idea how you're going to build an organization that can go from field to street corner?" His father sounded curious and almost excited. He'd been in search of the easy money for as long as he could remember, and Jerome was about to hand it to him. "It took Delarosa and that asshole Luis years to get there."

"I'm not that patient, and I don't want to settle on the pittance we can make selling it and turning over the profits to the men gutsy enough to take chances on this side of the border." He finally closed his eyes as they hit the interstate.

"You don't trust me enough to tell me what you have in mind?"

"Come on, Dad," he said and laughed. "The reason I wanted you with me is to keep me on track. You're the only person in this world I trust, but we need to be smart before we make any kind of move."

"That's what I want to know. What direction are you thinking will be the best? You've been at this long enough to make an educated guess." His father never raised his voice, but he managed to get his point across.

"If we want to skip recruiting and building a network, we have to take one that already exists. Like we talked about before. All we need to do is research which one is the most vulnerable." In his mind the best-case scenario was Hector Delarosa. The investment he'd made into completely blowing Hector's world to shit would eventually pay off, and he wasn't done with his plan to speed up that timetable.

"While you were gone, I was quiet about it, but I did some research as to what was going on from Florida to Arizona." His dad reached into his pocket and removed the small leather-bound notepad he'd used back when he was an agent, when he'd tried to reach into the dirty cookie jar too. "Delarosa is bleeding cash, and if the rumors are true, his supply took some serious hits. It won't be long before he's dead in the water."

"And we'll be ready to step in and fill the void he's going to leave. I doubt all the small dealers are going to care who they're working for as long as they're working. It's all about the laws of supply and demand." He turned his head without lifting it and smiled at his father. "Once all the rumors about what happened to him become a provable fact, there's going to be a war. The sharks will smell blood in the water."

"You did this?" his dad asked, his smile widening.

"I planned for a war, and if you plan, then you're prepared. All these idiots are going to kill to get to the top, but we've got the manpower to take that away from every single one of them. Everyone's going to learn that they'll either have to abide by the new power structure or die. Those are the only two options I'm putting on the table."

"That was brilliant, but who carried this out for you?"

There was a trace of skepticism in his dad's tone, but he didn't mind it from him. "Pablo sent some of our most trusted men. It didn't take many, and Delarosa was arrogant enough not to have a large force guarding his most precious asset."

"We need to be careful. You've started sawing through the head of the snake, but it's still poisonous. He's poured money into finding out who's responsible for his problems, and I'm talking from Colombia to here."

He didn't respond as they crossed the line into New Orleans East. There was no denying the cold tingly sensation that ran down his back. Nothing in his life had given him the rush that the last year had and outsmarting his old workmates had given him solace. Despite all that, there was that little part of his brain that embraced the fear he didn't want to lose because it would keep him sharp.

"Hector Delarosa plays the role of a gentleman well, but he's an uneducated butcher at heart." He hadn't forgotten that Delarosa had at first agreed to meet him, then told him to fuck off. That kind of disrespect had to be repaid. "His successor will take less than a year to blow up the business because she's even more mindless than he is. I just gave them a nudge in the right direction."

"What about Nunzio Luca and Carlos Luis? It's my guess that they're the two who've made the most inroads here and along the southern coast." His dad referred to his book again, and Jerome smiled.

"Luca lost his head to some bitch who ended up with Delarosa, and from what I hear also lost his grandfather, Santino. Carlos Luis is the only one who worries me. He stood silently behind his father for years, and he learned the business much better than his idiot cousin and aunt." The city skyline was visible from the top of the high-rise bridge over the intercoastal canal, and he stopped to admire it. "Instead of making a play for his share, we might have to meet to form some sort of alliance."

"Is there anyone or anything else that worries you?"

"Jasper Luke and Vinny Carlotti have the backing of the alliance Casey formed with old man Carlotti and the Jatibons. Casey says she doesn't dirty her hands with drugs, but she protects those two with everything in her arsenal." He stretched his hands out from the fists he'd formed and took a deep breath to calm down. "There's no way in hell I'm going to stand for her or her cronies benefiting from everything I've put into motion."

"Sounds like we have a lot to do," his father said, patting his shoulder.

"We do, and our first step is gathering all the information my guys have been getting for me. After that, we need to find a place to operate from that isn't a hotel room."

"You're planning to stay here? Is that a smart move?"

"I'm planning to leave someone like Pablo here, but until we're so insulated that we're untouchable, I'll need a place to lie low when I have to visit the States." The smart play would be to find a place out of the way of all the players, but he was no coward. If you were going to play the game, you had to be close enough to study your opponents.

"I'm with you all the way, no matter what."

"Then we're going to be impossible to beat."

CHAPTER TWELVE

"From what I understand, this place was once the most bugged place in Chicago," Cain said as they sat in one of the booths in Joe's Stone Crab. The restaurant was in an old building and had been an old mob hangout in its day.

"I'll try to refrain from laying out my plans for any criminal activity while we're sitting here, then," Emma said as she leaned over and kissed her cheek.

Their meeting with Nathan had ended, and they'd made their reservation time. The rest of the night would be all about Emma. "Good idea, lass, and I'll follow your lead." She picked up her glass of wine and waited for Emma to do the same. "To the most beautiful woman in this world, and the fact she's mine. I love you."

"You make me feel good, mobster, and you can stop worrying. I'm not going to crack up on you. I promise." Emma put her hand on Cain's thigh and squeezed. "I'm a little off balance, but no postpartum depression. I just want to be with you as often as possible."

"If that's the case, we should talk about having a few more." She was joking, but Emma glanced at her, looking hopeful.

"Do you mean that?"

The question surprised Cain, but not really. Emma loved children as much as she did.

"I keep telling you that I'll gladly welcome all the children you'd like to have with me. You can't ask me not to worry, though. That's part of my job, and I can't help it since you've gotten the worst part of these bruisers we end up with." She didn't care how crowded the restaurant was—she put her glass down and pressed her hand to the side of Emma's cheek. The kiss was as passionate as she ever got in public, but she couldn't hold it in. "You are the most important thing in my world, so take some time before we decide."

"Let's let Billy turn one, and then I'll be ready again. I think the best sign that one more is a great idea came when your brother's gift to us at the sperm bank was one of the things that survived that damn hurricane." Emma slid her hand up a little, really close to her crotch. If she hadn't promised Emma dinner, they'd be on their way back to the hotel by now.

"Excuse me, Ms. Casey," their waiter said softly as if really loath to bother them. "There's a diner who says she knows you and would like to come by and say hello if that's okay with you."

"Sure," Emma said for them, but not moving her hand.

Cain was as surprised as Emma looked when Judice O'Brannigan came to their table looking hesitant. Their first conversation—when Judice had admitted she'd had Cain's father's child—hadn't gone well. Fiona O'Brannigan was a New Orleans police detective, and Cain still didn't know if there'd come a day when she'd accept Fiona as family. As a sister.

"I hate to intrude, but I didn't want to be rude and not come to say hello." Judice was a petite beautiful woman who'd spent most of her life in California being sheltered by Cain's cousin Colin Mead.

"Judice, please sit and have a glass of wine with us," Emma offered. "What brings you to Chicago?"

"I really can't discuss it here, but Colin is meeting me tomorrow night. Will you still be here? I'd think he'd love to see you." Judice always seemed like she was ready to bolt at any second if things went bad.

Their relationship still wasn't what Cain would consider totally friendly, but she'd come to tolerate the woman for Colin's and Fiona's sake. Not that her relationship with Fiona O'Brannigan was great, but she didn't want her as an enemy either. Fiona spent most of her days aggravating the piss out of her, but things had changed considerably after Hannah's kidnapping by Emma's mother, Carol.

Cain believed that Fiona had come to see her as a parent that day and not just as the head of a mob family. And she'd repaid the favor silently by saving Judice's life. If Judice wanted to tell her daughter about that, she wouldn't stop her.

"We're only here for the night, but I'll call him and catch up. I haven't heard from him in a few months. Is everything okay?" Cain didn't know if Judice was worried about something in particular, or if high-strung was just her normal state.

"I can see tonight is special, so I won't stay long, but could I perhaps call you tomorrow? Talking behind Colin's back isn't something I do, but I think he might need your guidance with some issues he's got coming up."

"We're at the Ritz-Carlton until early tomorrow afternoon. I only have one meeting set, so call whenever you want to. Colin is family and I love him, but the man can try anyone's patience. Thank you for looking out for him." Cain smiled, and it seemed to relax Judice some. "I'm glad things worked out after all that stuff that happened, but are you okay? Are you worried for yourself or for him?"

"I doubt he told you, but he and his wife have legally separated. She's devoted to the church, so it might take death to part them, but he's made his intentions clear about how he'd like to live going forward." Judice lowered her eyes to the tabletop, and her voice got softer as she went on.

"I understand why you never got involved with anyone while you were raising Fiona," she said when Emma squeezed her thigh again as if prompting her to open her mouth. "Fiona's to a point that she loves you, but she's got her own life. You're young enough to claim some happiness before it all disappears, and there's nothing wrong with that." Colin had not only sheltered Judice, but he'd been interested in her in a romantic way for a very long time.

"How can you say that after what I told you about me and your father?"

"Had you told me that right after he was killed, I doubt forgiveness would've come quickly, but I have children. I realize what I would do for them, to keep them with me, and to keep them safe. Even though I think you were wrong, how can I condemn you for that?"

"All those things I said that night," Judice said, her voice still soft. "I loved him, and I mourn him still. Despite what happened and how we ended, he was a good man, and losing him was what made me want to punish him. You can't force someone to love you, though, can you?"

"You can't," Emma said, "but I find that when it's right, you'll see the difference. What we thought we couldn't live without is really only a learning experience, and it's what you gauge the real thing against. Sometimes you luck out and find the right one on your first try. Turns out the right one for you is a little louder, and way more persistent."

Emma smiled. "If anything, your life will never be boring. And if it counts for anything, I really think he loves you."

"That's what he says, but the man has a famous roving eye."

"I think those days are behind him," Cain said, and Judice's smile finally widened. "It took him a lot of years to mature, but I think it's finally come."

"Thanks for talking with me. Have a great evening." Judice stood and waited as if to be dismissed. "I never expected your kindness, but you've been more than gracious."

"Call in the morning, and give Colin our love if you talk to him tonight," Cain said. They watched as Judice walked away to a small table close to the door. "What do you think that's about?"

"It's Colin, honey, so it could be just about anything. I love your family, but I'm praying none of the kids take after him."

Cain thought of the big man who seldom thought much about what he was doing, and even less about what came out of his mouth. He was reckless, quick to temper, and way too immature for a man his age. "Let's hope my mother hears your wishes and has the power to grant them. If you think he's something now, you should've experienced him growing up."

"I can about imagine, but I have a feeling we'll get our share of that with Hannah. That kid can drive you to drink at times, and she's only five."

"She's high-spirited, is all."

"You're a generous grader, my love."

They enjoyed their meal and the walk down the Miracle Mile to do some window-shopping. It wasn't something they got to indulge in often, and she liked having Emma all to herself. They'd shared an interesting life up to now, and she loved imagining the years that stretched out before them. They rode the rest of the way to their hotel in the car Lou had rented, and they waved to the guards as they closed the door on the suite.

Emma kicked her shoes off. "Turn your phone off for an hour," she said as she presented her back so Cain could unzip her. "You need to concentrate for the next part of the night."

"No one is calling tonight—don't worry about it."

She stared as Emma let her dress pool at her feet. The matching bra and panties looked like silk and lace, and she wanted to hurry and rip them off her, but she'd go at Emma's pace. It was hard to not take charge when Emma took her jacket off and threw it across a chair, but she held back.

"Do you remember that beach house you took me to when we first got together?" Emma asked as she ran her hands from Cain's chest down to her belt buckle.

"I do," she said and kicked her shoes off, not wanting to get tangled in her pants when they hit the floor.

"You touched me in a way that made me think I'd die if you ever stopped. I was already in love with you, but that weekend you proved to me that I could crave another person. You touched me, and I would've done anything for you never to stop." Emma seemed to love unbuckling her belt. It was like declaring her intentions. "You took my breath away." Emma started on her buttons next. "And you still do."

"You do have a way with words, my love, and those early days will always be special to me. I think it was the balance of wanting to ravish you and trying not to scare you." She waited until Emma was done before taking her shirt off and stepping out of her pants.

"You never scared me," Emma said, pulling her head down and kissing her. "You are everything I want in a partner, and I love you. Sharing a life with you, having children with you, makes me feel so fortunate. Sometimes I'm afraid of losing a single minute with you."

She put her hands on Emma's ass and lifted her up. "I want you to keep talking to me about whatever's on your mind because I love you, and I want to take care of you."

"You do a good job at that," Emma said, "but that little spot in my brain that reminds me how fragile life is makes me want to never let you go."

"You never have to, and right now I think it's time to recreate that first night at the beach house." They headed to the bedroom, and she kept the blinds open on the floor-to-ceiling windows. Their room had an unobstructed view of the lake and was high enough that no one would get a look inside. "And as beautiful as you were then, you're more beautiful now."

"You're good for my ego, mobster, but you're getting lucky no matter what." Emma straddled her lap when she sat on the bed and combed her hair back as she pressed their bodies together. "I need you to touch me. I need it more than ever."

"Fuck," she said, unable to help herself. Emma took her hand and put it between her legs.

"I need you to put your fingers in and fuck me," Emma said,

moving back but not too far. "Remind me of who I am to you, and prove to me you're mine."

She closed her eyes for a second at how wet Emma was. If she'd ever needed proof of how much Emma wanted her, here it was, and she couldn't hold out any longer. She moved her hand so it was palm up and positioned her fingers. It was the only invitation Emma needed. They both moaned when Emma came down on them and squeezed her shoulders as if to keep herself in place.

"That's so good." Emma moved her hips slowly, put her hands to the back of Cain's head, and pulled her hair hard enough to get her attention.

Cain moaned when Emma's tongue entered her mouth, and her clit was hard enough to make her lose concentration, but Emma released her lips and moaned, sounding out of breath. If Emma kept up this pace, she'd come sooner than either of them wanted, and Emma seemed to read her mind when she slowed. The self-control Emma was still capable of made her think it would be one of those nights that would last for hours. Emma was in no mood to be rushed or deprived.

"I need to feel you over me," Emma said before she bit down on her neck. "Give me what I want."

She lay back without moving her hand and rolled them over. Emma's nails raked up her back, and her thrusts were harder and deeper in this position. There was nothing better in life than the little grunts Emma made when she was this turned on. She sped her hand when she felt Emma open up to her.

"Oh…" Emma ran her hands down to Cain's ass and opened her legs farther apart. "Like that, baby, like that."

She lifted herself a little to give Emma what she wanted. The sound of skin slapping against skin and Emma's moans filled the room until Emma finally screamed. "I'm coming, oh my God, I'm coming."

She kissed Emma when she stiffened beneath her. "You okay?" she asked when she rolled off. She kept her hand in place when Emma closed her legs, trapping it there.

"I might wear you out and kill myself, but I'm hoping my hormones don't balance out anytime soon." Emma sucked in a breath when she pulled out, and she doubted they were done. "Feeling you like this calms my restless soul."

"You sound like a poet out of time, but not to worry. I have plenty of stamina, lass, so I'll keep up." She lay on her back as Emma moved over her and started down her body.

"You're right about that. I've never had any complaints about your stamina." Emma dragged her hardened nipples down Cain's abdomen until she was kneeling between her legs. "You make me feel so good, and that deserves a reward."

She jerked when Emma put her mouth on her and sucked her in hard. It was as if Emma understood there was no need for buildup. Touching Emma was a privilege she never took for granted, and it drove her insane and made her hard.

Emma interlocked their fingers and raised her head, making her groan. "Let go, lover, and give me all of you."

There was no need for more words as Emma went back to what she'd begun, and that tightening in her belly started and she didn't want to slow down or stop. Emma had ratcheted up her need to the point that the orgasm she craved wouldn't be held back even if someone had put a gun to her head and demanded it. Her wife was the only person in the world who stripped her of every ounce of control, and she loved her for it.

"Fuck," she said as she gripped Emma's fingers tighter. Emma responded by sucking harder, and it was almost too much. "Fuck," she said again as she moaned when the pleasure got intense. "Fuck… fuck…fuck…" She released to the point of lethargy. She flinched again when Emma softly kissed her clit before moving back up to lie half on top of her. "You have a way of making me sound like a repetitive idiot, and you know how much I love repeating myself."

"I wouldn't say that, and it's kind of humorous that you only use the word *fuck* when we're in bed." Emma kissed her before resting her head on her shoulder and rubbing her stomach in soft circles. "I think I say it more than you do when your kids are driving me nuts."

"My kids?" she asked and laughed.

"The dynamic trio, who all look and act like you. They certainly didn't get all that hyperactivity from me."

She was about to tease Emma about that when she turned toward the buzzing phone on the nightstand. "The world better be on fire," she said as Emma moved to answer it.

"Hello," Emma said and glanced back at her, listening to whoever was on the other end of the line. "Hold on, Lou." Emma handed her the phone and got out of bed. A few seconds later the shower started. That didn't bode well. She'd brought Emma here to give her some truly undivided attention. Since the baby's birth, that had been what seemed to be driving Emma's happiness.

"What's going on?" She sat up and put her feet on the floor.

"The pub got hit again," Lou said, and she could almost feel his anger. "Josh was there with the contractors about the expansion."

"Fuck," she said, clenching her fist. Josh had been with her for years, and she trusted him implicitly. When a business was mostly cash, you either had to be there all the time or you had to trust the people who ran it for you. Bars were great places to work if you liked to skim. Josh was not only loyal and honest, but he was smart enough to realize what a bad idea that would be. "What happened?"

"It was late this afternoon—"

"Why are we just hearing about this?" It wasn't Lou's fault, but she couldn't help but interrupt him.

"Sanders Riggole just finished with the police and called me. He called me on the way to the hospital with Josh."

"So." She took a deep breath. Josh was a good man and a friend, but Emma loved him like a big brother. "Is he going to be okay?"

"Sanders said he was critical, but he's young and healthy. He's a fighter, boss, so I'm sure he'll pull through. The contractor got winged, but the guy with him was unharmed since he was taking measurements behind the bar."

"That's fortuitous."

"I talked to Sanders and called Dino." Lou referred to his nephew who was now Emma's driver. Lou had left him behind looking out for the house and the business as a way to see what he could do under pressure. She liked the young man who'd taken such good care of Emma and had gone out of his way to be friendly with Hannah. "He'll keep Josh safe from any other attack and from any questions from the cops until he's ready."

"Give me thirty minutes and get in here."

"What's going on?" Emma said as Cain opened the shower door and joined her.

It was hard to beat down the rage, and Emma seemed to sense that when she walked to her and placed her hand over Cain's heart. "Someone shot up the pub again, and Josh got caught in the crossfire. Sanders is with him."

"Who the hell did that?" Emma asked, her hand pressing down harder.

"We both know who did it the first time, but someone took the opportunity to add on. Shooting up my own places was supposed to make me look weak, but it wasn't an invitation to do it again." She took

Emma's hand and led her under the shower stream. "My redecorating technique was meant to be the beginning of laying a trap, and this proves it worked too well. Whoever did it, though, is going to pay for what happened to Josh."

"Do you want to head home?" Emma asked.

She didn't move as Emma ran her soapy hands down her chest. "I'm going to have to trust Sanders to keep everything under control until we're ready to come home. I'd rather not cut our vacation short, but I'm going to send some of the guys back to keep the peace and protect our territory. Nothing is going to happen at the farm, and even if it does, we'll see them coming and we'll be ready."

"Is Josh seeing anyone? I feel bad that I haven't really talked to him lately. If it wasn't for him, I would have never met you." Emma's eyes became glassy with tears, and Cain held her.

"Josh has never been open about his private life, and I've never pushed it." She got them out of the shower and threw on a robe. Lou knocked a few minutes later, dressed pretty much the same way.

"You want to go back?" Lou asked.

"Not yet. I need you to call the other families and tell them to tighten security. I don't want anyone to get caught by surprise if this is only the beginning." She took a couple of small bottles of whiskey out of the minibar and poured drinks for Lou and Emma before pouring one for herself. "Call Katlin next, and tell her to pick half of the guys we have at the farm and send them home. The next asshole that takes a shot at any one of our people better be dead on the street, so make sure she gets that across to every single person going back. This doesn't happen without someone paying a price." She had to gain the upper hand again before Emma or the kids became the next target. Losing any of them would kill her will to live.

"What about Josh?" Lou asked.

"I'll get in touch with Mano and see if they can spare someone. If not, Sanders can sit with him and trade out with someone else from Muriel's office. Even if Mano sends someone, tell him I either want him there or someone else he trusts. I want him talking to Josh before the feds or the cops get ahold of him."

"I'll take care of all that, boss. Get some sleep. If you want to head back earlier, I'll change our tickets." Lou put his empty glass down and stood.

"We have some guests coming tomorrow, so don't change anything." Cain mentally scanned the puzzle pieces, trying to work out which one to pick up next. "I need to talk to Judice to see what she's worried about. You know Colin as well as anyone, so it could be about anything. And the last thing we need is Colin and one of his great new ideas that becomes my problem." She waited until Lou had gone back to his room before waking Mano up. He promised he'd have someone posted on Josh twenty-four hours a day. "Make sure you do the same, Mano. I want to make sure your family is careful as well."

"If everyone thinks someone shot up all our properties the other night, why would someone else do the same thing? I still don't understand that," Emma said, dropping her robe and getting back in bed.

"Sometimes it takes a little while for the whole picture to come into focus, but I doubt this is Nicola Antakov." She got in next to Emma and put her arms around her when Emma came closer.

"Why?"

It probably wasn't wise to overshare her thoughts about something like this, but she'd promised no more secrets between them from the day they'd gotten back together. "The day Antakov hits, it'll be with what she'll consider a kill shot. That's who her family is, and I don't see her changing her way of doing business. Why send a warning shot when a kill shot eliminates the problem?"

"Why do you think she holds you responsible for her parents' deaths?" Emma asked even though they'd talked about this before. "I know they had to have had more enemies than just us."

"I was the last person to see them alive. They'd come for a very specific request, and I was in a position not only to help them, but to understand what they were asking me. Our lives are vastly different when it comes to business, but they had the same devotion to family I do. The only major difference was that I'm not going to raise my kids to be pimps. For them, though, it's all they've ever known. Exploiting trapped women was something they'd become immune to."

"There's no honor in what they did, and I'm not sorry you gave Finley the opportunity to remove that threat from Abigail and her children's lives."

"The problem is that I opened them up to another greater threat, so we'll have to see this through no matter what." They were quiet for a moment, lost in their own thoughts.

"Then who's responsible for Josh?" Emma finally asked. "And shooting up the buildings?"

"We'll have to wait and see who's stupid enough to gloat."

"What if they don't?" Emma asked as she got comfortable against Cain.

"The word to concentrate on, lass, is *stupid*. When someone runs up the hill and declares themselves king, they want the world to know it." She kissed Emma's forehead and tried to bleed off the anger still strumming through her body. "That's when they figure out there's already a king of the hill, and she's not at all forgiving."

CHAPTER THIRTEEN

Nicola closed her eyes as the private plane they'd chartered started its descent into New Jersey. She wasn't ready to fly commercial yet, not wanting to put her face out there any more than she had to. It was better to stay dead until her miraculous resurrection.

Her problems now were so much more than what she faced with her family. The name her girls had put on their schoolwork was seared into her brain, and she had to open her eyes to dispel the image. Whoever Finley Abbott was, one thing was clear. Abigail had moved on, and her children were in total lockstep. Some other woman had taken what was hers.

"Where do you want to start?" Nina asked.

She curled her hand into a fist and counted to ten before stretching it out again. "Call Sacha and set a meeting. Tell him to bring only two of his representatives, and we'll do the same."

"You know he's not going to do that, and if you set up a meeting, he's going to take it as an invitation to take you down."

Nina, she realized, issued these helpful hints because she cared about her, but she was tired of giving orders over and over again. "Call him and set it up. I've known Sacha for most of his pathetic life, and I know how ambitious he is. If I don't do this, he'll try to use my hiding as proof that I need to be taken down. Showing weakness isn't the Antakov way."

"I'm only trying to protect you."

She turned and faced Nina and waited for her to nod. It took longer than she was comfortable with, but Nina gave her what she wanted. "I'm going to show him that taking things that don't belong to him could cost him his head. So make the arrangements."

Forty minutes later they taxied to a private hangar, and they were able to get into the waiting cars without anyone seeing them. They made their way into the city and her apartment in Trump Tower. "Call me when you set up the meeting," she told Nina when they exited the cars in the garage.

"Let me walk you up," Nina said, walking around to her side.

"I have someone waiting, so head home. Once I'm done, I'll call you." She walked off with two of her men and left Nina standing there.

The elevator took them quickly to her floor, and she smiled when Svetlana Dudko held up a drink when she let herself in. She was grooming Svetlana to take some of the pressure off Nina, but she still had some things to learn. The best part of Svetlana, though, was her eagerness to please. That was readily apparent in how accomplished she was at killing. The other good thing was Svetlana didn't ask many questions or expect much, so the sex was easy.

"Nico." Svetlana handed her the cold vodka and kissed her before she could take a sip. "I missed you."

"I missed you as well, but I hope you were a good girl and did everything on the list I left you." She went into the bedroom and sat in the leather chair close to the windows. "I'll be disappointed if you didn't."

"You know better than that, baby. It's the most fun you've let me have in a long time." Svetlana stood before her and stripped naked. "Did you get everything on your list?"

"In good time, and we don't have time for that now." She motioned to Svetlana's body, but perfection was hard to ignore. The woman had been a gymnast, and the discipline had left her with a strong, fit body that she enjoyed touching. "With any luck, Sacha will be in the mood to meet tonight."

"Then we'll have to be quick, but you deserve to go in there with a clear head." Svetlana dropped to her knees and opened her pants so she could slide them down to her ankles. It didn't take long for Svetlana to get her off with her mouth as she touched herself.

They showered together and had another drink before she called Nina. "He can't wait to see you," Nina said. "All he needs is a place."

"Tell him the old club downstairs. The cops closed it down after New Orleans, but we shouldn't have a problem getting back in."

"Okay, and I'll be up in a minute to plan."

"I doubt you could add anything to what I already have planned.

Wait for me." She hung up and smiled when Svetlana beckoned her to the refrigerator.

"Your gift," Svetlana said, pointing to the clear bag on the shelf.

"Excellent."

They headed downstairs to the club with Nina two hours later and unlocked the door to the left. Both sides of the entire floor belonged to her father, and this had been one of the most successful sex clubs in the country from the time the building had opened. After what the feds had found in New Orleans when her parents had died, the government had seized this property and the one in Miami. The places she had in Las Vegas, Los Angeles, and San Francisco were incorporated differently, so they were still in operation.

The space was a mess, with paper covering the floor and the furniture stripped of its cushions as if they'd been looking for evidence everywhere they could think to search. Nina and Svetlana put together enough seats for everyone, and Nina stayed on the phone with their people to make sure Sacha played by the rules.

"He's getting in the elevator," Nina said as she checked her gun for the fourth time.

"Good, we can go ahead and get this over with." She crossed her legs but only for a moment because of the pain it caused. The plane crash wasn't something she had many memories of, but the aftermath was well cataloged in her head. The physical therapy she'd endured was like crawling out of the pit of hell, one slow inch at a time.

"Nicola," Sacha said loudly when he walked in with his hands over his head as if happy to see her. "I can't believe you fucking survived that crash. Your father showed me the pictures, and he pulled off that grieving parent thing like a Broadway actor."

She took a step back when he moved to hug her. "It's a shame he couldn't live long enough to enjoy my return. That's not why we're here, though." She pointed to the chair across from her, and he hesitated but finally sat down. "You don't agree with what my father wanted?"

"How do we all know what your father wanted?" Sacha said, no longer smiling and any pretense gone. "None of us knew you were alive, so how do we just accept that he had knowledge that you were and wanted you to take over?" His eyes narrowed and he leaned forward. "We talked, and he wanted *me* to take over the business once he knew you and Fredrick were dead."

"But I'm not dead, am I? Sacha, your problem has always been wanting more than you're entitled to. Your position in the business has always been to be happy with what we give you, but your mother put ideas in your head that could get you killed."

"Don't bullshit me, cousin. You're in no position to make demands or try to push yourself on us." The way Sacha spoke made her think there was something he wasn't telling her. He was the type of man who would rather run from a fight than engage. "I've been running things ever since your parents got hit. Where were you when they needed you most?"

"Sacha, you never did learn to keep your mouth shut, and what the consequences could be when you don't." She glanced at Svetlana, and she lifted the cooler from the bar and walked to Sacha with it. As she got closer Sacha's men reached for their guns, but Nina removed hers first and pulled the trigger twice so fast they didn't have a chance to respond. "I brought you a little gift."

"You fucking gave me a guarantee of safety for me and my men," Sacha ranted as he took the cooler Svetlana handed him. "What the hell is your word worth?"

"My word doesn't apply when it's some piece of shit who's trying to steal what rightfully belongs to me. You overreached, and now's the time to confess." She stood as well and accepted a gun from Svetlana. "Who filled your head with such shit that you're about to drown in it?"

"My mother—"

"Your mother should've known better. She's family, but all she did was accept a check every month until my father died. If it wasn't for my father, you two would be living on the streets." She moved toward him and flicked the top off the cooler with the gun.

The head inside belonged to the old guard who had watched over their cousin Linda Bender, and who had obviously thrown his support behind Sacha. Nina had told her it was this old fucker who had helped Sacha gain all the ground he had in the last months.

"Oh my God." Sacha threw the cooler away from him and the man's head rolled out onto the floor.

"God has nothing to do with this. It's all on you." She pressed the gun to his head and cocked it. "You killed him and plenty of others tonight, but here's your chance to redeem yourself. You've got one opportunity to pledge your loyalty to the boss, and that's never going to be you."

"What if I don't? After tonight I should declare war and pay you back for that." Sacha pointed to the head. He didn't get any closer to her, but he didn't back down either. "Face it, you aren't your father, and you don't have the balls to keep what he built."

"I'm not my father," she said, tilting her head slightly. "I'm much worse, so believe me when I say this is your last chance."

"Or what?" He laughed. "You're going to kill me? Is that the message you want to send out to the rest of the family? Fall in line, or I'll take you down even if you share my blood?" He shot the questions at her like bullets from a machine gun. "They'll join together and take pleasure in cutting you into small pieces."

"The rest of the family doesn't seem to be a problem, Sacha. Only you think you have the right to rise above your rank." She pressed the gun harder against his head and waited. "I need your answer before we leave here."

"Whatever you want, Nicola. You want me to do your grunt work, I'll do it." His answer was quick, and his smile suddenly widened.

"Just like that?" She hated herself for asking but the words came out before she could censor herself.

"You're Yury's daughter, and I'm not. It's that simple." He lifted his head as if daring her to pull the trigger. "Is that all you needed to hear? All I did was try to keep the family together and on top. You can't lay blame for having pride in who we are."

"Get out of my sight," she said, lowering the gun. In her bones she knew it was a mistake, but he was right about one thing. They were family. He didn't even glance at his dead guards as he went skittering from the room like the bottom dweller he was.

"You let him go?" Nina asked, sounding incredulous. "There's no way he gave in that quick."

"You think I don't know this?" she said through gritted teeth. "He'll stab me in the back the first chance he gets, but then the rest of the family will know what a snake he is and won't blame me for killing him when he strikes first."

"So this is the excuse you need to solve your insurrection problem?" Svetlana asked. "Very smart."

Nina stared at Svetlana contemplatively, like she didn't appreciate the ass-kissing, but it might be good for her to see there was some competition to stay at her side. Not that it would ever be Svetlana, but it was good that it might be a possibility.

"What's next?" Svetlana asked.

Nina put her gun back in the holster and slid her hands into her pockets. It was obvious there wasn't going to be anything else coming out of her mouth. Nicola didn't really have time for hurt feelings or petty jealousies.

"Nina, call a meeting with the family. It's time to get us all back on track, reopening some of our businesses, even if we have to relocate some. We have loyal enough clients that they'll search us out no matter what." She pointed to the head still on the floor staring up at her. "Svetlana, take care of that and the others and wait for me to call you."

They waited for Svetlana to place the head back in the cooler and wave as she headed out. She knew Svetlana would take care of the cleanup and disposal of the bodies. Once the door closed, there was nothing but silence, and it seemed strange in this space. From the time it opened there had been music and people laughing as they enjoyed everything the Hell Fire Club had to offer.

"What do you think?" she asked.

"About what, specifically?"

"What Sacha said, and what the family's reaction will be," Nicola said, trying not to get angry. "I've been away for a while, and you were at my father's side all that time. In some ways you might have a better feel for the family than I do."

"They're your family, and like you said, you're Yury's daughter." Nina's tone was cool, detached.

The answer was evasive and not at all what she wanted. "That's all you're going to say?"

"You don't approve of anything I say, but I'd like to keep working for you," Nina said as if that should've been apparent. "You're the head of the family now, and it seems like that's how you want to run it. I'm okay with that now that I know the rules."

"So you'll have no more opinions?" She found that hard to believe. She'd come to expect Nina's comments and arguments, and she couldn't go on without them. To be successful, she couldn't live in a bubble, but she wasn't used to open defiance. She'd have to find a balance.

"I don't need to have an opinion, and I've only offered them up till now to help you, not undercut you. It was never to disrespect you." Nina took her hands out of her pants pockets but left them at her side. "Is there something else you'd like me to do?"

She'd have to let it go for now. "Have you heard anything about Finley Abbott?"

"My contact said she was working on a special project out of one of the precincts and she was with the cyber unit. She's gone, but the woman she was partnered with is still there."

"Have the partner picked up, and make sure it's quiet. I don't usually mess with cops, but I don't mind killing one if that's what's necessary to get the answers I need."

"Sure," Nina said but sounded like she'd rather take a job flipping burgers. "I'll call you once we have her."

"Nina, now is the time to tell me you're unhappy," she said and Nina just stared at her. "I'd never let anyone just walk away, but I'm sure there's got to be some other job you might like better than this one."

Nina's jaw clenched. "If there's something you're not happy about with me, I'll be happy to move. Remember that, no matter what, I'm loyal to you."

"We'll see." It was a shitty thing to say, but she wasn't in the mood to placate anyone.

❖

"Are you sure you don't want to press charges?" the deputy asked Muriel as she stood close to the only two cells the small jail had.

The four federal agents stared at her as they held the bars. It was all she could do not to laugh.

"I think Cain wanted to press charges."

Muriel shook her head. "She's had time to cool off after these people tried to ruin her vacation. It's okay to release them with a warning not to do it again," she said, looking right at Shelby. "Just a reminder, people, the guard dogs aren't going away, and the signs on the property have been doubled when it comes to warnings about trespassing."

"You're going to pay for this," the new blond agent said.

"For what, exactly? You didn't have a warrant, you've been warned before, and you chose to ignore all that. If you try that again, I'm going to let you rot in here while I appear before a federal judge." There was nothing worse than a sore loser. "Make sure your friends bring you up to date on all things Casey before you go around making threats. The first agent that led a team out here ended up shooting my cousin on the order of a known criminal. That's not something we'll take lying down again."

"Is that a threat?"

"Not at all. It's merely a promise that we'll do whatever it takes to completely destroy you, within the parameters of the law, no matter how much it costs or how long it takes. Believe me, I'm that good, and my team is exceptional."

"Muriel, may I speak with you?" Shelby asked. "Privately."

"Deputy, if you don't mind." The young man unlocked the cell holding Shelby and the other woman but only let Shelby out, even though there weren't going to be any charges. "What can I do for you?" she asked as she led the way to a private room.

Shelby closed the door to the small interrogation room. "The dogs are a little much. Do you really think you can keep us off the property?"

"Do you have a warrant?" She held her hand up when Shelby went to answer. "You and I both know you don't. There's no warrant to arrest Cain, no warrant to be there, and no warrant that I know of to eavesdrop on any of her communications. I'm not naive enough to think there aren't blind warrants, but if you want to come near us, then you're going to have to be satisfied sitting on the highway."

"Why are you acting like all of a sudden this is a big surprise? Our agents could've been seriously injured by those dogs today and would've been within their rights to shoot them." Shelby appeared angry and at the end of her patience. This was the exact reaction Cain loved, and every FBI agent in New Orleans had yet to figure that out.

"If you'd done that, there would've been consequences even you couldn't fathom. And why are you acting like it's surprising we don't want you around?" She lost her smile and her own patience. She wanted to finish this and get back to Kristen. "Let me put it as simply as I can. When we're in New Orleans, you're not allowed on the grounds unless invited. Think of this as the yard in New Orleans without the neighbors. You're not allowed in the yard, and if we find any equipment you've left behind, Cain will forgo the skeet machine. Do we understand each other?"

"Yes, but you and Cain used to have a much better sense of humor," Shelby said in a softer voice.

Muriel wasn't falling for that. "Our sense of humor is fine, but you and your pals have a way of wearing out your welcome. Just to give you a heads-up, Cain is out of town, so don't bother to come back tonight."

She walked out and stopped to shake hands with the sheriff. He'd turned out to be a good friend and often drove by the house Cain had built as well as Ross's place to check on everything himself when they weren't there. Now, though, she wanted to spend the night with Kristen in the cabin Cain had assigned them.

Her phone rang as she opened the door to one of the farm trucks she'd grabbed to come into town. "Muriel Casey," she answered.

"Muriel, thank God," Sanders Riggole said as he let out a long breath. "I called and talked to Lou when I couldn't get you, and he's calling Cain."

"I was in the sheriff's office, and the signal is shit in there. What's going on?"

"Someone shot up the pub and hit Josh as well as the contractor he was meeting with. Josh is in bad shape at the hospital, so Cain ordered me over there."

"Is he awake?"

"He's going into surgery. I had one of the pub guys ride over with him while I dealt with the police."

She started the truck and headed back to the farm as fast as she could without getting pulled over. "Run by the office and call me from the secure phone there. I should be back to the farm by then, so if I don't answer the number I gave you, wait and call me back."

"You got it, boss. What the hell is this?" Sanders wasn't real quick to excite, which meant whatever had happened had freaked him out.

"We'll figure it out, but I need to talk to Cain after I talk to you. Hang tight until then, and don't do anything without talking to me first."

"You know it."

She'd known Cain's plans, but for once they might've backfired and hurt someone that they all cared about. Josh had been at the pub since her uncle Dalton was alive. She didn't pray often, but she offered up a few words on Josh's behalf as she turned off the highway and onto Cain's property. Kristen opened the door and waited for her inside in what looked to be an oversized sweater and nothing else.

"What happened?" Kristen asked as she handed her a drink.

"I dropped the charges against the feds, so that's done, but something happened at home I have to deal with. Why don't you go to bed, and I'll join you once I deal with all this?" She'd bypassed the main house and everything seemed quiet. The rest of the cabins were far enough apart to ensure privacy but still within walking distance of each other. When they'd been built, Emma decorated each space to create a comfortable feeling for the people who'd use them, and Kristen had loved theirs from the moment they'd walked in.

Kristen shook her head and put her hands on her hips. They hadn't been together long, but that pose meant nothing but trouble. "I'm not asking to sit in the room with you, since Cain wouldn't like it, but I'm also not some toddler." She kicked at a spot on the carpet.

She put the drink down and lifted Kristen's chin. It didn't take a relationship genius to know that Kristen was mad at her. "I'm not treating you like a toddler, baby, and all I need to do is make a few phone calls. After I'm done, I'm coming to bed and seeing for myself what's under this sweater." She ran her hands down Kristen's sides down to her butt. "As an incentive maybe I should give myself a hint."

Kristen grabbed her hands before they went any lower. "Not so fast, lover. You're a smooth talker, but you're going to have to do better than that."

She smiled as Kristen traced her lips with her index finger as she ran her foot up her leg. "Give me an hour, and I'll make it up to you. One of our people got shot, and he deserves our attention."

"Take your time and let me know if there's something I can do to help you. I hope he's going to be okay." Kristen kissed her, and it made her wish her night really was done.

"Your being here is making it okay. I might not say it enough, but I'm glad you're with me. I didn't think it was possible to be this happy." She kissed Kristen again and let her go.

"In case you didn't know, I really like it when you make these romantic declarations. They'll get you out of trouble every time."

"Good to know," she said as she headed for the office Cain had built in this cabin. The phones as well as all the spaces in each building on the property were swept often to make sure all their conversations stayed private. She called Lou first, knowing he was next door to her cousin and had undoubtedly visited her.

"Muriel," Lou said, sounding wide awake. "Did you talk to Sanders?"

"I told him to head to the office and a secure line before I tell him everything he needs to know. Have you talked to Cain?" She sat at the desk and put her feet up. After all the bad things that had happened to their family, she didn't like being away from Cain when something like this happened. It wasn't that she didn't trust Lou and Sabana to take care of her cousin, but peace of mind came when there was a wall of people around the head of their family. They would never survive without her.

"I just left their room. She's staying until tomorrow. We ran into Judice O'Brannigan when we were at dinner tonight. Colin has gotten into something new, and it must worry O'Brannigan enough that she wants to talk to Cain about it, and Cain is wondering if he's brought some madness our way. She's trusting Sanders to keep it together until she sends a group of guys back tomorrow on the first flight we can find."

"Don't worry, he's up to it. There's no hints on Colin?"

"He's your cousin, so you tell me," Lou said and laughed.

"I'm not the imaginative one in the family, so who the hell knows? What we need to figure out is who hit the pub. Even with everything else going on, this takes precedence. I doubt this will be the last shot they take at us, and I don't want any other innocents hit."

"Believe me, Cain wants the same thing. She was *pissed*. I'll call you and let you know what time we head out. I'm sure Cain is going to want to talk to you first thing, so call her at the hotel. I'll make sure it's a good line."

"Thanks, Lou, and call me if there's anything else." She hung up and checked in with Katlin and was glad the guys she'd picked were packed and ready for a flight at five in the morning. She called the hospital next, and was relieved to hear Josh was hanging on but still in surgery.

"Hey, boss," Sanders said when she called him next, because she wanted to finish her evening and get to Kristen.

"Listen, I know it's going to be time-consuming, but you've got to camp at the hospital. When Josh comes out of surgery, you need to be the first person he talks to. You also have to make sure no one tries to muscle the people Cain is sending to look out for you guys."

"I like having a drink at the pub when I can, and Josh is a good friend. I'll be happy to sit with him until he's ready to go home. You have to know he's not going to talk to anyone whether I'm there or not. Josh isn't that kind of guy."

"I know," Muriel said, "but there's no reason to take chances. Once our guys arrive tomorrow, point them in the right direction when it comes to the contractor. We need to figure out if there's any connection. The rest we'll talk about when I call you in the morning." She left the light on the desk on as she stood and stretched. There was something in her gut that told her this was only the beginning of what was coming.

She stopped at the bedroom door and saw Kristen sitting up

reading. The big sweater was gone, replaced by a silk nightgown with two very thin straps. Kristen put her bookmark in place and put the book in her lap. "Is your guy okay?"

There had been women before Kristen, but she'd never met anyone this compassionate. Perhaps it was because of her strange upbringing, but Kristen had a sense of empathy not shared by many people, especially someone this young. Looking at her made Muriel think of all the things Cain had said about Emma through the years. Love was the best healer as well as a shield to face the world when you had it.

"He's still in surgery, but I'm hoping everything will be okay."

Kristen got up and began unbuttoning Muriel's shirt. "Can you tell me what happened?"

"Cain was planning to expand the pub in the Quarter, and Josh, the manager—"

"Oh no, it was Josh?" Kristen stopped what she was doing and glanced up at her. "He's so nice when we go in there."

"He was meeting with the contractor, and some asshole shot the place up. That isn't a normal occurrence even if it's happened twice, so we'll have to do some research to make sure it doesn't happen again." She relaxed when Kristen moved to her belt and zipper next.

"Is that the kind of research Remi does?" Kristen asked the question that didn't really need an answer in a teasing tone. "You don't have to tell me, but promise me you'll be careful."

"I'm the in-house counsel for my family's business, honey. The only thing I'm in danger of is a papercut from all the paperwork I shuffle around daily."

Kristen put her fingers into the sides of her boxers and pulled down. "It's so funny that you expect me to believe that, but I'm not in the mood to argue with you."

She kicked everything off and waited for Kristen to take off her shirt, but she held the open sides and pulled her closer. "I'm glad you think I'm so exciting, but my days are pretty boring. You, on the other hand, are the exact opposite of boring." They'd taken things slow in the beginning because she wasn't sure if Kristen was ready for anything long-term. Her college graduation was still a year away, but it was impossible to keep fighting what Kristen kept saying she wanted, and she'd given in.

"What's going through that brilliant legal mind?" Kristen asked when she pulled her down. "If you bring up our ages again while we're almost naked and on a family vacation, you're sleeping on the sofa."

"I don't think about that anymore…much," she said, making Kristen laugh. She went along willingly when Kristen pulled her to the bed and pushed her into a sitting position.

"My sister gave me the broad strokes about Remi's family business. Don't worry, nothing too specific, and since Cain and Remi sprouted from the same family of trees, I have a general idea of what I'm getting into." Kristen stood between her legs and combed her hair back. "Do you have the complete picture of where we came from? And I mean really, where me and Dallas come from?"

"I helped cement your identities, but I didn't ask for specifics. It's not that I didn't want to know," she said and kissed between Kristen's breasts. "I thought too much information would mean prying into something that you and your sister might want to keep private. If you need to talk about what you went through, I'll listen and won't judge. But if you don't want to talk about it, I'm okay with that too." Their conversation had veered into something much more serious, and she wasn't sure why, but it seemed important to Kristen.

"How do you know you wouldn't judge?" Kristen's hands stilled and she didn't shy away from looking her in the eye.

"My father was the best man I ever knew." She placed her hands on Kristen's hips. "He taught me a lot of important things before he died, but the most important was to not judge anyone by the experiences that helped them survive. What you and your sister went through, even when your father came back, makes you strong." She caressed Kristen's cheek and patted the bed next to her so she'd sit. "Other people might've quit, but you got out of there and made your way to me."

"It was all Dallas. Without her I'd still be Sue Lee Moores from Sparta, Tennessee. I lucked out in the sibling department. Because of her I didn't grow up with an abusive prick of a father who wanted his daughters as bed warmers and moneymakers." Kristen opened her mouth but turned her head away before she said anything else. "It's what makes me think that you'll eventually pat me on the head and send me on my way. I'm some stupid kid who had to have her sister fight all her battles for her."

"Don't put words in *my* mouth or believe anything like that. You're incredibly special, and I realize that, even if most days I think I'm holding you back." She put her fingers over Kristen's lips when she started to disagree. "The thing you should think about instead of all this gloomy stuff is that it might be me who's scared that you'll eventually think all those nights of watching old movies at home with me is one boring existence."

"I'm sorry I called you brilliant. You're such an idiot sometimes." Kristen pulled her hair hard enough to get her to cock her head back. "If I wanted a college-aged fool who only thought about going out drinking and partying, I'd be with them right now. What I want are those nights with you, cooking for you, and sleeping next to you. I might be young, but I'm old enough to know what I want. Is there some reason you can't understand that?"

"My heart knows you're not going anywhere. Sometimes my head just gets in the way." She smiled wider when Kristen pulled her hair harder and kissed her. "It's a good thing that you're so patient."

"I'm not that patient," Kristen said and laughed. "All I wanted to say was you can trust me. I'm never going to betray you or your family, even if you decide to kick me to the curb."

"There's more of a chance of you doing that, honey, than me." She pulled Kristen closer and licked one of her nipples. "How about we forget what an idiot I am and try to enjoy the rest of my night? I have a feeling tomorrow is going to get a little nuts, and I might get busy."

"Don't worry—I have homework, and I know how much you love me saying that."

Muriel had to laugh at that. "Maybe I should start thinking what a stud I am and pat myself on the back more often."

Kristen laughed as she pushed Muriel back on the bed. "You are that," she said as she stretched out on Muriel and sucked in a breath when Muriel squeezed her ass. "Now try to keep your foot out of your mouth and stop talking."

She rolled them over and kissed Kristen again. "How about I use my mouth for other things?"

"That's your best idea yet."

CHAPTER FOURTEEN

Cain woke first and squinted at the wall of glass. It was still early, and they'd had a later night than she'd planned, but now it was time to go back to work. She reached for her phone and texted Sanders, wanting an update on Josh. It only took a minute for him to respond, and it was good news. Josh had done well in surgery and had been placed in intensive care for a couple of nights to assure close monitoring.

"How's Josh?" Emma asked, moving her hand in her usual small circles on Cain's middle.

"He's stable, and guess who did his surgery?" That had been the other part of Sanders's message.

"Do we know a lot of doctors outside our GP guys, pediatricians, and Sam and Ellie?" Emma asked, snuggling close when she did a little rubbing of her own.

"You'll remember Mark Summers. He put me back together after my shooting, and I work pretty good. It'll be nice to see him again. I'll call him later and ask him to limit Josh's visitors."

"Are you worried about something? What could he tell the police? It's not like he was doing anything wrong." Emma yawned and patted her thigh. "He was meeting with a contractor, for God's sake."

That was true, but when something came across as strange, she never ignored it. "When Sanders first called and reported what happened, there was one thing that didn't sit right. He said the contractor got winged and is home already, but the guy with him chose that particular moment to measure behind the bar."

"You don't buy it?" Emma raised her head and kissed her shoulder. "The guy could've just lucked out."

She considered it for a minute and shook her head. "I'm not moving the bar. I might add another one, but the one in there comes from Ireland, so I'm not messing with it. One of Da's friends sent it as a gift when he heard we were planning to open the pub, and it's old as hell."

"Why was he measuring it, then?" Emma asked, sitting up.

"We need to do some work before we go asking questions like that, lass. I like knowing the answers before I think someone is lying to me. But it's something to look into." She got up and followed Emma into the bathroom.

"You would've made a good attorney, honey. I think that's one of the rules before you go to court." Emma got their toothbrushes out.

"The problem is, once *I* ask those questions, a lot of those folks never make it to court."

They showered together and ordered breakfast sent up. Their day would start soon enough, and it'd be nice to enjoy the few hours they had left before the world demanded in. Lou came in and gave her an update on all their businesses and another one on Josh. Mark, her surgeon, promised no one would get into intensive care to question Josh, and his visitors' list would be limited to Sanders and Dino.

"Nathan Mosley called this morning and asked if he could have a few more hours. He's working on a lead and wanted to wait to see if it panned out," Lou said as his phone rang. She motioned for him to get it. He listened and gave a simple answer. "Send her up."

"Is Judice early?" Emma asked.

"She's downstairs and doesn't mind waiting if you're not ready, but I thought you might want to get the news on Colin and get this over with," Lou said.

"Good, since I'm dying to know." Emma laughed.

Lou excused himself once Judice arrived alone. Cain had ordered some more coffee and drinks and was surprised Judice relaxed enough to take a cup. It was an opportunity to study her while she fixed her coffee and to think about Judice with her father. Judice was completely different than her mother in coloring, and her hair a much brasher shade of red, but that probably wasn't her real color. She was different, but still a beautiful woman.

"Has everything worked out since we took care of Colin's problem? With Salvatore out of the way, Colin's business should be good," she said as a starting-off point.

"Yes, and you left so soon after all that, so I didn't get to thank you properly. It still shocks me that you did so much for me after I treated you so horribly. I'm ashamed that I had that reaction, but I've spent my life running from fear, and that's so hard to let go of." Judice seemed sincere. "I'm so sorry for everything, especially my behavior."

Apologies, her father used to say, were merely words if they weren't backed up by something to make you believe it. *I'm sorry* was easy to say, that was true, but she understood Judice's motivations. She didn't like them, but she couldn't find fault in her reasoning.

"The way I see it," she said, and Emma reached for her hand, "you most probably wanted a life with a man who loved you and your child. My father would've wanted to know Fiona, but he would've never taken her away from you. You're never going to believe that, but my mother understood what it was to bring children into the world. She would've never allowed Da to turn his back on either of you."

"I was young, and being pregnant back then without a husband was terrifying. It was a mistake, but all we can do is go forward. What I don't know is how Fiona would react if she ever knew the truth. I've lied too long now to ever gain her trust again."

"We'll never share your secret," Emma said. "You've carried it long enough, but Cain and I will never turn her away unless she means the family harm."

"I don't think after what happened to your daughter that you'll have a problem with that. Thank you for saying it, though." Judice took a sip of her coffee as if for courage and took a deep breath before she started talking. "Fiona seems happy where she is, so she doesn't concern me. I am worried about Colin. I don't want to smother him, but I also don't want anything to happen to him."

"He should be happy with the business we left him. Is he branching out into something else?" Cain had to give herself a small pep talk to stay calm.

"He's coming to meet with Cesar Kalina, and from everything I've heard, he's a scary man. I don't want Colin to think I'm going behind his back, but you're his family. Could you talk to him?"

She didn't have an extensive amount of information on every drug lord out there, but Cesar Kalina she'd heard about. "What is he thinking?"

Judice stared at her as if not knowing how to take the question. "You know what's happening on the border and beyond it, right?"

"I do, and I'm not upset. I just don't understand what he hopes to gain by this. We just got him out of a situation with one partner he didn't have a handle on. His dead partner is a pussycat compared to Kalina." She didn't understand her cousin and his need for more when he already had more than most.

"From what he said, Hector Delarosa has very little time before his operation gets swallowed by someone who wants his territory. Kalina wants to capitalize on that, but he needs help on distribution. That's where Colin would come in."

She nodded, but there was no reason to bring in more new players to their lives than they had to, and it was time to remember the people they needed to keep on their side. She'd have to think of a way to have a conversation with Hector about this. "I'm sure he did, but what Colin needs to remember is it wasn't Kalina who got his ass out of the crack his old partner put it in. If he wanted to partner with someone new, that's who he should've started with."

"I reminded him of that, but it was Kalina who approached him," Judice said, sounding almost relieved. "He hasn't heard from Carlos Luis."

"Don't take this the wrong way, but Colin can be an ass at times, and he needs someone to kick him in the butt." She made a fist, then flexed her fingers. "You need to be that foot in his ass before the guy gets himself killed. I love him, but he could try God's patience. It's like he goes from one situation that might kill him to a worse situation that will guarantee death."

Judice actually laughed. "That is true, but I love him. It's been hard to hold him off all these years, but I couldn't help but fall for him. The problem is that I can't deny him any longer, but I want to keep him alive. His children aren't ready to take over the business, and even if they're not interested, the world he lives in will never let them keep what they have."

Cain toyed with the mental puzzle pieces. "There's no way he can back out of this meeting now, but I need both of you to come to our place in Wisconsin before you head home. You're welcome, but I need you to know that the feds from home followed us there." She waited to see what Judice would decide. Not that it would change her mind one way or another, but it seemed like she was coming into her own even if it was late in the game.

"If you mean that, I'll be happy to accompany him. Will you tell him what I'm worried about? I can't help but feel that I'm being disloyal to him."

"All he needs to know is we saw you at the restaurant, and I invited you to coffee. We'll cover the rest after that, but he'll be the one fessing up to all this. Don't worry about it. I'll leave one of my guys behind, and he'll escort you there once you're done with Kalina." She stopped when Emma squeezed her hand, letting her know she had something to say.

"Don't worry that Cain will use your worry against you, and we have a place for you to stay if Colin wants to spend some time visiting with the family. It'll be a good time for you to meet everyone." Emma did a good job of putting anyone at ease, and even Judice seemed charmed by her. "Colin and Cain, like the rest of the cousins, are different in a lot of ways, but they're also a lot alike, and it'll be nice if you can see that."

"Thank you both." Judice smiled and placed her hand on her purse. "I won't take up any more of your time."

"Cain," Lou said, coming in and pointing to his phone. "Your next meeting is ready."

"Good, tell someone to bring him up." She stood and held her hand out to Judice. "Remember that I'm always a call away. Lou will give you my card."

Judice took Cain's hand in both of hers and held on. "Thank you."

"I'll see you both tomorrow, and I'll take care of it, if you want, by calling him and extending the invitation." That made Judice's smile widen, and she nodded. "Good, now if you'll excuse me."

"See you soon, Emma," Judice said before following Lou out.

It took Sabana a few minutes to get to their room with Nathan, and Cain almost laughed at the bright yellow overcoat over the soft green suit. She wondered for a moment if Nathan was perhaps colorblind and his clothier used him to get rid of these outlandish clothes. He quickly shed his coat, shook her hand, then moved to Emma and gave her a much longer greeting by kissing both her hands. Had he been anyone else, that would be a sort of death wish. Not that she would beat him, but Emma didn't appreciate anyone taking liberties with her.

"Good morning, Cain," he said when he sat in the same chair he'd chosen the day before. "And you, Mrs. Casey."

"Nathan, thank you for your time. Did you find anything?" she asked, but Emma pinched the top of her hand.

"Would you like some coffee, Mr. Mosley?" Emma offered as she stood with their cups.

"I would love some, and please call me Nathan."

"Then it's Emma, and feel free to go ahead and start talking."

He removed a file from the bag that matched his suit perfectly. "It's going to take some more time to pinpoint where Ms. Bender ended up, but it is possible to do my job in reverse. I'm not going to bore you with how I narrowed your scope, but I think I'm on the right track."

"Bore me a little bit," she said, not wanting to waste her time if Nathan was wrong.

"When a person runs from a life they don't want, it's much easier to do alone. Those are the ones who are almost impossible to find, but Ms. Bender ran with her brothers. Two brothers who are still in school," Nathan said with his finger up. "There's a way to search for new students in schools."

"That's got to be a large number to get through," Emma said, saying what Cain was thinking. "And if it's that easy, then she's not safe."

"It is if you don't narrow your search, and sometimes people who have no experience with this don't want to put in the legwork to find that needle in a whole country. What you have to think is that Ms. Bender didn't do all this to stay in New York State. Anything close to home would make her easy to find, but I checked New York just in case. No, I think she'd feel more comfortable with some distance between her and her family."

"That makes sense." She glanced down at the file he handed her. "Where do you think she is?"

"I've narrowed it to three possibilities. There's a small town in Arizona, a smaller town in Montana, and a place in Wisconsin. That's a start, but with some time I can narrow it enough that it'll be easy to find her."

That was good news, but it also made her worry. "Like Emma said, exactly how easy would it be for someone else to do this? I don't want this woman dead before I can talk to her."

"It's not impossible, and we need to consider that whoever else is looking for her has someone like me. If that's true, we need to hurry. Once I find her and you talk to her, I can do for them what I did for Dallas and Kristen."

"Whatever it costs, make sure you find them." She gave him the file back and sat back. "I think it's time we cement our relationship, Nathan. Name a price and I'll pay it. After Dallas and Kristen, I didn't think we'd need to meet again, but I'd like to have you on retainer to make sure things like this are taken care of."

"We don't need a retainer for that, Cain. I've made enough in my life to live the way I want, and these jobs are a way of staying safe in my retirement."

"I'd never move against you," she said, shocked that he'd think she'd do something like that to him.

"I think you misunderstand me," Nathan said, putting both hands up. "These favors I do for you, with you picking up the fees, I think of as me being able to call you when I have a problem."

That made more sense. He was savvy that way. "Sorry, and that's a given. Dallas and her sister are family to us, and without you, both of them would still be out there struggling. Let me know if you need anything, and I'll take care of it."

"Maybe the fee I'll take this time is dinner with you and your lovely wife. I figure she won't go with me alone," Nathan said with a wink.

It took Cain a second to smile, but she did when Emma pinched her hand, harder this time.

"I'd consider the invitation if I wasn't so happily married," Emma said with a small laugh. It was obvious Emma thought of Nathan as harmless.

"Find her," Cain said, "and I'll treat you to whatever you like... within reason." There was nothing wrong with putting down some parameters, especially when it came to someone infatuated with Emma. "That woman did something important to bring down a sick empire, and she deserves the fresh start she wants."

"I'll find her, and I promise to rush." Nathan stood and buttoned his jacket. He took the opportunity to kiss both of Emma's hands again before he left with another promise to call as soon as he was done.

"He's kind of hilarious." Emma laughed and shook her head.

"Yeah, a real riot," she said before calling Lou back in. "Hey, see if you can get us a flight. We're done, and I'd like to get back and do a little more legwork on some stuff."

"If we push it, there's a flight in an hour and a half," Lou said, texting someone as he spoke. "I think we can make it since we all packed light."

The cars were waiting, and they were dropped off right at the gate by the two men Lou was leaving behind to deal with Colin and Judice.

They walked right to the gate and boarded ten minutes before they closed the door. They'd get back early enough to play and have dinner with the kids.

"What are you thinking?" Emma asked once they were in the air.

"There's got to be an easier way to consolidate all this stuff, but hell if I can think of it. It's like having a bad casserole shoved in front of you and being forced to eat it." Cain lifted Emma's hand and kissed her fingers one at a time.

"I'm sorry, but I don't understand that at all."

"Think of a crappy casserole that you're forced to eat. You have no choice, but once you're done it makes your problems go away. If you're forced, it's not a matter of eating it or not, but of deciding where to start. Is it the edges first, or do you start in the middle for something different?" She licked the tip of Emma's index finger and smiled. "It's all about the execution, and I mean that literally."

Emma laughed and leaned in for a kiss. "Because it's you, baby, I totally believe you'll figure out the edges are the best, and you'll work your way in. I think that's also true in so many things in life. Don't you agree?"

"You do have a way of putting things, lass, that makes me look forward to every crappy casserole I have in my future."

❖

Shelby sat in one of the cars they'd rented and looked through the binoculars, sweeping the fields of the Casey property within view. They'd had to trek back to the airport for another couple of vehicles so they could split up and cover more ground. There'd be no more getting close without chancing a dog bite, and Cain's dogs meant business. Dylan was still complaining about the death of her favorite jeans.

"See anything?" Joe asked when she answered her phone. They were taking the afternoon and early evening shift. Dylan and their other backup would come on after that so they could run to the airport in the morning to pick up Lionel and Claire. If anyone could figure out how to monitor what they needed from a distance, it would be those two.

"I see cows and a dog sitting under a tree as if daring me to step in the yard so we can play." The dog suddenly stood and almost came to attention, and it made her look in the direction he was facing. The helicopter made her heart race as it flew over her car, low enough to make the windows rattle. "I have incoming."

"Incoming what?" Joe asked with a laugh as if she'd lost her mind. "If it's coffee, have them fly over here and not forget the sweetener." He stopped talking and it sounded like tapping from his end. "You think that's our target?"

"She's the only one I've known to love helicopters. We made it easy for her to leave town." The night in jail was still bugging her, but they all should've known better. After all the time spent watching the Caseys, maybe they were getting sloppy. Or desperate.

"Whoever it is will be visible when they land if they put down where the pilot is circling."

She could hear the click of Joe's camera, and she waited, as she could barely make out the helicopter over the trees. Once it landed, it would be out of her sight. "Think she'll invite us in for wine and cheese and tell us where she's been?"

"It's more like she'll invite us over to see if we can outrun the dogs. They've landed, and big Lou is out first. It looks like Katlin Patrick is waiting to drive them back, but there are plenty of her suits around too."

The large number of men didn't make sense. Cain, though, always had a reason for what seemed unreasonable. "If she'd turned that great brain to something like medical research, we'd have a cure for cancer by now," she said softly. The areas she could see were still quiet.

"Did you say something?" Joe asked.

"No, talking to myself. Wait," she said when a car drove up and parked behind her. A sliver of fear made her blink, but she saw Dylan getting out and walking toward her door. "Never mind. Is it her?"

"Yep," Joe said, sounding as if he was on his speakerphone. "She's being chivalrous and carrying Emma to the car. I wonder where she went?"

Dylan stood outside her door, waiting for her to put her window down, but the phone buzzed with another incoming call. "I guess we're about to find out," she said to Joe and put up a finger to Dylan. "Hello."

"Hello, extra Special Agent Phillips," Cain said sounding cheery. "How's the grind on the highway?"

"Uncomfortable, but what choice do I have, considering you're being so inhospitable?"

"If it was just you, I'd have invited you inside, but your new friends are a tad on the surly side." There was laughter from the other end, but it was higher pitched than Cain's, and Shelby figured it was Emma. "I thought I'd check in and tell you I took my wife out on a date night to Chicago. You say I'm inhospitable, but I just saved you hours of trying to figure out what I've been up to. Please make sure to report a good time was had by all."

"Thank you, I appreciate that. Are you sure you didn't meet with anyone?"

Cain laughed again. "That would make me sort of an asshole if I piled on a lot of work on a date night, Agent. If that's the type of person you're dating now, you could do better."

"Thanks, but I could do without the dating advice."

"Your loss, and call if you need something warm. I'll have one of the guys bring you out a hot toddy."

The line went dead, and she finally had to laugh as she lowered the window. "Hey, the Caseys just landed in one of the open pastures. According to Cain, they were in Chicago for a date night." She spoke into her phone but loud enough for Dylan to hear.

"Wait, she called and told you that?" Dylan asked.

"She did, and if you're ready, I need to go and meet Joe. Do you need anything?" She waited for Dylan to shake her head and then drove off when she didn't say anything else.

"She called me too, and I have no idea how she got my number," Joe said when he got in her car. He couldn't leave until his replacement showed up. "It's always surprising to hear her voice."

"It's called poking the bear with a stick," she said.

"You see us as the bear in this scenario?" Joe asked and smiled. "That's the true definition of optimism. Let's go pick up the rest of our team. I see my backup driving up."

He got back in his car and followed her to the hotel. They had a couple of hours, so they decided to have a cup of coffee before they drove to the airport. The café was open, and they noticed Cain sitting alone at a booth with a steaming cup in front of her. There'd been no call from Dylan, so they could only assume she'd followed Cain into town. It was strange to see her out alone without Lou's large presence behind her.

"Is it against the law to buy you a cup of coffee?" Cain asked, pointing to the other side of the booth when they stared a moment too long.

"You got here fast," Shelby said, sliding in first. "We spoke to you like forty-five minutes ago."

"Your friend sitting outside followed me here, so I kept to the speed limit. God forbid I break the law when I'm under your microscope. And I'm only in town because my father-in-law is buying feed and introducing his girlfriend and showing off his grandchildren to all his old buddies. I have some time to kill. Seeing you, though, reminds me that we need to have an off-the-record conversation."

"Agent Gardner is recording this, which means I can't guarantee it's going to be off the record," Joe said.

"Joe, when was the last time you recorded a conversation I wanted to keep private?" Cain said, giving them that smile that had probably gotten her more women than she had time to deal with before she'd married Emma. "I'm lucky that way, and I'm almost sure my luck will hold out. The only way we don't talk is if you're not in the mood to do so."

"What would you like to talk about?" She held up two fingers when the waitress came over and warmed Cain's cup. With any luck they'd get a hot cup for a change.

"Let's talk about your friends—old and new," Cain said, pouring what looked to be hot milk into her coffee. They'd only ever gotten the powdered stuff, which seemed strange for a part of the state that was mostly dairy farms. "The thing about me is I seldom forget anything that's important to me."

"If you need to talk about your feelings, that's not our field, but okay," Joe said.

"Does that mean I'm your field in other ways?" Cain asked as the waitress put down two cups and poured their coffee. "That's so flattering, but you have a tendency to miss things when you're constantly watching me."

"We communicate, so we seldom miss anything," she said, aggravated by Cain's poking.

"Okay, no need for snippy. It wasn't *your* wife tied to a table waiting to be assaulted, and I wonder sometimes if you've forgotten about Anthony Curtis. That he helped Juan Luis carry that out is something I'm never going to forget."

This had to be a trick. Cain Casey was never this talkative without a reason. "You think we've forgotten about Curtis?" Joe asked, and Cain stared at him with a patient expression.

"Please, Agent Simmons," Cain said, exhaling deeply. "If you like,

I can leave you to your iced coffee and kick you out of my sandbox. I'm not being patronizing—I'm asking a question."

"You seldom ask us anything," Shelby said, "but if you need reassurance, we haven't forgotten Curtis. I know exactly what he did, and he deserves to be punished." Shelby pushed her cup away and Joe followed suit. The waitress nodded when Cain held up two fingers and they were finally served something at the right temperature. "Thank you," Shelby said to the waitress, but all she got was the back of her head as she walked away.

"Enjoy it while you can, but back to my question."

"Why are you asking now?" Shelby asked wrapping her fingers around her cup.

"I told you. I'm waiting for my father-in-law. You're here, and I'd like to remind you about what's important, to me at least. Following me around when all I'm doing is taking my wife on a date makes me think you put the important things aside."

"We're capable of doing more than one thing at a time," Joe said.

"You're preaching to the choir on that point, Agent Simmons. I wonder what's happening in your world that some of you decide to moonlight. You've lost two agents and counting to the dark side. Barney Kyle was bad enough, but Curtis really took to it. Like father like son, am I right?" Cain picked up a butter knife from the table and twirled it through her fingers with practiced skill.

Cain's voice was deep and soothing, but Shelby tried to remember exactly who they were dealing with. Granted, Cain had given her the greatest gift she could've delivered, but this was her job. "If we could find him, we'd love to do that, but he's missing. Do you know where he is?"

"You'll be my first call if I find out. I'm pretty sure killing a federal agent is a crime," Cain said, putting the knife down and tapping her finger on the table. "And when I say killing, it's just a figure of speech. Even if he was instrumental in Juan's efforts to rape my wife, the courts deserve their shot."

"I doubt Juan is a problem any longer. From what I hear, he and his mother are dead. Do you have any idea how that happened or who's responsible?" Shelby's question stopped Cain's fingers.

"None whatsoever. Do *you* have any idea who's responsible?"

She wondered if Cain played tennis. The quick lob answers made her think she'd be good at it.

"Like I said, that's not our job, but Gracelia Luis was in town trying to take over her brother's business. Gracelia was eventually found holding her severed head, and her tongue was shoved into her vagina. Juan Luis has never been found, but is also assumed dead," Joe said after briefly glancing at her.

"Wow, that's graphic," Cain said, and her smile seemed to widen a tad.

"It is, and no matter her crimes, no one deserves that," Joe said.

"I agree, but I'm not privy to the dealings of the cartels. That's their signature when it comes to people they want to make examples of. See, Agent, maybe it's better the devil you know. You think I'm the devil incarnate, but am I really, in comparison?"

"Tell us about some of your crimes, and we'll let you know," Shelby said lightly.

"My only crime is liking really cheesy music," Cain said. That meant the stuff they'd be subjected to would reach new heights of annoying.

"So you only invited us over to ask about Anthony Curtis?" Joe asked.

"I'm only here for the excellent coffee, and you two sometimes look so dejected, it seemed like I should make an effort. I'm sure there have to be much more interesting things you could be doing for the bureau than skulking after me. The reason I asked about Curtis has to do with fairness."

"What do you mean?" Shelby asked.

"Your job is to catch me doing something you can lock me away for. I get that. I understand that. This game we play will go on for as long as I'm alive. You being outside my door and ten steps behind me is like blinking. It's something we do, some of us less than others, but still something that's a part of our lives that we can't change," Cain said, and she and Joe smiled at the dig. "My problem is the shortcuts some of you take to provoke a reaction that will finally bring me down. When those shortcuts involve my children and wife, that's beyond the parameters of our game."

"We agree with you on that, and we are actively looking for him," Joe said.

"I believe you, but that doesn't account for Hannah, does it?" Cain spun the knife on the table.

"Wait." Shelby held her hand up. "What do you mean by that?

Emma confronted me about it, but you can't seriously think we'd try to get to you by using a kid in kindergarten, do you?"

"Surely not, but then I have a bullet wound scar from an FBI-issued weapon. I also didn't think one of your little buddies would take the side of an animal like Luis, so what the hell do I know?" Cain pushed her cup aside and held up three fingers this time. It didn't take long for some warm apple pie to arrive.

"It's hard to argue when you put it like that," Joe said.

"Try," Cain said and laughed. "I thought you were the FBI," she said the letters slowly. "What's impossible for the FBI? Tell me how low you're willing to go to get your man."

"All I can tell you is that neither of us has ever done anything close to what you're suggesting," Shelby said. "We can't deny there've been bad people working for us, but it has nothing to do with me or Joe."

"That's true, but everyone has a breaking point, Agent Shelby. Take your partner here. It wasn't that long ago that his anger drove him to distraction. Not everything that happens leads to my door, but there you are banging away when something does happen."

"But a child? You really think we'd do that?" Joe asked in a defensive tone as if trying to excuse himself for his behavior after the Eatons were killed and he'd blamed Cain.

"What's hard to believe? That you'd stoop that low after all the shots I've taken because of your organization?" Cain asked, and for once she let some heat bleed into her voice. "It's up to you to figure out which one of your people would use my child. If I don't get a reasonable answer, then I'm going to take care of it, and Annabel isn't going to like the way I do it. And before you accuse me of threatening any of you, fighting my battles in the arena of public opinion is more of a promise than a threat."

"We can't take care of something if we have no idea what you're talking about," Shelby said. These circular conversations were aggravating as hell.

"Like *I* said," Cain echoed Joe's words, "you're the FBI. It shouldn't be that hard to figure out, but come after my children again, especially Hannah, and you'll be sorry."

"That does sound threatening," Shelby said softly. "We can't be blamed for something we don't know, and I give you my word on that. I know better than anyone we're on opposite sides most of the time, but I've never lied to you."

Cain's gaze was probing as she stared at them for a long moment before she nodded abruptly. "I believe you two, but that's as far as my faith goes." Cain took a bite of her pie and glanced at her phone on the table. "Enjoy your hot coffee while you can, and remind Annabel that the clock is ticking. If you'll excuse me, my father-in-law is done."

"How about one hint before you go? You sound like you know a little about the people responsible for what happened to Hannah," Joe said.

"You want me to deprive you of the pleasure of doing your job? You're supposedly the best investigators on the planet—figure it out."

Cain got up and handed the waitress some folded bills, and the woman kissed her cheek. There were probably more bizarre situations in the world, but Shelby couldn't think of any that would top the last twenty minutes. Cain Casey was a multifaceted enigma who had a way of confusing them beyond what she accomplished on a daily basis.

"Do you have any clue as to what the fuck she was talking about?" Joe asked.

"There has to be something to it. Emma Casey cornered me in the bathroom at Vincent's, and now Cain. Someone did something to that little girl, and they're blaming us." She tapped her finger against her chin and wondered if this was another one of Cain's mind games. "I'd say she was bluffing to distract us from something, but it rings too true."

"No agent in their wildest imagination would approach a kid to do anything for them. This is bullshit, and you know it." Joe cut off a piece of his pie and shoved it in his mouth. It was like he was pissed but wanted to enjoy the little bit of normal food while it was sitting in front of him.

"There's no reason for both of them to lie, Joe. Come on and think about this rationally. She prides herself in distracting us without the subterfuge of a story like this." She took a sip of her coffee and waved the waitress off when she held up the pot. The damn stuff in the woman's hands was probably yesterday's brew now that Cain was gone. "She seldom gets out of joint unless it's to do with one of her kids, so she believes what she's saying, enough to say it to our faces."

"Come on and we'll call Agent Hicks on the way to the airport. If Casey believes this, then she's also serious about the threat."

"Let's go." She finished her pie and coffee quickly before putting her coat back on. "If someone actually did it, I'm going to beat Cain to the punch when it comes to punishing this kind of stupidity."

"I'm with you on that one, sister."

"Save the amens and hallelujahs until we have something, and according to Dylan, we don't get too much of anything."

CHAPTER FIFTEEN

"Mom, did you see my snowman?" Hannah asked Cain as everyone sat around the fireplace in the large family room in the main house. Dinner was over, and everyone had stayed for the next chapter of the book Emma was reading the kids. Billy was asleep against Emma's chest, and Hannah had curled up on Cain's lap so she could talk softly to her.

"I did," Cain said, kissing Hannah's forehead. "You did a good job. Are you having a good time?" she asked as Victoria came closer and joined Hannah in her lap.

"I'm having the best time, Aunt Cain," Victoria said before Hannah could answer. Cain loved talking to the expressive little girl who reminded her of Hannah in so many ways. "Hannah said she's my best friend. Isn't that great?"

"Victoria said she's going to be my best friend too," Hannah said, her lethargy seemingly gone. "Tomorrow can we go show her and Liam the cows?"

"We'll go see the cows and then go sledding. Maybe Finley would like to race down the hill with you, Victoria, and I'll go with Hannah." She laughed at the loud screeching and the look Emma gave her when Billy startled and lifted his head. "The only way we can go is if you guys go to bed and get some sleep."

"Mama," Victoria said loudly, "can I stay with Hannah?"

"I swear, you're worse than Fin," Abigail said as she made a lower-the-volume motion with her hands in her daughter's direction. "She loves to rile these guys up right before bedtime."

"I do not," Finley said as she held Liam by his ankles upside down. Once Emma stopped reading, all the kids seemed to come to life.

"Emma can tell you that good girls never rule the world, and she was the best at being a good girl when I met her. Look at her now," she said and winked at Abigail. "And tomorrow we're going sledding, followed by hot chocolate. Tonight, though, it's time for bed." She stood with both little girls in her arms. "Go and kiss everyone, and I'll walk you two upstairs."

"I'll come with you," Abigail said as she rose and kissed Sadie's forehead as she started putting her coat on. "Go with Fin, baby, and I'll be right there."

"I'll walk you over, Sadie," Hayden said, and Sadie appeared thrilled.

Cain nodded and was proud of their kid. Hayden seemed to understand that Abigail's kids needed the extra attention after everything they'd been through. Sadie was young, but she'd found a good friend in Hayden, and they spent a lot of time together talking about books and movies. Hayden was Cain's heir, and while that would take strength, she also wanted him to be compassionate when necessary.

"Come on, monkeys," she said after the little girls said their good nights. She and Abigail got them ready for bed, and Victoria borrowed some flannel pajamas from Hannah. Cain told them a story of her father and his siblings, which was how she'd started teaching Hayden about their family. Victoria was an Antakov by birth, but with Abigail and Finley's help, she'd create a new history they could be proud of.

She stopped talking when both girls had fallen asleep holding hands. Abigail was sitting on the other side of the bed and was staring at her with an expression she couldn't decipher. "Everything okay?"

"This is a wonderful place," Abigail said as she ran her hand along Victoria's hair. "And your family is great."

"I think so, but it's okay to tell me if there's something on your mind. I'd like to think I'm not that scary, and I don't ever mind questions."

Abigail laughed at that and took a deep breath but kept her eyes on the sleeping children. "I want more than anything to enjoy this second chance at happiness. Finley is who I should've waited for—shared children with. Nicola was such a mistake, but I can't ever see my children that way."

"Your children love Finley, and I can see it's very much mutual. Children are a gift, but sometimes you get them after that infant stage. That doesn't mean we love them any less." She pointed to the girls and their joined hands. "Hannah doesn't care that Victoria just got here. She loves her, and they're family. Emma and I feel the same way, and I'm thrilled to finally be an aunt. Life stole that from me, but I'm done with loss."

"Can you really prevent that, though?" Abigail asked in a whisper.

"Nothing in life is certain, but if it's in my power to prevent something from happening to you and your family, I'm going to do it."

"My fears have nothing to do with you or your family, Cain. Please don't think that."

"I know. Nicola is still lurking out there, ready to mess this up for you. That's what scares you, right?" She stood and motioned for Abigail to follow her to the seating area Emma put in their room. The lake they looked out on was lit up, but the windows were treated to keep prying eyes out. "I'll admit your problems aren't easy to fix."

"You're making me feel so much better," Abigail said, laughing as Cain handed her a glass with a little bit of whiskey. "Fin likes to gloss over the danger, so I won't worry, but the thought of losing my kids makes me crazy. That Nicola so readily embraced the life she had disgusts me, but not as much as the fact that she wanted the same for our children."

"Rosy pictures aren't my specialty, but there's a way to deal with Nicola that'll bring her back into the open. I can't take a kill shot unless she pokes her head out of whatever hole she's hiding in." She sat across from Abigail and lifted her hand to Emma, who'd come in quietly.

"Will you have a problem with that?" Emma asked, obviously having heard her question. "Nicola is the mother of your children."

"My children think she's dead, and their grieving process was short. You can't miss what you never really had, and Nicola was only involved in a small way when she was alive." Abigail made air quotes. "It was me and my stupidity that tried to create an image of her for them, but I gave them a picture of someone who never existed." Abigail's hands clenched into fists, and Cain could sympathize. That level of frustration could drive you insane.

"Emma makes a good point, but I understand where you're coming from," she said as Emma sat on the arm of her chair. Finley was at the door and hesitated, out of Abigail's sight. Cain waved her in.

"I should be concerned, considering I wouldn't have my children without Nicola, but I think of who she was—who she is. If that's what Cain had done with her life, would you have one single doubt your kids would be better off without knowing anything about her?" Abigail rested her head against Finley's hip when she came over and put her hand on Abigail's shoulder.

"We need to have another conversation, then," Cain said, liking the way Emma was rubbing her back. "Did Nicola ever talk about her family outside her parents and twin brother?"

"She mentioned a few people, but we never saw any of them. The only socializing we did with her family revolved around her parents and Fredrick. I think the only time I ever met a cousin or some other relation was on one of our trips to Miami when we were there on vacation." Abigail closed her eyes as if trying to concentrate better. "It was a guy, and I remember Nicola laughing at me because I thought he looked scary."

"We'll get back to him, but did you ever meet Linda Bender and her family? We have a picture to help you." She waited for Finley to show her the image on her phone.

"She was at my in-laws' place sometimes but only to drop stuff off from work. We were never introduced, but I've seen her." Abigail held the phone and stared at the woman who might hold all the answers that could help them. "Who is she?"

"Linda is Nicola's cousin and the keeper of their ledgers. For a business that should have virtually no paper trail, the Antakov family kept ledgers that contained a roadmap of their entire operation. Linda turned all the records over to the FBI before running with her brothers. She didn't want them being raised in the family business." Finley gave her the rundown, and Abigail handed her phone back.

"I wish I had met her," Abigail said. "She sounds like the only one who got how crazy all this is."

"But you never spoke to her, right?" Cain asked.

"No, and I'm thinking that's the wrong answer here."

"There are no wrong answers, so tell me about the cousin you met," Cain said, and Finley sat on the ground and left her phone out.

"He wasn't Nicola's favorite, from the way she treated him, and his name is Sacha, I think. It's been a few years so I can't be sure, but he came for drinks with us but didn't stay for dinner. I don't think his last name was ever mentioned."

"Fin, you have anything on that?" she asked, knowing Finley kept a copy of the case she'd been working. Maybe Linda wasn't the only one who'd lead them to the answers she needed, and Abigail had found another way in.

"I'm going to have to check my laptop, but that name sounds familiar. The best way to get all the information is going to be talking to my old boss, but I'll hold off as long as I can. I'm not ready to give him a complete review of what I've been doing since I left. The files I turned over have surely been updated by now, and there's no way for me to access that information." Finley typed something into her phone. "I doubt they've made much progress aside from closing down the businesses they know about. With David Eaton and the evil twins gone, I doubt there was much to find at any of those clubs. That leaves the rest of the pecking order and how that's fallen out with the two top guys gone," Finley said.

"The family has a definite pecking order," Cain said, "and there's no way to know how it got reshuffled once Nicola supposedly died, and then David Eaton and his wife were killed. They were the top of the totem pole. The only way to know how the power structure got scrambled is to talk to someone inside. That's never going to happen unless you torture it out of someone, and even then I don't know if you'll ever know the complete truth." Cain spoke what she saw as the truth.

"I wish I knew more to help you," Abigail said.

"We'll get there, but there was a reason they were so successful for so long." Everyone stared at Cain as if she was giving an interesting lecture.

"What do you mean?" Abigail asked.

"It was a family business. That part I think the FBI got right, but it was run in pieces and not as a whole. I can't know that for sure, but for a business like this to be successful, you have to keep it as simple as possible to keep your risks low. Each player knew only their little piece, and the only ones who knew the entire game board were David Eaton and his wife along with his children. That makes Finley right—if we find someone who'll talk to us, they'll only know their little piece."

"That's what makes Linda Bender so important," Finley said.

"Right. From what we know of Linda, her father was David's brother, so that's how she got her job. Her brothers were too young to take over, so her old job has to have fallen to another one of the cousins now that she's in the wind. Outside of the Eatons, Linda was the only one with a view from the top of the mountain." She was thinking out loud, but they all seemed to be following along. "Now all we need to figure out is two things. Who took Linda's place, and what's the most important thing to Nicola Antakov?"

"What do you mean?" Abigail asked.

"Is it the return of her throne or her family?"

"That's easy, her throne." Abigail didn't hesitate. "She couldn't have given a crap about us."

"The problem with your argument is Sadie."

"Even I don't understand that one," Finley said.

"Sadie is about to turn eleven in a few weeks, right?" Abigail and Finley nodded. "Nicola has years to teach Sadie the business, or at least it will seem like years, but it's over in a blink. In Nicola's game, it has to be finessed. To be successful, Sadie's education has to start early."

"How can you teach a child to want that?" Abigail asked.

"Easy, by stripping away her humanity. All Nicola needs is you out of the way."

"Over my dead body," Abigail said with venom.

"There's going to be a dead body—it just won't be yours."

❖

Emma lay still with her head on Cain's chest, and she seemed to be listening to her heartbeat. "Are you sure you don't want to wait until we all get home? What can you and Remi do in a couple of days?"

Cain moved her hand up from Emma's butt to her neck. "I need some answers about what happened with Josh, and going alone will give me a jump on the guys outside. You and the girls will be fine, and you know I wouldn't leave you behind if it wasn't something I had to do. If I can, it'll be a day, and I'll be back." She was loyal to the people who were loyal to her, but her family came before all that. Getting answers would give her a way of ridding herself of any problem that could threaten her family. To do that she'd walk through hell and back.

"Try for that. I've been looking forward to this vacation, and I don't feel good about letting you out of my sight." Emma pushed up and looked at her. "Promise me you'll be careful. I know you don't take crazy chances, but don't take shortcuts because you want to make something happen."

"I promise, and shortcuts are a way to get caught. This is a way to start small and knock the cobwebs off," she said, pressing her hand to Emma's cheek. "I want you to know that you are the love of my dreams. There is no way I'll ever do anything to lose you or, more importantly, my time with you."

"Good, and you are my world. If you ever do anything that would take you out of my life, I'll never forgive you. I'm not that old, so a lifetime without you would really piss me off." Emma kissed her before touching her until she forgot everything for those long minutes. They were late for breakfast, but she didn't care.

"You coming back, Mom?" Hannah asked after they finished sledding and sat down to a late lunch. Only her briefcase was by the door, and that seemed to make everyone feel better that her absence wouldn't be for long.

"I am, but remember I said I had a surprise for you?" She smiled but Emma rolled her eyes. They'd discussed it and decided they'd put a cleaning service on speed dial to protect Emma's rugs.

"I get a surprise?" Hannah bounced on her knee and it was hard to deny this kid anything.

"Yes, but you have to promise me and Mama that you're going to take care of it and share with Hayden and Billy." Lou brought in a small pup that was the runt of Jerry and Maddie's latest litter of prize hunting beagles. The only hunting in the little guy's future would be her shoes.

She and Emma cringed when Hannah screamed loud enough to shatter glass, but from the reaction, she loved the gift she'd requested months ago. "I love him," Hannah said as she carefully took the wiggly puppy from Lou. "I'm going to name him Buddy."

"That's a great name," Emma said as she lifted Hannah and the dog off Cain. "Now kiss your mom good-bye for now, and go show everyone your special gift. And make sure you keep him on the pads we put down until he learns he has to go outside to use the bathroom."

"Listen to your mother, or we'll both be in trouble." She gave Hannah a hug and gave Hayden one before she met Jerry in the kitchen. "And you stay out of trouble," she said to Emma when she walked into her arms. "I'll call you on the burner I left you but not until late tonight. If you want, I'll make it early tomorrow morning."

"No, call me, I don't care what time it is. Give Josh a kiss for me, and don't forget us."

"Trust me, that'll never happen. I love you, lass," she said and kissed Emma long enough that Jerry blushed.

They took the four-wheelers Jerry used to round up the herd with trailers hauling feed, in case her watchers could see them. The way they were dressed and what they were doing should throw them off long enough to allow them to drive away from the adjacent farm.

Remi's plane was waiting at a private airstrip, and they strategized on the way home. Remi and Simon were going to pay Brandi Parrish a visit and check if she'd had any problems. She and Lou would deal with Josh, and they'd all make sure their people were ready for another attack that probably wasn't far off. And they were all going to start getting answers.

"Call me if you have any problems, and I'll meet you later," Remi said as they came to a stop in their private hangar.

"You do the same."

The ride back to Muriel's place was quiet and free of watchers. Silence was at times deafening when it came because it was so rare, but it gave her a chance to think. Her family was safe for now, she was free to do what she had to, but that part of her that belonged to Emma craved her presence. Maybe she was getting soft, but she doubted anyone would tell her that to her face.

When they arrived, Dino gave them both a hug and an update on Josh.

"He's talking, but it's going to be some time before he's back behind the bar. That shot nicked his liver, so the doctor said not to rush getting back to work. Doc said to make sure you get that across to Josh. He's already chomping to get back and oversee the reno," Dino said as he adjusted the guns he wore in his shoulder holster. "I told him you'd want to talk to him about what happened, but I found the guy who didn't get shot."

"And?" she asked as she sent Emma a quick text to let her know she'd arrived.

"I got some of the guys watching him, and he's been spending money he shouldn't have."

"Pick him up right now, but tell them to be invisible about it when they do. Deliver him to the office, and we'll have a chat with him later." She motioned to the back door, and Dino handed Lou a set of keys. "Good job, Dino. There'll be a bonus for everything you took care of while we were gone."

"No need for that, boss. Me and the boys did what you asked, but it wasn't fun to shoot up the places we like to hang out. Felt wrong." Dino reminded her of the first time she met Lou. Her longtime guard was a big quiet man who hadn't really said much until they'd gotten to know each other well. This was the first time she'd ever heard Dino string this many words together at once.

"They're coming back, and once they're open, the drinks are on me for you and your boys." She and Lou left out the back and drove to the hospital. If there was anyone still watching Josh, she didn't spot them, and Josh sat up straighter when he saw her. The move appeared to cause a lot of pain, so she walked to him quickly and took his hand. "Relax, old friend."

"Cain, I'm so sorry about what happened," Josh said, sounding pained but not from his wounds.

"Forget about all that and tell me what the hell happened." She knew all about the first shooting, but that was something she wasn't going to share, even with Josh. It was the second round she was interested in.

"I met with one of the guys you had on your list, that guy that did the house, remember?"

"Jimmy Pitre is hard to forget, and I'm sure that's what he says about me too," she said, laughing. It was probably a given that his asshole puckered every time he saw her or heard her name.

The macho guy had tried to intimidate Emma until he'd met with Cain, and she'd given him a lesson in intimidation. While she'd been recovering from Big Gino's attempt on her life, Jimmy had allowed a bunch of FBI agents to blend in with his crew. The agents had taken advantage of the open walls and planted enough listening devices that they could have heard her thoughts. It'd been the bugs in her and Emma's bedroom that made her think of the worst punishment she could fathom to hit Jimmy with. She'd made him shove thirty of the things up his ass and swallow the rest. There was no chance that Jimmy Pitre was ever going to forget her in this lifetime.

"He said he'd done some work for you and promised the same deal as before. We met for him to get a sense of what we wanted, and he brought one of his crew with him to help measure. They'd finished all the stuff I told him about, and the guy said he wanted some measurements of the old bar so they could replicate it in the front section."

"Was he on the phone before this happened to you?" She doubted Pitre had it in him to exact revenge by trying to get one of her people killed, but people's stupidity surprised even her at times.

"The guy said he had to call the next appointment to tell them they'd be a little late. Like five minutes later the place was a hellhole. I got shot before I could hit the ground, and Pitre pulled me behind the bar with the other guy even though he'd been shot. Do you know how he's doing? I owe him a drink for doing that."

If Pitre had pulled the others to safety, that meant the point hadn't been to kill anyone. Unless Pitre wasn't involved. "He got winged, and he's out of the hospital. I'll make sure to let him know you appreciate his efforts." She squeezed his hand and blew him a kiss. "That's from Emma, so don't get any funny ideas. Your job now is to relax and get better. All I need to know is if you have someone at home who can take care of you."

"Yeah, but the doc said it's going to be a week or so before he lets me go. He was waiting on you to move me to a private room."

"That will make visitors a lot easier, but some of the guys are going to stick around and watch so nothing else happens to you. Your first set of visitors is probably going to be the NOPD. Any place getting shot up in the middle of Mardi Gras is going to be a priority case, so tell them what you told me, minus the guy behind the bar. On that point you have amnesia."

"Tell me if he set this up he ain't getting away with it." Josh tugged on her hand a little and he sounded serious.

"He won't be a problem, but that's all I can say. Take care of yourself, and don't worry about anything. I'll handle all of it. I'll be back later to check on you to see that you're set up in a different room that doesn't feel like a fishbowl." She patted his chest and walked out with Lou. For the next part of their day they needed Dino's services and dark tinted windows.

It didn't take Dino long to pick them up and drive them to the office. Pitre's flunky was tied in the room below the office that was empty because of the water table fluctuation. The business here before them used the large space as an off-loading spot when they received barge loads of goods off the river. Now you could smell the water rushing under it, and the floor and walls were almost always moist.

She had to give the guy credit for displaying the correct response to being forced into a car and tied to a chair by a group of angry young men. He looked terrified, and from the appearance of his clothes, he'd already pissed himself. Dino had learned well from Lou and Katlin and had the guy's wallet on the small table he'd brought down with a chair for her. It didn't really matter what his name was, but she was sure someone cared what happened to him. Depending on what he had to say, those people might actually find him when all this was over.

"How much?" she asked, not wanting to waste time on the long, drawn-out process of shooting this idiot one small piece at a time. "How much did you make to have my friend almost killed?"

"Who are you?" the guy asked, sitting like a limp doll. Usually people were trying to get out of the bindings for all they were worth, like they could actually break the ropes around their wrists and ankles.

Not displaying the urge to escape made him either stoned or stupid, and Cain wasn't sure which it was yet.

"I'm a person who doesn't like repeating themselves, so answer the question, or I'll put a bullet through your head right now if you tell me you don't know what I'm talking about. Once I do that, I'm going to hunt down your mother, sister, girlfriend, and any other family you have and shoot them in the head for your choices." She sat and crossed her legs. Her intuition told her he worked for Jimmy Pitre doing trivial shit, and he'd seen the chance to make a little fun cash.

"It was a quick five grand, but the guy said someone had already shot the place up. I didn't know until right before it happened that it was going down *while* we were in there. The bar was the safest place, but I couldn't tell those guys what was about to go down without having to tell how I knew." This was the easiest interrogation she'd ever sat through.

"Start from the beginning. Who called you?"

"After the place got shot up that first time, someone called me and asked if I worked for Jimmy. He got my name from a buddy of mine who works for another contractor, and they offered me the money to call if we got the chance to bid the job. I didn't ask anything, and the guy handed over the money once the job was done." His words were coming slower and not panicked, as if he bought into the idea that the truth sets you free. He really was stupid if he thought he was leaving here breathing.

"What guy?"

"Everyone calls him Lizard. I don't know his real name, but he works for Cypress Construction. He called me and a few other guys who might bid on the pub job. Whoever made the call first got a grand bonus."

"And did you get your bonus?" she asked and smiled.

He smiled back but it was tentative. "Yeah, but I'm sorry that guy got hurt. I swear—I didn't think anyone would get hurt."

"Did Jimmy know about your little deal?" It never hurt to have some leverage over the idiot with the Confederate flag tattoo.

"No way. He'd kill me for sure if he knew I got him shot. He's home getting over it, but he can't move his arm for six weeks."

"One more thing before I let you go," she said, standing up and taking what was left of his blood money. She handed the bills to Dino. "I owe you considerably more than that, but I thought you might want to take your girl out to dinner tonight."

"Hey, that's—" The guy stopped when she stared at him. "It's okay, take it."

"Did Lizard tell you who hired him for these phone calls he asked you to make?"

He blinked a few times. "He wasn't giving up his source. He said he didn't want none of us going around him and trying to cash in."

Cain nearly sighed out loud. Stupidity rankled. "I don't believe you. No one goes behind the bar *before* making the call unless they knew exactly what was going to happen. You must believe I'm some asshole with no brains if you think I'm buying that. Didn't you consider I'd talk to the guy who lived?" She tapped the closed wallet in her hand and raised her voice a little. "Asshole, you should realize I know all the answers before I ask the questions."

"Look," the guy said, sitting up straight but not fighting the bonds. "Okay, yeah, I knew they were going to shoot the place up, but it was five grand to whoever made that call first. I got bills, and your guy's going to be okay."

"Do you think someone sprays a building with automatic weapons to scare people, or to kill? Remember, honesty will set you free."

"I didn't mean anything by it."

"Doesn't answer my question, and I'm not going to repeat myself." She took his license out of his wallet and held it up to read the information on it. "A good friend of mine got seriously injured because you wanted a little bit of money."

"Hey, five grand's a lot of money," the guy said loudly.

"Is it worth dying over?" she asked, curious what his answer would be.

"Hell, no."

"Precisely, but here we are." She said the words that signaled the end of his life, and Lou got his gun out. "The only reason my man lived was because of your boss, Jimmy. That phone call you made for so little money is something you can't take back, but you will pay for it."

"Let me, Uncle Lou," Dino said, holding his hand out. "I gotta do it sometime, and I'd rather it be with you."

"Are you sure?" she asked. Dino idolized Lou, but she also knew Dino's dad and his objections to the path his son had taken. "Once you pull that trigger, there's no going back."

"My loyalties are to you, Cain. You never have to doubt me and what I'll do for you." Dino took the gun and didn't flinch as he pulled the trigger. They all ignored the man's final pleas, which were nothing more than white noise.

"Lou, make him the crew boss of the guys you put him with, and give him the bump in pay that goes with it." She embraced Dino and kissed his cheeks. "And you know my loyalties are with you, Dino. Never doubt the lengths I'll go to keep you and your family safe, because now you're my family as well."

"Thanks, boss, and we'll be back here with whoever this Lizard is."

"Good. Put this guy on ice. We'll deliver him as soon as Lizard tells us who the money fairy is."

CHAPTER SIXTEEN

Hector opened his eyes when the plane touched down in Cozumel. The place survived on tourists, but Carlos Luis lived with his bride a few miles from all the resorts. The house that sat on the private beach was one of Rodolfo Luis's favorite getaways. Carlos had taken over all of his late father's estates, and no one was left to challenge him. Hector admired him for that, and for the way he'd taken revenge for the cowardly way Gracelia had killed her own brother.

"You okay?" Tracy asked. She reached over and rested her hand on his thigh.

"I was thinking about the very dead Rodolfo Luis," he said as they taxied to the stairs they were rolling to the edge of the tarmac. "He had a son outside of marriage."

"Plenty of people do that, baby." Tracy stared at him as if she suddenly didn't know him. "You've never told me the whole story about Marisol, but she doesn't belong to your wife. She's no less yours because you weren't married to her mother."

"I'm not being judgmental about how Carlos got here, and all you had to do was ask about Marisol. It's not a secret, but since you two don't get along, I didn't think you'd be interested." An immigration official came on board when they got the doors opened. The man did a short check of the cabin and stamped their passports, allowing them to deplane.

"What about Rodolfo, then?" Tracy grabbed her purse and briefcase. No matter what they were doing, the woman never stopped working.

"He had a son who is a good businessman, and a nephew who was nothing but a moron, yet he didn't acknowledge Carlos until right before his death. I have Marisol, or I did, but she wasn't my first choice.

None of my other children want to take over the business, though, so what else could I have done?" There was a car by the hangar, and a young man got out and started toward them.

His guard Tomas reached into his coat, but the man put his hands up and smiled. "Señor Delarosa, welcome. Señor Luis wanted me to come and pick you up. He hopes you and Ms. Stegal will be his guests for the time you're in town. He'd like to introduce you to his wife and have you join the celebration of his new baby."

"That is cause to celebrate, but we won't inconvenience his family." He put his hand on Tracy's back and waited for her to get into the car. "Could you stop in town? If there is a new baby, we must have a gift."

The driver promised to wait in the square as he pointed to a jewelry store he knew of in the center of town. "Let's not take too long," he told Tracy.

"Why do you think the old man didn't claim Carlos as his before he died?" Tracy asked, not forgetting their conversation.

"I don't know, but the only reason I can come up with is to keep him safe. He kept him close but not out front for someone to take a shot at. It's like Rodolfo taught him the business from the moment he was born, and put Juan out front as his heir almost like an easy target. That might be the reason Juan turned on him in the end even if that was the worst mistake he could've made." He asked the woman in the store where their baby section was, and Tracy chose a rattle and a silver frame they could engrave within the hour. It gave them time to have a cup of coffee.

"That makes sense, and since we have time, tell me about Marisol." Tracy ordered for them both, and he loved that she paid attention to his likes.

"When I met Marisol's mother, I was young and angry at anyone who looked at me too long. I was just coming up, and the rage kept me alive. I'd gotten married, and my wife was already pregnant and demanding. It was like I was suffocating and needed someplace to go where no one wanted anything from me." He twirled his demitasse cup in the saucer and smiled. "The place wasn't cheap, but for a fee I could ask for whatever I wanted, and there were no strings, as you Americans like to say."

"So it was a brothel?" Tracy asked, but she had a wide smile on her face.

One of the things he appreciated about Tracy was the way she understood him. They were lovers, and she worked for him, but if he needed a change of pace, she wasn't the jealous type. "It was, and this one particular girl became my regular. She was fun, sexy, and she seemed to like fucking. I know all prostitutes are supposed to pretend if they're good at their job, but she was either a decent actress or she loved me touching her." She'd been his exclusive girl for six months when she told him something that made him want to kill her. "After all that time she told me she was pregnant, and it was mine."

"Did you believe her?" The way Tracy asked was tactful, but he knew what she was trying to say.

"Did I believe a whore who makes her living on her back when she said that she was carrying my baby?" He didn't like telling this story because it made him sound like a *pendejo*, but it was part of his history. You could deny plenty in your life, but not your history. "No, but I made her a deal if she wanted to continue to claim the baby was mine."

"What was it?"

"I told her that if it was mine, I'd let her live and take the baby and raise it. If she lied, I'd kill her and her bastard as soon as it drew its first breath. That was the best motivation I could give her to tell the truth."

"She obviously didn't back down if Marisol is still with you," Tracy said before taking a sip of her coffee. "And she looks like you, so there's the other piece of proof you needed."

There might be a tinge of jealousy in the way Tracy was talking. This was the first time he'd heard her express that, and it released the small worry he had that perhaps she was only with him for the money and to avenge her sister. "I wasn't an asshole who depended on what the kid looked like. It took a paternity test for me to believe it, and my wife wasn't thrilled she had two babies to raise instead of just ours, but what choice did she have? Marisol came to live with us, but I did allow her mother to see her." Those visits weren't frequent, but he wanted his daughter to know where she came from. "It was a good lesson about where you could end up if you didn't conform."

"Her mother's still alive?" Tracy's smile was back when he took her hand.

"She is and is now the madame at her own place. Like I said, she was a woman who was good at her job, and she's made a good living at it." That bit of truth was hard for Marisol to accept, but he'd tried to teach her that her future was with him. It was a waste of his time to try to teach someone who had too much of her mother in her head.

The woman was successful because she knew how to fuck, but she was still an idiot. "I had more children with my wife, but none of them are ambitious. It's a flaw that will get them all killed if something happens to me. My life and the way I live it aren't something you walk away from. That I am good at what I do is the only reason they are safe."

"But now you're worried," Tracy said, staring at him intently. "Someone targeted you, and we have to do whatever we can to find out who it is. You're a strong man, and I have faith in you to fight until you're back on top."

"What happens if I can't?" he asked, not losing eye contact with her. Women like Tracy were attracted to the power and what you could do with it. She'd left Nunzio Luca's bed and gotten into his because he was the best chance she'd get at carrying out her revenge against Remi Jatibon and Cain Casey.

"We die together." She leaned over and kissed him.

"Even if I won't give you what you want most?" he asked as she settled back. "Cain Casey isn't someone I'm likely to move against."

"I know that, and I've known it from the moment I realized she helped keep you in power. She says she doesn't want to do business with you, but I think she doesn't want to see you fail, either. It's strange."

"Your sister was important to you, and that's something I understand," he said, not wanting to let the subject go. "Sometimes death is the only way to release the pain."

"Kim was my only family, and she died at Casey's order, but it was Nunzio's stupidity that got her killed. Letting go of that is the price I'm willing to pay to be with you." She kissed him again and put her hand over his crotch. "I'm not leaving."

"Good, but don't make promises that might be hard to keep."

"I wouldn't say it if I didn't mean it. I'm loyal to you, and I understand what you need from me. I'll never ask you to give more than you can." Tracy squeezed him enough to get his attention, then let him go.

"Don't you want a family of your own?" She was too young to realize the ramifications of what she was saying, and he was too old to start over with an infant.

"Like I said, Kim was my family, and I never thought about children. Don't worry, I'm not going to trap you with another person you don't want." She laughed and kissed his chin, leaning back when the woman from the jewelry store walked toward them. "Are you done?"

"Sí, señora. We gift wrap for you."

They went back to the store to pay for everything, and Tracy smiled when he added a bracelet to his purchases and put it on her himself. "Never be afraid to ask for the things you want. I might surprise you."

The driver headed out of town, and the ocean side road was beautiful. After a few miles the beach was no longer visible, and on the right side of the road were endless tall walls topped with either broken glass or razor wire. Their driver started to slow at the upcoming gate, and Hector tried to remember the house itself. He'd only been here once, and he'd walked away with a deal that he and Rodolfo would stay out of each other's way.

"Hola, Señor Delarosa," Carlos Luis said as he waited at the bottom of the steps that led up to a wide porch. The gardens were spectacular, and there was an older woman sitting in one of the rockers admiring the view, but really she seemed to be studying him and Tracy.

Carlos held his hand out, and Hector gripped it between his. The one thing he wanted to get across was the desire to become friends. "Thank you for having us," he said in Spanish. "This is my associate, Tracy Stegal."

"I met your sister," Carlos said, then stopped before taking Tracy's hand. "I am sorry, do you speak Spanish?"

"I do," Tracy said with that accent Americans never seemed to lose when learning another language. "You have a beautiful home."

"Gracias, and please come inside. I'd like to introduce my mother, Reyna Santiago."

The older woman didn't stand but did smile at them as she lifted her hand in their direction. It was obvious Rodolfo's cook was living a much better life now that her son had taken over the top spot. They followed Carlos to the back of the house where the glass doors opened to a large pool and a magnificent ocean view. There were enough guards scattered from the beach to the covered patio that anyone would be foolish to try anything.

"This is my wife, Paloma, and our son, Esteban. It was my father's middle name and also the name of Paloma's father."

The beautiful young woman was holding a baby, and she smiled when Tracy handed her the gifts they'd brought. A woman who seemed to be the nanny took the baby, and Paloma opened both boxes. She stood and kissed him and Tracy for their kindness and offered them a drink in Carlos's office inside.

All four of them sat in the beautiful room that still held traces of

Rodolfo. "Please, Señor Delarosa, feel free to tell us what it is you'd like to talk to us about. Paloma is much more than my wife, and I would like her to sit in on this." Carlos handed him a drink, and Paloma handed one to Tracy.

"Then we have something in common. Tracy is much more than my associate, and she is free to answer any questions you have."

"My father would laugh at us for being so evolved," Carlos said and smiled as he lifted his hands. "No?"

"Perhaps that will be the secret to our success," he said, raising his glass. "For me, though, there hasn't been much success lately. Someone has declared war on me but is hiding like a bitch."

"You and my father made a deal to not do business years ago, correct?" Carlos asked. "I'm not asking to insult you, but to refresh my memory."

"Rodolfo and I came up about the same time. He was ahead of me in business and established himself first. He concentrated on Mexico while I grew my business in Colombia. Our deal was safe transport though Mexico until we were on US soil. Other than that, we stayed out of each other's way." He finished his drink and waved Paloma off when she went to reach for his glass.

"That seems to have worked out well for both of us," Carlos said. "These others in the cartel never can accept that there's enough business for everyone."

"You're right, and to get what's mine, someone has destroyed my fields. There's no way I'm giving up what I worked for that easily."

"I think you're right, and if they succeed, it will start a war that will be good for no one. There are men like you and my father, and you made it to the top," Carlos said as Paloma took his hand. "But for every one of you, there are a hundred small dealers who want to kill everything and everyone to get to where you are."

"That's why I'm here." He glanced at Tracy before he said anything else, and she seemed to understand that he was having trouble verbalizing what he wanted.

"Señor Luis—" Tracy said, and Carlos lifted his hand.

"Please, we are friends here. Please call me Carlos."

"Carlos, whatever deal your father had with Hector isn't possible any longer. It's time to build new alliances, because if whoever these—" Tracy stopped and smiled. "I'm sorry, I'm not sure how to say cowards in Spanish."

"*Cobardes*," Paloma said.

"Thank you." Tracy continued in Spanish. "These cowards had the guts to take Hector on today, but I doubt they'll be happy with only that piece of the action if they think they can have it all."

Carlos tilted his head in assent. "The strange thing about all this is how quiet everyone is about what happened. It's almost like the government destroyed your business, but between the both of us, we have enough people in government on our payroll to know that's not what this was. And that means there are powerful people working against you, which puts me in line next." Carlos stood and offered him his hand. "If you want my help, you have it."

"Thank you, and I do need your help," Hector said, feeling like this was the first step to right his world.

"Let's have lunch, and we can finish our talk." Paloma rang a small bell, and they made their way to the veranda.

Reyna was the one who put all the food on the table and left them to their meal. "I should tell you I had a talk with Cain Casey yesterday." Carlos put a tamale on his plate and didn't look up when he spoke.

"You know Cain?" He tried to hide his surprise, but his question gave him away.

"Cain helped me avenge my father, and we are friends, not business partners. Her cousin Colin Mead, though, is a business partner, but he and Cain only have blood in common. I don't think she likes him."

"Who's Colin Mead?" This was like discovering a whole new world, and it made him feel like an idiot. "If you can't answer, I'll understand."

"His partner was Salvatore Maggio. Maggio turned out to be skimming from more than one distributor and was taken care of. Colin took over the business and has been a good partner in moving our product. I still have my dealers, but I don't have to worry about how my stuff gets to where it needs to be once it's in the US."

"I've heard about Maggio, but I never did business with him. My business handles my product from field to the corner dealer." It was interesting that Cain had more than Vinny and Jasper under her protection. How far did her grip reach?

"I'm not telling you anything that Cain wouldn't tell you herself, and I hope you don't mind, but I told her I was meeting with you."

Fantastic. If he hadn't come off as a weak asshole before, that would do it. "That's no problem."

"She called me because she felt Colin had made a misstep, but it was an interesting mistake. One that might benefit us both by knowing."

Carlos smiled at Paloma as she placed a plate in front of him, and Tracy did the same for him. "Colin was approached for his services by Cesar Kalina."

Kalina was a smaller dealer than Hector but still had a sizeable crew. There was no way he had the balls to move against him, but maybe Kalina had lost his mind. "What business did Kalina want to do?" It was interesting that Cain hadn't mentioned any of this.

"He wanted to take advantage of what happened to you by moving more into the US, and he needed help doing that. Colin's only business is moving product, and he's not involved in selling anything. That's a deal he made with Cain, and with me. She'd rather her family, her whole family, stay out of this business, but she didn't want to cut Colin off." Carlos was talented at putting things so they didn't sound patronizing. "If you want my opinion, Kalina wasn't the one who did this to you. He just knows about it and is making use of it."

"Cain didn't mention any of that to me." He didn't want to act like a petulant child, but stumbling around in the darkness was starting to get on his nerves.

"She only found out a day ago, but she hasn't talked to Colin about it. Her call to me was out of respect, and when she has the whole story, she'll let us both know. The meeting with Kalina hadn't happened yet when she was told about it." Carlos picked up his glass of wine and took a sip. "This information is useful going forward, but it doesn't answer the question of who's moving against you."

"Do you have an idea? I've put out enough money to have an answer by now, but…" He shrugged.

"I have no idea, but you're right that we need to form new alliances. This business is full of jackals, and we both have people to protect. By offering my help now, I can count on you to do the same when I need it."

"You have my word on that."

"Then you have mine that I'll return the favor whenever it should be needed."

It was the best deal Hector was going to get, and he almost didn't mind the price he'd have to pay for it. All he wanted was a name, so he could rip their balls off for this. "Thank you, Carlos."

"There is one more thing, and before I say it, please take no insult from it," Carlos said, and Hector was impressed by this guy's backbone.

"I'm here asking for help, so I doubt anything you say will insult me."

"It has to do with your daughter, Marisol."

Those simple words were going to make him regret the decision to bring Marisol into his business, but it was too late to undo his mistakes. "I've cut Marisol out of my business and my life. You have a child now, and with time you'll come to see that they don't always heed your advice. Think of all the time your father spent teaching Juan, and in the end he threw all that away. My hope for you is to never know the betrayal of a child."

"Thank you, and that is my prayer as well. Our future lies with our children, and Paloma and I will work to make sure ours is bright. Marisol made threats against Cain when she partnered with Nicolette Blanc." Carlos appeared dead serious when he stared him down. "Cain is my friend—a friend I owe a great debt to—so I won't tolerate anyone moving against her."

He felt Tracy shift ever so slightly beside him, and he knew what she must be feeling. But they'd talked about it, and it was what it was. "Cain likes to say we aren't friends, but we aren't enemies either. Our lives are separate, but we can coexist and respect each other. As for Marisol, she understands what will happen if she makes any threats or moves against my interests. She's my daughter, but there's no place for rabid dogs in our world, and there never will be."

Carlos's smile held a hint of pity. "Thank you for not taking offense. I believe we too can coexist while building our businesses, but we must remember our friends." Lunch was cleared away, and they declined more drinks, so Carlos called for the driver. "We'll talk again before you head back to New Orleans to iron out our plans. The first thing you need is product, and that we can provide. A shortage will drive up prices, and it'll allow the DEA to strengthen their position against us. No one cares for dead bodies on the streets because we can't get along."

"My people are still in place, and I can pay you for the supply until I get my crops back." This would be the answer to his problems if Carlos had the amount he needed to stay viable.

"Good, then we agree to a long and prosperous arrangement." Carlos shook his hand again and walked them to the door. "If you need anything tonight, please call me. I'll see you both tomorrow."

"Thank you for everything, and we're looking forward to it."

Hector waited until they were in their hotel suite to shed the happy facade, and he savagely pulled at his tie to get it off. There was nothing worse in life than to be scolded like a misbehaving schoolboy by a man who was no more than a boy himself. All of it because Marisol couldn't follow fucking directions.

"You knew this wasn't going to be easy, and it only has to last as long as it takes to regrow those fields," Tracy said as she rubbed his shoulders. "This will keep us in business so we can find out who tried to destroy you and kill them."

"You don't understand. I gave my word, and reneging on it will destroy me faster than everything that's happened to us. Once the fields are viable again, I'll have to cut a new deal." He sat and closed his eyes when she increased the pressure of her massage. "I did this to survive, but Carlos will expect me to abide by what I promised, and I will. Today we got attacked, but there's no saying it won't happen again. Those fields won't grow overnight."

"Next time we'll be ready," Tracy said, kissing the side of his neck. "And if we make an example of who tried this time, there may not be a next time."

"Let's hope."

CHAPTER SEVENTEEN

Remi was waiting for Cain when they finished with the asshole who'd set up the hit on the club that hurt Josh. She had Mano with her, and he smiled when she walked in with Lou. "Sorry to run off on you when we got here, but I wanted to check on Josh."

"Any news on that front?" Remi asked.

"Someone paid to be told when someone would be in the pub to set up the hit. They didn't care who as long as they worked for me. I need one more piece of that puzzle, and that'll lead us to the bank. Sounds like someone poured a little cash among some little minds, and it did wonders." She pointed to the kitchen where Muriel's housekeeper said dinner was waiting.

"So you don't think it's Nicola?" Mano asked.

"I could be reading her wrong, but this doesn't strike me as something she'd be behind. If I'm right, she's waiting for us to be out in the open and weak before she makes her move." All the Chinese she ordered was in the oven, and Lou went to get plates. "We need to find her before that happens because none of us wants to spend months looking over our shoulders. But the request for information out there, the hit on the pub...someone else is after us. Not just her."

"I might have some news on that front," Mano said as he handed her a file. "Finley went through Nicola's information and found Sacha Oblonsky. The FBI doesn't know if Oblonsky is Nicola's cousin, but he's made quite a few moves to take over the family. Seems a likely prospect."

"I wonder how hard Mr. Oblonsky is to get in touch with, and can we do it quietly?" she asked.

"I don't know about quietly. He's become the focus of the feds now that the Eaton family is dead. They finally connected that the Eaton name was just a front for the Antakov family. After the shooting in New Orleans, our friends in gray knew exactly what they were about." Mano opened the file and showed her the guy's picture.

Abigail was right—he was a scary-looking dude. "The bastards didn't even send us a thank-you note for opening that pit that was the Hell Fire Club," she joked as they sat to eat. "Has Oblonsky taken over? I don't want to waste time on him if not."

"The family seems torn, but he's got the upper hand by claiming to be the next in line to David Eaton. He'll have some rebuilding to do if he does land on top. The FBI and local authorities have shut down every business they had, according to the information Linda Bender gave them," Mano said.

"We all know that there are the things we own in our own names, and the things buried under layers of bullshit that will never be found in this lifetime," Cain said. "The Antakov family hasn't been this successful without putting some safeguards in place. We either have to find what those businesses might be or wait for Nicola to show herself and put a bullet in her head before she gets to one of us. Once she's dead, I doubt Oblonsky or anyone in the organization will be interested in Abigail or us."

"She's buried all that, so finding it will be impossible," Mano said. "But you're right. If we can get rid of Oblonsky's biggest problem, he might actually owe us a favor."

"It'll take time, but it'll be a good way to find the new and improved Nicola. She's had to leave that name and identity behind. Who is she now?" Her cell rang, the burner that Finley had given her. "Give me a minute."

She walked to the front of the house and glanced out the window. It was nice to not see anyone waiting in the shadows hoping to hear a conversation she shouldn't be having or doing something that would give them the excuse they were waiting for.

"Hi, honey," Emma said.

"Hey, lass, I'm sorry for not calling sooner. We got some news on Josh, and I was working through that." She sat on the sofa and dropped her head back. "The bastard with Jimmy got paid to make a call."

"Please tell me Jimmy wasn't that stupid." Emma sounded mad and it made her smile.

"He got shot too and still managed to pull Josh to safety. That might get him the job with some heavy supervision." She could hear the others in the kitchen, but she concentrated on Emma. "Are you doing okay?"

"I miss you, but the kids are wild and keeping us busy. Once we get them to go to sleep, we might open some wine and talk about our better halves."

"I'm sure Muriel and Finley will love that since they're still there. Go easy on me." The way Emma laughed made her miss their nights together. She was getting softer by the minute.

"Finley and Muriel are banned but I doubt they'd notice. Both of them have been working since you left, and there might be a mutiny soon because of your taskmaster ways."

"Tell the girls it's for a good cause, so go easy on them too."

"You'll find them in the same condition you left them, but I'm sure there's going to be some lessons taught. It's best not to ask questions." Emma laughed again, and Cain was glad Emma had friends to share time with. "I didn't want to bother you, but I wanted to hear your voice. Call me in the morning, okay?"

"I will, and the good bottles are at the bottom of the wine cooler." She paused and heard Emma exhale. "I love you, lass."

"I love you too, so tell Lou to keep a good eye on you."

She hung up and pressed the phone to her chin, thinking. It was still early enough to get something done, and she was hoping Dino's crew had found Lizard.

"Everything okay?" Remi asked, leaning against the doorway.

"Emma was just checking in. They're about to have a girls' night, which means God help us when we get back." They laughed and went back to the kitchen. "Let's get back to what we were talking about," she said, going back to her plate. "We have two leads to get more information on Nicola, but one is in the wind. Oblonsky, though, might be open to a meeting if we dangle a carrot for him."

"If you want, me and Papi can take care of that," Mano said.

"That would be good. It's simple for him. Once Nicola reappears from the grave, she's going to demand what she believes is hers. How successful she'll be depends on how the family falls out. Her father was an asshole, which means he made enemies even within his ranks." She glanced at Oblonsky's picture again and thought of this asshole with a number of young women under his thumb.

"The whole business is disgusting." Dino spoke up, then ducked his head and stared at his food.

She smiled and was glad he had the same makeup as Lou. Speaking your mind wasn't always a wise move, and he seemed to realize that after the words had come out. He was smart enough to stop talking, but his head was in the right place. "You're right. The fact that the guys follow *us* around all day, hoping to catch us doing something that'll justify their existence, makes me laugh. Liquor and cigarettes are what we do. There's no one being held against their will, and I'm not asking anyone to degrade themselves so I can live a good life. They're watching the wrong people."

"That's what I'm talking about," Dino said. "Finley showed me some of the pictures from the day she met Abigail. They killed all those women because one of them sent out a text message. That's sick."

"It's good incentive for all of us to concentrate on finding Nicola. Any luck on Lizard?"

"Lizard?" Remi asked, laughing. "That's the best nickname he could come up with?"

"Maybe someone gave it to him, and we can put him out of his misery once he tells us who paid him." They all laughed, and Dino seemed more at ease.

"My guys asked around, and he's working on some project uptown. Once they finish for the night, they'll ask him to come over for a talk," Dino said.

"Good, then let's finish here, and we'll take a ride later." She pushed her plate aside and glanced at Remi. "Has Brandi had any problems?"

"There's been someone chatting up her girls about a better opportunity, but no concrete promises have been made," Remi said. "I added some muscle to the guys you left over there."

"Good. Brandi and the people who work for her deserve to be left alone."

They finished dinner and talked about business and the casino until the call came from Dino's crew. He was about to drive them back to the office when her cell rang again. Something had to have happened for Emma to call twice. "Lass?"

"Hey, I wanted you to know that Nathan called and needs to talk to you. Don't worry, he followed all of Fin's directions, but he wouldn't tell me what he found. He did tell me he misses me," Emma said.

"Nathan's about to swap all those fancy clothes for a hospital gown," she said as Emma gave her the number. "Thanks, and this might bring me back sooner than I planned."

"I can't complain about that, and if it does, I owe Nathan a kiss."

"Let's not make it so I have to kill the little guy. He might be handy in the future." She promised to call as soon as she talked to Nathan.

"Want us to take care of this guy you've got waiting?" Remi asked. "Sounds like something might've panned out."

She could trust them to get the information she wanted. "Would you mind? If Nathan found Linda Bender where he thought she was, we need to head back as soon as we can."

Remi took Mano and Dino and called to make sure the plane was ready to fly whenever they were done.

"Nathan," she said when he answered. "Thanks for getting back to me so fast."

"I think speed is the best thing in this case, Cain." Nathan sounded echoey, and it made her pause.

"Where are you?" If this little guy had double-crossed her, she was going to bury him in one of his loud suits.

"Sorry, I'm in my workroom, and it makes the reception sound funny. If you like I can come to you and give you this in person, but I think someone else is getting close to the woman you want." Nathan didn't seem like the type to turn, but you never knew what people were capable of until they were cornered.

"I do want to meet, but give me a location and a name. If she's in danger, it's time to pick her up and offer her some help."

"She's in Wisconsin," Nathan said, giving her the town. "The woman you're looking for is Lorna Green." He gave her an address and phone number, and she hoped this was the right person. "Someone accessed her information along with six other women who fit the profile of who I was searching for. Hopefully, they haven't narrowed it down yet. And no, I couldn't tell who else was looking. Just that they were."

"Are you sure she's the one?" After hearing what Linda had done and why she'd taken her brothers, she was willing to buy her freedom. "I'm not questioning your ability."

"You kind of are," Nathan said, chuckling.

"What I mean is, I don't want to pick wrong, and Linda gets killed because we missed."

"I know, and don't worry about it. If I'm wrong, it'll weigh on my conscience, but I'm not wrong. You need to get to her and convince her to move before someone less friendly comes along."

"Thanks, Nathan, and I'll call you as soon as I find her. Once we talk, she'll need your help to truly set her free." She glanced at all the information she'd written down and hoped he was right. Linda's reward for what she'd turned over to the feds shouldn't be hours of torture before she got a bullet to the head.

"I'm ready, and I'll make sure she'll never be found."

"He found her?" Lou asked when she hung up and folded the paper to put in her pocket.

"He did, but it sounds like he's not the only one. We need to leave as soon as possible." She glanced at her watch. If they left in the next few hours, they could head toward Linda and reach her before sunrise. "Remi shouldn't take too long, so we'll fly after that." She called Emma and told her what Nathan had said. Emma was familiar with the area, and it was a miracle that Linda had landed an hour's drive from them.

"Do you think Linda held something back from the FBI?" Lou asked.

"She wasn't in a position to need a favor," she said as she sat in Muriel's study. The pictures of her father and uncle were sitting on the desk, and she had to smile at the expressions on their faces. It didn't seem that long ago that she sat in their room and listened to the two brothers tease each other and laugh at all their memories of growing up. "You only give up the house when you need a favor."

"So why she'd do it?"

"There's nothing better in life when you need to run than to blow what's making you run all to hell. What Linda did rocked the business to its core, but it wasn't completely destroyed. In the chaos of the blast, though, she ran somewhere she thought no one would ever find her." The front door opened, and she stood. Remi walked in with Mano and Dino and they all appeared frustrated. "Did he not say anything?" She found that hard to believe—if they questioned Lizard in the right way.

"He said plenty, but it's going to take a few more of these meetings to make any sense of what that idiot said." Remi twirled a cigar between her fingers, and she sounded angry. "Whoever ordered this put a doberge cake of layers between them and the two idiots we talked to. It was a low-level dealer who hired him, and it wasn't one of Jasper's. My gut tells me that we're going to go through a few levels before we get to what we want to know."

"We're going to have to put that off for now. Nathan came through, and Linda Bender is closer than you're going to believe." She explained what Nathan had said and what he was afraid of as they drove back to the airport. "Katlin," she said, making one more call before they took off. "I need you to take a drive." She gave Katlin the address and name

Nathan had provided. "I'm coming back, and I don't want to take the chance that someone beats us there."

"I'll take Merrick with me, and we'll sit on her until you get back. Are you driving out there tonight?" Katlin always sounded ready to go.

"That'll depend on you. I'll call you when we land, and if Linda's still up, I'll head your way and try to talk her into coming back with us."

"I'll wait to hear from you, and I hope it's her. Abigail deserves to be done with all this."

"It's not like we're giving up, cousin. Not until Nicola's truly dead."

"Make sure you let me know if you find out anything," Jerome Rhodes said as he scanned the street outside the house he'd rented in the French Quarter. He'd made a few contacts in town, and some of the players who moved product from Mexico to New York had been in touch. All he had to do now was sit and wait to make sure the people he decided to do business with would be the best fit.

"Yes, the man you need to talk to call you," Pablo said.

Pablo was on the east side of New Orleans, and from his description not much of the area had been rebuilt or even touched after the storm. That had made it a perfect place for drug dealers to squat and carry on their business with very little police interference. The flooded-out houses had also become a haven for users to squat in and get high, ignoring the mold-ridden interiors, and the only way they moved to the next place was when the stench of death became overwhelming.

"Forget about that for now, and get back here. I have an appointment with someone else in an hour, and I don't have time to mess with something that small." The street was fairly deserted, and the only person he saw walking around was the mailman. The guy appeared miserable enough to make him believe he really was a postal worker.

"I know, señor, but you should call. The man, he sound mad."

"Call back and tell him to give me two hours."

His father came in as he was finishing his call and sat in one of the leather chairs. The house had come furnished, and the antiques and high-quality furniture made him want to buy the place. The luxury was something he thought he deserved. It wasn't going to take him much time before he'd have so much money he would have to think of new ways to spend it.

"Problems?" his father asked when he ended the call.

"Pablo is worked up about some nobody that called. I hope he'll learn that we can't bow down to anyone." He had an important meeting in an hour, and he really needed to calm down before the guy got there. To do that he needed that teak box that he'd inherited from Gracelia. There was no way he was going to do that in front of his father, so he poured himself a drink instead. "He does good work, but Pablo is a nervous little guy."

"Don't put him down too much," his father said, shaking his head when he went for another drink. "You'll need people around you that you can count on."

"Why don't you call him and take care of this?" The excuse would get his father out of the house until he was done with his day. "Once you're finished, we'll meet for dinner."

"Are you sure you don't need me here?" He appeared hesitant to go.

"This guy who's coming is the nervous type too, and he'll feel more comfortable if we don't have a crowd here. I'll be okay, and we have enough people in the house that nothing is going to happen to me." He was glad when his dad stood and nodded. He waited until he saw the car carrying his dad pull away before he unlocked the safe in the bedroom and opened the box full of coke.

Pablo was good about filling it once they were on the northern side of the border and never spoke of it. He checked himself in the mirror once he was done to make sure there was no powder left on his face. The kick was immediate, and it was almost like the world had regained its color and beauty. This was the best thing Gracelia had introduced him to and the reason he'd kept her box. It was the only thing that would tie them together, and the only thing worth remembering.

"Señor Rhodes," the guard who'd been on post in the kitchen said, "your guest is early, but he asked if you're ready."

"Send him up." He took a deep breath and held it to get a grip on his nerves. The man who followed the guard in was tall and bulky, and his face held traces of redness usually associated with someone who'd been drinking for years. "Thank you for coming, Mr. Mead. It's good to meet you."

Colin Mead stared at his hand before shaking it. "I'm not sure what you've heard about me, but I don't talk to people I don't know. How about you tell me what's on your mind." Mead sat down and stared at him like he was trying to decide the best way to kill him for taking up his valuable time.

"My home is in Cabo San Lucas, and I'm in a delicate business that could use your expertise to get my merchandise over the border. Once it's across, I'll need transport to New York, Chicago, Tampa, Phoenix, Seattle, and here. If that's something you can do, we'll talk numbers." He opened the humidor on the coffee table and offered Colin a cigar, but he waved him off.

"First of all, tell me how you got my name. I'm only in town for the day and have a few clients to see."

His abrupt tone was irritating, but at least there was no preamble. "Your name was given to me by an acquaintance. Hector Delarosa said that if he was in the market for someone to act as his carrier, you'd be his first choice. He's having some trouble right now, so we'll pick up the slack until he's back to full production." It was all a lie—there was no way this guy did business with Delarosa. The cartels who kept him busy would prohibit him from talking to anyone else, but with the promise of enough money he'd take transporting product off his to-do list. "If we can come to an agreement, I give you my word it'll be mutually beneficial."

"And you'd do business with someone you've never heard of? I'm sorry, Rhodes, but what you're talking about comes with some stiff penalties if you get caught working with the wrong people." Colin leaned forward and placed his hands on his knees. "And if you're legit, you might want to think about having someone introduce you. Cold calls aren't going to go over well with anyone, and if you ask the wrong person, it can get you killed."

"Are you threatening me?" He thought about what consequences there would be for shooting this asshole for his disrespect.

"Not at all. Call it free advice. This is a private club, so you're going to need a reference." Colin laughed and it only made him madder.

"I just gave you a reference. Considering it's the head of the cartel, that should carry some weight."

"Hector is bleeding to death, and we've never done business. He doesn't know my name. If you're a cop, go ahead and write that down, so you don't forget it." Colin leaned farther in.

"Why'd you come if you weren't interested? This has been a waste of time."

This was going to put a nail in his plan, but Mead was the only one he remembered from his FBI days. He was just getting into the business when he'd left, and he didn't have the whole story on him. Mead was out of their jurisdiction since the guy was in California. There wasn't much known about him back then, but from what he understood, he'd carved out a niche of the market because he was good.

"I was curious, that's all. You're getting into a dangerous business at a volatile time, Mr. Rhodes. If you're starting like this, you aren't going to last long enough to finish one of your fine cigars." Colin stood and buttoned his jacket.

"You aren't going to talk about what I have in mind?" There was no reason not to give this fucker another chance. If he turned it down, it would give him the excuse to take the asshole out the first opportunity he got.

"Come back with some mutual friends and I'll be happy to. Until then, good luck. You're going to need it." Colin walked away without offering his hand and didn't look back.

"Goddammit," he yelled when he watched the big man get into a car parked out front. "You're going to be sorry you treated me like a punk." He headed back to his box and took another snort. "I'm going to fucking burn you to the ground." It was something he was going to add to his list, along with taking Casey down.

CHAPTER EIGHTEEN

Emma poured four glasses of wine and laughed at the story Abigail was telling them. They'd put all the kids in the den for a slumber party. Her conversation with Cain earlier had left her tense, but the night was starting to chip away at that.

"I'm telling you, the woman couldn't believe little boys could pee as far as hers did. I had to explain that you had to place the diaper immediately over his wee-wee. She also had a problem saying penis," Abigail said, laughing as she chopped vegetables for a salad. "People are strange, and then they have children so they can perpetuate their strangeness."

"Hayden was the worst, but Cain thought it was hilarious. She's had a little practice now that Billy's come along." She set the table as Kristen smiled and stirred something she was cooking on the stove. Emma never realized how much the sisters looked alike despite one being a brunette and the other blond. "You can laugh, girl, but you just wait," she said, pointing at Kristen.

"I tell Muriel I want kids now, and it'll put her into a catatonic state. She wastes lots of time every day thinking about the age difference, and I'm not about to whack her over the head about it."

"I think it's sweet," Dallas said, and Kristen threw a towel at her.

"Yes, it's so sweet when your girlfriend suggests that maybe you should be out sowing your oats. It's a pain in my ass, but it's about to become a pain in her ass."

"Muriel has always been a thinker, but if it helps, the way she looks at you when you don't realize is telling," Emma said, handing Kristen a glass. "I doubt anything going through her head has anything to do with you being with anyone else. If it helps, both Dallas and I went through the same thing but for a different reason."

"Oh yes, and if you're smart you'll do whatever Emma tells you. I did, and I ended up with a ring and my dream partner," Dallas said, kissing her sister's cheek. "The only one here who has superpowers to hypnotize the perfect woman for her is Abigail. Finley fell to her knees and into line the second they met."

"Please, that pout of hers makes me want to stand on my head to make her happy. It's good to know that I got it right the second time around. I didn't think I could be this happy," Abigail said, and Dallas kissed her cheek too. "I'm sorry if I put you guys in danger because of all my shit."

"Believe me, you're marrying into the best problem-solving, danger-prone family in the history of the world," Emma said as they sat down. "Do you mind if I ask where you met Nicola?"

"I was at Tulane, and I saw her one afternoon when I stopped for coffee. She was nice looking and she was charming, at first. She was a lot different than anyone else I'd dated, and I see now that after a few dates, she became much more demanding. A year later we were married, and I was in medical school." Abigail stopped to take a sip of wine, and none of them said anything. "After Sadie was born, I got wrapped up in her, and that made me stupid to everything else. Two more kids, a medical practice, and I totally missed that I was married to a pimp."

"Honey, you need to forgive yourself. I doubt any of us would've been any different. When we fall in love, we don't tend to see the bad in them," Dallas said.

"My second mistake was thinking Finley and her family weren't going to be a good idea."

"I'm glad she was able to convince you. I got in by pouring a tray of beer on Cain and not sleeping with her for a year. Sometimes I think I wore her down by turning her head to mush," she said to lighten the mood and make Abigail feel better.

"A year?" Kristen asked. "I'm surprised you didn't kill her."

"If you ask her, it almost did." They laughed and all got up when Dallas declared everything was ready.

There was a knock, and Finley stuck her head in. "Is it safe to come in?"

"No, and if you wake up any of the kids, I'm going to bury you in the snow outside," Abigail said as she kissed Finley's cheek.

"I'm just here to let you know Remi and Cain should be home in three hours, but they've got an errand to run when they land." All of them stared at Finley as if daring her to skip the details.

"Errand?" Emma asked. "Come on, Fin…"

"They think they found Linda Bender, and she's not that far away. According to that guy Nathan—"

"We're not the only ones looking for her," Emma finished for her. If Cain was going to meet with this woman, she wanted to go, but she trusted Remi to handle it.

"Yeah, so it might be a good idea for all of us to spend the night in the main house. That was Cain's idea, and since the kids were already here, that shouldn't be too hard to do." Finley kissed Abigail again and waved as she stepped away from her. "I'll leave you to dinner and pick one of the rooms upstairs."

"Try Hayden's at the end of the hall to the right," Emma said as Abigail reached out and touched Finley one more time before she went upstairs. "That's good news," she said, lifting her glass, "and it deserves a toast."

"To all our great tomorrows. We all deserve peace and love," Dallas said.

They ate and tried to stay away from any deeper subjects. It was fun and something they planned to do often even when they were back home. The fact that they could be open without fear of retribution or betrayal was freeing. Emma understood now why Remi and Vinny had been such important friends to Cain when she was growing up.

Kristen was laughing at Abigail's description of Finley and her first experiences with her children when the house phone rang. It wouldn't be Cain, and she couldn't imagine who else would call this late. "Hello," she said motioning for the others to go on up without her. They were going to finish their wine in the sitting area of the master bedroom to enjoy the view and not disturb the kids.

"Emma?" a man said, but she couldn't place the voice.

"Yes, who is this?" Her question stopped Dallas and she walked back to her.

"Sorry, this is Levi Layke from Hannah's school."

Having Levi call her in Wisconsin this late was like finding out you were related to Bigfoot. It was unbelievable in a bizarre sort of way, and it spelled nothing but trouble. Emma took a breath and greeted him. "Levi, hi," she said glancing at Dallas. "Are you enjoying your break?"

"I was, until I got a call from the security company at the school.

You know I wouldn't bother you unless it was important, but I think Cain is going to want to hear this." Levi, as always, sounded like a nervous puppy in fear of a beating. "Can I talk to her?"

"She's out at one of the cabins playing cards with her friends. What's this about? It's okay to tell me, and I'll give her the message."

"We had a recent talk about Abigail Eaton and her daughters. Cain told me how important they are to her, and if something strange happened, or someone came by trying to remove them, to make her the second call after the police."

The clip of Levi's words made her want to sit down. It couldn't be horrible news, though—Abigail and her kids were with them. "They're good friends," Emma said, "and Cain was worried about them after what happened to them in New York a few months back." She pinched her forehead and wanted to rush Levi, but she needed the whole story and for him to understand how much Cain meant what she'd said. "I'm not sure if Cain told you, but someone tried to kill Abigail and take her kids."

"Believe me, Emma, we learned our lesson with Hannah. It'll take an act of God to get a child out of here, but I understood where Cain was coming from."

"Good," she said, moving the phone so Dallas could listen in. "What does that have to do with why you're calling?"

"There was a trigger of our alarm system a few days ago," Levi said, and she and Dallas looked at each other. "The police came out and walked the perimeter of the building. There were no broken windows and no apparent forced entry, so they figured it was a false alarm, and the security company reset the alarm."

"But you don't think that?"

Levi hesitated, but he started talking when she cleared her throat. "I was out for a few days visiting my brother and got the message when I got back. You guys were the main contributors to the alarm system, and it's sophisticated enough that I doubted it triggered accidentally. Today I walked every inch of the school and found something that Cain needs to know about."

"Tell me, Levi," she said ready for the end.

"It wasn't anything like vandalism, but in Sadie Eaton's classroom someone crumpled some of her work and threw it on the ground. That made me call Victoria's teacher, and we went through her work. The picture she did of her family is missing from her room's bulletin board, and it's the only one that's missing." Levi stopped and took an audible breath. "I checked their files in the office, and they're missing too. That had all their information on it."

"Abigail put their home address on that paperwork?" If she had, they should've reconsidered that.

"Just a PO box, but Finley Abbott's contact information was on it too. And the name change in progress for the kids. If this puts them in any danger, please tell Cain to watch out for them. I emailed the video footage we got. The police have it as well."

"Thanks, Levi, I will. Please leave your phone on, and answer if Cain needs to talk to you. If you don't mind calling Sept Savoie and sending her a copy of that video, I'd appreciate it." She hung up and squeezed the phone when Dallas pressed their shoulders together. "Fuck," she said. The last thing she wanted to do was tell Abigail and Finley this.

"Fuck indeed, but you have to tell them," Dallas said as if reading her mind.

"Let's go." They climbed the stairs and she went to Hayden's room before facing Abigail. She was going to need the support.

"What's wrong?" Finley said, looking up from her laptop.

"Come on, I only want to say this once." They entered her bedroom. "Levi Layke just called us," she said, telling them the whole story. "Let's take a look at who this is." They all followed her to the office next door. She'd wanted Cain close when she was working from home so she could remind her to take a break, and she'd furnished the room with some things from home to make her comfortable.

She opened Cain's computer and put in her password. They all squeezed together behind her and watched as four people moved throughout the school as if not worried about anything. Abigail put her hand on her shoulder as if needing to steady herself when she watched the tall woman stare at the picture Victoria had done before crushing it in her hand and tossing it away.

"Nicola. Oh my God, Fin, we need to call my parents." Abigail turned and spoke in a loud panicked tone. "If she looks into you, she's going to use them to get to us."

"The house is listed under a dummy company that has so many layers it'll take years to wade through them, but you're right. I'd feel better if they left and went somewhere safer." Finley put her arms around Abigail and held her as she started crying.

"I'll send one of the guys to pick them up and bring them to our house. That's where you two and the kids will be staying until this is over," Emma said, putting a hand on each of their shoulders. "This is the proof we needed that she's close, but there's no reason to make it easy on her."

"She's never going to stop until she's dead," Abigail said, and the anger overtook her tears. "Damn her, she's never going to stop."

"Baby, listen to what Emma is saying. Why do you think I left the bureau and came back to my family?" Finley cupped Abigail's face and gently shifted so she could look at her. "I want to keep you safe, without you having to give up your life."

"All I want is you, the kids, and to be happy. Is that too much to ask?" Abigail's question was so laced with misery, that it made Emma sad.

"No, it isn't, and none of this is your fault. How in the world would you have known what Nicola was before you got together with her if she kept that side of her a secret?" Emma hoped Abigail would start asking herself that question enough times that she'd finally start to understand she bore no blame. "Cain isn't someone who abides by the law, but she was up-front about who she was. She gave me the chance to either accept it or walk away."

"So was Remi. She and Cain both let us make that decision," Dallas said. She reached over and took her sister's hand. "That's the same decision you and Kristen are going to have to make, but at least you get to make it. The women we love aren't hiding behind the facade of a fake name and a fake life."

"I know, and in my head I know you're right about all of it. My heart, though, was broken from the moment someone shot at me in the street because they wanted my children." Abigail rested her head on Finley's shoulder. "They wanted my children to keep this disgusting business going."

"With any luck, they'll be interested in computers instead," Emma said, and Abigail finally smiled.

"I have a feeling Sadie will be more interested in helping Hayden run the family business. She's got a huge crush for someone who's too young to know what the hell a big crush is."

"You've got years to worry about that, but think of how gorgeous our grandbabies would be," Emma teased her, and Abigail moved from Finley and hugged her.

"Thank you for everything. I'd have gone nuts by now without your family."

"This is your family too. That ring on your finger means you willingly decided to join, and Cain takes that commitment to family to heart."

"Thank God for that," Abigail said, squeezing her one more time before letting go.

"Well, the FBI thinks of her more as the devil incarnate, but *I* think she's heaven-sent." She picked up the phone again and called Cain, but she didn't answer, meaning she was tied up with something. Cain wasn't in the habit of ignoring her. "As soon as I get in touch with her, we'll put something in place to find Nicola and finish this. You deserve peace and a happy future, and I plan to give it to you."

❖

"The guy I put on this narrowed it to eleven locations," Nina said.

Nicola sat in her apartment with her eyes closed, trying to will the headache away, but nothing was working. She didn't have time to take the medication the doctor had prescribed since it knocked her on her ass for about ten hours. The meeting with Sacha had only made it worse, and she was waiting for his retaliation. That would be the excuse she'd use when she cleaned house and started over. All this waiting and planning was getting on her nerves.

"Eleven locations?" She cracked an eye open and stared at Nina. Svetlana wasn't ready and would never be as good as Nina, but Nina was starting to slip. "Are you being serious by bringing me a list that long?"

"Things like this take time, but he's certain that Linda is one of these people. When she ran, she did a good job of hiding her tracks." Nina placed the list on the coffee table and sat across from her, but on the edge of the chair like she was nervous. "He wanted to know if you thought any one place would be better to start with. Linda's your family, after all."

"Linda *was* my family. She decided to kill off the person I knew, so now she's just my next target." She grimaced when she reached for the paper and glanced at it before putting it down beside her, not wanting to move again. "California is a good place to get lost in." She spoke softly to minimize the pain, but she felt like someone was jabbing an icepick in steady intervals. "That's where I'd start."

"That's what I thought you'd say, but we did get some information from our contact about Cain Casey. Her wife is from some small town in Wisconsin where her father owns a dairy farm."

"How quaint," she said, making a motion for Nina to lower her voice.

"It seems strange to me that Casey would've gone for someone like that, but it matters now because one of the names on the list is in a town in Wisconsin about an hour away from Casey's father-in-law's farm."

"Fuck!" She pressed the heel of her hand to her head when she screamed. "That can't be a coincidence. Get someone there now, and tell them if they let her slip away again, I'll kill the lot of them."

"That's what I thought, but I didn't want to give the order until I checked with you." Nina made a phone call and gave Zoya Levin the information.

Nicola loved that it was Zoya going. There was no way Zoya needed a lot of hints as to what had to happen. She'd bring Linda and her brothers back so she could kill Linda slowly and painfully.

"She'll charter a plane if she has to, but she'll get there."

"Good. Anything else?" She wanted to lie down and sleep for an hour to see if that helped.

"Just one question. If Linda is that close to Casey, it makes me think it's not a coincidence," Nina whispered. "My question is, though, how did Casey know anything about Linda to help her?"

"That's a good question, and we'll add that to the list I have. Stay and take the couch if you want to, but I've got to sleep for a little while. Wake me, though, if you get any more news."

"Will do," Nina said, appearing concerned when Nicola had trouble getting up. "Is there anything I can get you?"

"Tell your guy not to ease up on Boris. I want him found so I can hand him his dick once I rip it from his body. I'll follow that by ripping his heart out of his chest."

"I remind him of that every time I talk to him." Nina followed her into the bedroom and pulled the covers back for her. "I'll call you in a few hours, but really, why not try to sleep for the rest of the night? You can trust Zoya to take care of anything and come back here."

"Fine, but keep me in the loop. Don't wait until morning if something comes up."

She took deep breaths until the pounding receded to a throb, and her mind filled with images of Abigail. The woman she'd chosen to have her children had been mesmerizing in college. Her blond hair and blue eyes attracted her from the first time she'd seen her, and Abigail had been easily swayed. It hadn't taken much effort on her part to get her into bed, and that had been more of a test to see if she'd get easily bored once they were in the same house together.

The day they'd had the ceremony, Nicola knew Abigail was in love with her. She didn't waste time on that kind of emotion except when it came to her family, but she gave Abigail credit for finishing medical school and her residency with a toddler and a baby. They'd have to have one more until they had a boy, but children disgusted her even when they were hers.

They were a compromise to who she was and what was expected of her. It was her responsibility to keep the Antakov line going, and she was glad to have Fredrick. He was responsible for the conception, but the children were hers, and everyone knew and accepted that. Her brother had been her double in every sense except for his sex. They were raised together, and they'd shared one mindset. It was their job to grow the operation and crush anyone who stood in their way.

There were perks to the family business. She liked fucking and demanded someone whose job it was to fulfill her every desire, in or out of bed. That the world wanted to punish them for this was idiotic. Her father always said there were people born to rule and people born to serve. It was the law of nature, and if you didn't understand that, it meant you were born a sheep.

Abigail's body before the kids was something she'd enjoyed, but the ravages of pregnancy were hard to hide. In the end she'd felt more of a desire to choke the life out of her wife than any desire to touch her.

"When I find you, I might ignore all the flaws and fuck you one more time before I kill you. That'll be your final lesson that you're mine, and no one else is allowed to touch you." She'd do it in front of Finley Abbott to show her the mistake she'd made in getting involved. "Once you see me fuck Abigail, I'm going to put a bullet through your head."

It surprised her, but the headache had gotten better. "Finding the two of you should be the cure," she said and laughed.

CHAPTER NINETEEN

"You think this woman is armed?" Remi asked as she put her guns on before they landed.

"I would be," Cain said as they started their descent. "Bender has to know that if Nicola catches up to her, she's dead. The sad part is her death will come with the blessing of Linda's mother, who wants her sons back." She yawned as she finished her coffee, knowing they had plenty to do before she'd get home to Emma and the kids. "My mum would've never sacrificed one of her children no matter what we'd done."

"It cements what we've thought about these people all along. They're proud of who they are, which will make this a nightmare until it's done." Remi put her jacket back on and sat next to her to buckle her seat belt. "The one good thing that's come of this is we'll be family if Kristen and Muriel work out."

"I owe you for finding Dallas. Who knew back then that her sister would be the cure for Muriel's heartbreak?"

"She's still thinking about that fed?" Remi seemed surprised.

"Shelby is dead and buried as far as Muriel is concerned. No, I'm talking about the death of my uncle Jarvis. The way things ended was rough on her because she thinks he died being disappointed and angry with her." She took a breath and made eye contact with Remi. "Trust her to treat Kristen the way you'd want her treated. The way I saw it, Muriel needed someone who'd lower a ladder into that dark pit she'd dug for herself, and Kristen had enough courage to do that."

"You know how protective I am of them. I don't know anyone who had a rougher start than Dallas and her sister, and now all I want is for them to never know that kind of fear again." Remi closed her eyes for a moment.

Cain knew Dallas's history. She'd done what she'd had to do to keep Kristen safe. "The sacrifices Dallas made for her little sister are something I admire. You'll do what you have to in order for all that to stay buried for her, and Muriel will do the same for Kristen." She offered Remi her hand and smiled when she took it. "And I'll make you a deal—the liquor is on me for both weddings."

"That I'll hold you to. I'm at my limit with all these plans, but I keep my mouth shut no matter what. She's having the time of her life planning with Emma, and that gives me all the patience I need." Remi laughed, and the captain announced they'd be on the ground in a few minutes.

She took her burner phone out and called Katlin. "Are you there?"

"We got here a few hours ago, but the house is quiet. They're not in there, and I'm not going out looking in case I miss them." Katlin spoke in a soft tone as if the neighbors would hear her. "This town isn't much, and I'm shocked no one's called the cops with us sitting out here. You know how these small towns are."

"That's one of the things I love about Haywood. Strangers don't blend in. They either know you, or they don't." The wheels hit the tarmac, and she pressed her feet into the floor as the pilot bled off speed. "Take off and use the binoculars. If you're too close, you're going to spook her when she comes back from wherever she is."

"Okay," Katlin said, and Cain heard the engine start. "Are you on the ground?"

"We just landed, so we'll be about a half hour. Call me when she gets back." They came down the stairs of the plane and waved to Jerry. The man who'd married Emma's best friend in her hometown was a good man who didn't ask a lot of questions. "Hey, thanks for doing this."

"I had to almost tie Maddie to keep her at home when I drove off. She thinks I'm out having fun without her." Jerry's dually truck was beat-up, but that's what they needed. The fastest way to get people to call the police was to appear slick. "I brought my gun in case you need some more backup."

"Thanks, but I'm hoping this is a simple conversation," she said, smiling at his enthusiasm. "Do you know where you're going?"

"Yeah, Katlin called and gave me directions. I buy stock there a couple times a year." Jerry handed Lou a hat like his, and the big man sat in the front with him.

She didn't mind getting in the back with Simon and Remi, but if this was Linda Bender, one of them would have to drive back with her. "Do you have any idea where she might be?"

"The only thing that would keep her out this late is if she's involved in school sports. It's wrestling season, and the matches go long sometimes. The kids are out of school right now, but they host some meets to get a whole season in." Jerry started up the big truck, and the diesel engine was louder than a regular one. "I thought this woman is older."

"She is, but she's got two brothers who are excellent wrestlers, if I'm not mistaken." That had been in Fin's report about the family. "Let's drive by the school and see if that's what's going on. If this woman runs again, I have no clue when we'll find her."

"That's kind of crazy to give up everything and everyone to run."

"Think if JC was in danger," she said of the little boy he and Maddie had adopted.

"I'd run to hell if that's what it took."

"That's what she did, only this is much quainter than hell." The number of cars in the high school parking lot made her relax a little. Manhunts were only exciting to bounty hunters. "Park over there," she said, pointing. "We'll wait and let her go home and take care of her brothers."

It took another twenty minutes before people started heading for the parking lot. It wasn't a crowd, but they seemed to split by the school colors they were wearing, and everyone seemed happy. This place reminded her of Haywood—it appeared to be a tight-knit community. The only three people who didn't look like they belonged hung back and talked only to each other.

"Is that her?" Jerry asked.

"That's her," she said. "Wait for her to drive out before pulling out slowly. It's almost eleven, so she's heading home. There's nothing else open."

Cain noticed how Linda scanned her surroundings. Because of what she'd done, she'd be doing that for the rest of her life. The only out was to find someone who could help her vanish, but Linda's problem was finding someone she could trust. You could pay someone to erase your past, but if Nicola paid more, you'd never be free.

Lou instructed Jerry and let a few cars go before they started after them. Linda was driving a Jeep covered in mud as if she was trying to blend in to her surroundings. The house they pulled up to was a large but older place that was a few miles from the school and had a snowman in the front yard.

"I'd like to leave this lady to the rest of her life, but that's not going to be possible," Cain said, getting out of her truck and buttoning her jacket. She was dressed much more casually than usual, but the country was no place for cashmere. "Wait for me, and make sure no one gets past you. According to Nathan, it shouldn't be too long before Nicola's goons show up."

"Are you sure you want to go in there alone?" Remi asked. From her expression the answer *yes* was not the way to go.

"I need you out here with Lou to keep an eye on the road in. My gut tells me we're almost out of time." She put her hands in her pockets to keep them warm, and she glanced at Lou. "Take care of the truck, and everyone put on a hat."

"What?" Jerry asked as Lou got out and took a screwdriver out of the bag he had with him.

Lou placed another license plate on the truck and placed a skullcap on his head. If something happened and one of the neighbors got the plate number, it would come back to a truck of Jerry's description, only owned by one of the larger farms north of them. Once they hit the highway, they'd change it back.

"You want a gun?" Remi asked.

"I'm going to try kindness first and see what that gets me," she said, smiling.

It was starting to snow, and the wind was picking up as she walked down the street. The house had a few lights on, but the places around it were dark. If something did happen, it was good that there were only four other houses to worry about. Linda had chosen a place close to what was considered downtown, but despite that, the pool of witnesses would be small.

Her knock sounded loud in the stillness, and the sounds from inside died quickly, but no one answered the door. "You can either let me in or sit and wait for whoever Nicola sent to get your brothers back. We have trying to get your cousin out of our lives in common." She glanced at her watch and decided on five minutes before she walked away. They wouldn't leave, but they'd have to wait Linda out and save her from herself.

"Who are you?" Linda asked through the door.

"My name is Cain Casey. I'm not sure if you've ever heard of me, but I'm from New Orleans, and my cousin is marrying Abigail Eaton. I know you're familiar with Abigail. All I want is a conversation, and if you want me to go, I will."

There was a pause, but the door opened with the security chain still on. "Are you alone?"

Linda Bender was a smallish woman with soft brown eyes and full lips. "People like me never travel alone, but I don't want to overwhelm you, so they'll wait outside. No one will bother us if you let me in."

The door closed again, and she heard the chain sliding off. Linda appeared wary when she opened the door but stepped aside. "How did you find me?"

"I have a friend in Chicago who specializes in helping people disappear. He used his talents in reverse, and here I am. The problem is that Nicola found her own friend, and I think she found you as well." She looked past Linda, and the two teenage boys standing there, looking scared and ready to bolt, made her want to hustle them all out to safety, but she couldn't force someone to take the help she was offering. "Whoever she sends isn't going to be offering you the same deal I am."

"What's that?" Linda said, sounding tired. "Work for you or you'll kill me?" The boys came closer and stood by their sister. "That's why I ran. I don't have it in me anymore, and I want better for my brothers."

"Ms. Bender," Cain said, standing away from them so she didn't crowd them. "I'm as different from your cousin as two people can be. All I want is your help, and for that I'm willing to share my friend with you. If you accept, this time when you disappear, it'll be permanent, and you can go anywhere you want to." She took her hands out of her pockets and placed them at her sides so Linda could see she wasn't armed. "If you help me, maybe the day will come when you don't have to hide behind a fake name and a fake life. Do you understand what I'm saying?"

"I think it's you who doesn't understand. Nicola's dead, and you're full of shit. What do you really want?" Linda turned from wary to angry in a second.

"Let me show you something." Cain took her phone out and found the video from the warehouse that had been destroyed with a bomb blast. "It's date stamped so you can see it was shot well after Nicola's accident."

Linda watched it and replayed it after it was done. "This can't be right."

"You never see her face, but the one person in the world who knew her best aside from her family assured me the person walking around my place is Nicola Antakov. The name Eaton is as fake as whatever you're using now." She took her phone back and motioned for Linda and her brothers to sit. They all took the worn couch, and she sat across from them. "Abigail has had to run for her life, and when her in-laws were killed, she figured she was free of all this, until our security system picked this up."

"Where the hell has she been?" Linda asked, staring at her as if she'd told her that Satan was real, and he was on his way over for drinks. "My uncle never said anything."

"I can't answer that because I don't know. My best guess is she was recovering from the accident since that part was real. Her death, though, was staged to protect her from the investigation that was getting too close." She checked her watch and could guess the freak-out level outside if she took much longer. "Right before you left New York, Abigail was in the city with her three children."

"Uncle David talked about it a few times." Linda averted her attention to her brothers, and their expressions were unreadable. "He mentioned that Abigail was planning to move to the city."

"With everything you were planning, you might have missed what happened next." She stopped and gazed at the boys as well. "You might want to hear this alone."

"We know what our family was, Ms. Casey," the older boy said. "Linda promised us we don't have to be a part of that."

The soft maturity in his voice reminded her of Hayden. "Listen to her. While Abigail was in the city, someone tried to kill her twice. She was shot the second time, and in the first attempt a bus full of women were killed so none of them could testify against your uncle." The way Linda's eyes widened made her stop.

"What women?" Linda said after a long, awkward moment.

"The ones from the quarry. One of them got a message out, and David made them all pay once he found out." She looked at her phone again and put her finger up as she sent Remi a quick text.

"I didn't know that, and I'm not sure why you're here," Linda said as her brothers each placed a hand on her knee.

"I want you to come with me. The only way to keep you safe is to get you and your brothers out of here. I've met Nicola only once, so you know her better. If she has someone on her payroll looking for you, do you think it'll be for a friendly visit?" It was the brutal truth, but she didn't have time for niceties. "You don't know me, Ms. Bender, but I'm the best option if you really want out."

"Forgiveness is out of reach for me now even if I wanted it, and I don't." Linda nodded, but she appeared exhausted. "Tim, get the bags and leave everything else." The older boy stood and moved to the front closet quickly.

"Is there any paperwork you need to bring with you?"

"Like what?" Linda asked seeming wary, but that hadn't really changed.

"Anything that's important to you and might lead someone to you if you had another identity in mind."

"I'll have to start over because Lorna Green is dead as of tonight, if you found me this easily. If you're not who you say you are, do me one favor." Linda spoke softly as the boys gathered a few more things since no one had stopped them.

"I'm exactly who I seem to be, but I do on occasion grant favors. Only save it for when you really need one. Tonight you don't. I'm here because our futures might be mutually beneficial."

"I'm not quick to trust, and if your plans are to kill me, please don't do it in front of my brothers. They're nothing like our father and uncle, and I'd like to keep it that way." Linda picked up her purse and stopped when Cain's phone rang.

"Yes," she said. When Nathan promised fast and easy, he wasn't kidding. They'd be back in Haywood before midnight.

"We've got company. There's a car driving slowly up the street and it doesn't fit," Remi said, her voice even. "You know what I mean?"

"Just one?" Linda didn't have many neighbors, but a shootout would be hard to miss.

"One so far, but I sent Merrick and Katlin through town to make sure." Remi stopped for a minute, making Cain hold her breath. "They pulled over a house down from you, but they're not getting out. It's too dark out here to see how many are in there."

"Linda, what's behind the house?" she asked with the phone still up to her ear.

"Pastures for the farm that's about three miles from us. I picked this place because we could always run out the back if we needed to." Linda gripped the strap of her purse and stared at her like she could drill a hole in her skull with the sheer will of her eyes. "Why?"

"Someone's outside, and they're not with us." She moved and

turned off the lights in the room and motioned for the boys to do the same in the rest of the house. "I thought we had a little more time, but everyone stay low."

"Who is it?" Tim asked, forcing his little brother down beside him by the couch. This kid seemed way older than his physical age, and it pissed her off. Kids were only kids a short while, so they should enjoy that time as long as possible.

"I don't want to go out there and introduce myself, so let's wait them out."

"Are you armed?" Linda asked her.

The question made her regret Remi's offer. "I'm not. I didn't want to make you uncomfortable, and I seldom carry a gun."

"You're like Nicola, then," Linda said. "She's never armed either. It's a lot easier to let someone else do your dirty work."

"I'm in the bar business, Ms. Bender, so I'm nothing like Nicola. I'm also stuck in this house with you, in case you've forgotten that little fact." She understood fear and stress, but there was no reason for Linda to blame things on her.

"I'm sorry. This proves I was crazy to think I could outrun her and the family." Linda's eyes watered, and she sat with her brothers on the floor.

"Don't worry about it. How many neighbors do you have?" She moved to a window and glanced out a crack in the curtains. It was easy to spot the two people walking in the grass at the edge of the yard.

"There are five houses on the street, but two of them are empty," Tim answered.

"Which ones?"

"The one next door and the one at the beginning of the street. This is the last one before the pasture butts up to the dead end." Tim pointed to the house to his left.

"Thanks, kid. Remi, pull the truck into the drive next door, and get out like you're coming home. The place is empty." She kept her eyes on the two coming closer, but there had to be more in the shadows. "How many of them are there?"

"We counted four, but I'm not saying there aren't more. What do you want me to do?"

"I need you to do what you do best. Snake eyes doesn't need my advice," she said, laughing. "Those two are getting close."

"Hang on, and remember to listen to me next time," Remi said, and the truck started.

She watched Remi get out of the passenger side with a gun in each hand, and without a sound the two people in the yard went down. "Does this place have a basement?" she asked Linda.

"Yes." Linda looked like she might be starting to panic, and Cain wanted to avoid that.

"Does it have a way to the outside?"

"No." Tim answered this time, and he put his arm around his sister.

"Good. Get down there, and wait for me to come back. Even if I'm gone for a bit, don't come up." She looked at all three of them until they all nodded. "Do you have a gun?"

"They're in the bags," Joshua said.

"Can you lend me one?" He reached in his pack and handed her a Glock that appeared well taken care of. "Take the other ones along with those bags down with you. If someone else makes it in here, I want them to think you're gone."

"Please come back," Tim said.

"I will, and you'll all be fine." She went out the back after they disappeared down a dark stairwell. It was amazing how dark it was, considering they were in the middle of town.

She stood outside the door and let her eyes adjust as she called Remi back. "Do you see anyone else?"

"Simon took care of the people in the car, so we should be good," Remi said. It sounded like she was walking.

"We need to get the two in the yard into the house next door. That'll buy us some time before we get the hell out of here." She stepped around the corner and inhaled sharply when a knife went through her right bicep. Her other hand came up in reflex as the woman dressed in black went for another strike. The pain was intense, but she didn't let go of the woman's hand as she put all her weight behind her efforts, and this time the knife was aimed at her chest.

Remi came up behind them and smashed the butt of her gun into the asshole's head, and she dropped like a rock, but not before the woman managed to pierce a spot above her right breast. "You okay?" Remi asked.

She lifted the hand of her injured arm and pressed it to her chest, trying to keep from bleeding on the ground. It wouldn't be good to leave any trace of herself here if she could help it. "Drag all these fuckers inside. Including the two in the car."

"We need to get that bleeding under control first," Remi said, opening the back door for her.

"We also don't need a nosy neighbor glancing outside and seeing any of this. I'll be okay, and I promise I'll tell Emma this wasn't your fault." She took her coat off and grimaced at the amount of blood already soaking her sleeve but tried to put the pain to the back of her mind. She opened the door to the basement and called down. "It's Cain. You can come up."

Tim came up first, and his eyes widened when he looked at the blood on her shirt, and Linda's expression was the same. "What happened? Are you okay?" Linda asked, coming closer.

"One of your visitors was upset I got here first." She sat down and took deep breaths. Pain was relative, she always thought, and she did her best to put it out of her mind. "Do you have a first aid kit, by chance?"

"I'll be right back," Joshua said, taking off down the hallway.

"I don't want to upset you, but we need to bring the bodies in here. The people with me bought us some time, so use it to get anything you want out of this place. It'll never be safe enough to come back to, and unfortunately it's going to have to become a pile of ash after we're gone." She watched as Linda wrapped a bandage around her arm.

"Do you think Nicola will think the bodies are ours?" Linda asked softly.

"She will until her people don't call back, but like I said, this will buy you some time, and she doesn't know you're going to end up with me." The front door opened, and she turned to see Jerry, looking seriously stressed.

"Goddamn," Jerry said, dropping the dead guy he and Simon were hauling like a sack of grain. "What the hell happened? Maddie's going to kick my ass if I let something happen to you."

"The four in the car were actually five, and I was lucky enough to find the last one. Are you doing all right?"

"These assholes were here to kill everyone, so they got off easy with a bullet to the head. That Remi's a good shot." He went back to help Simon roll the guy over and take everything out of his pockets as Remi and Lou came in with the next guy. "Katlin and Merrick are watching the one at the back, so I'll be right back."

"For a dairy farmer he's taking this well," Remi said as she looked through the wallet of the guy they'd carried in. "All these Russian names gives a clue who these guys work for."

Linda and her brothers sat as if they were waiting for coffee, but that changed when Jerry dropped a woman on the floor in the middle of the room. She let out a moan when her back hit the hardwood.

"Zoya Levin," Linda said. She gripped the side of the sofa with white fingers as if all of a sudden this had become terrifyingly real. "She's on the Antakov payroll."

"Does she moonlight as a chef at a hibachi? That's who cut me," Cain said, accepting the knife from Jerry. "Thanks, man. Why don't you go and pull the car to the back and take the boys with you?" Jerry seemed hesitant, so she took him into the kitchen. "I need to wake that bitch up and hear whatever her last words are going to be. Do you understand?"

"Yeah, but I hate to leave you. I'm supposed to be watching your back."

"Thank you. Making sure nothing happens to those kids *will* be helping me." She looked him in the eye and tried to gauge what he was thinking. "Are you okay with all this? There's me and what I do in concept and quite another to have it thrown in your face. I don't want to get you into this any deeper than I have to."

"I grew up in foster homes, and all I ever wanted was my own family. You gave me and Maddie that. I told you the day you handed me my son—I'll follow you to hell, and someone will have to put a bullet in *my* head to get me to betray you."

"Thanks, Jerry. You're a good friend, but please don't think you owe me anything. JC is where he belongs, and I know you and Maddie are the best choice of parents for him. His father was a lot like these people. His birth mother, though, was an innocent who lost her life because of the asshole she married." She accepted a bottle of water from him when Linda came in, dropped two Tylenol in her hand, and walked out. "You're all that little boy is ever going to need to become a good man."

"Don't worry about me. This is a lot more exciting than putting out hay, for damn sure."

She had to laugh at that as she followed him out. Tim and Joshua seemed reluctant to leave Linda, but she talked them into going with Jerry. "Zoya is one of Uncle David's killers," Linda said after the three walked out the door. "Sending Zoya means Nicola knows where we are."

Cain handed Lou the knife, and Zoya woke up with a start when he used it to cut off her index finger. The gag Lou had put in her mouth kept her quiet, but Zoya glared at her until she seemed to notice Linda in the room. That's when she started to struggle, until Lou did away with the middle finger. The ropes from Jerry's truck weren't going to give.

"You bitch," Zoya said when Lou pulled out the rag, but she appeared to be talking to Linda.

"All I wanted was out, but none of you could accept that." Linda's tone was even and didn't give away any emotion. "When my father was alive, it was only women who wanted to be in the business, and that was bad enough. Now, though, it's nothing but people who have no way out. I'm not letting my brothers get dragged into that."

"You're going to fucking die for what you did," Zoya said, her Russian accent probably thicker because of the pain of her missing fingers.

"I've said that on occasion," Cain said, dragging Zoya's attention back to her. "But when you're the asshole bleeding on the floor, you have no advantage."

"You think killing me is going to stop Nicola from coming and coming until she cuts you and everyone you love into little pieces?" Zoya's laugh was grating. "You're a peon she's going to have fun with until she gets tired and kills you."

"You wouldn't happen to know where she is, would you? It'll cut down the time until all the fun you mentioned." She could feel the blood soaking the bandage, and her shirt looked wet again. She was going to need stitches, but all she had to do was hang on. This wasn't going to kill her, though Emma might. Once they got home, Abigail would take care of her.

"You can't cause enough pain to make me talk to you. You sound like an amateur for asking."

"And you sound like Natasha from *Rocky and Bullwinkle*," Cain said, making Remi laugh. "It's making it hard to keep a straight face." She motioned to Lou, and the next finger came off. Zoya didn't scream at all. The only outward sign that it might have hurt was the wince when Lou brought the knife down. The woman was hard-core, no denying that. "Tell me where she is and I let your—" She accepted a picture from Remi and studied it before going on. "Is she a girlfriend or little sister?" she asked Linda.

"Little sister," Linda said.

"Let your little sister go free. She'll never see you again, but she can dance ballet and be safe from anyone cutting her and your mother's throat." She showed Zoya the picture of the young lady in a beautiful ballerina costume with an older woman smiling next to her.

"My brothers will kill you if you touch her," Zoya said with venom in her voice. She strained against the ropes hard enough that the tendons in her neck bulged.

"I'm not going to kill her, but I will promise that I'll make it impossible for her to stand on her toes." She put the picture in her shirt pocket and pointed outside. "The car you're in doesn't have room for Tim and Joshua, so you were here to get rid of Nicola's problems—all of them."

"You bitch." Linda grabbed the knife from a surprised Lou and drove it into Zoya's side. "If there was a way for you to tell Nicola I didn't give the feds everything, I wish you could, if only to see her face. But you're not walking out of here alive if I can help it. Once I do, I'll be happy to tell Cain where to find your family."

The admission that Linda had held back crucial information was what Cain was waiting to hear. "Tell me where Nicola is. I'm not wasting any more time here," she said, patting her pocket. "I don't need you. Linda can give me all the information I need about your family."

"Nicola is in New York," Zoya said. The glare she was giving them was almost comical, but Cain really was done wasting time.

"That's like telling me she's in the middle of the ocean. I'll make sure and tell your sister and mother it was you who's responsible for what happens. While they wait for your brothers to save them, I'll take pleasure in letting them know you got them killed as well." She stood and had to take a moment to get her balance as the pain intensified. Her light-headedness meant she might've lost more blood than she thought. "Lou."

"Wait, fucker!" Zoya said at the top of her lungs. "I don't know where she is, but my orders didn't come from her. It was Nina Garin who sent me, and she's in Trump Tower in the city. David Eaton put her up in an apartment there."

Cain glanced at Linda, who nodded.

"Nina Garin was Nicola's number two when she was in New Orleans," Linda said. "When Nicola supposedly died, she moved back to the city and went to work for Uncle David. If Nicola rose from the dead, Nina is by her side."

"Good, then we have a starting point," Cain said.

"Wait, give me your word you'll leave my family alone," Zoya said.

"You have my word, but unlike you, I'd never hurt women and children. My family has honor, and you're going to die with none." The second the words left her mouth, Linda slit Zoya's throat and stood over her as she gurgled and coughed until she was dead.

"Thank you," Linda said, gazing at the expression of terror frozen on Zoya's face for the rest of time. Linda was pale, and her hand was shaking as she dropped the knife. For all that she'd wanted to do it, there was no question she wasn't a hardened killer.

"Thank you for believing me. Now we need to know what bedrooms are yours so we can put all these people in your beds." Cain sat again as Lou made the trips up the stairs with Linda. He looped his arms through Zoya's to keep her blood off him. Simon followed Linda out to the truck, and Jerry came back to help Lou with the rest. The pain in her side was starting to give her a massive headache, but she understood Zoya and what she'd done before Linda killed her. Even the most vicious of people had their soft spot, and Zoya's, like hers, was her family.

If the day came when she was in Zoya's position, she'd give her captors whatever they wanted to keep Emma and her children whole. There was never a doubt about that. Right now, she wasn't in that position, but she did feel like shit.

"I turned the gas on," Remi said as the guys went up with the last body. "We're going to need more than that if we want this place to burn down to the ground."

"I got that covered," Jerry said. He got a hose from the basement, and they watched him cover the floors of the first floor in some kind of oil. "These old places don't have gas heaters. They run off heating oil, and the propane for the stove has a big tank outside as well. I'll rig that next."

"He's a handy guy to have around," Remi said when they went out at Jerry's insistence.

"He's a good friend." She got into the back seat with Linda, who was waiting with her first aid kit, and the boys were in the next car.

"Let me tie it tighter. You're going to need to see a doctor to get the bleeding to stop."

"Tie it so it lasts an hour," she said, closing her eyes briefly. The only thing that made her feel better was that she wasn't going home empty-handed.

"Okay," Jerry said fifteen minutes later. "All we need is a trigger."

"Get us to the end of the street," Lou said, getting his gun out. Jerry leaned back as Lou aimed out the driver's side window and fired with a silencer on. The fireball that went up at the impact of the bullet was impressive, but they weren't sticking around to watch the inferno.

"Think of it as your next step to the life you want," she said to Linda. "Eventually, you'll get to where you want to be."

CHAPTER TWENTY

The truck is in the lab, ma'am," the young agent said to Special Agent in Charge Annabel Hicks.

Annabel had been in New Orleans for five short years, but they seemed like a lifetime when she thought about everything that had happened in that time. "What did the coroner say?"

"He ruled it an accident when you consider the blood alcohol level. There's no doubt Newsome was drunk, but our lab said it was no accident." The guy placed some photos of Newsome's car on her desk and pointed to various spots.

"Someone bumped him over the guardrail?" The old white sedan was a piece of shit, but the white paint was a godsend. Nothing on the guardrail would've left streaks of blue along the driver's side of Newsome's vehicle.

"Someone did, and the cameras along the bridge got a license plate."

The next set of pictures were of what Annabel guessed was a blue SUV with Louisiana plates coming up beside Newsome's car. "Did the bridge police have any video?" The Causeway had its own police force, and years of tolls had given them an impressive budget to spend on things like being able to do surveillance on the whole span.

"I emailed it to you, which makes me curious as to why the coroner ruled it an accident. Of course it could be that their office didn't show up with subpoenas either, so that might have done it."

"Newsome put in a call to me and said he had some information I would want, and he was willing to trade to give it to me. He said the FBI agents he was working with had ruined his career." She flipped through the pictures again. "There had to be some truth to it if he thought it would get him his job back, and then someone ran him off the road. Who those agents were wasn't something he was willing to give up until we talked."

"I wasn't on that case, but Shelby gave me a quick rundown when I sent all this to her."

"Give me a minute," she said, buzzing for her assistant and asking her to get the NOPD police chief on the phone.

"Annabel," Chief of Police Fritz Jernigan said, sounding cheery. "How are you?"

"I'm actually reviewing one of your former officers, and I need a favor." She smiled at the agent still sitting in her office, then put her finger to the side of her head and tapped. Local law enforcement in the city was pretty good when it came to working with them. "Are you feeling generous today?"

"For you, always," Fritz said and seemed to pull the phone away from his mouth to cough. "Sorry, this is my yearly head cold. What can I do for you, and who are you talking about? Please tell me I'm not about to be the leadoff story on the news tonight."

"Remember Elton Newsome?" she asked, and she got silence from the other end.

"You found him?" Fritz sounded surprised. "I've had a search going for a while with nothing."

"We found him, but he's not talking."

"Let me at the asshole, and we'll see. We're still having to deal with the fallout from all that shit."

"He's dead. Someone drove him over the side of the Causeway as he was on his way in to talk to me. He called and said he had some information that would get him reinstated." She remembered the report Shelby had written when she'd been called to Hannah Casey's school. Emma Casey's mother had walked out with her and had been in town at Elton Newsome's urging. Why people like Newsome tried stupid things like that to get a rise out of Casey was something she never could understand.

"He went outside the chain of command to bring in some old woman who was supposed to help him do what none of us have been able to do since we were wet behind the ears." Fritz sneezed three times in a row and cursed. "Muriel Casey has brought a case she can't win, but hell if it's not costing us a fortune in defense. The only way he was getting reinstated was if he could tell me all the winning lottery numbers for the next year."

"He was pretty confident," Annabel said, "but he wouldn't tell me where he was. I talked him into coming in, and by the looks of it, that's what he was doing. Someone stopped him before he reached me." She studied the picture of the items they'd found in Newsome's pockets.

"What's all this got to do with you?" Fritz asked.

"I want to take the investigation off your hands," she said and waited. "But you know I have to be invited in."

"If he went off the Causeway, I'm not the one you should be convincing. You know how those guys are."

"I need you to make some phone calls and explain what you've been going through with Muriel. If they smell trouble, they might turn this over with no problem, but Newsome was your guy. If you want, I'll keep you updated, but there's a case here, and I want to run with it."

"Let me see what I can do, and I'll let you know how it goes. The chief over there owes me a few favors, which means you'll owe me a few if I come through for you. You think Casey had something to do with this?" Fritz asked, sounding like he couldn't believe it, but it had to be considered. "She was like a caged animal, from what Sept told me, the day her kid went missing. Sebastian and I had to go over there and kiss the ring." Fritz referred to Sebastian Savoie, the Chief of Detectives. He was Sept Savoie's father and had another five boys on the force.

"I doubt it. Sept will tell you that Casey is way too smart for that, and she'd know that damn bridge is wired for action."

"Give me ten minutes and I'll call you back."

"Thanks," she said, ending the call. "Did the coroner turn over Newsome's phone?" she asked her agent.

"He said there wasn't one."

"Ma'am," her assistant said over the intercom. "Chief Jernigan is on the line for you."

"That was fast," she said before picking up. "Fritz, hello."

"Those guys can't wait to hand this off to you, so you have your case. They'll send over all the paperwork as soon as it's done. Just remember your promise to keep me updated. I'd like to be able to put this behind us and report that the NOPD had nothing to do with it."

"Thanks, Fritz. I'll call when I have something." She handed all the pictures back and motioned for the agent to follow her. "Let's start with the coroner. There's no way Newsome died with no cellphone, and I'd like to know why someone forced him off that road. The first thing that tells us is someone knew where he was the whole time and moved in before he said something he shouldn't have."

"You're coming with us, ma'am?"

"There's something about this, and I'd like to know what it is. Newsome wasn't a good cop, and he had sensitive enough information that someone killed him to keep him quiet. That's especially true if it was something he thought would exonerate him." That last conversation with Newsome kept replaying in her head. Whatever Newsome believed he had just might tie back to Casey. Could this finally be what they'd need to put Cain in their done file?

"Do you think we should talk to Carol Verde?" the agent asked.

"I doubt a farmer's wife has it in her to kill someone, but Carol Verde is a different kind of woman, so yeah. Find out where she ended up, and we'll see if there's anything there. Our first step is the coroner, and then we'll track down that car. All this might turn out to be a late Christmas present."

❖

"What happened again?" Abigail asked as she started putting stitches in.

"It was the freakiest thing," Cain said as Emma smiled at her. "I decided to take a moonlight walk last night, and some woman with a large knife took exception to me invading her space." After Abigail had numbed the area, she could think straight again. The throbbing was starting to get to her. She'd lost enough blood to make her feel like crap, but it wasn't life-threatening, so the stitches would be all the first aid she'd need.

"Do you want me to stab you again?" Emma asked the rhetorical question as she sat holding her hand. "Sit here and look handsome."

"Does this happen often?" Abigail never looked up as she continued to work. "Is this, like, a common thing in your family? Finley comes home with something like this, and there'd better be some great explanation to go along with it."

"You're in for a lifetime of fun, but these guys do attract trouble wherever they go. Having a doctor in the family is the best thing to happen to us." Emma smiled, but the lines around her eyes were tight.

"I guess the fact that they're good-looking is a plus when it comes to putting up with them." Abigail cut the sutures so she could wipe away the antiseptic she'd cleaned the area with. She wrapped a fresh bandage and tied it off neatly before starting to clean up her mess. "There you go. Keep them dry, and I'll check it tomorrow and change the bandages for you. I'll give you a shot of antibiotics, and that should do it. They were both clean cuts, and it doesn't look like they hit anything really important."

Abigail left them alone, and Emma unbuttoned her shirt for her. It was ruined anyway, so Abigail had cut the sleeve off to get to the wound. "I told you to be careful. You know it freaks me out when you come home covered in blood."

She put her good arm around Emma and kissed her temple. "That bitch came around a blind corner, but Linda made it so she can't ever do that again. This time was a surprise, and from the sound of it, Linda can help us with our mutual problem."

"The fact that Nicola Antakov thinks like you worries me." Emma put her hands on her chest and gazed up at her. "You getting hurt is never the outcome I expect."

"There's plenty of differences between me and Antakov." She cupped Emma's cheek and ran her thumbs along the smooth skin to wipe away the tears that had fallen. "Our children aren't in our lives simply to take over for us one day. All three of them and you are the most cherished things in my life. That's the biggest difference between me and Nicola, and my desire to grow old with you is why we'll win."

"You are the most romantic thing when you want to be, but I'm not forgetting that you came home covered in blood. I'm not that easy."

"I am," she said, making Emma laugh. "And I'm sorry. I should've taken Remi up on her suggestion to arm myself, but who knew there'd be killers in the yard?"

"Like I said, you attract trouble, my love, so take the gun next time."

They had time for a couple of hours of sleep, and she wasn't worried about Linda since Katlin had driven her to Ross's place and was staying with Merrick to keep an eye on her and the boys. Finley had released a long breath when she saw that Linda had come back with them, and Cain could almost feel how anxious her cousin was to finish with all this.

"If you leave this bed without me, you're not going to like my reaction," Emma said after she kissed her good night.

"I promise I'll be here for the good morning kiss, and we're staying here for as long as we can get away with. I'm exhausted." Hopefully, the pain shot Abigail had given her would last, but for now the throbbing was gone, and she was comfortable as long as she didn't move.

Three hours later Emma showered with her to keep her arm dry, and the kids were happy to have her back. Hayden hadn't looked happy, but she'd had a private conversation with him, and it eased his mind. Carmen and Ross had delivered breakfast to Linda and her brothers, and she was giving them the morning to decompress from the hellish night. Whatever they'd accomplished in the small town they'd settled in was burned to the ground, like the house. Starting over was never easy, but she'd try to make it as painless as possible with or without Linda's help in return.

"You guys help Mama clean up, and I'll be back in an hour," she said to the whole family. Everyone had stayed in the house that night, but it was time to return to a normal routine. "Fin," she said, and her cousin jumped out of her chair.

"Did she tell you what kind of help she could give us?" Finley asked when they were outside.

"Not yet, but we'll get to that in a bit. Our job today is to make this woman as comfortable as we can, so she'll hand over the rest of what she's holding. The only thing we can't do is try to intimidate her. I think she's had a lifetime of that."

"Before we go, there's something you should know." Finley walked them back inside and upstairs to the office, and whatever it was, it required Emma and Abigail to come along.

"Last night, Levi called," Emma said. "There was a break-in at the school while we were here."

"And this is our problem how?" Cain asked. Levi had been a nervous little Nellie from the time they were in grade school, and manhood had done nothing to quash that. "We wrote the damn check for the security system."

"I know, and I wanted to call you, but I didn't think it was a good idea. You were supposed to be here, remember?" Emma rested her hip against the desk and poked her with her toe. "Burner phone or no, I didn't want to take a chance, and I didn't want to distract you."

"I can't imagine what he thought you could do about it."

"Baby, believe me, I thought the same thing until he sent the video footage from the hallway and office. And it was good he did." She explained what else Levi had said.

She stared at the screen once Finley had cued the video up, and she watched Nicola's every move. The woman, who was pissed enough to destroy her child's artwork, had changed from the time she'd known her, and it hadn't been for the better. Here was someone who was somewhat broken, judging by the way she limped and moved slowly. Whatever had happened to her, she'd become a bit unhinged, if her actions were any indication. Nicola had lost everything, and the only thing she had left to fill the hole was her children and killing Abigail.

"Last night, the woman who stabbed me told us that she didn't know where Nicola was." She started the video again, needing to study her opponent.

"How persuasive were you?" Finley sounded like she didn't think she'd done enough. "I know you and what you're like when you need to know something. This is my family, Cain."

"You don't think I know that?" She pressed her hand flat on the desk but tried her best to remain calm. "It's the entire family, not just yours."

"Cain, please," Abigail said but stopped when Cain put her hand up.

"I didn't say that because I want you to feel guilty we're in this spot. I was never blind when I did what I did, and I'd do it again and again. Trust me, I gave Zoya the best incentive to tell me what she knew, and she didn't know. Her orders didn't come from Nicola—they came from some woman named Nina."

"Nina Garin," Abigail said. "She was Nicola's manager when we were in New Orleans."

"Zoya said Nina went back to New York after Nicola's death and worked for David Eaton. She's got a place in Trump Tower, and she sent Zoya and four others to kill Linda and her brothers. If we hadn't been there, none of them would've walked out." She took Emma's hand when she offered it and smiled at Finley and Abigail. "Don't ever think that I don't know what you feel or, more importantly, what you fear. I do."

"Sorry, but I want this bitch dead," Finley said, and Abigail nodded. "It makes me crazy to think of something happening to Abigail or one of the kids."

"Let's go talk to Linda and see what she has to say. With any luck we walk out of there with some leverage you can use for our next step."

"Our next step?" Finley took Abigail's hand.

"I try telling Muriel all the time that there's a time and place for everything, so pay attention. The most important thing is finding Nicola, and the more people looking, the better." She stopped to kiss Emma before standing as well. "Perhaps it's time for your old boss to know that there's been a miracle and Nicola's risen from the dead."

"If she gets arrested or spooked before we get to her, this will never end." Finley frowned, her body tense.

"No one is untouchable no matter where they are, cousin. But before you get your undies in a twist, let's go visit our new guests."

Finley drove them down the road that connected the two places, and she waved to Ross, who was coming out of his barn riding a tractor. Carmen was on the porch with a magazine, and she smiled when they joined her. "They're waiting for you inside, Cain, but Katlin said it was okay to come out with Ross."

"Take it easy, Carmen. It's your vacation too. We'll take care of dinner tonight, but if you're too cold, come inside until Ross has finished whatever he's doing." Cain squeezed Carmen's hand, and her group followed her inside. Tim and Joshua were watching TV, and Linda was in the kitchen having coffee.

"You own this place?" Linda asked. She was dressed in leggings and an oversized sweater. In no way did she resemble a woman on the run. "It's beautiful."

"Hi." Emma held her hand out to Linda. "I'm Emma, Cain's wife, and this is Finley and Abigail."

"Abigail," Linda said, standing and facing her. "You might not remember me, but we saw each other a few times."

"I do remember you, but forgive me for not knowing you were related to Nicola. I'm not sure why she kept all but her immediate family a secret, and I'm so sorry for what she did to you." Abigail bit her lip and took a deep breath. "Nicola is someone neither of us will ever understand. I'm begging you, though, for your brothers and my children, that if you have something that could help us, please share it." Abigail took Finley's hand and pulled her forward. "This is my fiancée, Finley Abbott, and she's proof there is a possibility of starting over."

"Weren't you with the NYPD?" Linda asked, but she shook hands with Finley. "I remember David talking about you. Not to me, but to Boris."

"Boris St. John?" Finley asked, and Linda nodded. "Do you know what happened to him? That's who Eaton sent to New Orleans to find Abigail and the kids. I recognized him from the files we had."

Cain realized she had to look over Finley's files and familiarize herself with all these people. "Are your brothers going to be okay?" she asked. They were ready to begin, and she wanted to see how far Linda was willing to go, but she didn't want to do it standing in the middle of the living room where the boys could overhear them.

"They're watching television to see if there's any news about the house last night. They made some friends on the wrestling team, and they didn't want them to worry. There'll be no calling, though—they know better than that." As a group they moved into the kitchen, and Cain closed the door behind them.

"I believe your next move will be for good," Cain said as she pulled out a chair for Emma at the table. "They can make all the friends they want, and you can stop looking over your shoulder."

"That'll be a hard habit to break. I've been doing it all my life, and I think it was something I learned from my father. He married into the Antakov family, but he knew what kind of man his brother-in-law was. David Eaton might have fooled plenty of people in high society, but he was a butcher I blamed for my father's death." She tore at a paper napkin, shredding it to pieces. "My mother idolized her brother and only acknowledged her Antakov roots. It's what she wanted to nourish and foster in us, but I tried to teach Tim and Joshua a different way."

"Cain said that from what she could see, you've done a good job," Emma said.

"What we all have to understand is that the Antakov empire will never completely die away," Cain said and Finley nodded. "It's got too many fingers into too many things, but we can slice away and kill the parts that are a threat to all of us. If you can't accept that, then now is the time to say so."

"I agree," Linda said immediately, and Abigail nodded. "What do you need from me?"

Finley gave her a rundown of what had happened in their warehouse, followed by the school sighting of Nicola. Those were the only two times they could confirm Nicola was indeed alive and plotting. Linda watched the film and rhythmically opened and clenched her fists.

"What I need from you is a hint of how to find her. There has to be something in the ledgers that will lead me to her," Cain said to Linda. "The Hell Fire Clubs are officially closed, but there's no way Nicola and her father didn't diversify. Did they put that in the ledgers, or were they only to record the business run by the entire family?"

"Nicola and Fredrick were responsible for those clubs as well as the lowbrow places that finally drove me to run. They would set up trailers in low-traffic areas and fill them with the girls they were trafficking." Linda's disgust was obvious. "Twenty-five would get you a quick session, and a hundred would buy you a couple of hours. I can't tell you how many girls died by chewing through their wrists because they couldn't do it anymore."

"Jesus Christ," Abigail said. "I think I'm going to be sick."

"Christ had nothing to do with what your ex was capable of. The souls of all those girls in unmarked graves are on her head, and she'll have to answer for them."

"That's what brought in the bulk of the money, I'm guessing. Those two businesses kept the family in power," Cain said. "The feds, with our help, eliminated the high-end part, but the other side is still operating. That's too mobile to keep up with even with the power and scope of the feds."

"You're right, but Nicola and Fredrick started something new about five years ago, and David was furious they'd gone behind his back. At least, he was pissed until they cut him in for a percentage. They opened clubs that were similar to the Hell Fire Clubs, but under five different bogus owners."

"Did you keep their records?" Finley asked.

"Once David complained about it, he didn't see why I shouldn't be trusted to do that. Putting me as the bookkeeper assured him that his percentage would be correct. He was the head of the family, so there was no way they could disagree." Linda removed a ledger from the box at her side and placed her hands on it. "There are ten clubs and plans to expand to about thirty within the next year. Their agreement with David was no more than fifty to keep the heat off them."

"Is it a franchise, or are they all different?" Cain asked. If it was her, there was no way she'd go the same route throughout. Once the authorities were able to infiltrate one club, the others would be on the chopping block.

"Every one of them is different, but all run on the same principle as the Hell Fire Clubs. The one in New Orleans is Madame Laveau's in the Warehouse District." Linda handed over a smaller file with the names of all ten places.

"That's two blocks from Emma's," Emma said. "It's never as crowded as our place, but it does a steady business."

"The bar downstairs is a diversion for what's happening on the next four floors," Linda said, taking out two more ledgers. "I kept a ledger for each of them, and David kept a master with him. What happened to that one, I don't know."

"Are any of these set up under a different name?" Cain asked as she skimmed the list, with Finley reading over her shoulder.

"None of them have the names Eaton or Antakov associated with any of the paperwork. That, too, is different for each club. They're using different aliases for each one." Linda handed over another thicker file with all the red tape associated with opening a bar. If the whole thing was set up under corporate shells, it would take time to trace back to an individual person. "This is all I have left to bargain for the lives of my brothers. I'd gladly sacrifice myself if it means they are free of all this shit."

"That's noble but totally unnecessary." Cain put the file down for now. "Martyrdom isn't my thing, and I'd never ask it of anyone. All I want is to borrow these to find out who Nicola is now."

"What about Fredrick?" Abigail asked. "Did he really die in that accident?"

"That's a good question, but we need to figure out some other things before we can follow the money. As far as I know, Madame Laveau's is still open and making money. Where that's going is the question of the day."

"From the look of her, the accident was real," Linda said. She pointed at the screen of Finley's laptop where the frozen image of Nicola was still up. "Maybe she wasn't the only one who survived, but they didn't walk away without scars. Fredrick might be alive, but is he up and walking?"

"They were twins," Abigail said. "Even if we find Nicola and cut her into small enough pieces that she'll never be found, he'll retaliate as soon as he's able."

"That's true, but I don't plan to stop until we're done." Cain glanced at each one of them, so they'd know she was serious. "When we're done, the Antakov family will be a small piece of history not worth remembering."

"Amen," Abigail and Linda said together.

CHAPTER TWENTY-ONE

O ur best bet is to start with the club in New Orleans," Finley said. Abigail seemed to be reading through the information about the sex club Nicola owned in New Orleans, and Cain wondered how long she'd continue to pummel herself for someone else's sins.

"I'd concentrate on the spots where there was already a Hell Fire Club and compare," Linda said.

Tim and Joshua had come into the kitchen and introduced themselves, and Emma invited them back to the house so they could meet Hayden. Both boys were older than their son, but they seemed eager to come back with them. Cain got the feeling they were relieved to be surrounded by people rather than on their own. The boys went back to watching TV.

"There's no way of knowing exactly where Nicola has been, but you're right—none of these places seems to have closed."

"David Eaton probably took them over when Nicola was out of commission, and she took them back when he was killed. Finding her might be as easy as following the money."

Finley laughed and kissed Abigail's cheek. "That I can do. It was my job for the last eight years."

"Finley is the black sheep of the family," Cain said to Linda. "She decided to become an FBI agent instead of going into the family business, but all that training might come in handy."

"You're the one who was investigating Nicola?" Linda finally showed some emotion by laughing. "That's why you were undercover with the cops, right?"

"I was trying to figure out if someone in that precinct was dirty," Finley said as she took notes.

"If you met Captain Brock Howard, you found him. He's been on David's payroll for years and is probably the reason you never got very far. That type of information is in one of the ledgers I kept, if that's useful."

Linda had brought a total of three large bags with her, and they meant the death of whatever world Nicola had left.

Once again, Cain considered her own life and information and thought about holes she might need to plug. Her phone ringing got everyone to stop talking. She looked at the screen. "Go ahead, but I have to take this." It was Colin, and she was wondering if he was going to turn down her invitation. "Colin," she said, and Emma smiled.

"Hey, sorry I took so long. Judice said you saw her in Chicago, but I had one more meeting I wanted to take before we joined you. The invitation's still good, right?"

Another meeting wasn't what she wanted to hear, and if she had to make another call to Carlos, Colin was going to need stitches. "Where are you?"

"In your stomping grounds, but I'm done. Tell me the closest airport to you, and I'll have Judice book the flights."

"Call Mano Jatibon. He's waiting on you. The FBI hasn't figured out you're related to me yet, and I'd like to keep it that way. If you fly privately, we'll get you to the house without anyone laying eyes on you." She could feel the headache coming on, but her mother's admonishment of not being able to kill family, no matter how aggravating, went through her head.

"Great, and make sure there's plenty of booze on hand. This has been a long-ass day, and it's not even noon yet."

"Try to lose any tails you have before you get to the airport, and fly safe."

Emma joined her at the counter and pressed their bodies together as she put her arms around her waist. "He's coming?"

"Yes, and I'm almost afraid to ask what other shit he's gotten himself into. I have to question if we're really related sometimes." She turned to Finley. "You guys okay? If you are, we'll drive the boys back, and you can come to the house for dinner. Ross can bring you when he's done checking his domain."

"Let us know if Colin gets here before then," Finley said. "We'll come back so I can introduce him to Abigail and the kids."

Cain got behind the wheel of the SUV, and Emma faced the back to talk to Linda's brothers as they headed back. The two were quiet and respectful, and if things worked out the way she wanted, she wouldn't mind Linda ending up in New Orleans. Hayden had plenty of friends, but these guys needed a few in their lives.

Hayden welcomed them in, and he and Sadie disappeared into the den with their new guests without any prompting from her or Emma. "Want to go for a walk before my blood pressure hits a dangerous level from Colin's exploits?"

"Sure," Emma said, leaving her coat on.

They headed to the lake outside and followed the bank. This was what their vacation should've been, and she wondered if Emma minded all the stuff that was happening around them. Sometimes it was too much even for her.

"What are you thinking so hard about, mobster?" Emma looped her arm around hers and slowed them down.

"I was thinking that I need to start checking things off our list and not adding any more. I wanted some downtime with you." They stopped at the small shed she'd put in for the rowboats they'd gotten. There was a rope and pulley system that took the boats out of the water when they weren't in use.

"We've had some downtime, and I'm not complaining. You should know by now that one of the reasons I love you is because you help people like Linda. Think of what would've happened to her if you hadn't gotten there in time." Emma stopped her and pulled her head down by the neckline of her coat. "Now stop wasting time in your head, and kiss me. If you do a decent enough job at it, I might let you show me what a stud you are in that shed."

"The other kids are sledding with our friends a hundred feet from here, and we'd never live down the teasing if we aren't quiet. How about some sledding now, and I'll take a few runs at your slopes later?"

Emma stuck her tongue out at her but didn't stop her when she kissed her.

"You guys give it a rest," Remi said, laughing as she walked up behind them with the kids. "Come take a turn hauling these guys up the hill."

They played until Emma declared it was too cold to be outside, and they all went in for hot chocolate. Emma did some more reading when the kids all settled in front of the fire. She was surprised when Tim and Joshua joined them and smiled at the story Emma had chosen that was too young for them and Hayden.

"Who do you need to know to get a drink around here?" Colin said loudly when he came through the back of the house. Emma snapped the book closed and shook her head.

"He does know how to make an entrance," Emma said. "You guys want to watch a movie?"

"I can keep reading for you, if you want," Tim said shyly.

Emma gave him a wide smile. "Thank you, and I'm sure these guys would love that. If you get tired, you all vote on the movie, and Hayden will show you where the popcorn is."

They headed into the kitchen and hugged Colin. She offered Judice her hand and smiled to put her at ease. "Welcome to our home, and I hope you guys decide to stay the night."

"You have a beautiful place," Judice said. She held Colin's hand and followed them to the sunroom that Emma loved in the summer.

"Thank you, I grew up a couple of miles from here."

They talked about pleasantries for another half hour before the rest of the family arrived, and they pitched in to help Carmen with dinner. Colin went out with her to stand at the pit, and she stopped him from telling her about his meetings. When they got into it, she wanted Remi, Katlin, Muriel, and Finley to listen in.

Linda and her brothers appeared a little overwhelmed when they sat to eat, but they rallied, and Linda seemed to find Judice easy to talk to. They sat together and appeared to share a long conversation while Colin made the rest of them laugh. The kids left for the movie Emma promised them, and Emma took Dallas and the others next door to Muriel and Kristen's cabin for an after-dinner bottle of wine.

Once it was quiet, Cain got to business. "How did your sit-down with Cesar Kalina go?" She didn't want Colin to waste time getting to what she wanted to know.

"He's hot for Hector's territory and promised me the moon if I worked for him and pointed out where Hector's vulnerable." Colin sat next to her in the office upstairs.

"You think he hit Hector's production line?" There was no way they could afford getting in the middle of that.

"I think Kalina is an opportunistic little prick. He acted like a tough guy, but I'm shocked he's still alive. He's about five feet tall and sounds like he's about twelve. No, whoever did that to Hector had more cojones than this little guy."

Colin laughed but she didn't join him. This game was way too dangerous to play because the cartels had an unlimited number of soldiers who lived to kill whoever the top guy aimed them at. One wrong move and you ended up getting tossed in the street without your head as an example to anyone who dared make the same mistake.

"He'll either end up dead or with more than he has now because of his drive to win." Colin shrugged. "It's a toss-up."

"Colin, you can't go around putting your finger in every pie. Eventually someone's going to get pissed, and no one will be able to keep *you* alive," Katlin said.

Katlin saved Cain from having to tell him the same thing, and she was tired of acting like a scolding parent when it came to Colin. "It sounds like you like this guy, but not that long ago you needed help with Salvatore. It wasn't Kalina or anyone but us and Carlos Luis who got rid of that for you. If you want respect, you've got to give it."

Colin shook his head and held his hands up. "I'm not reneging on Carlos. You know I'm not an asshole, Cain. I also don't want to go through life being out of the loop. Meeting with people like Kalina lets me keep my head on my shoulders by knowing who's out there." He talked like he knew she was pissed. "I'm not going to forget my friends. Carlos and I have a good thing going, and that only ends if he decides that."

"So how did this meeting make you conclude that Kalina wasn't responsible for Hector's headaches?" Cain asked. She accepted a glass of whiskey from Muriel and waited for Colin to take a sip.

"He was happy about whoever blew Hector's world to shit, and he's the kind of guy who'd be thrilled to take credit. All those guys love to take credit, and they don't give a shit who knows, but he didn't do it. Believe me, he wants to corner what Hector has, but he didn't do it. He doesn't have the cojones." Colin seemed to sense she wasn't convinced, so he calmed down and got down to trying to do that.

Cain wiped at the condensation on her glass as she mentally shifted the pieces around. "We ended up with the best deal when it comes to Carlos. The drug business isn't something I'll ever be interested in, but it won't hurt if the new king of the cartel is friendly. It'll go a long way to keeping the peace." She'd always keep true to their heritage, and people like Carlos were doing the same thing. "Drugs are something we all have to contend with, but I'd rather work with a guy I can talk to if there's a problem. So let's try not to mess that up."

"Agreed, and Kalina understood that when I turned him down. He wasn't happy about it, but I was honest." Colin held his glass up and Muriel poured him more. "That's not our problem, but you might have one brewing back home."

"What's that mean?" Katlin asked. They had enough people on the streets that they should've heard if something was up.

"I'm late getting here because I flew to New Orleans to take another meeting. I should've told you, but I wanted to get what the asshole was about." Colin used a lot of hand gestures when he spoke, and it made Cain smile. He really was hard to stay mad at.

"What asshole?" Finley asked.

"You ever heard of Jerome Rhodes?" Colin's question made Cain, Remi, Muriel, and Katlin stare at him. Finley appeared curious but Rhodes wouldn't have hit her radar when she was still with the bureau.

"That's who you met with?" Muriel asked.

"Yeah, you know him?"

Cain had only seen Rhodes that day on the levee, and her mistake had been thinking Carlos would snap him up when he took Gracelia Luis. If Rhodes survived, he was the last link to Juan and his mother. With that side of the Luis family gone, Rhodes must've taken over. Someone else trying to make his mark from what Gracelia lost would have a lot of ground to make up.

"What did he want?" Cain asked.

"Same thing Kalina did. He said he's getting ready to move major product into the country from Mexico and needed safe transport to a few places. The list he mentioned would make him viable in pretty much the whole country." Colin put his glass down and rubbed his hands up and down his thighs. "I told him to fuck off, so don't get mad. I would've ended it like I had with Kalina, respectfully, but this guy's a prick."

"I need you to tell me exactly what he said." If Rhodes perpetuated the hatred that side of the Luis family had for hers, this was going to be yet another problem.

"I got a call from his man, Pablo Castillo. I never heard of the guy, but he told me Hector Delarosa gave his boss my name. That wasn't something I believed, so I flew down and met with him. I wanted to know if this was going to be a problem for you."

"Where was he?" Cain asked. "And did you talk about Hector aside from him telling you that's who recommended you?"

"He's got one of those big places in the Quarter, and he tried to sound sympathetic to Hector's problems. He said he was picking up the slack until Hector recovered." Colin stared at the ceiling as if that would help him remember better. "That's all he said, but he insisted Hector was the one who recommended me."

"Who the hell is this guy?" Katlin asked.

"That's a good question, and one we should ask Hector. If they've met, then all the stuff he told Colin makes sense. If he didn't and that was his in, we need to figure out why he lied, and if he's the one who hit Hector's crops." Cain didn't like mysteries, especially when they were so close to home. "Let's start with someone who should know." She picked up the phone and asked to speak to Carlos.

"Cain," Carlos said, sounding happy to hear from her again so soon. "Gracias to you and Emma for the baby gift. You must meet my son."

"Congratulations again, and thanks for taking the call. I have Colin with me, and he has an interesting story. Is Paloma with you?"

"She feed the baby."

"I'll have Remi tell you, if that's okay?"

"Sí, if you think interesting, I want to know."

Cain put the phone on speaker and handed off to Remi, who switched to Spanish, and Carlos didn't interrupt her. He obviously felt more comfortable in Spanish and responded quickly. Cain was only able to catch a few words, but whatever else he was saying, it was animated.

Remi explained, "Rhodes was in business with Gracelia, but Carlos isn't sure exactly who he is, and the guy seems to come out of nowhere. He wasn't there, back when they went to the hotel to pick up Gracelia. Whoever he is, Rhodes has started making deals with small-time guys," Remi said as Carlos agreed from his end. "He wasn't anyone to worry about cause he was so small, but now with what happened to Hector, Rhodes has emerged."

"He's using Gracelia's old contacts?" Cain asked.

"Sí, but only the stupid people I do not want," Carlos said. "Gracelia think she take over for my father, but the people stay with me."

"Thank you, Carlos." She thought Jerome Rhodes would be worth looking into.

"I meet with Hector. He call like you say, and I help him."

"Good, it's not going to be a bad thing if Hector owes you a favor. Take care, amigo, and I'll be calling again when I have more on Rhodes."

"Gracias, and I will ask too." Carlos hung up and she glanced at Katlin.

"Colin, what's your schedule for the next week?"

"I'm here for the night, then going home. I don't like being away from the business too long, but if you need me to do something, I will."

"There's one thing. I need you to go into business with Jerome Rhodes." Her statement made everyone look at her like she was crazy. "The sooner the better."

CHAPTER TWENTY-TWO

W hat do you have?" Cain asked Finley a week later. Their vacation seemed like a year ago since they'd been slammed from the time they'd arrived at home. She wanted some answers before sending Colin back to meet with Jerome Rhodes, and a week should've been plenty of time to find something.

"Aside from the location of Nina, a whole lot of nothing. I checked with my contacts, and Jerome Rhodes doesn't exist. The first time he hit any radar was when he flew in from Mexico on business, but that's been a while ago. There's no record of him going back, or any activity here." Finley read from her laptop. "The house where Colin met him is being leased by a corporation, but I can't find any physical address for that either, except for a PO box in Mexico."

"I think it's time to invite our neighbor for a chat," she said. They were having breakfast after the kids had left for school. She'd sent a few more guards with the kids, with Levi's blessing. "I know you don't like Hector, but he might have some clue we haven't found. Dino did us a solid and worked through the layers the person who ordered the hit on the pub put between themselves and the moron who made the call."

"What'd he find?" Colin asked. He'd sent Judice back to deal with the business, but she was coming back that weekend. With Finley and her new family staying with them, they had a full house.

"The last guy gave up the name Pablo Castillo. I have no clue who that is, but Castillo put out some cash as well as promises about a new supply chain of crack and heroin, and the lowlife jumped at the chance to do business with him. The only other time I've heard that name is when you mentioned it," she said, pointing at Colin.

"Castillo is who called me," Colin said.

"You don't have friends in the DEA, do you?" Finley asked Cain.

"I have plenty of friends, but that's one section of law enforcement where I haven't needed any. Sept Savoie may be able to help us out if Hector doesn't know. I'll give her a call if it's necessary." She put her arm around Emma's waist when she poured her another cup of coffee. "Until we have everything we need on all this, remember to be careful, and don't go out alone, any of you."

"Is it okay for me to go to work?" Abigail asked. This was the first time Cain had seen her dressed for work since they'd gotten back. "The hospital and clinic should be fine, don't you think?"

"It should be okay, but how about you make Finley and me feel better by having someone keep you company?" She pointed to Shaun Quinn, who was standing with Dino. "Shaun promises not to bother you, but he'll be inside with you until you're ready to come back. There'll be a few more outside, but like Shaun, they'll be invisible."

"Thank you," Abigail said, her eyes on the tall blond young man. "I'd tell you I don't need anything like this, but I'll feel better not making it easy for Nicola."

"Shaun, don't let me down, and don't scare any of the kids," she said, making Abigail laugh.

"Fin, let's make that call and get Hector's take on all things Rhodes."

Everyone stood, and she kissed Emma as Fin and Abigail said their good-byes. "Are you going anywhere today?" Emma asked.

"I'll be home all day, but let's see what Hector has to say. Once I get the pub and Josh sorted out, we might need to make a trip to New York." She hadn't forgotten Sacha Oblonsky and his ambitions. "Just for a night, but like Chicago, there might be time for dinner and some fun."

"That's a good way to make me forget that you're inviting that asshole and his bitch of a daughter over for coffee," Emma whispered in her ear.

"Such colorful language, Mrs. Casey." She chuckled when Emma slapped her ass. "And I promise—no coffee unless his story's good."

It took forty minutes for Hector to make it to the house. The weather had changed from the blue skies of the morning to a downpour that had dropped the temperature into the forties. That was unusual for the city, but it was nice to light the fireplaces every so often. She stared into the flames until Hector walked into the office, and she wasn't surprised to see Tracy Stegal with him.

"Hector...Ms. Stegal, welcome." She pointed them to the chairs that faced her desk, and everyone else took one of the seats Katlin had brought in. "Hector, my apologies for not calling sooner, but I'd like to go over some things with you."

"Yes, my trip to Cozumel let me learn things I should learn from you." Hector sounded pissed, and he did a good job of burying those emotions, but gritted teeth were hard to ignore. "Carlos Luis likes you."

"It's mutual. I understand what Carlos has been through because of what happened to his father."

"How about my sister?" Tracy asked, biting off each word. She shut her mouth when Hector glared at her.

Cain felt a chill go through her, and her first reaction was to put a bullet through this bitch's forehead. She understood loss, but she understood controlling yourself in business even more. "Your sister was Nunzio Luca's fault. He sacrificed her to save himself, but I'm not in the mood to explain it again. I'm also not going to sit here and take shit from you in my house. If you want to know who destroyed your fields, figure it out yourself." She stood up and leaned over her desk. "And if you don't understand the rules of the game, you shouldn't play. Kim did, but she decided to play with an idiot, and it got her killed. The only explanation for that is that she was in love with Nunzio, and love made her stupid as well as blind."

"Cain, that will not happen again," Hector said. "You have my apology, and I take responsibility for Tracy." Hector reached over and squeezed Tracy's wrist to the point of her wincing as he was talking.

"First Marisol and now her," she said, nodding in Tracy's direction. "I can't be a friendly neighbor if I have to be worried about being shot by the women in your life every time I go out."

"My apologies, Ms. Casey, but Kim was my sister. She was the only family I had, and my anger over her death isn't completely gone." Tracy wasn't exactly contrite, but she was civil. "I'd never do anything to harm you or your family, and I'd never betray Hector by going behind his back."

The fury over Tracy's attack wasn't completely gone, but she took a breath and tried to let it go. "Next time don't believe everything Nunzio tells you to make himself look good."

"You want her out?" Hector asked. One more squeeze made Tracy hiss, but then Hector let go.

"Forget about it, and let's get to what my people found," Cain said, going into what happened at the pub. "We've talked to almost everyone involved, and their orders came from Pablo Castillo. Do you know who that is?"

Hector closed his eyes and shook his head. "I have never heard that name."

"It was worth a shot, but we'll deal with him too once he's found. I know Carlos was going to talk to you about Cesar Kalina and what he offered my cousin, Colin." She waited until he nodded. "Colin turned him down with the explanation that he was exclusive to Carlos."

"Carlos tell me this, but what does it have to do with my fields and business?"

"We're getting to that. Do you know Jerome Rhodes?"

Hector shook his head but was looking at Tracy. She stayed quiet until he waved her on.

"Someone named Jerome Rhodes called and asked to meet with Hector, but that was a while ago. It happened right before Gracelia Luis was taken out of the game by Carlos Luis." Tracy made eye contact with Cain as if daring her to look away. Her intimidation game was laughable. "He never showed after that happened, but the reason he gave for the meeting was that he could deliver what Gracelia could not. We've never heard from him since, so I doubt he'll be a problem."

"He called Colin for a meeting and gave your name as a reference, Hector. Apparently, you're working with him and letting him pick up your slack until you're back in business."

"What the fuck?" Hector put his hands on the arms of his chair and braced himself to slide closer. "Who you say he is?" His anger made his English slip a bit and she came close to smiling.

"Jerome Rhodes. Like Tracy says, he was with Gracelia, but there's no background on this guy. Using your name made me think about his conversation with Colin. Moving major product from Florida to Arizona, New York to Seattle, and everywhere in between means he benefited from what happened to you. There's a sudden opening, and he's filling it." She could see the rage building, and if she aimed him in the right direction, he'd burn a path to Rhodes, saving her the time.

"Gracelia couldn't even hold on to what her brother had, so how is some guy who was begging for scraps making a move on Hector?" Tracy's question was a good one, but Cain expected Hector to slap her from the way he turned on her.

"Easy, this guy's a planner," Cain said. "When you plan and you have the right people, you can do what everyone else would think insane. And I'm not saying this is the guy, but I have Colin meeting with him again to see what information we can get." She held her finger up when Hector opened his mouth. They'd never get anywhere if she let him build himself into a froth. "Once I have that answer, then I'm going to gift-wrap him and deliver him to you. I'm guessing there's no way to replant your fields and harvest before you run out of inventory, but I doubt anyone would stop you from taking what belongs to Rhodes, if he's behind what happened to you."

"Give me your word." Hector stood and held his hand out.

In that moment, she thought there were worse things than the devil, and Hector fell into that category. He was friendly enough, but he made her feel dirty.

"Hector, I've never lied to you," she said, her eyes on his hand. "Sometimes you get angry because I tell you the truth, and I'm not going to change that now." He gripped her hand when she accepted his. "All you need to remember is I'm not your enemy, and you need to remind everyone in your orbit that's the case."

"Marisol is gone from my life, and Tracy will never give you a problem."

She held his hand a bit longer and then let go, not really wanting an explanation about Marisol. "I'll be in touch as soon as Colin comes back from his meeting."

"I will ask about Pablo Castillo to see who he works for. Thank you, Cain. I owe you a debt if you find this man."

"Just give me your word that you'll wait for me to call. If you drive this guy underground before we get to him, we'll never find him. That's all I'm asking."

"I give you my word, and thank you."

Hector left with Tracy's hand in his, but it seemed more to keep her in line. If he acted like Cain thought, it wouldn't be long before he flooded the streets for information. He'd want his own people trying to find answers to cut down the favors he'd owe if she beat him to it. That would be okay with her. Once people started talking, it wouldn't take long for word to get to her.

"You know he's not going to be able to help himself," Finley said. She'd been sitting off to the side listening. "I don't know him well, but he doesn't seem like the type."

"I know, and he's going to keep hitting his head against a wall until he breaks something. If he's doing that, it'll give the guys outside something to watch other than us." She tapped the side of her head and smiled. "Da used to say that shiny things are hard to look away from, and for us, Hector is the biggest shiny thing I could find."

"What exactly does that mean?" Finley asked.

"Think about your old job. The feds are always watching, and I'd like them distracted as much as I can manage. There's something about Pablo Castillo and Jerome Rhodes that bothers me. Why would Castillo hire someone to hit the pub? Who told him to do it? And why would Rhodes call Colin when there are plenty of people who could do the job he's asking for?" She tapped her fingers on the desk and took a deep breath. "It's a curious thing, and I haven't figured it out yet."

"What's our next move?" Remi asked.

"We issue another invitation, only this one has to be private. I don't want to give Mr. Castillo the chance to say no once we find him."

❖

"The guy about creamed his pants when I told him we were on for a deal." Colin's smile was wide and genuine, and the skin by his eyes crinkled. He'd just gotten back from Jerome Rhodes's place, and it sounded like the guy had gone for everything Cain had in mind.

That smile had gotten him out of more shit than Cain could imagine. "Good, and did you talk about Hector some more?" she asked.

"If you believe him, he's grieving for old Hector, but he's not turning down the business it's throwing his way. We're on for dinner at his place to discuss everything." Colin took a cigar out of her humidor, but she shook her finger at him to keep him from lighting it. "I'll go if you need me to, but this guy gives me the impression he's always the smartest guy in the room."

"I love working with guys like that," she said, her own smile widening. "Let's see if we can find Castillo before you have to spend any more time with him. I like having some of the answers before I start asking questions."

"This time he had his dad sit in on the meeting, and the old guy was full of ideas."

"His father?" That was new. "He's part of the business?"

"Sounds like it, and they look pretty close. I still miss working with my old man."

"Focus, Colin," Finley said. "Who's the father? That might be a way to narrow down our search."

"His name's Patrick Rhodes, but Jerome introduced him as Patty. That's a nice Irish name, don't you think?"

Finley typed something in and waited. It took five minutes for enough results to populate. "There are twenty matches between this area and Cabo to look at." She turned the device so Colin could look at the screen. "Are any of these guys his father?"

Colin put on reading glasses and studied each one. "Nope, the guy I met was older, white hair with a little dark streaked throughout, and he was fit. I'm not sure how old he is, but the guy was sharp up here," Colin said, tapping the side of his head. "He tried to guide Jerome without making it seem like he was doing it."

"Cain"—Lou knocked on the doorframe as he entered—"you aren't going to believe who Dino found."

"I'll give you twenty dollars if you tell me it's Pablo Castillo."

"I'll take the twenty spot, boss. Dino sent a text message to Castillo from the phone of the last guy they weeded out. He told him it was urgent that they meet. He texted Castillo there'd been a break in the chain, and you were on to them."

"I like the way the kid thinks," she said, and Lou smiled.

"Yeah, and after the text, Dino positioned our guys to wait and see if anyone took the bait. It took an hour before an older man walked into that bar at the back of the Quarter." Lou showed her a picture, but she didn't recognize him. "He bought that the dealer sent Dino to deal with the fallout."

"Where are they now? And good job on that kid's training. Dino's going to be a good man to have around."

"I told him some stories about the place out in the east, and that's where they brought him."

"We should wait until dark, but we're leaving for New York this afternoon. The meeting with Oblonsky is set, and Remi got us an audience with the top of the food chain in New York. Angelo Giordano invited us for dinner, and I'm thinking you don't turn that down. Let's get this done so we'll be ready to roll later."

"We can drive to Emma's and take the tunnel out to the river," Lou suggested. "I'll have the boys leave a car close by."

"Good, let's go. It's been a while since we've been out there. It's still working after the storm?" She put her jacket on and let Emma know where she was going. Remi was providing her plane again, so it wasn't like they'd be late for their flight.

"It flooded in the back, but the rest of it is working. At least for what we need it for, it'll be good."

The bar that shared Emma's name was closed until the repairs from the drive-by could be done, but Muriel's firm was still working upstairs. Lou lifted the trapdoor behind the bar, and the only people watching when they reached the other side of the tunnel, hidden beneath the length of a city block, were the ones who worked for her. Lou got behind the wheel of the crappy car the boys had left for them at the exit to the tunnel and took his time and his usual circuitous route when he wanted to ensure there was no one behind them. New Orleans east was still desolate, so a tail would've stood out.

The processing plant in New Orleans east had been in her family for years, and it'd been about that long since it had been used for meat processing. Its history was much grimmer than when they lined cattle up in the small stockyard toward the back. There were only weeds growing there now, with litter washed up by the storm against the walls.

Lou pulled in through the large doors and motioned for the guys to close them. The small Hispanic man didn't say anything as she walked up and sat in the old leather chair across from him. Dino had put Castillo on the rollers that led to the grinder, and Cain was sure he'd been thinking about that since they'd arrived. If she was a gambler, she'd bet a flax seed wouldn't fit up his ass he had it puckered so tight.

"We haven't met, so let me introduce myself." She crossed her legs and placed a hand on her boot. "I'm Cain Casey." The guy stayed quiet, but she could see in the movement of his eyes that he understood what that meant. This was a trapped animal looking for any escape. "We haven't met, but you know me. I know that because you shot up my place and wounded one of my people." She tapped loudly on the alligator skin covering her heel and stared at him to see if he'd say anything. "My question is why? Why would you do something that has done nothing but piss me off?"

"I no understand." Castillo sounded like he wasn't outwardly concerned, but the excessive swallowing was giving her a different impression.

"You don't, huh?" She shook her head and put her foot down. "I usually have a system for this, Señor Castillo. I tie someone to a chair and put bullets in the most painful places in the body." His eyes widened, which meant he understood plenty. "I'm not going to do that today."

"I no understand why I here." He put his hands out like he was about to start praying. "I no know you."

"I'm not going to do that today, because I'm going to put you into that grinder feet first and take you a little at a time until you tell me what I want to know." She put her hand up when he took a breath. "If you repeat yourself again, I'll put you through that thing and make it last for hours. Just nod if you understand that." He did and she lowered her voice. "Why did you hit my place?"

"I no do that." Castillo's voice seemed to go up a few octaves, but that was about to get much worse.

"Lou," she said. Lou and Dino picked the guy up and placed him in the intake feed, holding tight as he struggled. "Trust me when I tell you I have enough stuff here to wake you up, so you're not missing a moment of this when you pass out from the pain." She stood and walked to the controls. "You have three seconds before your feet are coming out the other end, shoes and all. I should tell you this machine can handle an entire cow."

"Madre de Dios, no. I pay for you to stay away from my business." Castillo spoke loudly through his tears.

"You must think I'm stupid, Pablo." Dino handed her his passport, and she flipped through it. "You're not the boss. El jefe doesn't show up for a meeting with a low-level dealer. That's gangster lesson number one, and that you don't know it means you do deserve to lose your feet." She put her hand on the switch, and he screamed again.

"My boss! He no want you to mess with his business. He tell me to do it."

"Tell me who your boss is, and this ends. And before you lie, think about what'll happen if I already know the answer." She drummed her fingers on the controls and watched the snot drain from his nose. This asshole didn't care that Josh got shot. "You make me ask again, and I'm going to turn it on until I reach your kneecaps."

"Señor Rhodes, he tell me to do it."

"Jerome Rhodes?" She took her cell out and hit speed dial as Pablo nodded like a madman. "Emma, tell Colin not to meet with Rhodes. He'll know what I'm talking about."

"He's outside playing with the girls, but I'll tell him."

"Pablo, think carefully about this next question. I have everything

I need, but a wrong answer will make the crabs in the lake very happy tonight."

"Qué?"

"Was it Rhodes who hit Hector?"

"Sí, it make it easy to do business with Delarosa on his knees."

"Gracias, amigo." There was nothing more he could tell her that she didn't already know. She nodded at Lou, who shot Pablo through the heart. It was the least she could do for his truthful answers. "Send the cleaning crew, and make sure this place is locked up when they're done."

"You got it, boss," Dino said, taking her place at the controls.

They made it home the same way they'd left, and Colin was waiting in the office. "Call Rhodes and tell him you're ready to do business, but you'd rather have dinner at Vincent's place in two days. Tell him you love the food, but remember to wait the couple of days. We need to have a meeting with Rhodes, but I'm going to have to let Hector know about it."

The front door opened, and she heard Abigail come in and greet Emma. Finley had already left for the city, having arranged a meeting with her old partner. It was time the FBI knew Nicola was among the living. Finley was going to meet them at the hotel, and if her story was good enough, hopefully the feds would be useful for once. She only needed one shot at Nicola, just one.

"Are you ready?" Emma asked. "I know you have a meeting before our dinner, so you need to get moving. The sooner we get there, the sooner Dallas, Abigail, and I can go shopping while you take care of things."

"I'm ready, lass. Today's been kind of a grind, and I'm ready for a change of scenery."

CHAPTER TWENTY-THREE

Remember, none of you lose the guards," Cain warned Emma, Dallas, and Abigail when they landed. She'd brought plenty of people with them, but the thought of letting all three women out of her sight brought on a little nervousness.

"Stop worrying, my love, and we'll meet you at the hotel later. I promise you'll like the results," Emma said before pulling her head down and kissing her. "Be careful. I'm freaked out by where you're going and who you're going to see. Remember what happened the last time I let you go out alone."

"If someone stabs me, I'll give you permission to spank me," she said, putting her hand on Emma's butt. "I love you, lass."

Their trip into the city was slow because of traffic, and she was surprised by where Sacha Oblonsky wanted to meet. She'd been to the city plenty of times but had never set foot in Trump Tower, finding the owner and the place over the top, and not in a good way. There was a man just inside the door who took them up to the correct floor without a word.

They got out to a dimly lit corridor where two large wooden doors swung open. In any other scenario she'd have probably turned back and headed right back down. It smelled of a setup, but she'd brought enough manpower to fight her way out. Running had never been her style but neither had stupidity, so she was on high alert.

"Casey?" The large man who walked out had a smile on his face and his hands out as if he was about to embrace her.

"Cain, and you must be Sacha Oblonsky." She took his hand and introduced him to the others. "Thank you for meeting with us."

"You're very convincing, and you told me a lot of things that were good to hear." He walked them in, and the place was as tacky as the downstairs. Gilt as a decorating scheme should've died centuries before. "Welcome to the Hell Fire Club, or what's left of it."

"The FBI isn't subtle at times, is it? And this time they got too close to what's important to you." There was a container full of ice with a bottle of vodka at the center surrounded by shot glasses. Vodka wasn't her favorite, but today wasn't the time to complain about it. "Who do you blame? Yourself, the feds, or Nicola?"

"You're blunt for someone I just met." He scooted to the edge of his seat and poured a shot glass for everyone. The liquor came out slowly, as if it was syrup. That it had just come out of the freezer would make it more tolerable. "I like that. Sugarcoating is for children."

"The truth is something we all hate to face sometimes, but it's a part of life. You've had something precious taken from you, and now I'd like to know how you're going to respond." She held up her glass, glad Sacha was still smiling. "But first, a toast. To new friendships and the truth."

"I'll drink to that." He slammed the shot back and poured another. "What did you mean by losing something precious to me?"

"The business belonged to your family." She waved her hand. "It's gone, but you were in charge of what was left. That is, until recently. You lost out a second time." She wondered if he'd bite, and when he sighed dramatically, she slid another piece in place.

"My cousin Nicola has pulled off the impossible. She's risen from the grave and has been making demands from her first breath." He finished the second shot and shrugged. "If you're here to do business with her, then my bluntness will give her an excuse to finish what she threatened. I'm not the kind of guy who's going to live in fear until the bogeyman comes for real."

"That makes two of us. Nicola has aimed her guns at my family as well, so I think we can be friends if only for one brief moment in time. We want the same thing."

"What's that?" He sat back and stretched his legs out, seeming relaxed.

"To live doing what we love without someone hovering close by, without someone constantly threatening to take it all away." No one said anything for a good two minutes after she finished talking, but she expected it from Remi, Katlin, and Simon. She'd have to wait and see what Sacha's silence meant.

"You want Nicola dead," he said, not posing a question.

"Nicola's a problem, and problems at times fester into something that becomes unmanageable. The best cure for festering is removing the irritant."

"You have a talent with words as well as the truth." He shook his finger at her and gave her a big belly laugh. "The only truth that counts now is if you're here to ask my permission or my help."

"If you want the same thing I do, then it's time to commit. Only the simpleminded wait for permission." She shrugged and he laughed. "Nicola is something both our families want gone, so we should do it together. That way we can't push off the blame, and we both get what we want." She circled the top of the empty shot glass with her index finger and waited.

"She still has friends in the family. Me gunning down my cousin won't be something the rest of them will forget in a millennium. We're Russian—our memories as well as our grudges last forever."

"If you took over so easily, there have to be a few men you trust. Two cars and four men are all we need, along with a location." She looked him in the eye, and he didn't hesitate to hold out his hand. "Do you know where she is?"

"The bitch called me and handed me the head of my most trusted man. She did it because I tried taking what was hers, so she made sure I didn't forget the lesson by taking something precious from me." He punched his palm with his fist and made what sounded like a growl. "She should've stayed dead."

"Then tell me where she is."

"How do you know I can tell you?" His curiosity seemed to drown out his anger.

"Because you seem like a smart and reasonable man. If someone embarrassed me and killed one of my people, I'd make them pay. To cash in on my rage, I'd need to know where to aim." She pointed at him. "You're smart enough to know she's keeping an eye on you, but she's arrogant enough to not expect it in return."

"What happens to me if I agree to this?"

"Nothing from our end, but I can't predict how the other families in this city will react. That might change if they know our family helped you."

"Would you care if I took care of this myself?" He held his hand out again and waited. "It's my family and my responsibility. That bitch *has* been watching since our meeting but hasn't picked up the guys I have on her ass."

Cain gave him a quick smile. "Let me know if you change your mind and need help. With us in town it might take some of the heat off you once it's done."

"Thank you, my friend, but I don't mind heading into hell alone."

"Fair enough." She didn't protest when he hugged her and kissed both cheeks. "There's a little devil in us all to help us bear the heat."

❖

"It's time to go back. If you're telling me Casey's back home, that means so is Abigail, with my children." Nicola was sitting by the window in Delmonico's, in the mood for a steak even if this wasn't her favorite part of town. "Once we get that out of the way, we can come back here, but have someone start looking for a bigger apartment. I don't want the kids in my face all the time."

They'd taken some time to visit the new trailer setup in the section of town that had clusters of storage units. At night the area was dead, but she was glad to see their operation was as busy as ever. After a short conversation, the people they had running the show were aware she was back and were clear as to how they accounted for the money from now on. With an infusion of cash, she could start rebuilding. The one thing that had stayed the same were the two clubs she'd founded with Fredrick. Those had accumulated enough money for her to not have to worry about the future.

"School's back in session," Nina said, "and the people I left behind said the girls are in class again. We still haven't found where they're staying, and Abigail has found a way to change vehicles every day to throw us off."

"You can't follow a car home? I'm beginning to doubt you're helping me." She stopped when the waitstaff delivered their meals. There was another headache starting, but she hoped eating something would stop it from becoming debilitating. "How hard can it be to tail children?"

"We see them come in the morning but never see them leave. It's not a matter of following them—it's finding out how they're getting out of there. I can't be sure, but it's like Abigail figured out you're still alive." Nina spoke to her as if she didn't care what happened. "Did you contact her?"

"I'm not an idiot, and there's no way Abigail figured that out. She's not going to know I'm alive until I'm ready to kill her. Once we get back, I'll show you how it's done." She cut into her steak and smiled when Nina glared. Getting under someone's skin was entertaining, and Nina was never this easy to rattle. "What else have you heard?"

"I talked to our contact at NYPD and asked about Finley Abbott. She left the force after the attempts on Abigail's life. Where she is now wasn't something they could answer." Nina put her cutlery down and picked up her wine. "We know she's in New Orleans, so the only answer is that she followed Abigail back. The children have taken her name, which means she followed Abigail for more reasons than just protecting her."

"That's the only answer? There's more to it than that, and you need to find out what it is. Why in the hell would a cop leave her job for Abigail?" Her appetite disappeared at the thought of Abigail with someone else. The little bitch knew what was expected of her, and hopping into bed with someone else wasn't acceptable. The fact that she'd turned her children away from their true heritage was her real sin, though.

"Abigail and the world thought you were dead," Nina pointed out as if it should've been obvious.

"You just finished telling me she figured out I was alive." She waved Nina off from saying anything else. "Finish and let's get out of here." They ate the rest of their meal in silence, and she sat thinking as Nina finished paying. After she took care of her family, she was thinking of starting over in Florida. New York would always be the center of their business, but there was no reason not to take some time and let the kids get used to being with her again.

Nina's phone rang right after she stood, and she figured Nina would be right behind her as she left the restaurant. The weather outside was biting cold, and she cursed that the car wasn't waiting. She glanced up and down the street and didn't see much of anything—actually, nothing at all. Her gut made her turn around. The first shot hit as she reached for the door. Her only thought was that Nina wasn't standing beside her. The next hit knocked her to her knees, and the last one she was conscious of pierced her side.

Then there was nothing but darkness.

❖

Cain sat across from Angelo Giordano and laughed at the story he was telling. Remi had been right that Angelo was a lot like Vinny but with a much smoother delivery. There had been more than one story about her grandfather and his time in the city. Angelo's father had been a young man when her grandfather had taken over for his father in New Orleans, and they'd become friends when the older Giordano had come to the city on vacation.

"Cain, I'm glad you finally accepted my invitation," Angelo said. The waiter walked around the table and filled everyone's glass. "Remi and I had a great conversation in Vegas, and I think we can do business."

"Do you have any business in New Orleans now?" She smiled when Emma put her hand on her thigh and squeezed, even though she was having her own conversation with Angelo's wife, Jessica. The blonde, like Angelo, wasn't young, but she was still beautiful and seemed devoted.

"No, my holdings are here and in Vegas. Gambling is still a profitable business, and the rest of our operations are funding the expansion I have planned for Vegas and the Indian casinos here." He lifted his glass and waited for her to do the same. "Remi and her family have a good thing going with the Gemini. I don't want to intrude on that, but there's no reason we can't toast to the future. Am I right, Remi? Cain?"

"Life is much better with friends, Angelo. That's always been my belief, and we're always open to new opportunities." She tapped her glass against his, followed by Remi's. "We talked to Sacha Oblonsky earlier today."

"Please tell me you're not doing business with that trash." Angelo's expression changed, and he grimaced like someone was holding something rotten under his nose.

"Not in this lifetime," Remi said.

"Give us more credit than that." Cain told him the story of Abigail and why she'd gone to talk to Sacha. When the time called for it, she didn't mind stroking someone's ego, and Sacha had certainly acted accordingly. "Now all we have to see is if he has the guts to do something about it."

"That might be good for all of us if he does. Yuri Antakov and Nicola were vicious but smart, and with his death, if someone like Sacha takes over, the business will be taken a piece at a time. The feds will get their share, and their rivals will get the rest." He stood and pointed to the door of the private dining room. It opened to a quiet balcony that was glassed in. "If he takes your advice, it'll be me who owes you a favor. These assholes have been a pain in my ass for years.

Believe what you want about me, but I'm not into little girls and human trafficking."

"Cain," Lou said from the door. "I hate to bother you, but I need a minute."

"Excuse me," she said, glancing at Remi. Her friend smiled and offered Angelo a Cuban Cohiba.

"Finley called. There was an incident at Delmonico's. Someone opened fire, and there are two dead at the scene."

"Is Nicola one of those two?" Nothing in life was ever this easy, but you never knew.

"Oblonsky swears she went down, but the two dead are the valet workers from the restaurant. Fin is checking with hospitals, but the place is crawling with cops. I'll let you know if Fin calls with anything else. The two guys we sent to the scene pretty much said the same thing. The valets went down, but the witnesses said there were a few others who got shot."

"It's time to wrap this up, so get ready to move." She went back out and told Angelo and Remi what happened. Angelo understood her need to go and wanted to make a few calls of his own.

"Thank you for everything," she said, kissing both his cheeks.

"The next time we meet in New Orleans," Angelo said. "I think our families are meant to do business."

They moved out in three different cars with Lou and Simon seeming trigger happy. As they got in, Cain noticed the FBI team led by Joe and Shelby right across the street in an SUV. She could imagine the conversation going on in there as they tried to figure out what she was doing meeting with such illustrious company. The drivers Angelo had provided didn't stop until they were back at the hotel.

"She's not dead?" Abigail asked when they were in the suite. "Are you kidding me?"

"We don't know that, but according to her idiot cousin, she *was* shot. I've checked with every hospital, and she's not in the morgue," Finley said.

"You're asking the wrong people," Cain said. She took out the card Angelo had given her and called him. "I hate to bother you after such a great meal, but I have a question."

"Like you said, we're friends, so ask."

"Who's your doctor?"

"He's a retired surgeon from the Upper East Side. You just left, so don't tell me you need his services already." Angelo laughed, and it made her like him even more.

"Supposedly Nicola got hit, but no one can find her."

"He wouldn't cross the family to work on someone like Nicola. There are consequences to actions like that."

"Do you mind if I talk to him? Maybe he can point me in the right direction."

"Let me send one of the boys, and he can come to you. I have a feeling you're like us, and you've drawn a crowd since you've gotten here. Dr. Cecil Black is who'll be calling."

They waited an hour before someone knocked. A large tough guy pushed an older man inside and kept a hand on him once they were in the room. If the smaller man was Cecil Black, he appeared terrified. His hands shook as he held them between his knees when he was pushed into a chair.

"Tell them, or I swear I'll put a bullet in your head right now," the large man said.

"Does Mr. Giordano know I'm here?" Cecil seemed to think he'd found the question that would get him out of there.

"He's going to give me a bonus for killing you when I tell him what you did." The guy put a gun to Cecil's head and pulled back the hammer. "Talk."

"Three people showed up on my doorstep. I'd never seen them before, and two of them had been shot. The woman they said was their boss was in bad shape, and I removed four bullets. But the other woman only had a shoulder injury."

"I need a name," Cain said, and everyone stared between her and Cecil. "And if you want to walk out of here, you're going to give it to me."

"The man who carried the severely injured woman called her Nicola. All I had time to do was stop the bleeding. Once I did that, the other woman ordered her moved and they left. Nina was the woman with her, and she paid double my fee. Once she paid, they disappeared." Cecil combed his wispy white hair back with both hands. "If she doesn't get her friend to a hospital, I doubt she'll make it. I can't say for sure, but I think one of the bullets hit a kidney."

"Where else?" Abigail asked.

He counted off on his fingers. "Through her right side at kidney level, the shoulder, leg, and left arm. Before you turn me over to Mr. Giordano, the man with these women put a gun to my head and threatened me. From the Russian accent, I believed him. I swear, I had no choice."

"Where'd she go?" Cain asked.

"There's no way they could fly, but all Nina said was they had to get out of town, and they needed me to stabilize Nicola. I did, but it was patchwork at best. That's all I know."

"Wait here." Cain motioned to the bedroom where everyone followed her. "This is only speculation…"

"Your guesses are usually on point," Remi said.

"They don't have the numbers to fight another attack off, and Nicola doesn't trust the family to fight for her. She threatened Sacha, and I'm sure there were a few others on her list, but Nina knows better than to call them for backup."

"What are you saying?" Emma asked.

"They really are getting out of here, and we need to figure out where that is. If that old guy out there is right, Nicola is on borrowed time. If that's true, then we need to punch her clock." She sat on the bed and tried to think. "Fin, what did your boss tell you?"

"Russell is out of town, and I'm not going to trust anyone else with this information," Fin answered.

"How about your old partner? You trusted him to get Abigail and the kids out of town."

"Peter is okay, but do you want to give it to him first?" Fin walked closer to her as if to gauge her reaction.

"You tell your partner, and once he shares that with your old boss, Russell Welsh will beat us to New Orleans." Cain couldn't hide Finley from her orbit forever, and this might be a good way to bring her out of the shadows. "He'll be the best person to lead any team against Nicola, and it's about time you introduce your family. We'll think of a way to make sure it doesn't bite either of us."

"What about Nicola?" Abigail asked. "I don't know how much more I can take."

"I can't answer that, but I'll bet anything Nina and whoever this other guy is took her out of the city."

"They could end up anywhere," Dallas said. That was probably what everyone was thinking.

"Not really," Remi said, coming and sitting next to her on the bed.

"She's right," Cain agreed. "Leaving changes depending on how you're doing it. Nicola's hurt, so she can't get on a plane bleeding, and trains will be out as well." Cain was interested in keeping everyone calm, but this was the worst possible scenario. She wanted a clean kill so that she could stop obsessing over Nicola, and if she was truthful, that's what she'd been doing. "Abigail, is there a place the family liked to go? A kind of retreat or favorite spot that they went often?"

"The only places we visited were New York and Miami. The only change to that was our honeymoon. We went to Paris, but after that our world centered on those two places, but sometimes the family came to visit us."

"Miami was where Fredrick was, right?"

"Yes," Abigail said. She appeared more grief stricken by Nicola's survival than her death. "Do you think he could've survived that crash too?"

"That's going to take time, but we'll get there. Don't worry that I'll go back on my word. The world is a big place, like Dallas said, but when you're hurt, you have a tendency to run to the familiar to lick your wounds. We find the place a monster like Nicola feels safe, and we find Nicola."

They went back out, and the big guy had put his gun away, but Cecil didn't appear any less scared. "I need you to write down exactly what you did and what's wrong with Nicola. You can add what you did for Nina as well."

"How's that going to help us?" Finley asked. She didn't say another word when Cain stared her down. This was no longer an FBI operation where plenty of questions were helpful.

"I want a full medical report, so get to it." She sat and drummed her fingers on the arm of her chair with one hand while Emma held the other one. It took Cecil a half hour before he handed over what she wanted. "I'm not sure what Mr. Giordano has in mind when it comes to you, but working outside the parameters usually brings stiff penalties."

"I know that, but when you're having to put in stitches with a gun to your head, it makes you forget whatever promises you made." Cecil's laugh was grim. "Hell, Mr. Giordano might do the same and pull the trigger, but I knew what I was getting into. He's been good to me over the years, and I'm sorry I betrayed his confidence."

"I'm sure his man here will tell him that. But I need to know if, in your medical opinion, Nicola will survive."

"If I had to guess, the odds are less than fifty–fifty. You can survive a shot to a vital organ if you have it treated in a hospital. If she's traveling outside the city, I doubt she'll live past Jersey."

"Let's hope, for all our sakes, you're right."

CHAPTER TWENTY-FOUR

Emma ran her hands down Cain's back in the shower. The night before everyone hadn't left until almost one in the morning, and Cain had been exhausted by the time they finally got to go to bed. They'd all agreed to a later start in the morning, and they had to talk to Sacha one more time before they headed home.

"What are you thinking?" Emma asked when Cain turned around and rinsed the shampoo out.

"I'm thinking that I should've never left something like this to an idiot like Oblonsky. You know how I feel about loose ends, and Nicola will be a threat to the family until she's put down like a rabid dog." She took the bath sponge from Emma and returned the favor. "I'm sorry this trip didn't turn out like we'd planned."

"You think I'm worried about that?" Emma pinched her as she bit her shoulder. "There's time for fun and time for work. Right now, I need you to finish what you started. If Nicola is just wounded and figures out you had anything to do with that, she's really going to come after you."

"You can tell her yourself that I'm taken." She kissed Emma and pressed her against the shower wall. "I'm ready to get home and to familiar turf."

"You're on familiar turf right now," Emma said, dropping to her knees. She had to fight to stay on her feet when Emma did her best to drive her insane. It ended too soon, but she wasn't selfish and picked Emma up and pressed her to the wall again and slammed her fingers in. There was something to be said for fast and passionate, but she didn't want a steady diet of it.

"And you know your way around the terrain," Emma said with her legs wrapped around Cain's waist.

"I much prefer the scenic route, but I'll take you however I can get you."

They finished and had coffee in the main room of the suite, dressed in the hotel robes. Emma called home as she checked for messages, and she let Emma's voice relax her as she listened to her talking to the kids.

"We'll be home by the time school ends, so be good for your grandparents."

There was a message from Sacha as well as one from Angelo, both of them asking her to call. At the moment she was interested in talking to Angelo more than Sacha. Maybe if Sacha had the opportunity in the future to make the choice of accepting help from someone who knew what they were doing instead of going on his own, he'd wise up. She doubted it, though. People like Sacha went through life wearing the blinders their upbringing clamped on them.

"Good morning, Angelo," she said, stepping back in the bedroom.

"My man tells me you talked to the doctor."

"He did a lot of talking, and it was nothing I wanted to hear. That bitch is still alive, or she was last night." The street under their window was full of people, and all of them seemed in a hurry to get somewhere.

"He learned his lesson and got his leash shortened, but I do have news. There's an ambulance service that has ties to one of my brothers—one had someone charter a bus for an out-of-town client who was willing to pay for a long haul. The patient was a victim of a gunshot and couldn't fly."

"Do they have a destination?" If she was truly blessed, it would be as easy as following an ambulance and killing the patient.

"That's the thing. They were about fifty miles out of the city heading due south when two troopers called in three bodies. The whole crew of EMTs is dead." Angelo sounded pissed. "When we find these people, I'm asking you to be my stand-in when it comes to getting a piece of these assholes. Someone has to pay for the lives of three innocents."

"I give you my word on that, and I promise to send you some heads by special courier." She finished her call and turned to find Emma standing by the door, her robe hanging open. "I know we promised not to bother anyone before eleven, but we need to talk to Abigail."

"What, now? We just woke up."

She told her what Angelo had said, and Emma made the call. They had enough time to get dressed before Finley knocked on their door.

"Sorry to get you up early, but I need to know every address Fredrick was linked to in Miami. Try to remember every house you visited or read about while you were down there." If the ambulance was headed south, Miami had to be the destination, and she was willing to commit men to find Nicola.

"Cecil must've been telling the truth if they needed an ambulance to travel. Why kill the EMTs so quickly, though?" Finley asked.

"Keeping Nicola safe right now means limiting the number of people who know where she is. Nina either picked up someone who can monitor her as they go or is willing to chance that Nicola will survive." She took the list from Abigail and squeezed her hand to take that frozen expression off her face. "I'd be willing to bet that after they dumped those guys, they dumped the transponder that tracks where the ambulance is right along with them."

"This is a nightmare that never ends." Abigail sounded miserable, and no one could blame her. "The thing I'm most afraid of is the kids finding out she's still alive and trying her best to kill me."

"Kids are more intuitive and smarter than we give them credit for," Emma said. "They're also forgiving. I'm living proof of that. In your case, though, I think if they do find out, it'll be the excuse they haven't perhaps given themselves to let the past go." Emma hugged Abigail, and Cain motioned for Finley to follow her to the bedroom.

She dialed Sacha, and he answered immediately. He sounded a bit desperate. "Good morning," she said as she put the phone on speaker.

"Giordano called me this morning and told me about his doctor. That bitch is still alive."

"She is and headed south. We have to agree that Miami is where she'll end up if she survives the trip, and that we'll work together this time to make sure the job is finished. I'm sending my people there, so be careful not to kill anyone who's trying to help you."

"As blunt as ever, my friend. I can agree to that as long as your people agree to the same." Sacha laughed, but it sounded forced. "Do you think Nicola's woman will want payback for me moving against her?"

"Abigail will send you an edible arrangement in thanks if you bury a knife in Nicola's skull. The only one who wants Nicola alive is Nicola. Once that's done, you'll never hear from Abigail or her children again. The Antakov side of the family will be erased and will want no future claim on the family."

"You sound so sure, but there's still Linda's brothers to consider."

"Accept that I'm telling you the truth, Sacha. There's a new leader, and the only way anyone takes the crown away from you is if you give it away." She smiled at Finley, and the tension in her cousin's shoulders seemed to ease. Life was about meticulously lining up dominos with a steady hand for days, but it made it that much more satisfying when you flicked the first one over. "Do you want to give it away?"

"Fuck, no."

"Then long live the king."

❖

Nina sat in the uncomfortable seat in the back of the ambulance and tried to ignore the pain in her lower back as she watched the slight rise and fall of Nicola's chest. Her boss had yet to regain consciousness, but she was still alive. Once Nicola was able to form words, her first would be to order her death, of that she was certain. The phone call she'd received as they were leaving the restaurant warned her there were men in the kitchen waiting to kill Nicola, so she'd stayed inside to cover Nicola's back. That meant she hadn't been there when the first bullet hit.

"Fuck," she said softly. She'd been inside, and Nicola was outside, close to death. It'd been a good thing she'd had Dimitri with them, and he'd been able to carry Nicola to the closest car and hotwire it to get them to safety. Dimitri was one of David's trusted guards and had wept when he'd seen Nicola for the first time, glad she was alive.

"Nearly there," Dimitri said from the front seat. "I called, and the doctor is waiting."

"Good, I think we're running out of time."

"She's a fighter," Dimitri said with conviction. "She'll hang on so she can put a bullet in every person who did this."

She felt them turn and slow. Just as suddenly the back doors opened and the bright sun blinded her momentarily. Four people worked to get Nicola out, and they wheeled her off faster than Nina could follow. Her legs were asleep, and the pain of standing was crippling. She stood and stared at the house where they'd be stuck until Nicola crawled back to health, but she'd done it before.

"How did this happen?" The question was inevitable, and the man asking it might shorten the timeline to her death.

"Hello, Fredrick, and I can't answer that yet." She turned and faced him, trying not to give away her feelings of sadness at seeing him like this. "I received a call right before this happened."

From the moment she'd started working for the Antakov family, she'd fallen hard for Fredrick—a man too beautiful to describe. Now he was in a wheelchair with deep scars on his face, one hand shriveled up and useless. He shared his twin sister's view of the world, and also her unforgiving nature. She told him the entire truth and waited. The man behind Fredrick seemed to be waiting for the order to kill her for all her mistakes.

"Who knew you were going there that night?" Fredrick used the toggle on the chair to go back inside and out of the sun.

"No one. We were planning to return to New Orleans that night after dinner, and she was making plans for what had to happen once we got there. She even talked about buying a new place to make the children more comfortable." She stood, not wanting to overstep when he stopped in the large den.

"That makes no sense. There's a dozen people who know she's alive. It shouldn't be that hard to find who did this." He pointed to the teapot on the counter and the plastic cup with a straw. "She told me Sacha wasn't happy with their meeting. Do you think it could've been him?"

"No, I doubt Sacha had the balls for this." She fixed his tea and handed him the cup, touching his fingers. "I've been loyal to your family for most of my life. I'll accept whatever you want to do to me for this, but before you kill me, give me the chance to avenge her and give her a reason to fight."

"What could possibly do that?" He didn't pull his hand away, and he stared at her in a way that unnerved her.

"Let me kill Abigail and bring the children back here. Once she can see them and know they're safe, I'll go back to New York and force Sacha to tell the truth."

"Such ambition," he said, motioning her to sit. A young woman came in from the yard totally naked and knelt next to the chair. It seemed a programmed response, but there was no smile as she put her hand in his lap and touched him through his clothes.

Did he even have any sensation below the waist with his spinal injury? Another naked woman came in from another room with a comb in her hand and started smoothing down Fredrick's hair. How many more of them were there? "Not ambition, Fredrick, loyalty. I failed her in that restaurant, but it won't happen again. Just give me the chance."

"Go, and don't disappoint us again."

She was glad to get out of this house as yet another naked woman came out and fawned over Fredrick. They were probably from one of the clubs and were there to remind him of the virile man he once was, but Nina would rather shoot herself than be subjected to this daily humiliation. "Believe me—I won't." Once she'd killed Casey and Abigail, she was going to follow Linda's example and get out of this fucked-up existence. "I won't."

❖

Sabana and Shaun sat in Cain's office at home and appeared eager to leave after she finished telling them what she wanted them to do. "You're invisible while you're there. Do you understand that?"

"Yes," they said in unison.

"Sabana, I'm trusting you with this." Cain stared intently at the woman she'd come close to putting down for her attitude and actions. Sabana had a hard time following orders, but she seemed to be getting better as she spent her days watching over Hannah.

"We're taking two other people, and I'll be in touch with Lou the whole time. I'm not making any moves unless he okays them. You won't be sorry for trusting me to do this."

"Okay, get out of here, and drive safe. Don't forget to put on the Florida plates when you're out of Louisiana." The two guards were leaving for Miami in search of Nicola or anyone associated with her. Once they found them, she'd ordered them to do what anyone would do with a wounded animal beyond salvation. You put them down. All she needed was someone she trusted to tell her it was done.

Lou hugged both of them good-bye and spoke softly to them before they walked out. It appeared his relationship with Sabana was still ongoing. "Colin is waiting, boss," he said once they were alone.

"Welcome back," Colin said, bending to kiss her cheek before he sat. "We're on for tonight, and I've had the Rhodes fuckers watched the whole time you were gone. You don't know Jerome, so I had some pictures taken of the father while he was out. Maybe that might knock something loose in here." Colin tapped his head.

The picture of the older man made her stare. There was something vaguely familiar about him, but she couldn't quite grasp it. "This guy looks familiar, but I can't place him."

"We'll find out later, I guess. I talked to Vincent, and he's all in on letting us use the private room that leads down to the meeting room. I called Hector for you too."

"Good." She continued staring at the picture, but nothing came to her. Remi came in and she handed the picture to her. "Recognize this guy?"

"I've got no idea, but I have good news. The Biloxi casino is back at full capacity, and we've been approved for the hotel expansion we planned."

They sat and covered a few more things that needed both their attention before stopping for lunch and some more wedding planning with Emma and Dallas. Their job was to sit there and agree with whatever both women wanted. Cain listened and nodded when Emma looked at her, but that picture was still on her mind.

"We have everything we need for the yard covered, and the tent will arrive in two days, so they can start putting down the floor." Emma checked something off in a notebook, and Dallas did the same. "And we have your last fitting this afternoon."

"Kristen wants to come with us. Until I had you all, she was the only family I had, but this has been a blessing. Thanks for everything, you two," Dallas said, smiling like she was the happiest woman in existence.

"Goddammit," Cain yelled, a puzzle piece sliding into place. The outburst made them all jump.

"Derby Cain Casey, what in the holy hell is the matter with you?" Emma said in a tone that meant she was pissed.

"Sorry, and we are family, Dallas, but I just thought of something that should've occurred to me earlier." She went and got the picture off her desk. "Who does this look like if you darken the hair?" She handed the picture to Emma.

"He does seem like someone I should know," Emma said covering his hair with her hand.

"Does he resemble our rogue agent just a little bit?" Juan had changed his face to be able to come back for another try at Emma, but she'd dismissed the possibility when it came to Anthony Curtis. No one took their job seriously enough to have plastic surgery. In the back of her mind she'd always thought his dealings with Juan, and ultimately Gracelia, were a part of his undercover work for Annabel. No agent would permanently erase his identity like this unless he'd left that life behind. "Remember what Vincent told us?"

"Anthony's father had tried for years to get on Vincent's payroll.

It was one of the reasons he'd been released from the FBI," Emma said, cocking her head as she stared at the picture. "His son does look a lot like him."

"Jerome Rhodes is Anthony Curtis, and he's taken over what Gracelia had and expanded on it. It's like he fulfilled what his father failed at, only he's the boss this time. He's not taking orders from someone like Bracato."

"We should've thought of that when you figured Juan out," Emma said.

"I was certain he was working undercover, but I was wrong." She shrugged when Emma laughed. "Come on, it happens."

"You're saying Anthony pulled a Juan and changed his face surgically?" Remi asked, and she nodded. "Wow, that's messed up."

"Not really when you think of what his father wanted. Easy money and plenty of it was what he was after when he offered to work for Vincent." She tapped the picture and thought about the meeting that night. "This changes things."

"What things?" Emma asked.

"We should give the feds the opportunity to close their case," she said as she stood. "Lou," she called out the door. "Is Colin still here?"

"He's working in the sunroom."

Remi followed her out of the room, but Emma and Dallas stayed behind. "Colin, call Rhodes and see if he answers. You need to change the meeting for tonight."

"Why?" Colin asked, but he didn't sound like he was disagreeing.

"Because neither of those guys is leaving alive, but I don't want them to disappear. There's no way to move bodies out of Vincent's without someone noticing."

"That's new," Colin said, smiling. "Are we hanging them from the gates or something?"

"No, I have something completely different in mind."

They listened in as Colin told Jerome about his change of plans and asked if he could meet in his hotel suite instead. Getting them out of the Hilton Riverside was going to be a lot easier than Vincent's basement. Jerome didn't hesitate to agree and said he'd be there in a few hours.

"Let's finish what needs to be done wedding-wise, and we'll meet you at the warehouse in New Orleans east." Cain put her hand on Remi's back and aimed her for the door. "With any luck they'll let me give you a get-together to say good-bye to bachelorhood."

"You're crazy if you think that," Remi said and they both laughed.

It took them some time to pick up Hector and lose everyone's tail, but eventually they were on their way. Hector appeared amused as they drove in the crappiest car Lou could find to the most unpopulated section of town. That he'd agreed to come alone surprised her, but he seemed to need revenge more than safety. Lou pulled into an abandoned warehouse full of rotting food. Cain didn't want to give away the location of any of her places to Hector.

"If you plan to kill me, I have made it easy for you," Hector said.

"I plan to make you a happy man, so we'll leave the dying to someone else today." They got out of the car, and Colin opened the door to the office where the smell abated but not completely. "You wanted answers, Hector, and we're about to find some."

Jerome and Patty Rhodes sat with only their eyes moving as Cain and her crew entered the space. Dino and one of his guys held guns to their heads, which accounted for the stillness, but she did notice Jerome's eyes widen when he saw her come into view. It was an expression that didn't need the words *oh shit*, as they were definitely implied.

"Of all the movers in this business, Jerome, you picked my cousin. Of all the dumbass moves to make, you went straight for the most damaging." She slapped his face gently and laughed. "I've heard your name a few times since Gracelia's death, and I was amazed at your ability to make the right move time and time again."

"What are you talking about?" Jerome asked.

"You're new to the game, but you were smart and leapfrogged over quite a few people to position yourself to be successful. You were like a grandmaster chess champion, the way you maneuvered yourself close to the top spot. Like you knew exactly who all the players were and how they'd move. It was genius, but let's talk about something else." She took her father's switchblade from her pocket, and the sound of it flicking open made the older man breathe a little harder. "Like how the body has a multitude of fleshy parts you can stab over and over to inflict pain without killing."

"What's wrong with what I did? And you don't have the right to hold me here." Jerome looked her in the eye and seemed to be trying to keep his voice calm. "You would've done the same—have done the same, if I've heard right."

"True, but then my father taught me well. I've gotten to where I am because of my hard work and by using my head, and not because of the FBI's playbook. How many days of your life did you waste in the back of that shitty van, wondering what happened in meetings like this?" She pressed the tip of her blade on the inside of his thigh a few inches from his crotch. "Knowing all the time that I was as dirty as you imagined but could never prove…Is that what turned you? Did you turn your back on your old life for this one because it's so easy to get away with doing what you want?"

"What?" Jerome asked, his voice going up a few octaves. "I don't even know who you are."

She glanced up at Dino briefly and he cocked his gun. It was incentive to keep Jerome in his seat as she pushed the blade through the fleshy part of his inner thigh slowly until it hit the chair. Jerome gritted his teeth as she twisted it, pulling it out. "I usually shoot my way to the truth, but today I have time to kill."

Remi laughed at that. "I'd take her literally on that one."

"You watched and watched until you couldn't take it anymore, and then you found Juan. Little Juan, so eager to prove his manhood that he kidnapped my wife and tied her to a table. It was the only way he could get a girl to talk to him." She repeated the painful exercise on his other leg and was amazed he stayed quiet. "You helped him with that. Was he planning to let you have a turn?"

"I don't know."

Jerome swallowed and shook his head to clear the sweat from his eyes. The room was cold, but she could see the fat droplets caused by his pain and his fear. The sight quelled that part of her that had raged at what had happened to Emma. She'd gotten back the power she'd lost that day.

"I don't know what you mean."

She twisted the blade and pulled out again, dragging it until it was against his side. It made her think of Cecil and his declaration that you could survive if someone shot you through the kidney. "I don't think that was hard to follow. You made all these genius moves but followed them with the biggest fuckups you could think of."

"Leave him alone," his father yelled.

"Don't worry, old man. I have someone who's been dying to meet you. The plan to destroy Hector wasn't your son's idea. I've had time to think about it, and the only reasonable explanation is that Hector's position in the cartel made it seem impossible to topple him. To make a move on a man like that took planning and forethought, and we both know Jerome here doesn't have those talents."

"Fuck you," his father said.

"So unimaginative, and back to where we were. I'm sure your boy thought it was his idea, but he forgets all those whispered conversations in his ear guiding him along." She glanced at the door where Hector stood in the shadows. "What you didn't plan was what would happen if Hector found out. What would a man like that do?"

"I guess we'll never find out, bitch. We'll—" The words died in his throat as Hector walked in.

"You tried to cut my balls off," Hector yelled. "That's going to cost you yours, but first you will watch your son die."

"Cain, wait." Jerome's demeanor changed. The bravado was gone and replaced by palpable fear. "I'm not your enemy."

"You're right, you're not, Anthony. I know you don't like the nickname Tony, so Anthony it is." She put pressure on the blade and it sliced into his side like an arrow through wet bread. Anthony was trying to stay quiet, but he couldn't seem to help the moan that escaped. "Back to the subject of Hector and what he'd do." She twisted one way, then the next before pulling out.

"It was only business," his father said. "We didn't mean anything personal by it."

"Hector," she said, and Hector cocked his head slightly. "Did you take this as only business?" Hector seemed too enraged to speak, and he shook his head. "See, Matty, that particular line only works in the movies. Someone blows your world to shit, and it *is* personal."

"All you need to do is kill this bitch, and we'll give you all the product we have," Matty said to Hector. Jerome seemed to be working to breathe, his head bowed as blood seeped from various holes.

"You shut up," Hector yelled so loud that Cain was glad they were in a deserted part of town.

"Like I was saying, when someone blows your world to shit, it's personal. That brings me to the day you and Juan took my wife. What exactly was going through that tiny brain of yours?" She didn't have the same patience on the other side of his lower abdomen, and she slammed the knife in, making him yell for the first time. "What did you think I'd do to you the day I finally caught you? And believe me, I never forgot about you."

"I was trying to…to make…Juan trust me." Anthony could barely get the words out, and his hands went from his thighs to his sides as he tried to put pressure in different places. "That's all."

"That brings me back to another point. Like your father giving you the idea to hit Hector, Juan wasn't smart enough to pull off that perfect abduction. The FBI even told me how you covered your escape. It was all textbook FBI training that made it work so well. That wasn't gaining trust, you petty little fucker, that was aiding and abetting." She turned and looked at Lou and Dino. "Clear the desk."

The others held Matty down when they spread Anthony on the surface and tied his hands and feet to the bottom of the desk. Lou made quick work of his clothes with his knife, and Anthony had tears running off his cheeks when Lou was done. This did not at all resemble the guy who'd come to her house and tried to shake her down so long ago.

"Cain, please. If you think I'm this Anthony, that means you're going to be killing an FBI agent."

"You'll be my first." She laughed and tapped her chin. "That's not exactly true, is it? Your old boss had to be buried without his brains, and that was all me." She smiled when his eyes widened. "Confession really is good for the soul. Yes, Barney tried to kill me, and he paid. Cehan tried to kill me by slamming my head repeatedly into every surface he came across, and he's in Angola. From what I hear, he's become the favorite of the inmates even though he's in protective custody."

"You fooled them all, but you didn't fool me," Anthony yelled, tears and snot still running down his face.

"I didn't fool you because you're worse than I ever thought to be. You attacked people who'd done nothing to you. Emma and Hector weren't your enemies—they'd done nothing to you. That's the secret to survival, asshole. You mess only with those who mess with you."

"What did you do to Juan?" He started straining against the ropes, and Matty had to be held down.

"You're about to find out." She accepted a bottle from Lou and went through the ritual of dousing Anthony like she had Juan. "You're going to burn for touching something that didn't belong to you. No one touches Emma without her permission, and she didn't give it. What you did almost cost us our baby."

"You aren't going to get away with this. Shelby and Joe will figure it out."

She slid the match against the side of the box and watched the flame for a moment before throwing it on his genitals. The smell was almost instant as Anthony began screaming.

"Please...please let me go," he screamed. His body arched over the table like they'd run an electric current through it. He thrashed against the ropes, but there was no escape.

"Look what you've done, old man," she said to Matty, who looked on, horror-stricken. She took the gun Dino held out and pressed it to Anthony's forehead. "All your scheming and planning for the easy life. This is the cost of getting it wrong." She pulled the trigger and put him out of his misery, the fire continuing to burn. His father's sobs and threats were ignored by everyone there.

"Thank you, Cain," Hector said, putting his arms around her. "You have given me my life back, and I owe you."

"Do you have any problem with what we talked about?"

"No, and I would like to see their faces. First, I have some fun," Hector said, his eyes on Matty.

"Take all the time you need. No one will bother you here, and you deserve some fun." She put her jacket back on and accepted her knife back from Lou after he'd cleaned it. "Confessing is good, but nothing is better than settling old debts. Anthony has finally paid his in full."

Shelby sat at the conference table in Annabel's office with her original crew. Joe had given Dylan point for the night crew, and it was nice seeing Lionel Jones and Claire Lansing back again. It seemed like a lifetime they'd been gone. For once the city was quiet, and their job of following Cain had become boring. She'd been spending lots of time in the clubs that had been shot up, and with Muriel in her offices above Emma's.

"I called you here today to talk about something that can't leave this room," Annabel said. She sat at the head of the table and glanced at each of them. "It's the same as when we had to have our talks about Ronald Chapman. I think we have the same problem, but I can't figure out who's behind it."

"Do you think Ronald's back in town?" Shelby remembered when Chapman had come to town gunning for Cain, making everyone's life miserable, only to run from a field the day before Cain's wedding. He'd run and landed back in DC with no explanation. Whatever it was had Cain's signature on it, and none of them had complained. It was how she'd gotten rid of Barney Kyle. She'd exposed him for the slime he was.

"I'm not sure. Chapman's still powerful within the bureau, so I've had to be quiet about my inquiries. He'll nail me to a wall if he thinks I'm looking into him." Annabel handed them each a folder. "Keep these secure, but right now our focus is on former Detective Elton Newsome."

"Someone finally fire that loser?" Lionel asked.

"Someone killed him." Annabel held up a photo. "It was a professional job, no question. The car that did it has been found, burned out. The owner reported it stolen the day after Newsome went over the Causeway's guardrail."

"The guy was a screwup who ran, after what happened to Hannah Casey. Are you sure he didn't just mess up one last time?" Joe asked.

Annabel cued the film the Causeway police had sent and let them watch it on the big screen. "The night this happened, Newsome called me and wanted to come in and talk to me. He said the information he had would be enough to get his old job and pension back. The only hint he gave was that it was all our fault, and he wasn't responsible for the fallout."

"Responsible for what? Hannah Casey's abduction, or Emma's mother?" Shelby asked. She flipped through the rest of the folder and thought about Emma's accusations.

"I don't know, but to me it means the FBI, and not us as individuals. Newsome was on his way in, and someone killed him. I'd like to know why." Annabel was, as always, calm and focused. "I have absolutely no proof, but I think Emma Casey was correct. Someone used their daughter to try something that no one should've ever contemplated. It was illegal, not to mention unethical, and I think it's Chapman."

"You think Ronald Chapman is running an illegal sting in our city, and the bureau hasn't clued you in?" Claire asked.

It was a legitimate question. This sounded totally absurd, which was why it made total sense. "I think Agent Hicks is right. Emma Casey never allows her facade to crack—ever. That night at Vincent's, she was pissed." Shelby could tell how upsetting someone approaching her child had been to Emma. "She talked to me directly, and then Cain said the same to us in Wisconsin. How to prove it, though, is going to be tricky."

"Not really," Joe said, pointing at her. "I'm willing to bet my meager savings that Cain Casey has more information on this than we do. All we need to do is ask."

"You think it's that easy?" Annabel laughed.

"Yes," Shelby agreed with Joe. "All we need to do is tell her we believe her. She loves showing the world the underbelly of the bureau when she finds a dirty agent. That night when she handed Chapman that envelope, you could see the life drain out of him. Whatever she found, there's no way he wants that to go public. It had to be good, not only from his reaction but hers. She was pleased with herself, so whatever it was is devastating."

"Which gives him motive to strike back in a way that'll shut her down," Annabel said. "It's worth a try, but it goes no farther than our group here. And if it isn't him, then we need to figure out who it is."

Annabel's intercom went off and she answered it. "I'm sorry, ma'am, I know you said no interruptions, but there's a reporter from the *Times-Picayune* here with a delivery. He said you'd want to take it."

All five of them walked to the waiting area and recognized one of the reporters from the crime desk. He had two boxes with him that sat ominously on two chairs. "Can I help you?" Annabel asked.

"Special Agent Hicks, we received these in the newsroom today with instructions to bring them here. No one opened them, and before you process them, I should tell you there's a few sets of fingerprints from the people in our office who handled them." The guy took out his notebook and stared at them. "Any chance you'd open them now?"

"Thank you," Annabel said as Lionel and Joe each took a box. "Wait here."

They headed for the in-house lab and had the techs x-ray both boxes. Shelby shivered when she saw what was in them. "Who is that?" she asked as they all stared at two heads.

"Open them," Annabel ordered.

The technician laid both heads on the exam table and held up a note in a plastic bag. Each man had his genitals shoved in his mouth, and a frozen, terrified expression on his face. It didn't take a federal agent to know they'd died in pain.

"Read it," Annabel said.

"*Found something you lost*," the tech read. "*Your runaway has a new face, but his father should look familiar to you. Anthony and Matt Curtis are no longer vying for the top spot with the cartel. These fuckers were known in Mexico as Jerome and Patrick Rhodes.*"

"Shit," Joe said. "I'd have pegged Casey for this until that last line. She's a mob boss, but she never swears. It seems beneath her."

"Look for any trace evidence, and bring it directly to me," Annabel said. They followed her back to the waiting area. "How were these delivered?"

"Two kids with hoodies and big sunglasses. It had a note for me, and it gave me orders to bring them here."

"Thank you for following directions, and we'll call you first when we're ready to report anything," Annabel said. The conversation with this guy was over. "Keep Dylan busy with surveillance and perhaps looking for the bodies that go with these heads, but we start meeting regularly about what we talked about. Get with Casey as soon as you can."

"Yes, ma'am," Shelby said. Whatever this was all about, hopefully it wouldn't take them all down.

"What do you think?" Joe asked her once Annabel left.

"I think we should've chosen our words carefully when we said how bored we were. This is going to be anything but boring."

CHAPTER TWENTY-FIVE

Two weeks later, the Jatibon–Montgomery wedding date had arrived, and Cain got dressed at Remi's place along with Mano, Katlin, and Finley. They'd been thrown out of the house so the girls could have the Casey home to themselves. Their house was transformed, along with the weather. The last week had been nothing but rain and cold, but last night the clouds had parted, and the temperatures had gone up to a comfortable cool.

"This is it, my friend," Cain said, lifting a glass of aged Cuban rum. Ramon had dropped it off the night before, and he'd opened it for the celebration before the celebration.

"It is," Remi said and tugged on her bow tie.

"I remember the day you were born," Ramon said. He handed Remi a glass and held up his. "Your mother was holding you when they let me in. Your brother was sleeping in your abuela's arms, and both of you were beautiful. I swore that day to be the best father I could be—to teach you and guide you until my time with you was done." Ramon raised his glass higher. "Like your brother, you've found a new confidant, and a new best friend. Love her, and always treat her like the most precious thing in your life. If you do, your life will be as blessed as mine."

"I will, Papi," she said hugging her father.

"Then to money, luck, health, happiness, and love. May you have a lifetime of all these things, but most of all, may you be well-loved."

"Salud," the group said before drinking.

"Let's get you over there, now that you look pretty," Mano said. Remi slapped the back of his head, but they were all laughing.

"Congratulations, Remi," Cain said as they got in the limo Emma had ordered. "All I can tell you is that marriage is at times rocky, but do

what your father said. Just love her, and you'll be a happy camper. That
and have children. There's nothing like it."

"I'm glad you're happy. You and Emma deserve it, and I owe you
so much for all the help you gave us with Dallas and Kristen. I don't
often say it, but I love you like I love Mano."

"I love you too, and there are never debts between family. Dallas
has been a good friend to Emma, and Kristen has been Muriel's
salvation. If anyone has a debt, it's me. The Montgomery sisters have
been a good find."

They drove through the gates and waved to some of the guests
who were headed out back, and there were enough guards to fight off
an army, all of them looking good in tuxedos. The tent company had
laid a floor so no heels would get messed up on the soggy grass, and the
tent that held the chairs and altar for the ceremony was beautiful with
all the lit candles. Emma and Dallas had done a good job of organizing,
and Cain hoped the day was all Dallas and Remi imagined. The back
door of the house was lined up with the middle of the aisle, and that
was covered as well.

All they had to do was wait for the bride and the friends Dallas had
asked to stand with her. Dallas had found a family with them as well
as with the Jatibons, so her bridesmaids were her sister-in-law Sylvia,
Kristen, Emma, and Abigail. Cain shook hands with Bishop Andrew
Goodman, her father's oldest friend, and her new confessor. The church
didn't sanction this marriage, but Father Andy always preached that
love knew no color or gender, and he was happy to officiate.

"It's time," the wedding planner said.

They left Remi at the altar alone with Father Andy and moved
closer to the door. She watched her cousins escort Sylvia and Abigail
to the front and whistled softly when she saw Emma. The off-the-
shoulder, tea-length black dress fit Emma perfectly, and she looked
beautiful. "Do you have a date for later?" she whispered in Emma's ear
before walking her down the aisle.

"Yes, and I'm planning on bringing her home," Emma whispered
back. "Now behave."

Kristen and Mano performed their maid of honor and best man
duties, and there were a few tears when Dallas and Remi said their
vows. Cain's mind went back to the day she'd said her own, and it made
her smile. She'd never felt stronger in her life than the day she declared
to the world that Emma owned all of who she was and would ever be.

"Ladies and gentlemen, I present to you, Dallas and Remington Jatibon," Father Andy said. The guests applauded, and Remi and Dallas kissed one more time before heading inside.

Vincent's catering crew moved everyone to the next tent, and the band started playing. Remi put her hands on Dallas's waist and lifted her off the ground, twirling her in a circle. "You're mine now," Remi said, and Dallas nodded.

"That's what they want you to believe, but it's the other way around," Cain said, and Emma pinched her hard. "It's not a bad thing, lass."

"The smart play, mobster, is to be quiet and smile for the pictures." Emma twirled, her dress floating around her.

They took plenty of pictures before heading back out and sitting through the speeches and the cutting of the cake. Vincent's people did a great job, and Cain didn't mind them wandering around the first floor of the house. All of them knew doing any favors for the feds or betraying Vincent's trust would lead to an employee review they'd never forget.

Cain enjoyed watching Hannah dance with Victoria, and Hayden and Sadie kept an eye on Liam. Life wasn't all about work and figuring out puzzles, but about days like this when you could sit and enjoy the rewards all the work brought. She had a family she was proud of, and there was nothing that would change her opinion of that.

"What does a girl have to do to get someone to ask her to dance?" Emma stood behind her with her hands on her shoulders, and her soft voice was enough to make her want to carry her inside.

"I thought the coven was over there, planning out the rest of Remi's life. Or is it Muriel who's next on y'all's hit list?" She grinned.

"Coven?" Emma bit her earlobe. "You're in rare form tonight."

"I'm joking, lass." She stood and bowed over Emma's hand. "Would you do me the honor of this dance, bewitching lady?"

"I'm telling the bar to cut you off if you're getting this cheesy, but I'd love to dance." Emma allowed herself to be pulled in. "This has been a wonderful night. You and Dallas did a great job."

"The best night is still the night I got you to say yes, but Remi and Dallas look happy. Are you ready to plan two more weddings?" Emma nodded at Ramon and Marianna, glad to see Remi's mother appeared as ecstatic as the bride.

"That is one of my favorite memories, but you've given me plenty to daydream about. Watching our children being born, sharing my days with you, and the top of that list is the day I met you. I've always thought all those romance novels were pure fantasy when they talked about being thunderstruck at the sight of someone." Cain bent her head and kissed Emma gently. "But then I saw you."

"I don't say this often enough, but thank you for the life you've given me, my love. I can't imagine what my life would be if I'd never taken the chance to come here—I know I'd crave you even if I had no idea who you were." Emma dabbed at her eyes, but Cain knew they were happy tears.

"There's no need to think about what-ifs." She turned them so Emma could see her father. Ross was handsome in his tux, and he seemed happy as he led Carmen around the floor. "Your brave soul led you here, and you *have* bewitched me from the moment I saw you. That might sound cheesy, but it's true. Look around you and see what your leap of faith has brought us." She pointed to Ross and Carmen, then at the children who were dancing in a circle. "You gave us this."

Remi and Dallas joined them on the dance floor, and they switched dance partners. "Thank you for everything, Cain. This has been the perfect day," Dallas said as she kissed Cain's cheek.

"You're welcome, but all the credit goes to Mrs. Casey. Once you finish with your honeymoon, you can start planning your sister's wedding."

"It'll be nice to have a Casey in the family, as well as some Casey nieces and nephews." Dallas laughed, then gazed up at her. "I'd like you to know that today Katie Lynn Moores is at peace. She finally learned that dreams really do come true."

"That girl deserves peace more than anyone else I know. All you need to remember is that all her secrets died with her. You're Dallas Jatibon now, and also a part of my family. Emma thinks of you as the sister she never had, so we're in your corner."

"And I love you both for it," Dallas said, standing on her toes and kissing her cheek again.

"Hey, get your own girl," Remi said, handing Emma back. "I think it's time to go, so I can have my wife all to myself."

"I like the sound of that," Dallas said.

Cain laughed when Muriel caught the garter and the bouquet hit Kristen in the chest. "Have fun and don't worry about anything," Cain told Remi. "Mano and I have it all covered."

"Thanks, and you throw one hell of a party." Remi hugged her before taking Dallas's hand and waving to everyone as they headed for the front door. They were spending the night in the new house before leaving for Key West for the week.

The party went on past one in the morning, and Cain sat with Ramon and Vincent for a drink while Emma went up and put everyone under the age of fifteen to bed, with Abigail's help. The men finished their last glass before gathering their dates and wishing them good night. Linda Bender and her brothers had retired to the pool house, so all that was left was the catering crew. For outsiders, Linda and her family appeared to have had a good time, and she'd sat and talked to her once dinner had been cleared.

"Everything is picked up as far as food, Ms. Casey, so we'll be back tomorrow to box everything else up and get it out of the yard," the catering manager said.

"There's some cases of whiskey left, so make sure everyone gets a bottle. They deserve it for a great night." She took out the cigar Remi had given her earlier and stretched her legs. The party had been great, but the silence was nice too. She waited for the interruption she knew was coming.

It was late and she was tired, but she wasn't ready for bed just yet. She blew a stream of smoke upward and didn't turn around when she heard someone walk up behind her. It wasn't totally unexpected, but her shoulders still tensed. No one could be lucky forever.

"You can talk or sit, but don't just stand there." She blew another ring of smoke. "Don't worry, I'm not armed. If you knew me, you'd realize I never am."

"My boss always said how smooth you were in every situation," the woman said.

Cain didn't recognize the voice, but the Russian accent was unmistakable, and she wasn't going to give in to temptation and turn around. She wouldn't face death by losing her pride now. "Not every situation. I've come unglued every so often, so don't believe everything someone tells you."

"You have Abigail and her children here. Why?"

"Have a seat, Ms. Garin, or would you like a drink first?"

"You know me?"

The way Nina asked it made her smile. Lou or Katlin would've never made that mistake. "Not really, but you're here for one of two reasons." She used the cigar to point to the chair close to her.

"Entertain me, then, before I put a bullet in your head for David and Valerie." Nina moved into Cain's line of sight but didn't sit down.

"You're either here to avenge your boss's death by killing me, or you're here to get your ass out of a crack for not protecting her. Which is it?" She took another puff on the cigar.

"Nicola's alive," Nina said, waving the gun. "If you want to live, all you have to do is give me the children and Abigail. She needs to see them."

"You know you're asking the impossible. Unless you brought an army that can kill every one of my people as well as the FBI that camps out on my lawn, that's not going to happen." She crossed her legs, glad that this idiot had waited until now to do this. "How long have you been here?"

"Long enough to know you also took in that bitch, Linda. Once Nicola finds that out, she's going to kill your entire family." Nina laughed but not too loud.

Cain motioned with her cigar. "Tell me where she is, and I'll drive over and sit for a visit. If she can pull the trigger, I'll give her a free shot, but she can't. Isn't that right?"

"Shut up before I fucking shoot you for being such a smug asshole."

"Then do it. Kill me, and all your problems go away. If I'm dead, those kids and Abigail will be so out of your reach, it'll make Nicola kill you a thousand times. Go ahead," she said loudly.

The gun sounded like a canon even though it had a silencer, and the shot pierced her left arm this time. She cursed under her breath as the pain made her nauseous. Nina's body hit the ground with a thud, a red flower spreading from the center of her back. Finley lowered the gun she was holding and stepped over Nina's body.

"Were you waiting for her to shoot me somewhere more vital?" she asked Finley.

"I'll go get Abigail," Finley said, handing her a napkin. "Sorry, but I didn't want to take any chances until I knew I had a clear shot. She must have been about to pull the trigger."

Cain waited, keeping pressure on the wound and thinking about final puzzle pieces. Abigail glanced at Nina before turning all her attention to Cain. Emma sat on her uninjured side. "Lou, take care of that, but check to see if she's got anything on her to get us somewhere. And make sure there are no sidekicks lurking anywhere." Cain sat and took deep breaths as the anesthetic Abigail had injected around her wound took effect.

"You got it, boss." Lou pointed to some guys who picked Nina up and carried her off.

"When did you know she was here?" Abigail asked as she dug the bullet out and stitched her up.

"Toward the end of the reception, a few of the catering crew went out to get some stuff out of the van parked on the street. Three went out and four came back in. All the guards were hypervigilant to anything out of the ordinary, and someone let me know right away. I recognized her from your file when one of them pointed her out."

"What did she say about Nicola?" Finley asked. "I couldn't hear what she was saying."

"She's alive, but I doubt she's doing well." She told them her theory of why Nina had come, and Abigail was the only one who nodded. "Think about it. Nicola isn't in any shape to give the order to kill Nina for what she'll see as a betrayal, but Nina thought she'd eventually get there. Nina came here to do what Nicola couldn't. Showing up with your children and telling Nicola you were dead, along with me, was the only way to save her life."

"Has anyone ever told you that you're an interesting person?" Abigail asked, making Emma laugh.

"She is, and it runs in the family, and they'll pass it on to your kids," Emma said. "But that's not a bad thing."

"We'll talk about that later, but for now what we do know is Nicola isn't in any shape to come after you. That gives us time to deal with her. What we need to do now is figure out how Nina got here. Find the car or the hotel she was staying at, and it might give a clue as to where she started."

"We'll take care of it," Finley said. "You okay here? I'm sorry I didn't shoot faster."

"It's not your fault. Desperate people are hard to deal with." Cain pulled her bow tie loose and unbuttoned the top of her shirt. At this rate, she was going to have to order more. "It might not seem like it, Abigail, but tonight was a good thing. It brings us one step closer to cutting you free of your past." Her breathing returned to normal now that Abigail had again taken the edge off the pain.

"I hope you're right, and I'm sorry you keep getting the brunt of all my mistakes."

"Don't send me a bill for the stitches, and we'll be square."

❖

Emma undressed Cain once they were upstairs behind a locked door. They were both exhausted, but Emma couldn't get used to the sight of blood seeping from Cain's body from some new wound. Nothing in her life was more terrifying than seeing Cain hurt. The gunshot had made her heart jump to her throat, and only Cain's voice in her head had kept her from rushing outside blindly.

"You keep scaring me. I wish you'd stop getting new holes in your body." She finished unbuttoning Cain's shirt and wadded it up once it was off. She wanted no reminders of Cain's mortality.

"The thing you should keep remembering, my little hayseed"— Cain put two fingers under her chin and gently lifted her head—"is I always walk away breathing. You're not getting rid of me even if you try." Cain backed her toward the bed. "My mum used to say I walk with the angels, and today I finally figured out she was right."

"You are luckier than most, my love." Emma turned so Cain could unzip her. "And you're not getting lucky. You just got shot."

Cain nodded and watched her take off her dress, making a noise of approval at the strapless bra and matching panties. "You're right." Cain's caress meant she didn't really mean what she was saying. "But I bet if I do this"—she moved her hand higher—"you don't really want that to be true."

"Uh-huh." The feel of Cain's finger going under the side of her underwear made her bite her bottom lip. "Honey, you're hurt."

"But I'm not the one in pain, am I?" Cain said. "Take them off, and I promise I won't use my arms."

She got naked, lay down, and spread her legs. "Don't hurt yourself."

"I'm a professional—I know what I'm doing." As Cain lowered her head, the phone rang.

"Fuck me," Emma said louder than she meant.

"That's a given, lass, but give me a minute." Cain rolled off the bed carefully and reached for the phone. "Is the house on fire?"

The question made Emma laugh, but it died in her throat when Cain put her hand between her legs and flicked over her hard clit.

"Not nice, mobster."

Cain smiled and concentrated on the call. "Drive it in and park it in the garage. Check her pockets for a key card, and let's hope the name of the place is on it." Cain hung up and finished taking her pants and underwear off. "Now, where was I?"

"Right here." Emma reached down and spread herself open. The craving had definitely not died.

"My favorite place to be, lass." Cain put her mouth on her, and it didn't take much to reach the peak she loved. Cain came up and kissed her, and she could taste herself on Cain's lips. "Sleep now. Tomorrow will be soon enough to talk about what I have planned."

"Are you sure?" She yawned and gave Cain a sleepy smile.

"Unlike some of the people lined up against us, we have all the time in the world. Don't worry, I'll be here in the morning—every morning."

"As happy as I was for Remi and Dallas today, I'm happier for me. Thanks for loving me."

"It's hard not to after you've put this ring through my nose and tattooed your name on my ass." Cain pulled her close.

"You're lucky I love you." She put her head on Cain's shoulder and covered them both.

"That I am. That I am."

CHAPTER TWENTY-SIX

The next morning Cain got dressed and waited for Emma to finish with Billy. She held up Emma's coat and helped her into the car that Lou had pulled to the front. They were going for a drive alone, but their destination was well covered from both sides of the chasm. For every FBI agent around the spot she'd picked, she'd placed two of her people. She'd had enough stitches in this lifetime.

"We haven't been here in ages," Emma said as they walked into the Golf Club Restaurant in Audubon Park. The large wraparound porch was almost empty, with most of the diners eating inside because of the cold.

"Charles put us in the corner, so let's see what Annabel is up to these days." Cain shook hands with the manager and followed him to the secluded spot with two heaters, where Shelby and Annabel Hicks already sat waiting for them. "Two hot chocolates, Charles, and whatever the ladies care for."

"Thanks for agreeing to this, Cain, and hot chocolate sounds good," Annabel said.

"It's not often you thank me," Cain said and laughed. "Well, I'm sure I do take up more of your day than you care for, but a call so early makes me curious."

"We believe you," Shelby said, as if to cut to the center of things. "We believe you, and we're sorry that anyone approached Hannah. That is in no way protocol."

"Maybe, but it didn't surprise me. The *protocol* of some of your agents makes me believe they attended different training than most FBI agents. That's a topic for some other coffee date, though." She sat back and held Emma's hand.

"Why now? I told you, and you acted like you had no clue," Emma said to Shelby.

"The death of Elton Newsome convinced me and raised some flags," Annabel answered. "Someone killed him on the night he was coming in to talk to me. He wanted his job back and had information that would give him what he wanted."

"That almost sounds nonaccusatory." Cain smiled and winked when Annabel smiled back.

"This should prove to you that not all bad things that happen in town lead me to your door," Annabel said. "Someone killed Newsome to keep him quiet about something that might have been the FBI's fault."

"And that would be?" The way Shelby was staring at Annabel meant this wasn't their usual FBI procedure. Annabel shouldn't be divulging this, and she knew it.

"I don't know. Someone killed him. Someone also killed and delivered Anthony Curtis and his father to me, minus their bodies. No matter how long I'm in this job, it's very disconcerting to receive heads in boxes." Annabel shivered, and Cain hoped every agent in the office had the same reaction. That's what happened when you messed with people who wanted to be left alone.

"I'm surprised you're out here telling me all this, so what is it you want?"

"We think someone is trying to bring you down, Cain," Shelby said.

"I know—I'm buying a couple of them hot chocolate right now." She stopped when Emma squeezed her fingers. "Let me see if I understand where you're coming from. Elton Newsome came up with some wild idea involving my mother-in-law, to provoke me by taking our daughter. That backfired and sent Newsome running when Carol acted like Carol does, but it turns out Newsome wasn't the mastermind behind that great idea. And you think that mastermind is the person gunning for me. Am I warm?"

"You would've done well at this job," Annabel said. "And I have no right to ask, but how did you know someone tried getting to you through Hannah?"

She glanced at Emma, and Emma squeezed her fingers again. "Let's face it, Agent Hicks," Emma said. "If an *adult* had talked to our child without my permission, I wouldn't have needed Cain. I would've personally made that person sorry."

"A child?" Shelby asked as if she had never considered that.

"Lucy Kennison became Hannah's best friend and spent a lot of time in our home. As of the school break for Mardi Gras, Lucy has been removed from the school, and we've never heard from her again." Emma gave them the information without embellishment.

Shelby wrote that name down. "The problem is that Lucy, along with her parents Drew and Taylor Kennison, doesn't exist. Not before they enrolled Lucy in school and positioned her to get close to Hannah. Lucy is who told Hannah that if she didn't do what her parents wanted they couldn't be friends. Which meant planting a bug only big agencies use." Cain made a fist and bumped her knee with it. "People don't have such elaborate backstories or tech without help. Your kind of help, before they go undercover."

"And you had no idea about any of this?" Emma sounded skeptical.

"Not every agent is perfect, Mrs. Casey, and not every operation is made known to us," Annabel said. "Sometimes different agents work on operations that overlap, but we don't communicate about them."

"But you have that little inkling in your gut that points in one direction, don't you?"

"I can't speculate," Annabel said. "It does seem incredibly coincidental, though. But you have a way of dealing with problems internally, and I can't take that chance if I'm wrong."

"I'm not an animal, Annabel, and we're done here." She threw two twenties on the table and pulled out Emma's chair for her. "The smart play here was to ask me who I thought it was. Not what I was going to do about it."

"I guess it's too late for that—although if you do have an idea, that would save some time," Annabel said. "But if there are rogue agents playing outside the rules, again, then I want it stopped, and I want it done without bloodshed. Yours or ours."

"I'm not unforgiving, extra Special Agent Hicks. Shelby and Joe will tell you that, but today isn't the day for that." She buttoned her overcoat and handed Annabel one of her cards. "Let me think about the best way we can do this and stay out of each other's way. Once we've established the ground rules, we might get somewhere."

"I had nothing to do with what happened, but I am sorry," Annabel said, closing her hand over the card. "I've been honest with you this morning. Honest enough that it might cost me my job if you were to disclose it."

"I'm not that kind of person."

"I know, and I hope you see my honesty as my desire to work together on this," Annabel said, and Cain believed her.

"Trust me, Annabel. When the time comes, we'll take care of our mutual problem and do it to our mutual satisfaction. That's not going to be today, so have a good morning."

She and Emma nodded before walking away. They sat in the cold car for a moment before she turned the key, and Emma stared at her as if trying to figure out what she was thinking. "What happens now?" Emma asked, not wanting to wait.

"Now we wait. There's plenty left to face, to do, to finish. I wanted to be done with all this, but there are still pieces in play." There were a few golfers playing despite the cold, and she ignored them to concentrate on Emma. "Patience is the key, but I did lie about one thing."

"What's that?" Emma said taking her hand and kissing the back of it.

"Sometimes I am an animal, and she gave away that she thinks Lucy's parents, Taylor and Drew, are agents. Her admitting that not all operations are known to the local office proves that. When I find them, I'm going to bury them once they tell me all their secrets. Only then will we be done with what happened to Hannah. Their boss will regret he ever tried this."

Emma laughed and nodded. "You make me hot when you talk like that."

"Then all those intimate moments required to make that next baby shouldn't be a problem," she said, leaning over to kiss Emma. "Come on, there's life to enjoy on a beautiful day like today."

"Yes, there is. Take me home."

About the Author

Ali Vali is the author of the long-running Cain Casey Devil series and the Genesis Clan Forces series, as well as numerous standalone romances including two Lambda Literary Award finalists, *Calling the Dead* and *Love Match*. Ali's newest standalone is *One More Chance*.

Originally from Cuba, Ali has retained much of her family's traditions and language and uses them frequently in her stories. Having her father read her stories and poetry before bed every night as a child infused her with a love of reading, which she carries till today. Ali currently lives outside New Orleans, Louisiana, and she has discovered that living in Louisiana provides plenty of material to draw from in creating her novels and short stories.

Books Available From Bold Strokes Books

A Far Better Thing by JD Wilburn. When needs of her family and wants of her heart clash, Cass Halliburton is faced with the ultimate sacrifice. (978-1-63555-834-0)

Body Language by Renee Roman. When Mika offers to provide Jen erotic tutoring, will sex drive them into a deeper relationship or tear them apart? (978-1-63555-800-5)

Carrie and Hope by Joy Argento. For Carrie and Hope, loss brings them together but secrets and fear may tear them apart. (978-1-63555-827-2)

Detour to Love by Amanda Radley. Celia Scott and Lily Andersen are seatmates on a flight to Tokyo and by turns annoy and fascinate each other. But they're about to realize there's more than one path to love. (978-1-63555-958-3)

Ice Queen by Gun Brooke. School counselor Aislin Kennedy wants to help standoffish CEO Susanna Durr and her troubled teenage daughter become closer—even if it means risking her own heart in the process. (978-1-63555-721-3)

Masquerade by Anne Shade. In 1925 Harlem, New York, a notorious gangster sets her sights on seducing Celine, and new lovers Dinah and Celine are forced to risk their hearts, and lives, for love. (978-1-63555-831-9)

Royal Family by Jenny Frame. Loss has defined both Clay's and Katya's lives, but guarding their hearts may prove to be the biggest heartbreak of all. (978-1-63555-745-9)

Share the Moon by Toni Logan. Three best friends, an inherited vineyard, and a resident ghost come together for fun, romance, and a touch of magic. (978-1-63555-844-9)

Spirit of the Law by Carsen Taite. Attorney Owen Lassiter will do almost anything to put a murderer behind bars, but can she get past her reluctance to rely on unconventional help from the alluring Summer Byrne and keep from falling in love in the process? (978-1-63555-766-4)

The Devil Incarnate by Ali Vali. Cain Casey has so much to live for, but enemies who lurk in the shadows threaten to unravel it all. (978-1-63555-534-9)

Secret Agent by Michelle Larkin. CIA Agent Peyton North embarks on a global chase to apprehend rogue agent Zoey Blackwood, but her commitment to the mission is tested as the sparks between them ignite and their sizzling attraction approaches a point of no return. (978-1-63555-753-4)

Journey to Cash by Ashley Bartlett. Cash Braddock thought everything was great, but it looks like her history is about to become her right now. Which is a real bummer. (978-1-63555-464-9)

Liberty Bay by Karis Walsh. Wren Lindley's life is mired in tradition and untouched by trends until social media star Gina Strickland introduces an irresistible electricity into her off-the-grid world. (978-1-63555-816-6)

Scent by Kris Bryant. Nico Marshall has been burned by women in the past wanting her for her money. This time, she's determined to win Sophia Sweet over with her charm. (978-1-63555-780-0)

Shadows of Steel by Suzie Clarke. As their worlds collide and their choices come back to haunt them, Rachel and Claire must figure out how to stay together and, most of all, stay alive. (978-1-63555-810-4)

The Clinch by Nicole Disney. Eden Bauer overcame a difficult past to become a world champion mixed martial artist, but now rising star and dreamy bad girl Brooklyn Shaw is a threat both to Eden's title and her heart. (978-1-63555-820-3)

The Last First Kiss by Julie Cannon. Kelly Newsome is so ready for a tropical island vacation, but she never expects to meet the woman who could give her her last first kiss. (978-1-63555-768-8)

The Mandolin Lunch by Missouri Vaun. Despite their immediate attraction, everything about Garet Allen says short-term, and Tess Hill refuses to consider anything less than forever. (978-1-63555-566-0)

Thor: Daughter of Asgard by Genevieve McCluer. When Hannah Olsen finds out she's the reincarnation of Thor, she's thrown into a world of magic and intrigue, unexpected attraction, and a mystery she's got to unravel. (978-1-63555-814-2)

Veterinary Technician by Nancy Wheelton. When a stable of horses is threatened, Val and Ronnie must work together against the odds to save them and maybe even themselves along the way. (978-1-63555-839-5)

16 Steps to Forever by Georgia Beers. Can Brooke Sullivan and Macy Carr find themselves by finding each other? (978-1-63555-762-6)

All I Want for Christmas by Georgia Beers, Maggie Cummings & Fiona Riley. The Christmas season sparks passion and love in these stories by award-winning authors Georgia Beers, Maggie Cummings, and Fiona Riley. (978-1-63555-764-0)

From the Woods by Charlotte Greene. When Fiona goes backpacking in a protected wilderness, the last thing she expects is to be fighting for her life. (978-1-63555-793-0)

Heart of the Storm by Nicole Stiling. For Juliet Mitchell and Sienna Bennett a forbidden attraction definitely isn't worth upending the life they've worked so hard for. Is it? (978-1-63555-789-3)

If You Dare by Sandy Lowe. For Lauren West and Emma Prescott, following their passions is easy. Following their hearts, though? That's almost impossible. (978-1-63555-654-4)

Love Changes Everything by Jaime Maddox. For Samantha Brooks and Kirby Fielding, no matter how careful their plans, love will change everything. (978-1-63555-835-7)

Not This Time by MA Binfield. Flung back into each other's lives, can former bandmates Sophia and Madison have a second chance at romance? (978-1-63555-798-5)

The Found Jar by Jaycie Morrison. Fear keeps Emily Harris trapped in her emotionally vacant life; can she find the courage to let Beck Reynolds guide her toward love? (978-1-63555-825-8)

Aurora by Emma L McGeown. After a traumatic accident, Elena Ricci is stricken with amnesia, leaving her with no recollection of the last eight years, including her wife and son. (978-1-63555-824-1)